EMILY PRAGER'S

CLEA & ZEUS DIVORCE

"As with all men who are born sexually attractive to women, there was a quiet and caution in Zeus, a faint bewilderment that cloaked his body and clashed with the perpetually beckoning light in his eyes. Inside himself, he was always blushing, always a little turned off, always kindly denying his powerful but involuntary sexual message; a postural apologist for the shape of his shoulders, the slant of his cheekbones, the pulp of his lips. Except onstage. And except with Clea."

Clea & Zeus Divorce

Emily Prager

CLEA & ZEUS DIVORCE

VINTAGE CONTEMPORARIES

VINTAGE BOOKS

A DIVISION OF RANDOM HOUSE

NEW YORK

A VINTAGE CONTEMPORARIES ORIGINAL, OCTOBER 1987
FIRST EDITION

Library of Congress Cataloging-in-Publication Data
Prager, Emily.
Clea & Zeus divorce.
(Vintage contemporaries)
I. Title. II. Title: Clea and Zeus divorce.
PS3566.R25C56 1987b 813'.54 87-10456
ISBN 0-394-75591-X (pbk.)

Grateful acknowledgment is made to the following for permission to reprint previously published materials:

Chappell & Co., Inc.: Excerpt from the lyrics to "Gigi" by Alan Jay Lerner and Frederick Loewe. Copyright © 1957, 1958 by Chappell & Co., Inc. All rights administered by Chappell & Co., Inc. International copyright secured. All rights reserved. Used by permission.

New Directions Publishing Corporation: Excerpts from two poems from *The Orchid Boat: Women Poets of China* by Kenneth Rexroth and Ling Chung. Copyright © 1972 by Kenneth Rexroth and Ling Chung. Reprinted by permission of New Directions Publishing Corporation.

Warock Corporation: Excerpts from the lyrics to "My Mammy" by Walter Donaldson, Sam M. Lewis, and Joe Young. Copyright 1920 by Irving Berlin, Inc. Copyright renewed 1948 by Warock Corporation. International copyright secured. All rights reserved. Used by permission.

Author photograph copyright © 1985 by Ralph DePas

DESIGNED BY J. K. LAMBERT

Manufactured in the United States of America
10 9 8 7 6 5 4 3 2 1

For my grandmother and for Robit

There has been a coup
In the Kingdom of Thought.
Love now reigns
In the Idea Palace.
Fiery humeurs
Are burning books.
And mindless joy
Beheads philosophy.

LIU AH MIEN
Shanghai, 1935

Clea & Zeus Divorce

One

CLEA banged open the door of her dressing room. She bolted out into the corridor, encased in an aura of rigid control that protected the wispy innards of her femininity like an eggshell protects its developing egg.

As she hurtled toward the stage in her trademark deer-hoof boots, her waist-length punk mane streamed behind her. Her painted Betty Boop face was set and grim. The stagehands, who scrambled to get out of her way, were aware of her sexuality only because her breasts bounced in an obligation to physical science.

She was like one of the brightly colored Mexican saints backed by a silver oval that one sees at roadside shrines. Or a figure that's part of a feminine lamp. She dashed forward, oblivious to the many people around her, to the cables beneath her feet. Her arms stuck out beyond her rhinestone-studded cocktail dress in a clearly intended suspension of use. Her little fingers were open and poised. World War Three couldn't have gotten her attention. Or, maybe her attention, but never her emotion.

When she landed at the area adjacent to the stage-right wing, she turned off engines and addressed Miss Florie in a voice so calm and resonant it might have been sent by aliens. "Where are the radiation suits?" she asked.

Miss Florie bobbed her head, clucked something in the Xhosa dialect, and turned in the direction of Bobette the costume lady, who jumped right up and answered frenetically,

"They're right here, Clea. Hanging here. See, I have them."

She pointed, and Clea looked at them—hanging on the portable costume rack, hoods slumped over hanger necks, gloves pinned to sleeves, boots beneath, like two dead snowmen on a gibbet. Clea nodded at Bobette, glanced intensely at Miss Florie, and then glided into the wings. There, alone between the paint-smelling flats, she commanded the rigidity to leave her and she went limp.

ZEUS sauntered out of his dressing room, followed by Mr. Liu. A rush of awe as the door opened silenced the stagehands and dancers who loitered in the stage-left corridor. Now they alternated between staring at Zeus and trying to get a look at the hundreds of handmade toy sailboats that were crammed into his cubicle.

Roger, the lighting designer, happened by at this moment, and gesturing toward the door with a torn pink gel he had just replaced, said good-naturedly,

"Zeus, what is this thing you've got for toy boats? Why do you love 'em so much?"

Zeus smiled. Then he became aware that the entire corridor was awaiting his reply.

"Perhaps," he said, faintly embarrassed, warming the onlookers with his soft, heart-melting, almost British voice, "it is because my country is landlocked." And he turned his back.

"Jesus!" whispered Rita, a long-legged dancer who was leaning up against the corridor wall. She spoke to her equally endowed cohort, Peg. "He's so gorgeous. He's like a cross between Lord Byron, Robert Donat, and—"

"Frederick Chopin and Mel Gibson," said Peg.

"And he's funny. And he can dance." They sighed.

Mr. Liu retreated into the dressing room for a moment. Zeus, left to himself, began to summon the energy dormant inside his appendages. He shook languidly and then revolved like a tranquil dervish. He completed his turn in time to accept a hand-rolled cigarette which Mr. Liu was now offering him from a newly opened pack.

"Good fortune, Zeus," said Mr. Liu, and lit the smoke.

And Zeus replied, "Thanks." Then, putting one hand into his pants pocket so he could cup his bad hip and comfort it a bit, he meandered down the corridor toward the stage-left wing.

As with all men who are born sexually attractive to women, there was a quiet and caution in Zeus, a faint bewilderment that cloaked his body and clashed with the perpetually beckoning light in his eyes. Inside himself, he was always blushing, always a little turned off, always kindly denying his powerful but involuntary sexual message; a postural apologist for the shape of his shoulders, the slant of his cheekbones, the pulp of his lips. Except onstage. And except with Clea.

Clea. "Where are the radiation suits?" Clea. He heard her voice toll across the proscenium, and he halted and slumped against the corridor wall. He dropped his head on his chest, took a long drag on his cigarette, and abandoned himself to an anguish that rose up and flooded his eyes. "Jesus Christ," he muttered to himself. "Not now, mon, not now."

Down the corridor, Rita and Peg inspected this perfect man with his glossy black hair and his milk-white English skin and his Florida Keys blue eyes. They surveyed his big square shoulders in his gray nineteen fifties jacket flecked with black, and reappraised his long, black-suede-covered legs. And they thought, curled in the fetal position as he was, that Zeus reminded them of James Dean dressed up for church on a bad day. Or William Holden in a slump. Or any heartthrob they could name.

Only, different. Because he was a man who could move, and that was rare. A big, strong masculine man who could fire a gun and then dance like the bullet on its way to the bull's-eye. Their experience was of feminine men doing limp-wristed turns in jockstraps that hid only wounded birds. How Zeus had happened, they could never fathom, but they loved him for it. They loved him for his looks and they loved him for the gift he had been given—maybe by one of his African gods, maybe that was the difference.

"Do you think Clea will get through it without flipping out?" Rita whispered to Peg.

"I hope so for his sake. I hope so," Peg whispered back.

"They're right here, Clea. Hanging here. See. I have them." At this last, Zeus unfolded, dropped his cigarette and squashed it with his foot. He took from his pocket a small silver flask, unscrewed the top, and sucked on it until he felt the rough liquid stagger down his throat. It was time. It was time. He must resurrect.

Behind his eyes, as blue as the blue wheat beyond the Rift Valley, he dragged his mind back, back through the shutter reflexes of years to a dawn on a distant savannah. A newborn light on a drought-scorched, dun-colored earth. A sloping plateau that stretched beyond imagining, where tiny pools lay sparkling and drying, and here and there gazelle munched on primordial fern. He gunned the motor of his open Land-Rover over the tufted water—questing roots in search of lion. He squinted into the distance, identifying imperceptible flecks as warthog, jackal, and gnu. He turned off the engine and waited.

After a time, two young males loped over the rise, obviously hunting. Way before they saw them, the gazelle herd had turned. Heads down and chewing nonchalantly, every single one of them had turned to face their predators as if some inner instinctual choreographer had silently snapped his fingers. A series of cries, squawks, grunts and lows seemingly unattached to beaks and chops, rang out of the golden mist and gossiped of the present danger. With the infinitesimal creep of house cats after flies, the lions approached the herd. The gazelle went heads up now, their necks and noses straining, their ears twitching, their eyes stretched open with worry like a bunch of Bambi clones in a trap.

Slowly, slowly as the lion's crouch, he crawled onto the hood of his Land-Rover. The metal was thickly hot to the touch of his bare feet, and the burning rubber smell of cooling machinery rose about him in a vapor. He took a moment to be sure of his footing and then he straightened up A part of his brain detached now and followed his sinews down the back of his neck, through the vertebrae on his spine, over his buttocks, around the backs of his thighs and calves, and into his ankles and heels. It slid under the soles of his feet, up his shins, bumped over his knees, traversed his femurs, and roamed past his genitals, bringing life to them for just a moment. It caressed his hip joints, embraced his chest, flew out along his arms and back, shinnied up his Adam's apple, negotiated his chin, and finally retreated up his nose and back to his brain.

Its flight check done, the brain part reattached itself and a glow came over him, a pull of promised pleasure so strong, he had to know it. Slowly, he bent himself, letting his arms and hands drift with the graceful flow of his binary symmetry, and he bowed limply but courteously to his animal audience. Then he rose up.

"Take my life, please," he shouted at them. And, with a body snap that slapped his heart, he leaped five feet into the air and laughed as his feet cooled in the breeze. And he danced.

The lions drew back. The gazelle went still. The sounds of the savannah ceased. And all that was heard was the pulsing of human breath and the metallic thumps of his feet on the hood.

"Places, please, Zeus. Zeus?" Charlie, the stage manager, was tapping him on the shoulder.

"Yes. Yes, of course," Zeus said. "Thanks, mon."

And he darted into the stage-left wing and waited impatiently for his cue.

MISS FLORIE, her round, plump arms sitting on her hips like hens' wings, her hands clasped in front of her, her head bobbing to an internal rhythm of sorrow, made her way along the stage-right corridor toward Clea's dressing room. The stagehands were poised and ready to go, perching tautly, she thought, almost menacingly, like the totemic dance masks of her youth. Max, the producer, was hovering nervously in the corner by Clea's dressing room and approached her as she came along.

"Is everything all right, Florie?" he asked, knowing there was no answer.

Miss Florie paused for a moment. She thought of her grandmother stirring mealie pap over an open fire outside her kraal in the Transkei. She was grinning, the old lady, chuckling to herself. A husband and wife had fought in the night over another woman. Her mother's mother, from whom she took her name, was rolling her eyeballs and shaking with glee.

"Well, Max," began Miss Florie and smiled showing the gold tooth, a front tooth, her pride and joy, "when two elephants fight, the grass is trampled."

Max laughed weakly, and Miss Florie went in the dressing room door and gently closed it behind her.

MR. LIU hurried across behind the stage, carrying a needle and thread, a button, and one of Zeus' costumes. Behind the scrim, he moved silently and swiftly, his old guerrilla training still a part of him despite the gaining years. He had heard and seen much, Mr. Liu, but he spoke little, preferring to sift events through his mind, sorting them out in a neat row, then programming them into some Zen alpha-wave computer that seemed to be his by birth. To some he was fearsome, to some inscrutable, to others he was just the greatest tailor Hong Kong had ever produced. To Miss Florie, however, he was a servant, just as she was, with all the protocol that implied. And it was for this reason, and the fact that they had never spoken openly about Clea and Zeus, that Miss Florie burst into tears when Mr. Liu opened the dressing room door, came in, and sat down beside her.

"I'm too sad, Liu. I hurt," said Miss Florie, clutching herself like a backwards koala bear.

Mr. Liu put his arms around her and rested his head on her shoulder. For a long time he said nothing. Then he sat up, took his needle and thread, and began to sew.

Miss Florie wiped her hands on her skirt, and wearily rose to her feet. One by one, she began to take down and pack the items on the walls of Clea's dressing room: a pair of black satin toe shoes, the many maps of nuclear conflagration—the maximum ranges of the effects of a 150 kiloton bomb burst over New York City, a long long photo of the aftermath of Hiroshima, an eight-by-ten glossy of Clea and Zeus from the early days, a stuffed armadillo juggling plates on sticks, the plans for the fallout shelter. There were duplicates of these things in Clea's War Room at home, and Miss Florie handled them now with much avoidance, feeling on her hands the hot red burn of the poisoned female spirit. She had seen the blood and flesh of female sitting in her own pulp, deprived of the white bone maleness that provided coolness. She had seen the agony, the distaste for one's own juices, the wild grief, but she had seen worse too. Much worse. And so had Mr. Liu, which is why he said, after a time of watching her stacking the items in neat piles and putting them in boxes,

"End of love, Miss Florie. Not end of world."

"I think," said Florie haltingly, always careful lest the words that came out of her mouth affect reality, "I think"—an image was crossing over in her mind: Clea huddled under the double bed in a crumpled evening dress looking out, a wild screaming girl in the bantustan, quite mad, cutting herself with a rusty tin can—"it is for her."

"No, Florie," said Mr. Liu quietly, aware that the orchestra had started the overture, "not even for her."

"PLACES, please, Clea. Clea?"

Charlie, the stage manager, had slipped in between the flats and was now leaning over her, clipboard dangling from one hand, staring at her in a posture of fatherly concern. Disembodied voices emanated from his headphones, which he had taken off for this moment and which lay slung around his neck, like a talking noose. He took her hand.

"Clea? Are you okay? Is there anything you need?"

Slowly, Clea opened her eyes and peered at him through the heavily mascaraed prison bars that were her eyelashes. Beyond the curtain, the kettle drum began its inexorable roll and she started, throwing her head for a moment into a yellow shaft of backstage light that uplit her features and made them seamless. She had the look, Charlie thought, of a brain-damaged china doll.

Through her great blue eyes, which connected to her brain, which since childhood she had visualized as blue, Clea caught his thought and registered it. She explained with wistful good humor. "I'm one of those women men like to hold in their hands, Charlie. They like me to dance on their open palms while they examine me and take delight in me. I see their giant faces peering down, adoring me, and I caper and then when the dance is done, they lay me in a tiny velvet box, which they carry with them always. I don't mind. They mean well. They don't want me to get broken."

"I would, Clea, if I could," offered Charlie bashfully.

The orchestra was swelling, blanketing out the chatter of the audience, and Clea began to draw in. Her little round head swayed from side to side. Her delicate fingers plucked the air. And in her tiny deer-hoof boots, she began to glide across the concrete between the flats, backwards and forwards with invisible effort, as if in fact she had no feet but stood on casters.

Her years at Chinese acrobatic school and her years of Chinese dance had taught her to move without moving, to marshal her muscles like ducks in a row and to set them to sail. In an instant long ago, she had transcended her cumbersome bipedalism. In the southwest corner of the Moon Court during typhoon season, she had suddenly broken free, beneath the gaze of the Master Liu Ah To, in a high threatening wind, as the tittering maids watered the night-blooming tanqua plants with tea and epigrams. It was as if there had been a detonation inside her followed by an afterwave of perfect fusion, as if the boundaries between her senses had melted down. The flow, the liquid mingling of time and movement, seeped and drained from some burst epicenter of grace. Liu Ah To, seeing the shock on her face, took her in his arms and said softly and clearly,

"Clea, now that you have merged with time, you will find that your mind is both locked in and locked out. You have relinquished awareness for something much greater. You will need protection."

He turned to Mee-Lan, the great acrobat who had rushed to the Moon Court when he heard of the event. "Wire my brother," the Master said.

OUT IN THE control truck on Forty-fifth Street, the director was switching cameras for the opening. He was sitting before the intricate console, snapping the picture from closeup to long shot to closeup to long shot in the frantic hope that somehow this would give him the godlike perspective he would need to get through the performance. From time to time, he barked into the headphones, "Charlie? Charlie!," after which he would listen intently, hoping anxiously for a positive reply. Or any reply. He turned to the A.D. and hissed through puffs of cigarette smoke,

"Where the fuck is he? Why doesn't he answer? What the fuck is going on down there?"

He sat back in his chair and, between deep drags of nicotine, continued to switch the picture. On the line of monitors before him, opposing angles of the same picture existed simultaneously, toying unmercifully with his knowledge of truth. The set behind the curtain, shadowy in the rehearsal light; and then, the curtain itself— gold velvet with gold tassels, shining excitedly in the full wash of anticipatory brights. First minicam came over the 'phones and said in a discreet whisper, "He's in the wings with Clea. You want to see? Look."

Onto the line of monitors popped a poorly lit long shot of the stage-right wing. Clea was slumped against the flat. Charlie was staring down at her, mesmerized and deeply in love. It was really just the outlines of their bodies and the bulk of their mass that the camera picked up through its lens and transmitted. No detail. For the moment, it was no more than mood and attitude. Clea was limp with concentration. Charlie was fantasizing making love to her. His body strained slightly forward, taut, ready to spring.

Clea was like a puddle, an abandoned gelatinous mass of mixing emotions that confused at the surface of her skin. She had no consciousness of Charlie. She was fully emotional at this time but untouchable. Her skin was as hot as a farm animal's, but it did her no good. Her performing emotion was useless in a human context. She might as well have been a piece of ice.

"Cut to closeup," the director said. And on the monitor appeared the tightest of closeups of Clea's face.

"How does she look to you?" the director asked the A.D.

The A.D. glanced at the six faces of Clea on the six TV screens and laughed. "She's so beautiful, and yet she's funny. I don't know what it is."

"No—she look okay?"

Tighter closeup now. The two men checking the face for signs of fallible humanity, but on a screen, of course, bone structure is king. A deep eye socket can substitute for sanity, a smooth skin texture for innocence of evil . . . it was hard to tell. And then Clea's eyes popped open and the two men, because they were spying, felt shame at the fear they saw there.

"Shit," said the director, and sat back heavily in his chair.

Over the phones came Charlie's voice then, insistent and officious.

"Right," he crackled. "Let's get this show on the road. All systems are go. Who's on first?"

Clea's giant face on the TV screen broke up into a smile at this and she said, "For Christ's sake, Charlie. It's not baseball. It's the end of the world as we know it. We can survive. But it helps if you're prepared. As I am."

"She's looking good," said Charlie.

The director put his hand over the mouthpiece and turned to the A.D. "This guy is a complete idiot"—he shook his head—"but he's been in the business for thirty-five years. I'm gonna go with his reading. I'm gonna pretend like this show's the same as any show we've ever done. She's great. Zeus is in the pink."

Max, the producer, stuck his head in the door at this moment and asked weakly, "Is everything all right?"

The director laughed and said into the headphones, "Give me Zeus, Ben."

"Zeus is great. He's dancing," said a disembodied voice. And he was.

. . . .

Two

. . . .

A s THE houselights dimmed and the overture wound to a close, Clea stood up tall, closed her eyes, and inhaled the smell of her own makeup. She was all put together, all done up, as starched and defined as any girl could be, anytime, and she was damn proud of herself. She straightened her back and felt the power of being completely in command but able to cry at the drop of a pin. The phrase "Happiness is a precipice" bounced into her mind and out again, the result of the feel of the rhinestone-studded skirt on the surface of her poised little fingers. She glanced at her pink digital watch.

"Aw God," she whispered, crashing into a valley and shooting out again as on some trampoline of despair.

"What time is—aw God." She trotted to the mirror secured on the flat and peered at her image. Her heart-shaped face was perfect and painted. Makeup filled the suncracks in her eyes, suncracks she might have avoided if she'd cared to, that summer on the Acgean beach or by the Indian Ocean. She could have worn a hat, but it seemed so cumbersome, and with Zeus there to protect her from everything including the sun, especially the sun, why bother?

"Zeus. Zeus." She turned abruptly from the mirror and called across the stage in a hoarse whisper. Zeus was already looking at her, had been for some time by the stance of him. Lost in thought. Worried.

"Zeus," she stage-whispered, "are you my father?" Zeus laughed and executed a graceful bow of assent in her direction. This was the moment that the minicam picked up and sent to the control room, the moment the cameraman defined as dancing but which wasn't dancing at all. It was cover, the blatant cover of a man who had seen several worlds come and go and had never gotten used to it. The camera can lie, is the thing to remember here.

Then, as at the start of every show they had ever done since their first outing at the Cairo Hilton so long ago, Zeus stared at her across the vast expanse of stage, and winked. It was a simple action, the kind of thing a man watches his father do to his mother in his childhood and then repeats when he falls in love. The kind of action that makes a woman's, a sensitive woman's, heart weep.

"Miss Florie," Clea asked one bad day, sitting at her dressing table in the endless preening posture that had come to define her life, "it is true that men love more deeply. That's the real secret isn't it, the real tragedy?"

Clea winked back. The lights went out.

In the blackness, Clea and Zeus walked crisply to their illuminated marks on the stage floor. They positioned their feet, picking them up and setting them down as if they were props. They glanced at each other and, in that second of intensity, sprang simultaneously into the illusion of life. Like the monolithic statues of the pharaoh and his wife, they posed silently together and heard the whir of the curtain slowly lifting. The rush of energy from the darkened audience set their hearts pumping and their lips moving involuntarily with the words and phrases they were to utter in the hours to come. In these moments, they were like oracles on PRINT, coughing up input, mindless expositors of retrievable memory.

They stood counting inwardly, waiting for the light, 5-4-3-2-1—
the great spots splattered from above, bathing the pharaoh and his
wife in white gold. They stood about three feet apart from each other
on the stage, two lone spotlit figures of great comic beauty. When the
audience saw them, their dream lovers, they cooed and clapped. Clea,
her arms extended in mock fury, in spite of her illness, in spite of her
fear of imminent death, snapped into inner timing. Turning to Zeus,
she unconsciously measured the audience's coo, and when it was
just to end, she flipped her aura around like a laser weapon and cried
with passionate whimsy,

"I don't know which is worse: men like you or incest."

"I love you," Zeus parried with a casual but ironic anger. "It's like
being in prison."

Three

THE LIGHT from the rainstorm was purple and green. The smell
of hot, wet asphalt permeated the apartment. The sound of raindrops falling on the air conditioner was faintly like machine-
gun fire. Clea hurried down the long, twisting hall, her boot-heel
clicks defining the route to Zeus' wing.

She knew she had reached his territory when she sighted the
mercenaries. Slouching in the doorways, they were brotherly sen-
tinels, always affable, always available for heavy work except when
they were drunk, which they were today, a bit. Their eyes were beer
red against their peaches-and-cream English complexions. The rain
made them lonely for their farms. They missed Africa. The atmosphere was a little out of control.

Clea, nervously aware of the intrusion of her female presence, approached the seven young men cautiously. As she walked, she shifted inside her skin, back and forth between empathetic mistress and modest maiden, unsure of which would be in residence when she reached the border.

They were blond, all seven of them, and beautifully designed, with aquiline features and innocent expressions that decorated their rough interiors and gave their violence a boyishness, which, in America, was hard to understand.

She called them the Seven Golden Lieutenants. They were Zeus' bodyguard system. They had always been Zeus' bodyguards. They had protected him with thornwood swords in the Rhodesian highlands of their youth. They had stood their ground around his farm when revolution smashed their idyll. And later, when Zeus was famous and they had to flee, he had brought them to his city-state and they had sworn allegiance for all time. The fact that they always wore camouflage fatigues, and were known for concealed weapons, had made Clea and Zeus' contract negotiations legendary. They were the only couple in show business who had never been screwed. But this was no mafia. This was Anglo-Saxon steel tempered with an Enid Blyton whimsy that melted it to roux. This was a force that was well mannered and pleasing. In truth, it was only the memory of it that was invincible.

The seven young men were staring into space when Clea arrived and said warmly, the empathetic mistress,

"Howzit? Good afternoon. Miss Florie has laid the tea. And there is mail."

They rumbled, a lethargic cricket team, slowly moved aside, and mobilized for this familiar ritual. Clea trotted through them, pushed open the great wooden door, and entered the antechamber that led to Zeus' wing.

Doron Harrismith sat behind the huge wooden desk aiming his machine gun at dog walkers in Central Park, and talking on the phone to the booking agent for the Jed Harris Theater on West

Forty-sixth Street. Clea moved to the windows and followed the aim of his gun barrel down to some moving umbrella specks trailing minuscule Akitas along miniature bridle paths. From above, the park looked like some aerial reconnaissance photo of a giant, wet forest. It was almost spring. There were almost buds. The incipient growth burst was palpable, the romance of its rebirth enhanced by the purpling light.

It was four in the afternoon. Clea was wearing a black sequined evening gown. Her jewelry was cold and heavy, the metal radiating the draft. Her hair stood straight up from her head like a shaggy punk lion. She had painted her face so the doll was outside. No man could gaze on her without fantasy, no woman without awe.

Doron looked up from the phone and fantasized for a moment with her image. She paused for the moment and let him, and then grabbed a cigarette off his desk and lit it. She was uncomfortable. Her stockings prickled. Her bra cut into her back. And her makeup was a gooey mask. How many times had she been in evening clothes before the sun went down? She never got used to it. It was unnatural. These were the garments of the night. In the day, they were all theatrics. She felt like a ratty wraith encased in a glamorous bloom.

Doron hung up the phone, and leaned the machine gun gently against the desk. "We got the theater," he said exuberantly, "and for a bloody good price."

He made some notes in a leatherbound book, and as he did so, his straight, golden hair fell over his forehead and she had a vision of the first time she met him. Hunched over an outdoor café table in Athens, scribbling in a diary, his dirty khaki shirt and shorts hardly concealing his overextended aristocratic bones. He had glanced up and seen Zeus, and the confusion in his eyes became tears that louged down his alpine nose and blurred the ink in his book. He began to get up, but before he could, Zeus reached him and threw his arms around the spindly man, pulling him up out of the spindly wire chair, burying the sound of his sobs in a soundproof African warmth.

Doron was different now, self-possessed and golden, a land mine in the DMZ of American show biz, the tallest and perhaps the only Wasp manager in the game.

"We've got the theater for the tenth of September. That should give you and Zeus enough time to write the script, rehearse, perhaps even take a small vacation . . . Clea?"

Clea was staring at the door to Zeus' room. She glanced at a copper clock in the shape of Africa that sat on Doron's desk. Returning her eyes to the door, staring at the wood grain, focusing on its swirls, trying to penetrate its mass with the intensity of her suspicion, she asked coldly,

"Where's Zeus? We're supposed to be at the awards taping at five-thirty. Where is he?"

She flicked her eyes toward Doron and pinned him for a moment where he stood. But he got away and opened the desk drawer and took out the can of oil and the chamois cloth that he used to clean his machine gun. He set these on top of the desk, took up the gun and, gesturing toward the door with it, replied, "He's recreating the Battle of Salamis."

Clea took a long drag on her cigarette. "He's not going," she said, and began to nod to herself and tap her foot.

"Well," said Doron, beginning to disconnect the machine gun and place its parts on the desk, "about twenty minutes ago the storm had just hit. Xerxes was regrouping in the Bay of Eleusis. He's with his boats. You know how he is."

Clea was tapping and nodding and smoking, turning into a small volcano before Doron's eyes, but he was ready and said, "Billy Butler called, darlin' . . ." Clea looked up. "He's going to take you tonight. He's in town for the awards. You were in the War Room, unreachable, so I took the liberty . . . the limo's picking him up first. He'll be here at five. He's up for original comedy, you know?"

Clea stared at Doron for a long time, saying nothing. Once, she absentmindedly ran her fingers through her hair, and then muttered, "Shit," as she realized what she'd done and that she'd have to recomb it. Finally, she trotted over to Zeus' door and turned the doorknob. It was locked.

"When did the drugs arrive?" she hissed at Doron. "Last night?" Doron opened a box of Zimbabwean cigarettes that lay on his desk and lit one.

"You know," he began, fixating on the box, "they call these Madisons, but they are really Rothmans or something similar in disguise. Since independence, because of the foreign currency flow problem, they can't package them properly and the big cigarette manufacturers won't allow their smokes to appear in inferior packaging. So they give them another name. But they're the same cigarettes. Maybe they've always been. My first smoke was a Madison."

Clea rattled the doorknob of Zeus' door. "Last night?" she spat, "last night?" She released the doorknob, dropped her cigarette and, glaring at Doron, crushed it into the carpet with her toe. He could see she was all inside herself now, thinking fast, banishing disappointment, erasing the dirt marks of love. She was wringing her hands and keening around like Ophelia before she lept in. Doron spoke quickly. "Did you say there was tea?" he asked, rising and coming out from behind the desk.

Clea was plunging toward the outer door, the train of her evening gown fleeing after her like a scared snake. Doron sped after her. With his six-foot-seven-inch long-boned frame he reminded her of a secretary bird when he sprinted across a room as he was doing now: flapping his huge bony wing and seizing her bare shoulder with his huge bony claw. "Clea," he said with those long vowels that made everything seem classy, even despair, blood, and death, "you cawnt change him." There was bewilderment in his eyes, though his voice was sure. In some situations, Clea thought, all men are poets. "Zeus is the way he is."

Clea yanked open the great wooden door and flung herself into the hall. She shot along the dim, narrow passageway, her velvet silhouette receding so fast that the wood clop of her deer-boot heels lagged behind, a Doppler effect of a stampeding herd of faerie horses.

Doron caught up with her just before the doorway to the dining room and, keeping astride, asked in a calm, managerial voice, "Clea, what's the show to be about? Do you have an idea?"

Clea stopped short. She turned to Doron and saw, past his head, through the dining room arch, what seemed to be a perfect colonial photograph. Seven blond young men in camouflage fatigues seated around a great dark wood table. They were reading letters, all of them, intently, silently. The tea tray sat in the center of the table. Two oversize china teapots steamed from their spouts. They were white with gold embossing: the crest of an African farm. In the background, hazy, swathed in the shadows of a rain-dark afternoon, a Xhosa woman bore on her head a tray piled high with crumpets and fresh cream. Her eyes were averted, self-effacing, elsewhere. The whole thing had a grainy quality, like an art photo, like it was history.

"Look, Doron," Clea whispered, clutching his elbow, pointing with her eyes, "how ironic for Florie. It looks like everything she tried to escape. Look."

But before he could, the photo came to life. Florie snapped on a table lamp, set down the crumpets, took one, and pirouetted through the swinging kitchen door. One of the young men began to read aloud in a small, scared almost-British voice, "I love you, utterly. I yearn for you. I am paralyzed . . ." A letter from a lost wife.

Clea moved quickly down the corridor, past the dining room, and Doron followed.

"Clea," he persisted, "what about the show?"

Behind them, a door slammed, and out of Zeus' wing, coming toward them down the long hall, padded Mr. Liu. In one hand was an ashtray heaped with butts. The fingers of the other were jammed in the open mouths of five empty beer bottles. Liu's head was down; he was concentrating. When he reached the dining-room arch, Clea called to him, "How is he, Liu?" She said this sarcastically, her hands on her hips, like a living razor blade ready to cut and slash, foreseeing the beauty of blood.

Liu looked up at her but did not reply. She continued. "Let's see: a pack of cigarettes, six beers—I'd say we're at the end of Act One. The interval. Time to repowder, hey?"

Liu disappeared into the dining room. Clea checked her watch. Four forty-five, not much time, alone again, what do you do?

She laughed. "I've been tapping into NORAD, Doron. And it may be the last show, the very last show we ever do on the earth as we know it."

Doron took out a pack of Madisons and removed one, then lit it, never taking his eyes off the mad Celtic fairy they all fucked by proxy. In their waking moments, in their dreams and fantasies, her aura was so strong, it made them weak. "Clea . . ." He went to comfort her, but she flinched away.

"Don't fuck with me, Doron, I told you before. It could happen anytime, in any way: a nuclear accident, a difference of opinion, a wrongly pushed button. The end is near, the big bang and whimper, over and out. Gigi!" She threw up her arms and belted the words in a slurred French accent, Louis Jourdan in drag, waltzing around the corridor with joy.

" 'Am I a fool without a heart, or am I merely just too dumb to realize? OH, GIGI! Have you been growing up before my very eyes? AH, GIGI!—' "

"Clea." Doron was smiling in spite of himself. The Seven Golden Lieutenants peeked around the dining room arch with innocent curiosity, ignorant of the song.

"Ah, boys, boys." Clea was still speaking in a French accent. She fluttered her hands and pursed her lips. "As it will be the end, the end of efreetheeng we haf werked for, liffed for, loffed for, I theenk we should pay omage to thet and call the show 'Clea and Zeus Deevorce,' c'est juste, n'est-ce pas?"

There was a dead silence. The Seven Golden Lieutenants withdrew through the arch. Mr. Liu, who was coming out with a clean ashtray and a pack of unopened beers, paused, alert. A Xhosa click-phrase rang out in the dining room which, translated freely, meant "shit." And Doron, instantaneously catapulted into a hand-dug trench, sandbags around him, said in the calm, clear voice of a general between artillery bursts, "Are you serious? Does Zeus know?"

Clea was biting her nails like a small ape after lice. "I imagine he does," she said coolly. "He knows everything about me. He is me. He's a witch doctor, you know that."

"Clea—" Doron's tone turned as hard as the stone of the Great Zimbabwe ruins.

"Ah, detachment"—Clea's eyes flashed. It was hard to understand her between nail bites—"what I wouldn't give to have it. How I wish it were in my cells as it is in yours. It's a linkage to the Y chromosome, I'm sure of that. No, Doron, I've not told him in words, but then we haven't used words in a long, long time. But perhaps, after the Battle of Salamis, later tonight—"

"No, Clea," said Doron, "don't."

Mr. Liu moved forward. Balancing his burdens, he hurried up the corridor toward Zeus' wing.

"Doron,"—Clea was moving too, turning her back, trotting in the opposite direction down the corridor toward the War Room—"it doesn't matter. The earth is going to blow up. The only question is when. There may or may not be anything left. A divorce is good business. It's a great marketing principle. People will love it. And you know what? Like you, they'll refuse to believe it."

She had reached the sliding panel to the War Room now. She stuck out her hand and placed it on a small fingerprint security box that protruded from the wall. Its fingerprint analysis done, the door slid open and she vanished through it.

Left in the corridor by himself, Doron glanced at the framed publicity pictures and theatrical posters and playbills that lined the walls. *Clea and Zeus at the Cairo Hilton; Clea and Zeus in Love; Clea and Zeus at Carnegie Hall; Clea and Zeus Grow Up.*

He stood there and repeated to himself the name of the show he was doomed to promote. "*Clea and Zeus Divorce. Clea and Zeus Divorce.*"

Four

M UU-SIC! SLIDE!" barked the director, and with a swirl of
strings, onto the line of monitors, over the figures of Clea and
Zeus, flipped the yellow and turquoise title script: "Clea and
Zeus Divorce." Doron lit a cigarette. They were off. The show had
begun.

"Go!" the director barked, and the first credit slide snapped up.

The door to the control truck opened at this moment, and Doron
jumped, then grinned, as Ruth Ravenscroft hurried up the metal
steps aided by a chauffeur, who helped her in and then retreated,
closing the door behind him.

"Go!" barked the director again, and the second credit slide snapped
up, this time his.

"Yea, Al!" Ruth called, and the director glanced back and smiled
sheepishly.

Ruth was just two hours off the plane from Zaire. Dizzy with jet
lag, she dragged her knapsack into the corner of the truck where
Doron stood huddled, and collapsed against him.

"Hallo," she whispered. "I came as soon as I could."

"Hit it!" the director barked, and another credit slide snapped up.

Through the paintbrush script, Ruth peered at the two spotlit
images that were her dearest friends and tried to get a sense of them.
She passed her eyes from screen to screen over the six technological
two-dimensional replications of Clea and Zeus and couldn't see it.
Actually couldn't take it. She jerked her head and her blond hair
fanned around her like an angry cat tail.

"Sorry." Her breath feathered Doron's ear and gave him a momentary comfort. "I'm a bit weird from the journey. I literally came
out of the jungle, hopped on a plane, and I'm here. There were some
problems with poachers out of Kinshasa. They winged Muamar. I
only got your letter a few days ago."

Doron nodded glumly.

"Go!" hollered the director, and the final card snapped up.

"You love that ape more than me," Doron sneered. Without taking his eyes off the monitors, he crankily offered her a cigarette. She took the one he was smoking instead and inhaled it and handed it back.

"You're right," she replied, "I do. Simply dreadful about Billy Butler's death and the madness." She rattled on, trying to get used to the whir of the machines, the cold steel casings which it seemed had suddenly shot up around her. Vanished were the gentle stirrings of banana leaves, the crunch of a gorilla paw treading on a twig. "Which has more to do with the divorce?" she asked.

Doron shrugged. "I don't know," he muttered. "I'm only a man. I don't have intuition or heightened perception or much of a sense of future. I only look around me if I have to."

"Muu-sic." The director caressed the word and a poignant sting was heard. "One!" He snapped his fingers, and a closeup of Zeus appeared instantly.

"Clea," Zeus was calling in a strangled mixture of anger and anguish, his eyelashes wet with tears, or was it sweat? Ruth couldn't tell.

"Two!" the director spat, and up shot Clea.

"Zeus." Clea pushed the name defiantly, out of picture into the televisual void. Her lips were trembling. Her eyelids at half staff.

"I can't tell," murmured Ruth. "I can't—"

"Lights, three, go!" The stage lights bumped up. The spots were dimmed. The sting faded. And onto the broadcast monitor snapped a two-shot: Clea and Zeus posed, yearning, then sobering, becoming, in a sense, normal, turning upstage, heads bowed in thought, sauntering into the play. The director sat back and went limp with momentary relief.

They looked, Ruth thought as she watched them go, as they always had, like a handsome cartoon wolf and a gorgeous Peppi La Pugh. Zeus was rangy and fluid, his message a languid control. Clea, with her skunky punk mane coming to a point in the center of her back, was all kinetic precision and fiery feminine grace. They seemed the same, lithe and magnetic, black and pink velvet, a sequined beast with two backs, their fate predetermined long ago in a shadow play on the wall of a cave. You couldn't tell anything was wrong on the monitor. In two dimensions their effect was, if anything, surer, more defined, as if they'd never broken apart, never trusted anyone else.

"Blast!" said Ruth, frustrated and confused.

"Don't say that word, please,"—the director glanced back—"it makes us nervous." The A.D. giggled uncontrollably.

"What time is the . . . uh . . . nuclear detonation? What time does Clea say the bomb will hit?" Ruth turned to Doron.

"Ten. Three quarters of the way through the second act." Doron sounded numb.

"We hope she's wrong," the director added, "of course."

"Can I talk to her at intermission?" Ruth asked.

Doron shrugged. "You can if you can. Perhaps you can, Ruth. Perhaps *you* can persuade her to drop the radiation suits from the love dance, though I doubt it."

Doron massaged his face. His long, bony hands cupped his head like it was a basketball in a foul shot.

Ruth stared at Doron, and the sheer grittiness of being a human being in a human world, something she had avoided for some time now, washed over her like an acid rain. They were none of them cut out for it, never, not since the beginning. What drew them together was their innocence, their goodness, their all-consuming interest in the mechanism of love. It was when they got successful that it backfired on them. It was simply too precious for the hucksters around them to see, evidence of a fatal vulnerability. And so they tried to hide it, and that's when the trouble began.

Doron straightened up. "I'm going out in the house to check security. Come with?"

"Hold on them," the director was saying. "One, two, three—"

"Right," said Ruth, and followed Doron to the door, halting as he opened it to take a last look at the long shot of her friends as they walked upstage.

This was the last time she would look at them without emotion. When she saw them in person, she would see the ragged edges and— "I can't believe it," she said, her face crumpling, the phrase coming out a tearful squeal. She put her hands over her eyes.

"Four, five, six," the director was murmuring mournfully.

Ruth sniffed and said, "Uh, my stuff will be safe here, yes? There are some important notes about the younger apes—"

"God, we hope so," said the A.D.

"Brilliant set," she bravely told Doron as they clambered down the metal steps and onto Forty-fifth Street.

"Yah," muttered Doron, and thought of the design meeting when Clea announced, "I don't care what it looks like to begin with. I want it a nuclear void by the middle of the second act."

. . . .

Five

. . . .

OUT IN THE house, the Seven Golden Lieutenants were spaced around the theater, two flanking the orchestra, two, the balcony, three by the exits, legs spread, armed with machine guns. They wore their camouflage fatigues, of course, and heavy boots and berets, like the show biz mercenaries they were. The light from the fire exits gleamed off the metal gun barrels, making them phallic torches in the dark of the aisles. The audience had long ago accepted the Lieutenants. They were part of the entourage, part of an evening with Clea and Zeus, there to protect. The audience was glad of that, and found them roughly glamorous. Men and women chatted to them in the intermission, and it was reported in the *Times* once that they were lovely English boys, Rhodesians, yes, but terribly polite and charming, classically educated even, well versed in Virgil and the metaphysical poets. At this point in time, they were part of the performance. The audience would have fretted were they gone.

Everything was all right. On the surface, everything was calm. The audience was staring at the stage in rapt and excited attention, waiting, waiting as a Jungian consciousness for the answer to the question the evening's event had posed. Is it over? Really over? And why? Why? A woman crinkled the cellophane on a candy box and whispered anxiously to her seatmate, "I think if they get a divorce, I'll die." And popped a sugar almond into her mouth. Jim, the set designer, leaning on the orchestra wall, fixating on the stage, noting one by one the details of his set, the placement of objects, the relative blend of color, the power of the inanimate when engaged by the animate, laughed nervously at the comment.

The backdrop on the stage was a strange planetary sky. A giant flat painted a series of aqua blues and violets ran the full length of the upstage wall. Two great setting suns dripping with yellows and reds hung in the upper right corner. Roger's lighting was the precious gold of the afternoon sun on the wane, strong rays of light, and in between, deep shadow. Placed in a semicircle, beginning downstage right, along the upstage flat, and ending downstage left, were eight conical heaps of objects, the possessions of Clea and Zeus. Each object was tied separately onto one massive rope, which formed the heaps and coiled between them along the stage floor. Each heap was a mass of colors, shapes and textures containing articles of clothing, books, mementos, shoes, letters, furniture, and even some live things, a bowl of fish, a cockatoo and a Siamese cat. The colorful detritus of ten years of marriage and of art. The stage floor was the red rust of the African earth. The rope to which the objects were attached was Chinese yellow, the yellow of the Yellow River. It was an abstract Africascape littered with the maddest of tall termite hills, a lyrical outer space veld. Through the sweet, hot shafts of light, Clea and

Zeus sauntered upstage and then parted, Clea to the right conical heap, Zeus to the left.

Clea removed a bowie knife from the belt of her cocktail dress, and cut from the yellow rope a leather sled with attached dog harness, an American Indian artifact. She placed it downstage, where the audience could see it.

Zeus snapped a switchblade out of his coat pocket, and cut from the rope a dime store reclining lawn chair, a bottle of beer, a bottle opener, and a martini glass, which objects he sat on the stage floor opposite the leather sled. He unfolded the chair, opened the beer and poured it in the martini glass, and then settled himself in the chair with his feet up. Assuming the satisfied smile of a man whose lawn has no bald spots, he sipped his beer and began watching Clea. The audience tittered.

Clea was scrambling around the right conical heap, picking at it. As she was sifting through the objects, she could feel the energy ebb and flow around her, and without looking at Zeus, she chose the precise moment when the smile was played out on his face. She cut from the rope a large wing-tip shoe.

"This yours?" she asked, holding it aloft on one finger. He nodded. She threw it onto the dog sled, where it hit with a thud.

She addressed the audience. "We're getting a divorce," she said. The audience gasped.

"No, it's fine, really," she reassured them. "It'll probably be like *Scenes from a Marriage*: ten years from now we'll be married to other people but we'll be meeting secretly in a motel. Don't worry."

The audience laughed and then moaned audibly, "No. No."

"Yes, I'm sorry"—she was shaking her mane—"it's over. Isn't it, Zeus?"

She snapped her body toward him and the final *s* carried her words across the proscenium, where he caught them, palmed them for a moment, and then threw back a laconic, "Yah, mon."

"It happened," she went on, dragging the rope on which was hanging a massive collection of science fiction books over to the sled and cutting their connection so they fell down with a crash, "because of an infidelity . . ." The audience fell silent. "The question is whether it was his or mine. You never really know."

She cut from the rope an eyelash curler and then a mirror and began to curl her eyelashes. "This is the most magnificent makeup tool ever invented." She pointed at Zeus with her thumb. "He's used it. Don't kid yourself." She glanced over at him. "It's been a constant fight for control of the mirror. Don't ever marry a performer."

Zeus nodded. "Good advice, Clea." And then to the audience, "I wish she'd mentioned that ten years ago."

"Ha, ha, ha,"—Clea shook herself like a dog after a swim—"very funny. For a man." The audience began to relax. Maybe it wasn't true.

Clea lapsed for a moment and became aware of the heat of the light. She fixated on a bead of sweat on Zeus' upper lip and went blank, then cold. In the control room, the director flinched. Out in the house, Doron clutched Ruth's arm. Backstage, Miss Florie and Mr. Liu looked at each other and prepared for the worst. Zeus slowly turned his head, aware of the panic but loath to catch it. He caught her eye and smiled. And she remembered. The audience never knew.

"Zeus is a macho guy," she pronounced, pulling the rope, dragging more objects out of the heap. "Look at this."

She cut from the rope an African assegai and a small target glued to a stick. With a great effort, she carried the assegai over to Zeus, laid it in his lap, and then returned to the sled, putting the stick in her mouth so the target was suspended before him. She put her hands behind her back and waited. Zeus unfolded himself, stood up, drew the assegai back over his shoulder, and threw it.

"Hit it," barked the director, and first minicam followed the flight of the assegai as it took the target off the stick and nailed it to the proscenium wall. The audience clapped.

Clea walked over to the arrow and tried to pull it out of the wall. "I love him for this," she said, finally giving up, too weak to extract it. "I wouldn't want him to wash dishes. I'm not interested in domestication, really."

The inside of her lip was sore from where the stick had caught for a second before the target flew off. Though she had been prepared for it, the jolt startled her and she did a small turn away from the audience to allow some escaped tears to roll down her face.

Zeus laid the assegai on the dog sled. "All women," he said straightening up, grinning at the audience, "are interested in domestication, even if they fear it." He repaired to the lawn chair.

"Like Clea." He gestured toward her. She had resumed cutting items off the yellow rope: their poster from Carnegie Hall, a dried out bridal bouquet she had caught at a friend's wedding, an oversize packet of birth control pills as big as a record album. The poster she placed on the sled. The bouquet she attached to her belt by means of clips. The rest of the items she placed in a shopping cart, which now she cut from the rope. The album of Ortho-Novum made the audience laugh and she popped one huge pill out and chewed on it as Zeus said, "Clea, for example, dreams of motherhood."

Clea spat out the pill into the shopping cart, looked over at him and listened, waiting.

"But in reality, what would become of her career, her identity, her freedom?"

"You never wanted children!" Clea barked the line across the stage, addressing Zeus directly.

The audience gasped. Zeus picked up his martini glass and toasted the crowd.

"See what I mean?" he said, and downed the drink.

The sound of a doorbell electrified the stage, and the scenery began to revolve. The eight conical heaps, slowly whirling, began to descend beneath the stage floor. Zeus folded up the lawn chair and exited downstage left, carrying it under his arm. Clea, the golden light dimming and wavering around her, unbuttoned the front of her cocktail dress as she traversed the stage from down right to up left. She stepped out of it and dropped it on one of the heaps, which was disappearing beneath the stage floor. She continued up left, wearing now a pair of short shorts and a halter top and, of course, her deer-hoof boots.

From the wings three walls appeared, forming a room. In place of the conical heaps, several pieces of hotel furniture now rose up through the floor, a double bed, a couple of chairs, a dressing table.

Clea stopped and the lights undulated around her, creating a lyrical chaos. She watched the objects whirr. She listened to the mechanisms creak and transfused them into molecular change. She injected her heart and drew out first love and squirted it under her skin. Her eyes were closed and in her mind she conjured pictures, the nape of his neck, an earlobe, a swirl of hair on a toe, and many subtitles: his eyes were so . . . I wanted so badly to . . . my veins were pumping, are pumping. I am, I am overcome. I am only a girl. Oh Lord. Oh Lord. There is peace only in that . . . The lights bumped up. The mechanisms idled. Clea opened her eyes, fifteen years younger, fifteen years dumber, sweeter, newer. The doorbell sounded again and Clea bounced across the stage to what the audience could now see was her hotel room door.

. . . .

Six

. . . .

ZEUS squeezed through the wing into the backstage area. He thrust the lawn chair and martini glass into the extended arms of a propman on the run. All around him in shadowy lighting people were rushing, twirling, leaping, imitating the underground machinery, evolving toward the incipient scenes. Zeus threaded through them, sweat-logged, burdened by his wet wool jacket, his hair plastered to his head like a baby's cap. He emerged from the dimness into the glare of the backstage left corridor and stopped for a moment to adjust his eyes and remove his jacket.

The dancers were massing for the nightclub scene. The men sported galabias, army uniforms, and such, the different outfits of Egyptian male street garb. The women wore fishnet gowns of teal blue, red ocher, and mustard, the panoply of colors from the Valley of the Kings. These choicest of designer mummy wrappings outlined their barge-shaped breasts, barely concealing the nipples.

Zeus was so blank and drained that he became momentarily distracted. A tall, befuddled figure in this midst of pressing femininity, he reached out his hands, dropping his jacket, and like a baby near a moving cat, grasped a pair of passing tits and held them for dear life. He stared down at them, and then lowered his mouth to the nipples as if by instinct. A scream was heard. His hands were slapped. And Zeus came to before voluptuous little Peg, who had shrieked not out of piety, but out of fear that if he sucked on her she'd melt.

Many eyes from made-up faces stared at him, amused and silent. Peg, embarrassed and trying to recoup, seized his hands and tried to bring them back, to place them on her breasts again. But just then Mr. Liu appeared, the wraithlike tugboat. He dipped to retrieve the jacket from the floor, and steered Zeus away to his dressing room.

Mr. Liu closed the door and hung up Zeus' jacket. He unbuttoned Zeus' shirt and peeled it off him. Zeus sat down heavily in a chair in front of his dressing table. He noticed in the mirror that his torso was a different color than his head and neck.

"Look, Liu," he said excitedly, "I'm wearing a Zeus head."

He spread three tissues on the counter and pressed his face down onto them, first one cheek then the other, enjoying this private wallow. When he sat back up, one tissue remained stuck to his cheekbone, which he left dangling—a visible threat, till it finally fell off, at some point later, just in the nick of televised time.

"Ten minutes," murmured Mr. Liu, and turned up the sound on the monitor in the corner of the room. A bell was ringing.

Zeus glanced at the clock, ten to nine, seventy minutes to lift-off, no, ground zero, no Trinity, yah. In the mirror, Zeus could see

Clea on the monitor, bounding across the stage, answering the door to Eddie Witz. Eddie, whose rotund appearance and foghorn of a voice often reminded Zeus of the great actor Eugene Palette, was playing the part of Sid, Clea's road manager, in the evening's production. The scene was the Cairo Hilton, her first tour, July of '73, where it began. Eddie as Sid entered, followed by the Egyptian room boy who was wearing a caftan and clutching some towels. The boy beamed at Clea and, proud of his English, boomed, "Good morning, sir!" Clea nodded to him. The audience laughed.

"Come quickly," said Clea, and took Sid's arm and dragged him upstage onto a small balcony that protruded off the back flat. "Something important has happened." She scooped up a pair of binoculars from a nearby chair.

"You're pregnant," said Sid.

"No. Come!" She pushed him onto the balcony.

"Worse," he muttered. "You're giving up show business and going to law school."

"No, Sid."

She pressed the binoculars to her face and peered down at something below. In the control room, the director went to tape and onto the monitor in the shape of binocular lenses popped the pre-taped shots of Zeus sailing a toy galleon in the Cairo Hilton pool. He was wearing his third world brown suit, on his knees surrounded by bikinied women, maneuvering the craft with a bamboo stick.

"See that man?" Clea handed Sid the binoculars. "See him? I've fallen in love with him."

"Clea—" Sid began.

"No, I'm going to marry him. Find out who he is."

"Clea, honey, listen to me," Sid was mewling, "the guy's some kind of businessman, a straight guy, not your type, not my type. He's pretty, I give you, but, honey, honey, he's not an American."

"So what, Sid? He's still got a backbone. Look!" Clea prodded the binoculars in Sid's hand. "You can just make it out beneath his shirt."

Zeus smiled and then reached over and turned off the sound on the monitor. He watched Liu moving around behind him, laying out the brown suit and the garish short-sleeved shirt, the old-fashioned briefcase, the heavy brown lace-up shoes, the kit that used to define him before he was a star when he was just a citizen of the third world.

"My suits and I were handmade in Rhodesia, which no longer exists," Zeus said to him. "Perhaps I don't either."

Liu held out the trousers, and Zeus took them and began to dress.

It hadn't happened exactly as he and Clea had written it. They had taken, as they always did, poetic license with their life, theatricalizing it, decorating the tedious parts, so that often, when they sat in armchairs and looked back, they couldn't quite distinguish what had happened from what they had designed. It had gotten that complex. Or so they told the press. But the beginning one always remembers, perhaps because of the excitement, perhaps because of youth, perhaps because it is the seed pod of everything that follows. Zeus leaned down to the mirror to tie his vulgar tie and a memory assailed him: the first time that he saw Clea, in the baggage room at customs in the air terminal at Addis Ababa.

She was by herself, a slender child-woman with a giant, big-eyed head on a spindly dancer's body, all in black except for a safari hat. Zeus, ever on the lookout in these godforsaken places for beautiful women unattached to tours, felt he had caught the ring this time, and hovered near her like a gull to a surfacing fish.

"Where will you be staying?" a grinning Ethiopian asked her, pounding her passport with his big black stamps, transfixed by her attractiveness, giving her the greatest gift he had to offer: letting her go by without a search. She smiled and said, "The Hilton, for a week." And Zeus relaxed. The same hotel. No need to rush. "Bless the tobacco monopoly and everyone connected with it," he muttered to himself. "Perhaps it's had some purpose after all." He gathered up his boxes of tobacco leaves and prayed they'd let him through.

The Ethiopian despised him. Despite his British passport, issued to mask his origins, the customs man could smell him, scion of black oppressors, *baas* by birth, it seemed to be all over him like sweat. It would take an hour to rifle his luggage, then an interrogation, then the payoff to bring in the leaves . . . Zeus had resigned himself. The Ethiopian was motioning him aside when just then Clea reappeared, juggling three red bananas she had bought from ragged children in the road. She flipped them up into the air, spun them on her fingertips, and made them do a jaunty dance in space. The Ethiopian stamped his passport hurriedly and told him to be gone. Stepping from behind his pedestal, the man stood mesmerized by Clea, who, as a final gesture, caught the dancing fruits one by one as neatly as could be and offered them to the Ethiopian *en bouquet*. The other customs officers cheered and clapped. Clea bowed. The Ethiopian was thrilled and blushed through his café-au-lait skin. His neat blue-white teeth gleamed against his deep pink gums as he laughed with delight. And then she was out, nipped into a cab, off to the hotel. Zeus hurried out after her into the car provided by the tobacco monopoly. "Follow that cab," he told the driver, "to the ends of the earth."

Ethiopia was a mysterious place in those days before the coup, the last empire in Africa. Addis Ababa was the strangest of cities. It was surrounded by a eucalyptus forest which, when the rains were beginning, as they were when Zeus arrived, gave off a deep, dark herbal scent that, combined with the dusky incense that emanated from the Coptic churches, hung heavily about the streets like a veil. It was so dense, this pungent air, that in the back of the chauffered car Zeus felt his eyes watering and then the tears cascading down his cheeks.

Through blurred vision he could see lone donkeys grazing on the promenades before colonial buildings with a Byzantine touch. Here and there an Ethiopian dandy strutted by. The men were very tall and thin, with high cheekbones, brown skin, and narrow Caucasian features—a bit of both, like Nordics dipped in ink. The national costume was high style, white linen jodhpurs and shirts topped with linen shawls draped, with insouciance, over one shoulder. Accessories were lace-up shoes, slouch hats, and rain or shine, open umbrellas.

The effect was whimsical, like line drawings from an English children's poetry book of the nineteen thirties.

> E is for Ethiope
> Slender and proud.
> It isn't a cape he wears,
> Neither a shroud . . .

"Here," the driver said suddenly, "is Haile Selassie's palace in Addis."

"He has others?" asked Zeus.

"Oh yes," the driver replied, just a touch of sarcasm in his tone, "he has a palace in Debre Zeit, in Harar—" He gave a list and then he asked, "You speak Italian?"

"No," said Zeus.

"I do," the driver smiled. "I learned in the occupation." He paused and asked with promise of sympathy, "Why are you crying?"

"*Amore*," Zeus replied.

"Ah! *Va bene*," said the driver, nodding in understanding. "Where are you from?"

Zeus seized up, stopping himself before he inadvertently replied.

"Wiltshire," he said finally, fantasizing a rolling English garden and him on a lawn chair bouncing a red-cheeked baby. "Wiltshire," he said again, using the international code name for the unnameable place where he was born. "I'm a tobacco man."

As he remembered it, he had traversed the dark, cool lobby of the Addis Ababa Hilton and found her in the coffee shop. Sitting near a short banquet table festooned with breakfast cereals and local fruits, adjacent to some red bananas, she was absorbed, reading a medical text, a study of leprosy. Her energy was so contained, her concentration so focused, that she did not hear him as he stooped to her and spoke the only line that he could summon up in such a present presence.

"Is this seat taken?" he said again.

She looked up, he could see, guns ready. An enemy aircraft had violated her airspace. She went to fire but he was quick, jamming her radar with laser eyes. Blinded, she floundered, stating the obvious.

"No," she said. And immediately he dropped landing gear and glided smoothly into the seat opposite her.

She was so pretty, this girl, this human mouselet, that he was overwhelmed by a desire to crush her. He wanted to mash her narrow childlike frame against his body, to fling her little arms around his neck and wear her like fleshy armor. He wanted to slip inside her and then get up immediately, draping her over his shoulder like an Ethiopian shawl, carrying her with him everywhere as he went about his business. Her giant head would loll near his face and he would kiss her when necessary, drawing from her a needed strength. And with him still inside her, she would twitch from time to time, grabbing his neck from sensation, unwilling to let go. But in spite of these thoughts he simply asked, "Will you have dinner with me tonight?" And she considered it.

"I saw you at customs," he kept talking. "You were splendid. Are you a juggler by trade?"

Her eyes sparkled and she told him that she was indeed a juggler and an acrobat, booked into the Cairo Hilton for a month, but for the moment traveling, researching rhythms.

"So, will you come with me tonight?" he asked again. "The head of the tobacco monopoly and I are going to some nightclubs." She hesitated, weighing, he could see, the consequences of coming out, of breaking from her Zen-like focus. She was attracted to him, that was clear, and yet she was no party girl. Her books would do her fine, her fantasies, her little red bananas. She was a self-sufficient one, this little thing. He searched her for a crack, an unlocked door, a yearning he could satisfy. He had to have her. That was that, and that was very rare.

She was thumbing through her book, biding time, and he looked down at it and blurted, "Would you like to see some lepers?" And she was all attention.

"Yes," she chirped, "oh yes."

"Some lepers, then," he boomed, delighted. He was in. "Some lepers, dinner, and some nightclubs!"

"All right," she said, laughing softly with some personal irony, "all right."

That night, they traveled to the western part of the city to a street of nightclub shacks with little neon signs. The names were Hollywood, Las Vegas, Hot Hawaii, and the like, planetary monikers for good times without guilt. Inside were stark dance rooms lit by bare bulbs, with wooden banquettes built up against the walls and the occasional plastic chair. Clusters of very young and very beautiful Ethiopian women stood about, smiling and giggling modestly. Their slender girlish demeanors seemed strangely at odds with their Western miniskirts and high-heeled shoes.

"They are prostitutes, of course," Cieslaw Plundera, the head of the tobacco monopoly, explained to Clea. He winked at Zeus as he grabbed a delicate young beauty and planted her on his knee. "In Czechoslovakia, where I came from, it was a choice, here it is a life and death struggle against filthy poverty, the only job they will ever get." He pinched the young woman as he said this, and she giggled and kissed his cheek.

Cieslaw was a great favorite at the brothels. He tipped big and he was known to be kind. Zeus accompanied him whenever he was in town, and once, Zeus had bought a woman. But when she took him out back to the gritty little bunkers, the fucking rooms that smelled of human shit and animal death, he changed his mind. He gave the woman the money and bought instead a soda in a recycled pop bottle which he drank while he waited for Cieslaw. "I have too much oppression on my back as it is, mon," he had told the Czech.

"I love these girls." Cieslaw was shrugging. "And they love me. We have our bargain: they keep me sane and I keep them alive. Communist expatriotism!" and he laughed.

"But there are no clients," Clea said. She looked embarrassed. Fifty very young women were milling about the room, staring at the party, rocking occasionally to some weird third world disco band. "No clients," she went on. "They're so beautiful—why?"

Cieslaw was grave. "Ah, well, this is the terrible tragedy. No Ethiopian can afford a prostitute. Sometimes, on a holiday, a few Europeans, but really—not." He fondled the woman on his lap and she squeaked delightedly. "Get us some drinks," he said, squeezing her, and she got up and went outside. "So they are very innocent," he added philosophically, glancing resignedly around the room. "Here you can always have a virgin if you want one. A jaded businessman's paradise, eh?"

Zeus sat silent, studying Clea. The girls were examining her clothes, feeling the material of her dress between their fingers, peering admiringly at her earbobs and rings, trying on her strange deer hoof-shaped boots. She was smiling at them and laughing, holding out her hands so they could see, pulling her long dark hair behind her ears. Her normal liquidity of movement was absent, though. What she offered them was a genuine but superficial grace beneath which she was rigid, mortified, he guessed, by their predicament.

Cieslaw's woman returned with the drinks and Cieslaw spoke to her in Amharic. Then he leaned toward Clea and murmured, "Zeus tells me you are interested in lepers."

"Yes," Clea said simply.

Cieslaw appraised her, thoughtfully. "Perversion?" he asked. "Science? Tourism?"

Clea looked at Zeus and said nothing. She was, he could see, impenetrable, but waiting like a hyena near a fresh lion kill.

"My friend here"—Cieslaw gestured toward the girl—"will take you out back. There are some beggars of the district—but I'm sorry, my dear,"—he took her hand and kissed it—"I cannot accompany you. In some things I am very cowardly."

Clea nodded. Her face was alert but emotionless.

"Do you want me to come?" Zeus asked out of duty and a desire vastly different from the camaraderie it offered.

She looked at him. "Please," she replied, taking his hand and pulling him and herself off the banquette.

They followed Cieslaw's woman across the room and down some crumbling stairs to the back courtyard. The grisly bunkers were barely visible in the moonlight. The smell of shit was there, and garbage and animal urine. They padded past the door of an empty bunker. Cieslaw's woman cast a yearning glance at Zeus, just in case. They went around it, past a refuse heap of offal and glass bottles. They heard an infant scream, a donkey bray, a human moan, and then they saw them. Propped up against the bunker, four abreast, of indeterminate sex, wrapped in white cloth.

"Lepers," the woman said in Amharic, pointing, and stood by.

Zeus looked at Clea. She was frozen, staring. Then she seemed to shake herself, and approached the four, removing from the pocket of her dress a pair of black gloves. She pulled the gloves onto her hands and then removed from her pocket a wad of money, which she divided into four and handed out to each of the lepers. They took it with whatever part of their appendages they had left to them, two twisted fingers, an elbow cleft, three gnarled toes, a dying fist, and then grouped beneath her, waiting and watching. They didn't know what was in store for them. They didn't seem to care. They never got attention, these creatures of the sewers, not even of a negative kind. They knew their place by now and kept it. They lived in a plane between life and death, in some paraphysical rut. Nothing could happen to them now. You couldn't kill them. They had been killed. You couldn't give them life. It wasn't possible. In a way, they were the best of audiences. They were easily entertained.

Clea bent down and began to examine them. She turned to two of them, stuck out her gloved hands, palms up, and gestured with her fingers. The two stuck out their mangled paws and she took them, turning them over, peering at them as one might inspect a child's hands before dinner. With scientific detachment, she ran her gloved fingers over their toeless feet, their footless legs. She motioned them to move and they moved, some crawling, some limping oddly, some dragging themselves along the ground. She stayed with them near to the ground, tracking their rhythm, parodying it within herself. After a time, she stood up.

There was one who wore a veil, who, it had transpired during the movement, was a woman. Clea gestured for her to lift it up. Cieslaw's woman, who had monitored the proceedings with great interest, snapped her head away now, indicating to Zeus that the lepress had no nose. Clea gestured at her again, but the lepress just stared back at her, motionless, an emotion gathering in her coal black eyes. Suddenly the lepress screamed something out in Amharic, her anguish slicing the incense- and urine-soaked air. Clea was still.

"Uh, no," translated Zeus, terrified. Cieslaw's woman had run for the front of the bunker and was cowering there, shaking.

Clea peeled off her gloves and dropped them on the refuse heap. She turned, head down, and limped past Zeus. He followed and joined up with her and peered at her until she spoke. "I know this must seem odd to you," she said as they crept around the bunker and back to the courtyard, "but it isn't really. You see, I haven't seen my mother since I was a child. In a few months' time I will visit her for the first time. She lives in a leprosarium in Hawaii. I am preparing," she said, stopping, fixing him with a sad smile. "My mother is a leper."

. . . .

Seven
. . . .

ZEUS was leaning back in the chair as Mr. Liu patted his face with a powder puff. Liu dabbed over the piece of tissue still dangling from his cheekbone, and then dusted a few powder specks from Zeus' shoulder with a strange Chinese brush. There was a soft knock at the dressing room door and Liu cracked it and then opened it wide to admit Ruth Ravenscroft.

"Liu!" she cried, and kissed him on the cheek.

Mr. Liu giggled silently and stroked her hair. "Blessings, Ruth," he said. "Welcome."

· "Zeusee love!" She threw her arms around Zeus' neck and hugged him close. He bent his head back and looked up at her. "Howzit, my jungle bunny?" He managed a smile and the tissue sailed off him to the floor.

"Oh, Zeus,"—Ruth pulled up a chair next to him—"you are naughty. Someday you'll get us killed with such talk."

"Perhaps tonight." He raised his eyebrows and looked innocently hopeful.

"Do you really want to talk about this now?" Ruth asked seriously.

"Not really." He sighed. "It's just I fear for your spiritual safety. Most of us are here tonight because we have to be, not because we want to be." His eyes flicked toward the monitor. "Even Clea. It's just for the contract. The show must go on. She didn't find out when the world was going to end until after we signed the deal. This evening is a sacrifice for her, believe me. She'd planned to be in upstate New York when they nuked us, in her brand-new biosphere bunker."

Ruth stared at Clea on the monitor. Clea was joyfully doing a courtship dance for the room boy, juggling high heels, flipping them into the air, catching them on her feet, lots of different-colored pairs with spangles and spike heels. It looked dangerous.

"She's got the 1967 Volkswagen ready. She's driving up there after the show. I don't know if you know this, Ruthie, but the 1967 Volks is *the* postnuke survival car."

"Why?" asked Ruth, humoring his bitterness.

"Because"—Zeus was pointing at her like a guy in a commercial—"it's the easiest car to get parts for in a holocaust. I warned her there might be nuclear winter, but, like the Pentagon, she wouldn't listen."

"My God, Zeus," mumbled Ruth. She wanted to ask questions, find out about Clea's madness, the divorce, the death, but there wasn't time. He had to perform. She looked to Liu for guidance.

"Two minutes, Zeus," Liu answered. She took Liu's direction and changed the subject.

"Oh, Zeus! My apes are so great! They know their names now and that's pretty good—it's only been three years. I'm halfway through the book. After this show, you must come visit. I have a new tree house—it's bliss, truly."

Ruth was genuinely delighted. She had gotten right away from the doom. Zeus envied her. It was all that solitary confinement. She had a million things to discuss. She hadn't held a two-way conversation for months.

"Have you seen *Greystoke?*" he asked, rising, readying himself to leave his dressing room.

"What do *you* think?" she replied, annoyed.

"Oh, sorry. I don't think anymore, I just act"—this last with a great physical flourish, a graceful bend and a kiss to her cheek. "If I don't see you again," Zeus whispered softly in her ear, "goodbye, my darling friend. You made me feel sane for just a moment. Thank you for coming. I love you very much."

He went to rise, but Ruth caught his arm and pulled his face to hers. "This is a wank, man, you hear me. This is Clea's obsession, not yours. Don't fuck with it, Zeus." She let him go. He rose, straightened his tie, and walked to the small kiddie pool that lay, filled with water, at the end of the dressing room. A small Spanish armada floated on top. He moved several ships into new battle position, made some battle noises, and then turned and strolled determinedly out the door.

Ruth addressed Liu. "He's awfully cynical. He doesn't believe in her nuclear blast?"

"No," said Liu. "He was just sad now."

"Liu,"—Ruth's voice was harder—"why are you letting him do that drug? I can see it, Liu. It's in his eyes. I saw De Quincy in the audience."

Liu set about hanging up Zeus' discarded costume, and then suddenly he said angrily, "He is a man, and the men decided it, little sister. He had to have something to dull the pain."

"They're hungry," Ruth said quietly. Absentmindedly, she beat her breast with her fist. "That's what it is. They're both dying of hunger." She paused and then, as she reached over to the monitor and turned up the sound, she added, "The eating gorilla is one who comes in peace."

CLEA was just finishing juggling the high heels. She had three long sticks in her mouth and three in each hand. The spike heel of each shoe was balanced on each stick and Clea was bobbing rhythmically, which made the shoes appear to be walking. The audience was laughing and clapping. The music conjured up faerie women trotting.

Clea was focused on the sticks, fully absorbed, feeling their pressure as she bobbed them to the beat of the music. At the appropriate violin sting, she yanked them away and spat them out, suspending the shoes like a rainbow in midair. She said to the room boy, who was perched on the bed, "Catch them, please," and turned away. The audience laughed.

The room boy leaped to his feet and scurried to and fro trying to grab the nine falling high-heeled shoes before they hit the ground. The many-colored spangles on the shoes picked up the light, and the audience ooed. It was like a mini fireworks show.

Three of the spiked heels hit the room boy on the head and hung there on his headcloth just as rehearsed. Clea laughed with the audience, inhaling their delight, calming her beating heart with their approval of her magic.

Her blood was swirling at the surface of her skin. Her mind was alert and precise. The words, the stunts, the stage moves and crosses were perfectly in sequence now, flowing out of her just ahead of her conscious mind, acquainting her with rebirth. She was sailing around the stage on an endorphin sea and the audience was the wind that blew her sails.

The music stopped. The room boy collapsed on a chair, his arms filled with spike-heeled shoes, a lone one dangling off his white wrapped headcloth. Clea stamped her foot.

"Where is Sid?" she addressed the audience. "Where is my reconnaissance report? It's useless setting a trap unless you have the right bait."

She threw herself into two back flips and a twisted back somersault and exploded up the stage onto the balcony, which protruded off the back flat.

"There he is!" she said in a stage whisper, looking over the ornate railing. "Sid's down there slinking around, which he does very well, being a manager. But he's not on my side in this." She turned to the audience. "They don't want you to fall in love. They say love takes the edge off. And they're right. Except that there's a catch: without it, you burn out. You're like a cat"—she flicked the back of her shorts and a tail appeared, hanging—"savaging its own tail."

She fell to the stage floor and rolled around the stage in a perfect hoop. Her tail was in her mouth. She was chewing it madly.

"I love you," said the room boy suddenly and ardently, in a high-pitched Arabic voice. "Your face like Nefertiti's. You want to go to hashish party?"

She looked interested. "Sure, can I bring a date?"

At this moment, the door opened and Sid hurried into the room.

"I got bad news, honey." He was shaking his head. "The guy's a salesman and he's got a weird name."

"What is it?" Clea rushed over and searched his face, expecting the worst.

"Zeus."

"Zeus," Clea repeated this, at first softly, then louder and louder, rising up, leaping into the air, flipping around in space, merging her energy with that of the air. "Zeus? Zeus? Like the Greek god? Like the creator of the ancient Wasp world? Zeus." She landed upright on stage, looking at Sid.

"I knew you'd feel as I do," he said dryly. "It's a tragedy, baby, but it isn't in the cards."

"What does he sell?"

"Tobacco."

Clea thought for a moment. "Tobacco," she said and she bounded off stage. Sid stared at the spike heel hanging off the room boy's head. Clea reentered, wearing a giant box of Marlboros that covered her from her head to upper thigh. Her arms stuck out the side of the box, her legs out of the bottom. "Well, then, to get his attention, I can wear this." She did a little tap dance and a few high kicks just to prove her point. The audience laughed. Sid was deadpan. "Too obvious?" she asked, her voice muffled from inside the box. "Well, what else?"

"Well, his main passion in life is—and don't get too excited by this, babe, you've got a show to do—is toy boats."

There was a pause. The dancing Marlboro pack leaned against a chair. "Toy boats?" it repeated. The audience clapped. It was familiar with this fetish of Zeus' and applauded its entrance into the play. The cigarette pack shook. "Damn!" it moaned, "it's not going to be easy."

"No. Not unless you're on Quaaludes," Sid said. "Listen, kid"—Sid took the arm protruding from the Marlboro pack—"you deserve a guy with class. A guy like Frank Sinatra or Dean Martin, a guy with moxie and bucks, a guy—"

"In Christmas trees," finished the box.

Sid bristled. "What's wrong with being in Christmas trees? I was in Christmas trees for two years on the East Coast."

The pack rose and hugged him. "I know. I'm sorry, Sid. It's just you're putting down my fiancé."

Sid made for the door. "You're cracked, kid," he barked as he opened it. "Don't say I didn't warn you. The guy's a white African, he likes the ladies, and his sperm count's low. Need I say more?"

"How do you know his sperm count's low?" the pack asked haughtily.

"I haven't spent five years in show business for nothing," was the reply. "Happy hunting, kid. I'm lunching at the Valley of the Kings." Sid exited, closing the door.

The Marlboro pack turned toward the room boy. "You can go, thanks." He offered his armful of high heels. "You can keep them. Watch out for pelvic tilt, tho." The pack gestured toward the door. The room boy stumbled as he went and fell, puncturing his chest with the spike heels. He crawled out, wailing.

Slowly, Clea took the Marlboro pack off and set it on the stage floor.

"Ordinarily," she began, addressing the audience, "you go for clothing or makeup. Or you stick your tits out, you know, or talk knowledgeably about Sartre. Sometimes, you keep your mouth shut and go demure, but that's harder if you're a babbler like me . . . although I've done that, I've done it. These males, you know, they pin you with this force field and it's all you can do to exist. I've got these gatherer genes in me. When I fall in love, I want to rush right out and gather wild greens to make a salad."

The lights dimmed around her until she stood in the spotlight. The binocular tape of Zeus kneeling by his boats and surrounded by bikinied women came up on a huge video screen suspended stage left. First minicam dollied in for a closeup of her face. The set began to revolve around her. A sound effect of lapping water faded up slowly. She went on, warmed by the glare of the spotlight, focusing now and then on single faces in the audience, talking to them with as much sincerity as she had ever felt in her life.

"I don't know why I want to marry this man, this Zeus. I guess it's a chemical thing, hormones, peptides, amino acid flashbacks. Or you could say it's past life, if that's your gig." The picture on the screen began to change as she talked, featuring giant closeups of different parts of Zeus' face and body. "I mean, I was watching him all morning through my binoculars and without, just his movements. And his aura was so strong that it changed mine. See that?" She pointed at the video screen. "See that curve of his neck? I can feel some ionic reorganization going on in me as I look at that. You explain it. Of course you want to sleep with a man, that's a part of it. Don't underestimate the power of sex hormones. They can make you kill. I am, I am inhaling him now as if he were a closed bakery. But that's only part of it. I mean, I haven't even met this man and yet I'd be willing to bet that he's got a distant authoritarian father and a warm but submissive mother and he's looking for a woman who can flip-flop. That's been the analytical set of every man I've known. It's part of my M.O. So in some weird way, I'm a father figure—"

The audience laughed. It was hard for them to visualize this child-like, feminine woman in such a role.

"No, no, I am. I am. You learn these things from serial monogamy."

Very slowly and precisely, Clea now began to do a series of back walkovers up the center of the stage. The spotlight followed her and she continued speaking into a small microphone taped to her chest, softly and breathily now, in conjunction with the effort she was making. One hand grasped the stage, supported her weight, and then her feet were down and she was up. Over and over, never breaking the mood of the scene, with consummate fluid grace. The audience gasped. Clea was a genius at uniting mental and physical concentration. She was a genius at acting upside down.

"Toy boats," she murmured. "Toy boats. Ordinarily you stick your tits out, but in his case it's toy boats . . ."

The spotlight was fading. In the dimness, the hotel room walls slid off into the wings. The hotel furniture sank down below the stage. The stagehands pushed on a long, narrow machine that spanned the proscenium wing to wing. Up through the trap floor midstage appeared a pyramid, a camel, and two date palm trees. The music swelled an Arabic love cry. And Clea, upstage, upside down, purred in the dimness, ". . . and why I want to marry this man, this Zeus, remains life's mystery. It's between me and my double helix."

The lights faded out.

CLEA stood on the stage, shrouded in blackness, and underwent a change. Relieved momentarily of her duties as a symbol, she was hovering in a vacuum state, treading limbo, stripped for the moment of emotional servitude. Her hearing was still attuned to her memory. Her eyes had not adjusted to the dark. One full life had left her, exiting through her mouth and pores. Another, perhaps more real, perhaps not, was straining at the threshold, yearning to pour in and fill up the emptiness.

In this robotic state, one last message was transmitted by her brain: to leave the stage. She turned to do so and saw, in a shaft of wing light, Zeus, carrying a small galley ship and a box of tobacco leaves, surrounded by voluptuous women in bikinis, getting ready for his entrance. Unhinged by this vision, a sluice opened then and a deluge began of facts and feelings, of memories and dread, pushing into her skull. Gathering momentum, it became a tsunami, drowning her with sensation. She could not take her eyes off the crotches of the women, the little v's that had betrayed her, that would always betray her—all in a circle, guarded by smooth slender thighs that led to knees that stared at her, skeptical and bony. In the flood, a thought snagged on her brainstem that she was jealous not of their beauty but of their youth. Then the thought pulled loose and churned away.

In a few milliseconds, the change was effected. She was all filled up again. Another soul, another set of priorities, stuffed her skin. Sections of another personality crossed over in her skull and hooked together. The floodgates shut, one by one, and the rushing ceased. She looked over at Zeus and this time thought that soon it would all be over. A surge of love warmed her and she was glad Zeus had consented to wear the radiation suit, very glad. He was standing with the bikinied women, laughing and chatting, but it no longer bothered her. For in an hour and a half, by her pink digital watch, all bikinied women in the world would be burned to nuclear ash.

Eight

M ISS FLORIE was waiting in the stage-right wing for Clea to make her exit. The seconds were ticking by, and Clea had not appeared. Charlie, the stage manager, was pacing the stage-right corridor, glancing anxiously into the wing past Miss Florie and mumbling sotto voce into his headphones. Miss Florie, loath always to be noticed, disapproving actually of all publicity on the grounds that it courted ghosts, edged reluctantly to the end of the wing and peered into the blackness of the stage.

Clea was still standing on the spot where she ended the scene. Her eyes were fixed on Zeus and the dancers, who were entering quickly stage left. She seemed entranced. She was like a child Florie found once who had wandered into the bush and lost her way. There had been a procession that day. A young woman of the district had been betrothed. The child had followed alongside frolicking and then had become transfixed by a hummingbird skeleton that was lodged somehow in a cleft of a branch.

Florie had found her on the trek home from the bus stop. The child would not budge. Florie feared she had been possessed. After reasoning with the child until the shadows began to shroud the acacias, Florie had tied her suitcase to her body and dragged the child wailing and moaning to her home in the bantustan. That evening the child fell ill and never recovered. Although they might have, the child's family did not blame Florie. They regarded her as a benevolent interference but one that had come too late. Several weeks later, on her way back to the city, on her trek through the bush to the bus stop, Florie passed the place where the hummingbird skeleton was lodged in the branch. She found that it had crumbled to pieces. She never took that route again.

Florie darted onto the stage, grabbed Clea's hand, and yanked her through the wing and out into the stage-right corridor. Charlie noted with relief that Clea was offstage and hurried off down the corridor and around backstage to check on the entrances for the next scene. At first terrified, then furious, Clea grabbed Miss Florie by the neck. She would have throttled her, but Miss Florie yanked Clea's chin and rubbed her mouth soothingly with a finger, murmuring as she did so an incantation in the click language. Clea's hands dropped to her sides. Her head lolled on her chest. "Was I all right?" she whispered. Florie nodded. "Very good," she replied.

The stage-right corridor was empty save for Bobette the costume lady, a thin wraith cringing by the costume rack, and the rotund, full-hearted Eddie Witz. As Miss Florie propelled Clea into the corridor and becalmed her, Eddie boomed in his huge foghorn of a voice, "Know when to get offstage, honey," and made Clea laugh in spite of herself. Clea looked at him and corralled her laugh into a sly smile.

"Eddie," she said, shaking her head, "Eddie, Eddie I beg you to wear a radiation suit. We're going to need some laughs in the nuclear wasteland."

Miss Florie sniffed in disgust. Bobette giggled nervously. Eddie ignored the statement. "You were great out there, Clea. I had a great time. You were flying, baby." Clea beamed.

"It's not too late, Eddie. There are enough suits to go around." She glanced at Florie. "Florie is undecided because she claims the ancestors disapprove—both sides, patrilineal and matrilineal. Right, Florie?" Miss Florie nodded gravely.

Eddie grinned. "Listen, Clea, if we melt out there tonight as you predict, at the moment that you predict, as I'm standing in the wings here getting ready for my entrance into the love dance scene—well, darlin', it'll be so amazing, such a great clap of black humor thunder, that I'll be ready to go. I mean it won't get better than that, Clea. My career, to all intents and purposes, will be over."

"But then I'll be starting *Post-Blast Productions*, Eddie. You can get your screenplays produced right away. Anything you want. No problem."

Clea was taking his hand, speaking earnestly to him, searing him with her eyes, offering him a deal no humorist could refuse. Eddie replied seriously, negotiating.

"Let us remind ourselves of the circumstances here: your psychic in Las Vegas gave you this date and time for the atomic blast. Give me one good reason why you believed him so goddamn thoroughly."

Clea smiled and a strange, tormented look crept through her eyes. "What if I had ignored his prophecy, Eddie, and there was an atomic blast and out of bloody-minded gray-faced cynicism I wasn't ready for it. I died. We all died without having the chance to choose, and out of a fetishistic worship of nonchalance? I couldn't live with myself."

Miss Florie took Clea's shoulder and gently turned her in the direction of the dressing room. She spoke over her shoulder to Eddie before she was led away. "Mass destruction is in our souls, Eddie. That it should announce itself through the medium of a great guy in Vegas makes perfect American sense. Jerry's a true seer, Eddie. He's never been wrong about my career. Why should he be wrong about this? I do not intend to be destroyed out of a terminal desire for social acceptance, or an embarrassment with discordant image projection, or an ennui with humanity. If nothing happens tonight, then, as King Lear put it so succinctly, nothing will come of it. Period."

"Yeah," Eddie barked after her, "nothing except a few ulcers, several nervous collapses, the death of your marriage, the end of Clea and Zeus, the unemployment of fifty people, the termination of your performer's insurance, the schism of your husband's soul—"

But Clea was no longer listening. Miss Florie had by this time unlocked the dressing room door and herded her inside like a name-sake cow symbolic of the bloodline in her lineage.

CLEA took off her halter top and shorts and handed them to Miss Florie. Wearing only her bikini underpants and her little, deer-hoof boots, she sat down at her dressing table and stared at her upper body in the mirror. She had, for such a slender birdlike bone structure, rather large breasts. In order to perform her acrobatic feats, she taped them down with gauze bandage, according to some instructions given in a book of feminine etiquette from the twenties. She found it odd that a generation of women would flatten their chests to appear more attractive to men. Without clothes the bound effect was like the aftermath of a mutilating accident. With clothes it was mutantly childlike. Did women do it in order to offset the sluttishness of wearing short skirts, breasts and thighs being too much to handle all at once? And what did they do when they made love? She gazed at her torso and imagined a sexy dance in which she unwound the bandages and her breasts bounced free, reverse bondage, was that what it was? The twenties must have been a strange time for men and women, strange, dark, and filled with confusion.

Her narrow, birdlike chest looked so vulnerable bound in white gauze. So vulnerable that she instinctively rummaged through her makeup box, drew out a bottle of stage blood, and artfully began to drip it across the bandages, accenting the illusion of horror. She watched herself in the mirror as she was doing this until a strong brown hand reached into the picture and took the bottle out of her grasp.

"Hey!" she snapped, eyes whipping toward Florie. Florie shoved the bottle in her pocket.

"Hey what?" Florie replied.

"Hey, I'm doing something artistic here, madam," said Clea sullenly.

"You are going too far with these things," said Florie in her warm, snuggly full-hearted voice, "too, far. I cannot see these things. You are playing with fire."

Clea turned back to the mirror. "Where's my Hiroshima?" she barked, baiting. Florie pointed to a box on the floor. "I asked you to leave it up. I told you. I want to be able to look at it. I want to see what it will be like."

Florie shrugged. Clea leaped out of the chair, retrieved the photo from the box, unfolded it to its fifteen-inch length, and retacked it above the mirror. Florie watched in silence. When Clea was done, she stepped back and admired it.

"There. That's all I wanted: a very simple thing, a comforting thing." She glared at Florie. The short brown woman with the wrapped headdress and the simple calico frock was sizing her up with terrible uneasiness. Clea's stomach spasmed.

"Florie?" she asked, plaintive and childlike, "Florie?"

"I got to go see if the boat is ready," Florie said dismissively. And she hurried out the dressing room door.

There was chaise longue at the end of the dressing room, and Clea crept to it now and lay down, pulling her knees up to her chin. She pressed her hands together in prayer position and then draped them limply, like gloves, over her knees. She sneaked a look at the monitor, which was on in the corner without sound, and caught sight of some palm trees and pyramids. She flicked her eyes away quickly before she focused on the human figures in the foreground. She began to suck on her tongue and to rock back and forth, stopgap calming measures she had used since babyhood. She accompanied herself with a rhythmic hum. After a time, the discordant images of insanity began to flee, and the shadows of things earthbound were visible in the milk glass vestibule of her consciousness.

She saw again the little sand-floored adultery huts behind the pyramids. They were like children's playhouses, but separated one from another by vast expanses of sand. She and Zeus had been taken there by Mr. Abdul, the head of the tobacco monopoly in Egypt. It was late afternoon and they had come by camel, loping away from the great pyramid of Cheops. Riding first, Mr. Abdul, round-faced and cheery, gesturing with a cigarette, pointing out the historical sights: here, some conqueror pried the gold off the top of the great pyramid and melted it down for coins; there the broken nose of the great Sphinx shot off in target practice by Napoleon's troops; and right here—he chuckled—some little boys for sale, "Hallo, not today."

Buni, Abdul's rotund mistress, age twenty-five, dark-eyed and hawk-nosed, riding next, laughed uproariously at this and at everything that was said. She was happy in life, was Buni, or so it seemed. Kalil came after, Buni's cousin. Kalil chaperoned her everywhere, even to the adultery huts, silent and smiling, less intrusive than a pet. Then rode Clea, then Zeus, as yet just friends.

They had been drawn to each other in Addis Ababa by genetic link, by cellular lust. After the lepers, they had been unable to part, riding together in Clea's hired car, chatting about the state of the empire, the color of the light, avoiding the issue of flesh. She learned that Zeus was from Southern Rhodesia, that his country was censured, and that he was a sanction buster. And when he told her this, smiling sardonically, showing his three passports and winking with mock mystery, she had the sense that he was walking around with a phantom assegai cleaving the center of his skull.

Zeus was so physical to her that at night when they parted in the hotel corridor, she scurried away down the carpeted hall, only waving when her key turned safely in the lock, so she could bolt through the door and slam it behind her. In her memory, Zeus stood bewildered and amused at the end of the long hall, his hands frozen in a gesture of preempted affection. He looked as if the seal of his self-containment had cracked and he was dripping warmth slowly and inexorably, happily unable to stop himself up.

They flew together to Cairo, where, fate would have it, he was traveling next to sell tobacco. And when, as in some biblical tale, there was no room for him at the Cairo Hilton, she offered to share hers. And it was that selfsame afternoon, pulsing toward a night of no escape, that Mr. Abdul produced the camels and took them to the desert.

It was Mr. Abdul who called them the adultery huts. Buni laughed. Kalil smiled.

"The Egyptians come in the afternoons," he said, "but today"—he peered over the vast expanse of sand at the tiny monopoly houses dotting the dunes—"is a slow day. Hashish?"

He crawled into his hut, dug in the sand, and produced an earthenware vessel, which he brought outside. He opened it and inside was a pipe. While he set about lighting it, she moved next to Zeus.

"I've never actually smoked," Zeus said and then sheepish, "I'm rather dull."

Abdul handed him the smoking pipe and he inhaled, then he passed it to Clea. Buni did not smoke, nor did Kalil. They just laughed and smiled and stared into space.

The pure serenity of the setting sun on the Sahara Desert cleansed them like a baptism. The eave on the little hut cast a modest shadow in which they sat staring out, speechless. In one direction lay the pyramids. The rowdy village at their base was hidden by a dune and so the three giant perfect cones towered, it seemed, out of quiet sand, the greatest of tributes to death and rebirth, to the paranoia of man. In another direction the monopoly huts stretched in a line toward Cairo. All around them, the wind spun a cocoon of sound, its unceasing furry moan muffled their human thoughts.

Abruptly, Mr. Abdul got up. "I must take Buni home," he said. "I will come back for you in an hour."

Clea turned to Zeus. He seemed unable to speak and simply nodded. When they had first arrived Abdul had sent the camels back. Now, Abdul pointed to the road beyond the huts, where suddenly had materialized a silver Mercedes-Benz. It shimmered in the sun like a supersonic mirage. Clea watched the three Arabs tread softly toward the car, Buni trudging ladylike in her high heels though the spikes sank into the dunes. Then Clea turned back to Zeus.

Something was happening. Zeus was white. His lanky form was hunched over. Waves of fear were cresting out of him, breaking on the surrounding air, drenching her in their wake.

"Come on," she said, taking his arm and helping him to his feet, "let's walk."

He got up, smiled weakly at her, and then peered defiantly out at the endless sand.

"You're stoned, that's all." She stroked his arm reassuringly. "You feel it in waves, right? It's okay. It's all right. You won't die. Relax."

He looked down at her, rigid for a moment, uncomprehending, and then suddenly he relaxed, that too a sensation so palpable that she felt she was ankle deep in it. She stared at him. He laughed a bit hysterically and then sat down, shaking himself. She sat down next to him.

"I . . . uh . . . I had bilharzia once," he stammered, "Do . . . uh . . . do you know what that is?"

"A parasite?" she ventured.

"Yes. It entered my brain, and for a while, I had epileptic fits. I haven't had one for some years now, but getting stoned, at first it is the same sensation. I thought—" He laughed and then was so relieved that quite naturally and ebulliently he took her in his arms and hugged her for dear life. And then, she kissed him.

They crawled on all fours into the hut. They each removed their own clothes, modestly, tentatively, laying the different vestments out on the sand like a blanket of flattened male and female forms. They sneaked looks at each other's bodies as they did this and were pleased with what they saw. It would all fit together as they thought it would. When they had prepared their nest, they turned to each other and entwined and the bursting anticipation they had felt for so long exploded over them and bathed them in its hope.

And it was home when he pushed inside her and they lay there soft mouth to soft mouth, sparkly eye to sparkly eye, in such unutterable pleasure it moved them first to goose bumps then to tears. Home was what popped up between their ears amidst the howl of wind. Home, the dark black velvet cradle, home, the exquisite agony of pulpy trust. Home, the place to which you return again and again.

And after, disengaged, a bit bereft, he said, not looking at her, "There's something you should know about me. Last year, when our farm was attacked by rebels, there was an accident." The wind hooted through the hut. She stroked his back. "In the confusion . . . my father . . . shot my mother . . . in the face. I saw my mother murdered."

She clapped her hands. "Ah, now I know what it is we have in common," she said passionately. "I saw mine murdered too."

Nine

FLORIE hurried anxiously down the backstage corridor toward the prop area. She was upset, dangerously off center, vulnerable, in fact, to the malicious influence of outcast, mischievous spirits. The corridor, though momentarily clear, hummed with a low level cacophony. She shook herself. She didn't like it. The fat black television cables bumped along the floor beneath her feet like gnarled tree roots in a jungle. She tiptoed over them, gingerly at first, then stiffening with a darting fear that at any moment they might change into creatures animate and deadly.

Suddenly, her foot lodged in a clump of sound and picture and she fell. On her hands and knees now, a moment came back to her, a moment in a Zambian rain forest when she had fallen, so exhausted, so drained, that the force of life within her had shrunken down to spirit, pulsating, sacred spirit but trapped in a dead weight physicality that seemed impossible to budge. She collapsed, through with life, done, only to be awakened hours or maybe days later by many large pieces of fruit which whacked her on the head, the dead-on accurate missiles of a spider monkey suspicious of her presence. She ate the fruit, gave thanks to the forest and its creatures, and continued on her way. The omen had revived her and she had far to go; fifteen hundred miles, as it turned out, before she would encounter Clea and Zeus beneath the great statue of Ramses the Second at the sacred spot Abu Simbel, three quarters of the way through her trek out of Africa.

Florie tried to pick herself up and she fell again. Out in the control truck, the picture buzzed for a moment and the director screamed, "What the hell's going on? Someone's fucking with something."

The A.D. jumped. "What is it?" he snapped anxiously. "It's not airplanes or something, is it?"

"Maybe," the director said seriously. "Thank God I sent my wife and kids to the Oregon-Washington border. Clea says it's the safest place to be."

"Aw Jesus, you did?" the A.D. said. "I couldn't afford to. My kids are home."

"I'm sorry," the director said sadly, then broke into uproarious laughter. "Got ya, y'idiot."

The picture snapped again.

"Charlie," the director screamed into the headphones, "what the fuck is going on? Something's going on down there. Someone's fucking with something. Find 'em!"

"I AM," Clea once said in reply to a query about her profession, "the personal manager and agent of my own emotional system, a strange existence."

"But then who are you really?" the questioner asked.

"I am a natural schizophrenic, a human chameleon, a functioning Sybil, an anarchist puppet and its Nazi puppeteer."

"But are you ever One?" the questioner persisted.

"Well, I am One, you see, that's the hell of it." Clea smiled.

"No, but how are you able to perform so well? How do you do it?" the questioner continued.

"I don't know. And I don't want to know. But I suspect by depriving myself of human life."

"Thanks," Zeus called from across the room. The questioner was startled. He had forgotten Zeus was present.

"Oh, honey. You know I didn't mean you," said Clea, gazing at him with adoration. The questioner laughed.

"No, Clea," Zeus said after a beat, "what *do* you mean?"

"Well, it's just . . . I don't think I'm half as good at living life as I am at imitating it."

"I think I'd agree with that," said Zeus.

"Thanks," said Clea, pouting. Everyone laughed.

"What about you, Zeus?" asked Clea. "How do you do it?"

"Lust," said Zeus simply.

"Lust?" the questioner asked.

"Lust," Clea repeated. "Well, that's another way of looking at it entirely."

. . . .

Ten

. . . .

THE PICTURE on the monitor broke up and buzzed for a second and Clea, startled, whipped her eyes to the wall clock and then to her watch: eight-thirty. It wasn't time. It must be something else. Unless they were being attacked early, in which case Jerry would have seen it and called her from the bunker in Oregon. She looked around the dressing room for the hotline, the little red Princess phone that connected her with Jerry's command post, but she couldn't see it. Slowly, fuming, she patted the surfaces, lifting up papers and costumes, searching nooks and crannies, squeezing balls of cloth, and then she spied it: upended in one of Florie's packing boxes, wires dangling, unplugged.

Unplugged. She rushed across the room and grabbed it and tried to plug it in. The wires had been cut. Unbelievable. She giggled. The forces of literal sanity were after her again, had always been against her right from day one. She was laughing now, gesturing helplessly with her hands, showing the cut wires of the phone to a jury of invisible peers, and sputtering: you do not cut the wires of the hotline one hour and thirty minutes before Kennedy Airport is to be nuked. You don't do it, how can you do it? Unless you can't face facts, unless you'd rather shut off part of your brain than face facts, unless you'd rather die in agony than face facts, which—she slumped into the chair before her dressing table and laid the phone on the counter before her—God help us, is true of most of my company.

She stared in the mirror at the rock-hard set of her jaw and then pushed the button of the intercom that connected her to the control room.

"Hallo," said the Ice Princess, "this is Clea."

Out in the control truck, the director and the A.D. yelped and lost ten years of life.

"Yes, Clea." The director's voice was shaking.

"Someone has cut the wires of my hotline. Get Liu in here to fix it, now."

"Yes, Clea," the voice of the director reverbed through the dressing room and then he clicked off.

Clea ran over to the monitor, turned up the sound, and began to remove some important things from the boxes that Florie had packed: the armadillo juggling plates, the black satin toe shoes.

"This is ridiculous," she muttered. "This has been reduced to a child's game. I should be in my bunker as I planned, but then"—she snarled with bitter sarcasm—"so many goddamn jobs depended on me, so many goddamn jobs . . ."

She remembered screaming at Doron and Zeus. They were sitting in the library, heads bowed, glancing at each other from under droopy eyelids. She was pacing back and forth before the glowing fireplace, her movements driven by a steam of anxiety that no longer seemed to abate, that would drive her, she imagined, to the ultimate conflagration.

"There will be no more jobs." She was screaming. "There will be no more theater. It's the final curtain. The notice is posted." Her last scream garroted the atmosphere and the Seven Golden Lieutenants, who were guarding outside, actually put down their machine guns so they could clasp their ears.

"You're booked, moffie," bellowed Zeus in reply. "You've got a previous engagement. That's show biz." And the subject was closed.

On the monitor, Zeus was recreating the Battle of Salamis for the bikinied women. Across the length of the proscenium lay a bitubular revolving machine covered with aqua net and red rhinestones. When light was projected onto it, through tinted glass slides, and when it slowly revolved, the most magical of glistening rivers was created. A fleet of small galley ships flew from a pulley system above the machine, hung by invisible wire. Zeus pushed them with a long stick and they moved along their pulley tracks and skimmed the sparkling waternet like landing gulls. Upstage were two palm trees and a pyramid. Arabic love calls swelled the air. Two of the bikinied women were diving gracefully between the tubes and then surfacing again, diving and surfacing within the waternet in an elaborate mime of a sensuous swim. Behind the tubular waters was a wooden ramp covered with sand. The ramp was steeply raked so that from the audience anyone sitting on it seemed to be right at the water's edge. Zeus was on his knees there, dressed in his third world suit, cross-legged, stick in hand, flanked by Rita and Peg, who stared up at him with fawnlike ardor.

"It was vengeance," Zeus was saying with great intensity, "a son's vengeance for his father's shame. Darius the First had lost his balls on the Plain of Marathon. Sixty-four hundred Persians slaughtered, screaming, to a Greek loss of only one hundred ninety-two. His son, Xerxes, had no choice, you see that, don't you?"

Rita and Peg undulated sleepily, jostling their bulging breasts, and replied, "Sure, baby. Sure, baby."

"No! It's important," he went on, fired, determined. "Fifteen years had passed. Fifteen years of family ignominy and imperial wretchedness. When Xerxes got the throne, he had to move on Greece. He gathered men from Egypt, India, and Ethiopia. He built a massive army. War was it in those days, the only way of proving right to life." He tried to rise, but the women held him down.

"Not sex?" they cooed, and pressed themselves against him.

"Sex?" he repeated absently, and stroked the slender backs of his handmaidens. "Sure," he said kindly, standing now, the boyish warrior surrounded by his fleet, "sex was at the core of it. Can a man get laid when his father's shamed an empire? Only barely. His orgasms seemed to him like dreams. His hard-on wasn't hard until they sailed."

Zeus pushed the Persian trieres as he said this and they swept across the waternet.

"Xerxes built the greatest battle fleet the world had ever seen." Music came up now, Korngold at his best. Twelve hundred warships and three thousand smaller vessels, and on their decks, two million men. But what he didn't count on was—" Zeus raised the chains of the two women kneeling before him. "Was?" The women looked at each other questioningly. "Blueballs!" shouted Peg, and the two women fell about laughing.

"Close—" hissed Zeus. "Themistocles and his battering ram."

Zeus jumped into the air straight up, feet together, hands pointed toward the heavens and, dropping his stick as he pushed off, made a perfect swan dive into the tiny space between the two tubes of the waternet. The sound of a giant splash was heard as he penetrated the surreal surface, and the audience shrieked and laughed. A moment passed as the bikinied women worried over his disappearance beneath the tubular waves and then he surfaced again, shaking his head so swimmerlike that the audience would have sworn that he was soaking wet.

How he had landed and turned beneath the tubes was Zeus' magic. The audience was mesmerized. He would have had to be a tiny ball, spinning and unfolding his great frame in such a narrow little space, reappearing with no loss of grace at all, a swimmer in the long and storied Nile. He did the backstroke now. Back and forth, he swiveled and frolicked like a dolphin bathed in Roger's midday light which sparkled off the red rhinestones. The audience clapped with glee. In between the galley ships, Zeus bobbed and Peg called out anxiously,

"Be careful of bilharzia."

He stopped between the Greek and Persian fleets and treaded water. "Look here," he cried, grasping a Grecian galley by its hull.

"The trireme, prow designed for ramming, and on its tip a metal cap shaped like a trident, the weapon of the sea god, Poseidon, whom Themistocles knew well. A timber warship, light and speedy, driven by one hundred seventy oarsmen, volunteers, not slaves—this is important. There were two hundred of these ships and on each prow stood archers at the ready, couriers of projectile death."

He swam a bit and reached the Persian fleet. "And here: the Persian trieres, lumbering hulks, built not for sea battle but for landing and boarding, the old-fashioned way. Vast munitions, stores and soldiers stowed beneath the decks. Rows of soldiers' shields along the sides protecting oarsmen. Eight hundred ships that could not easily be turned, their victory lay in power and brute force."

The women stretched and yawned on the sand platform above the waternet. They took off their bikini tops and leaned back, bathing their exposed breasts in Roger's sunlight.

"Lighten up," they called to Zeus. "Lighten up, honey. Forget this war and come and play with us."

"Listen," cried Zeus, rising from the waves, pleading with his arms and hands, his face a tragic mask, "this is a tale of liberty, of freedom from an autocratic master. I know this story in my bones. This isn't just a man's adventure."

Rita and Peg leaned against each other, naked shoulder to naked shoulder. Their nipples were stiff and the light bounced off them like beach balls off a seal's nose. They stretched out their arms and moaned softly,

"Come here, pretty man, let us comfort you." The three other women continued their mime of diving on either side of the raked wooden sand at the edge of the tubular waters.

Suddenly, the light darkened. The sound man produced a clap of thunder. Roger set off a flash of lightning. There was a low continuous rumble of the kettle drum and Charlie, the stage manager, stood by as the special effects man flipped a switch and turned on rain. Rita and Peg hollered piteously, "Oh no, rain!" They squirmed with panic like cats in a filling bathtub.

Zeus struggled in the tubular waters. He was swimming violently, creating with his movements the distinct illusion that he was being buffeted by stormy waves. His voice rang out in the cacophony.

"Poseidon, the sea god, sent this storm. Outside the Salamis strait, the Persian fleet was massed for battle, eight hundred ships massed for attack. And then the storm hit, and the Persians foundered in the open sea and crashed upon the rocks. Four hundred ships were lost. Half the Persian fleet. And the battle had not yet begun."

"We're going in, Zeus," the women called unhappily. "We're getting wet."

"Why are women so afraid of rain?" Zeus asked. "What is it they know?"

"Colds and chills, infections, mud, wet clothes, wet wool, half-wet hair on neck—oh God, don't remind us." The women were leaving the stage.

"Wait! Don't go! My story will be over soon. I thought, if you wanted me, you'd want to know . . ."

"What?" the women, half naked, glistening with rain, inclined their heads. Zeus stood up between the tubular waves, a drowned rat, hair plastered to face, clothes wrinkled.

"I fought for freedom once . . . on the wrong side."

The women turned to each other. "Let's go," they whispered with distaste. "He's weird. Let's get out of here." And they exited, carping.

Zeus turned and, bedraggled, faced the audience. A shaft of sunlight after rain broke through the fantasy clouds and illuminated his shriveled form.

"I've never been in love," he began, softly. "I've never found the right girl, as they say. But then I've never had to look, not really. Girls fall on me, out of the sky, like leaking lost balloons. They like me for what they think they see. I'm everywoman's wet dream until I sail my boats. That turns 'em right off. That they fear, as if my little galleys were the children of a former marriage, evidence of a weighty link to something they can't change. I cannot live on kisses anymore, though once I did. Once, I made love in the tobacco fields in topping season, collecting all the hacked off flowers into bouquets, making the workers chuckle as I lured the young girls with my presents. The foreman and I kept tally, on a wooden plank inside the worker's kraal.

"'Ah, Zeus,' he'd say with deep and thundering laughter, 'you are the one for the girls, mon. You are the honey for the honeybirds. Ah, wow, wow, wow. Ah, *baas*. It is you.'"

Zeus paused for a moment and a great grief emanated from his person and lodged in the throats of the audience.

"But that was long ago," he went on brokenly, picturing a terrible scene in his mind, using a terrible piece of his life to fill this beat and make it memorable. The knowledge of this betrayal made him sweat.

". . . long ago, before I wore a suit and found that loneliness stuck with me like a number one wife."

Delicate Chinese pi-pa music faded up now, and out of the corner of his eye Zeus spied Liu, who had taken a seat in the corner of the orchestra pit and was strumming, absorbed, the instrument he was renowned for.

"She was betrothed to me when I was young, this Velvet Loneliness. I looked to her to push me into life. I thought that she'd fill up sometime when we were older. But now I find her vacuum's with me still. The trembling anticipation that she made me feel is gone, subsumed by dread. I may be like a cigarette with a hole in it, a mere promise of gratification, I don't know. But I long to find a concubine to join our family, a girl I could escape in, who would understand about my boats . . ."

With a deep, sad sigh Zeus looked away from the audience and off into the stage-right wing. Clea was there, ready, poised, okay. Behind her were the dim shapes of Florie and Ruth, sagging somehow, their shoulders slanted and uneven. After a beat, Zeus sprang up, taut. He glanced at the audience in astonishment, then back at the stage-right wing.

The audience gasped. Entering now, between the tubes of the waternet, sailing slowly but majestically to a lyrical flourish of pi-pa strings, came a three-foot-tall Chinese junk. Its fat brown sail crested past the trieres and anchored neatly near the triremes, stage right of a startled Zeus. The audience clapped and hooted. They knew it was Clea. Her upper torso and head encased in the sails, she moved her feet with such precision beneath the waternet that she created the effect of a junk sailing on water. The position of the sails was such that her person was invisible to the audience or television camera. Zeus could see her if he chose to look, but her control was so perfect, the illusion so real, that he narrowed his sightline and simply basked in the vision of this noble boat speared in sunlight maneuvering toward him in a sea of red stones.

"What happened then?" A lilting female voice floated out of the Chinese junk, and Zeus looked around him in astonishment.

"When?" he replied, tentative, as if not sure to whom or about what he was speaking.

"After the storm, when they went into battle." The junk backed up a bit and halted.

"Why?" Zeus asked, suspicious. "What's it to you?" The junk rocked back and forth and the sound of lapping water was heard.

"I adore sea lore," the voice said passionately.

"Oh," said Zeus, and glanced at the audience, bewildered. "Well, where was I?"

"The storm. Four hundred ships, half the Persian fleet was lost."

"Ah, yes, well—" Zeus turned to renew his tale and noticed that the junk was obscuring the trieres. "Uh, could you move?" he asked. The audience tittered.

The junk sailed backward to the end of the waternet, revealing the Persian fleet. It rolled a bit and quieted down. Zeus leaped straight upward into a flip and landed on the wooden sand platform. After shaking his hair back, he took up his stick and began.

"After the storm, Xerxes still had four hundred ships, twice that of the Greeks. At dawn he brought his fleet into the narrow channel between Salamis and Athens to smash the lightweight triremes of Themistocles. But there was no room. The high-sided Persian trieres, lumbering out of line, impeded each other, and could not navigate."

"Shame," cooed the Chinese junk, "they should have seen it coming."

Zeus stopped and looked thoughtfully at the graceful Asian boat. "Yes," he agreed, "but in those days strength was power. Themistocles changed that. He saw the uses of technology, that the power of invention could triumph over strength. He was the first techie."

"Or the first terrorist," said the junk.

"Is technology terrible?" asked Zeus.

"If it bites the hand that feeds it, yes. Go on."

"All right." Zeus poked the pulley wires with his stick and the trieres began to smash into each other. The pi-pa music faded and a violent Korngold sting struck up. The sounds of massive wooden collision topped it all.

"There was panic in the Persian command! Their ships were foundering. And at this hellish moment, Themistocles attacked. His lightweight triremes darted through the channel, maneuvering like craft rats. They drove the Persian ships against each other and battered them with their trident rams."

The triremes on the waternet crashed against the trieres. Zeus was like a great conductor, here, shoving with his baton, pushing and gliding, his body moving everywhere at once. Male screams filled the air now and the Chinese junk moaned and rocked. The lighting scissored and strobed and finally turned to red, the red of Persian blood.

"For twelve hours the bloody battle raged. Triere after triere was crushed and foundered. Throughout it all, Greek archers sent a teeming rain of sharpened arrow death. It was a marine screaming opera. The Persian chorus, doomed by heavy armor, sank with discordant harmonies beneath the waves. Over and over, Themistocles ordered his rams and plunged them through the trieres' hearts. The sea was like a body and boat soup, a hearty meal for a hungry devil. At sunset, it was over. The banks along the strait were piled high with Persian driftwood dead, the waters littered with a million Persian splinters."

"The Persians withdrew?" the junk asked as the screams died

away, the Korngold music stopped, and the pi-pa strains were heard again.

"Yes," Zeus replied, "crippled and defeated. Only two hundred ships remained of the original strike force. Morale was shot. And Xerxes' balls had spasmed into atoms, as had the territorial aims of the mighty Persian empire."

"Wasn't there a peace treaty?" The junk sailed forward now, blocking the wreckage.

"How did you know?" asked Zeus and, with a loud splash, he dove once again between the tubes of the waternet and came up treading water by the junk.

"I heard it once on the wind in my sails. I'm interested in freedom and its incarnations."

Zeus smiled. "Me too," he said. "Well, after some years, the Persians made a treaty. The freedom of the Greek city-states in Europe and Asia was assured, as was the independence of the great Athenian state itself. Victory for Themistocles in the Battle of Salamis! The end of autocratic rule."

"Amazing," mused the Chinese junk, "bloody amazing." And it began to sail toward the stage-right wing.

"Wait!" Zeus swam after the boat and clasped its prow with his hand. "Where are you going now?"

"Fishing," came the gentle reply. "Why?"

Zeus thought for a moment and then got up his courage and said abashedly, "I wish that you were human . . ."

The junk tipped courteously in his direction, and something fell off its deck and into the waternet with a splash. "I do too," murmured the junk, and sailed offstage.

Zeus dove frantically between the tubes and finally came up amidst the battle debris holding the object in his fingers. It was an earring, a golden chain on which was hanging a black heart.

First minicam zoomed in for a closeup of the bauble. The pi-pa music rang to a crescendo. Through the lens, the cameraman watched as the closeup faded from black heart to black.

Eleven

M<small>R. LIU</small> hurried through the orchestra pit and up the stairs into the stage-right corridor.

"Lovely solo, Liu," called Bobette from the costume room, where she was trying to extract Clea from the straps that enclosed her in the Chinese junk.

Liu smiled and nodded modestly. As he weaved his way through a bunch of actors in Egyptian military dress and then past the propman, who was handing out skeet guns, he was struck by a feeling of *déjà vu*. He stopped for a moment and watched the propman click open the rifles, load them with skeet shoot, and slam them shut again, and suddenly it was 1936 and he was twenty, there, at the Communist camp in the high mountains, being issued his first weapon. It was ironic his being issued a weapon, because he only wanted to write. He was a wunderkind in those days, a prodigious talent, high on the list of those voices the Kuomintang wished to silence. When they began arresting writers he had fled underground, hiding out for a time in the flat of a lovely woman in the French concession in Shanghai. Finally, he had gone to the Communists, hoping when the war was over, he would, once again, have the freedom to write. But writing, they said, handing him gun after gun, was too dangerous a weapon for him to fire. He was caught, as the great Lu Hsun once put it, "between two gates of darkness," and his talent and youth grew stunted from lack of light.

But for a moment he was back, standing in a long line of fellow intellectuals, shivering in the wind and saying to the peasant with the pile of rifles, "Give me one that shoots poetry, comrade." The peasant laughed, and then handed him a log of metal so heavy that it threatened to bend his dreams till they snapped. They never did, but under such weight, they grew into a grotesque shape, like that of a tree espaliered to resemble an animal that amuses the emperor.

"Liu?" Doron was looking down at him quizzically. "Zeus asks that you check the flying wires."

Liu nodded. "But first there is the matter of the telephone . . ."

"But Zeus—" Doron was prodding like a man directing a game of chance.

"First," Liu said firmly, "the telephone," and he hurried up the corridor to Clea's dressing room.

"Why is he fixing that bloody thing?" Doron muttered to Florie, who had appeared by his side on her way from the costume room. "He believes in fates, Mr. Doron," said Florie defensively. "I understand him. I too."

LIU picked up the severed wires of the hotline and began carefully to reconnect them. He wondered if he was going to die, if, in an hour, the world was going to end or if it was just a symbol expressing itself in a madness in Clea. Certainly, in one sense, their world was going to end. Clea and Zeus were parting. And, as he had put it once in a hidden poem:

> The end of love is like a fission bomb,
> A mighty crack that splits two souls to atoms,
> And burns to shadows those
> Who took the union all on faith
> And as a proof
> That they might know love too.

How long ago he had written that! How long ago he had finally left Shanghai, scurrying across the border into Hong Kong, forced to admit that it was his ironic fate never to be allowed to use the talent he was allotted. So if he died, the truth was that in some way he was already half dead, smothered at birth, his brain denied the oxygen of expression among his own, to all intents and purposes a supremely intelligent mute.

And yet, he thought, laying the reconnected telephone on the dressing table, in all the frustration, there had been Clea. He had been living in a Kowloon slum when he received the wire from his brother. For months he had lain upon his simple bed, smoking opium and considering his fate. Screams of children, crowing of roosters, and cries of street hawkers swirled round his brain. The odor of simmering tofu and the stench of thousand-year-old eggs permeated his half sleep. Once in a while, to make money, he had done some tailoring or taught the pi-pa, and, in spite of himself, had built up a following. His clientele spoke of him in reverent tones and praised his stitching or his strumming. It seemed his talent, like a population of hungry cockroaches, had squeezed out through tiny cracks in his skin and nested and bred in his other endeavors.

So when the wire came, he went down to his friend in Wu Pan Street and got himself a fake British passport, and soon after left for Taiwan. His admirers were devastated to see him go, but the wire had said, "Come quickly. There has been a rebirth. You are the only one that I can trust." And for the first time in years, he felt a quickening of curiosity in his intellect, a tiny flare of excitement in his heart, and he had to go see what his brother had found.

Clea bolted through the dressing room door, followed by Florie who was carrying an evening gown.

"The telephone is fixed," Liu said calmly to Clea, taking in her childlike, almost alien visage. Her head was wrapped in a white cloth. Her chest was bound with a white bandage that had been spattered, in the manner of a Jackson Pollock, with a liquid that mimicked blood. Her round dolly face was powdered and painted. She wore white underpants over panty hose, and her little deer-hoof boots. She was like a darling wounded refugee from a bombed-out dolly planet.

"What is this?" he asked, pointing to the fake blood on her chest. Florie sniffed loudly.

"A joke," Clea said, moving to the Princess phone, picking it up, and listening for the dial tone. "A political statement, a fashion first. It's hard to tell in this world, isn't it, Liu?"

"I saw your father in the audience—" Liu began, but the picture on the monitor broke up again, and Clea urgently punched three phone buttons. "Jerry?" she called into the receiver, "Jerry?"—again feverishly—"come in. Jerry? Come in please." Florie looked at Liu and shook her head disgustedly. "Jerry?" Clea continued. "Jerry? . . . Jerry! Thank God. Someone cut the wires, yeah, I know. I know. It's ludicrous. Okay. What's the time? Eight forty-two. Right. One hour and eighteen minutes. Right. We had breakup on the monitor. I don't know. Something else, I guess." She looked pointedly at Florie and Liu. "Okay. How's Oregon? Oh God, Jerry, I can't believe I'm not in my bunker. . . . But I have the suits, so it should—well, Soong's there anyway. Yes. I sent her up by chauffeur. I've never done a show without my cat here, Jerry." She began to cry. "I know. I know. Well, the Volks is parked down the street. Well, if it doesn't melt we should be there by—Zeus, who else? And maybe Florie and Liu if they decide to wear the suits and survive." At this, Liu bowed his head and hurried out the dressing room door.

· ·

Twelve

· ·

THE GREAT main room of Zeus' wing pulsated moodily in the purpling light. Zeus was slumped in his armchair, fixating on two raindrops that had suddenly smashed against his windowpane in a vain attempt at forcible entry. He was dressed in black tie, and freshly shaved. It was only the hidden look in his eyes that betrayed the fact he was stoned on laudanum. By his chair was an empty ice bucket, two cartons of Madison cigarettes, and two tiny old-fashioned drug bottles that had recently contained the tincture of opium.

Zeus' room, though odd, was very beautiful. Aside from the plush dark green carpeting that was meant, he said, to look like veld, it was an exact replica of the main room of the African farmhouse in which he had been born and then grown to a man. It was, therefore, that bizarre mixture of colonial English and tropical pagan, animal heads and antimacassars, dark wood paneling and faded chintz, assegais and needlepoint cushions, that makes the brain of a colonial boy incapable of assimilation in polite society.

In one corner, on a table, were lots of old photographs in ornate Victorian frames. Many of these old photos, specifically the ones of his mother and father during his childhood years, were turned away with their backs to him. Zeus permitted the world and himself a look at only two, which faced front defiantly among the defectors. One was a daguerreotype of his great-grandfather. A crusty old gent, he was standing on the prow of a boat stacked with rifles, which he was about to run up the Luangua River. The guns were a payment from the British South Africa Corporation to King Lobengula for one of Rhodes' quack treaties. In return for this mission, his great-grandfather had received a grant of land on which he built the tobacco farm where one hundred years later Zeus was born. The photo was brown and hazy like an old thought. The man was grizzled and wiry, grinning the wild, toothless grin of a low-class man about to make money, whose ship has finally come in. A floppy zebra skin hat was pulled down over one of his eyes, a rakish touch, and a pistol was strapped to his hip. In the background, Matabele tribesmen carrying rifles on their shoulders were boarding the boat. The sun was shining so hard that the humans had a universal squint.

The other photo was a black and white from the fifties, 1956 to be exact. It was taken at the Luangua Reserve in Northern Rhodesia, in front of the camp where they stayed on vacation one year. Doron, Ruth, and himself, all age eight, and behind them, their nannies, Beatrice Gwelo, Elizabeth Progress, and Violet Kwambe. The three black women were beaming toothy smiles, the smiles of servants barely supervised and on vacation in a pleasant place reserved for fun.

The children too were smiling broadly, their eyes almost closed against the glaring sun. They were all dressed in cotton safari suits, little shorts, and jackets. The boys posed like musketeers with thornwood swords carved for them by Elizabeth Progress' boyfriend in Ruth's parents' workers' kraal. Ruth held a baby spider monkey, cradling it to her chest like an infant. It was morning, the three sets of parents were out hunting. In the afternoon they would return and drink in armchairs by the river. During this vacation, the parents would always be laughing, always good-natured, always young, and always sane. It was the vacation the children, no matter how grown, no matter how jaded, would never forget. The one that would egg them on to marry and have children and haunt them when they couldn't do it. It remained, long after things crumbled, a memory hope of how life could be: sunny, carefree, sexy, and serene.

Along the back wall of Zeus' room was an ebony sideboard. Along its upper shelves were the royal commemorative plates: Queen Victoria, George the Fifth, leading up to Zeus' favorite, the one he had smuggled out when he left, the home-produced one celebrating Ian Smith's secession from Britain. Ian Smith's smiling face, where the pudding would be, hand-painted on a white background and the slogan: *No Majority Rule in My Lifetime.* "Look here," Zeus would say sardonically, pointing to it when giving a tour, "here's some real royalty, one of the colonial kings." And then, from the depths of him, he would growl, "He never loved Africa. He loved his own dick."

On the counter of the sideboard, beneath the plates, sat a battered old tin tool box from the thirties, Zeus' mother's makeup case from her days in English vaudeville. Though the key was long gone and the box unlocked, it was never to be opened, never to be touched, by Zeus' edict. It sat, as it had for the five years they had lived in the apartment, covered by an ever increasing layer of dust. And now, as Zeus sidled his eyes around to gaze at it, it looked like some furry thing, a sleeping rodent or a fat dead cat.

There was the tiny rumble of a key turning in a lock, and Zeus rolled his head on the base of his neck and stared expectantly at the door from Doron's office. Mr. Liu entered quickly. He was carrying five unopened beers and two clean ashtrays. He glanced concernedly at Zeus and then shut and relocked the door behind him.

"Thanks," murmured Zeus as Liu placed the beers in the ice bucket. "Thanks, mon."

"Florie is bringing the tea," Liu said, pocketing the empty laudanum bottles and setting down the ashtrays, "and there is a letter from your father."

Zeus smiled to himself. "Oh mon," he intoned. "Yes, mon. Yes, yes."

He closed his eyes and slept for a moment and the sound of the thunder and rain outside brought dreams of the farm and he was there, age ten, on the porch of the big house. It was dusk. And he was staring out through the screening, tracking the rivers from the rain gutters, a rapt audience for the honeybirds, who shrieked and flew and landed on the drenched English flowers. He began swaying in the grainy, wet air, keeping the rhythm of rain on a banana leaf, the faraway beat of drums in the workers' kraal. He jumped now emphatically but noiselessly as the workers had taught him, up and down, up and down, when suddenly there appeared from nowhere a lone kudu. The beige antelope with its lovely white markings, the most whimsical of warpaints, strolled slowly into view and halted just in front of him among the flower beds. It posed there, unmoving, save for its eyelids which, in protection of its gentle eyes, lowered slightly as the force of the downpour increased.

Perhaps it was a runaway from a nearby game reserve, perhaps it was a loner who had never been counted and simply roamed and grazed off the farmers' fields. He didn't know, but the majesty of the creature stunned him. It stood there in the violet rain, an ur-horse or mega-deer, about six feet high, its perfect musculature carefully sectioned with sweeping white lines, an award winner for the illustrators of the Creation, a wild African animal who had happened to cross his civilized path.

Behind him there was a noise and, very slowly, he turned. There in the doorway stood his mother. It was dark from the rain and the evening was falling, so at first, he couldn't quite make her out. But as he focused, he realized that his mother's face was painted shiny black. She wore white gloves, a nappy black wig, and carried a cane. The whites of her eyes gleamed out at him jovially and she rolled them around in her skull. She winked at him saucily and a violent shiver scissored through his body at which same instant the farm dogs, which had caught the kudu's scent, began barking hysterically. He snapped toward the kudu. The dogs streaked up the road toward the house and the kudu jerked, leaped gloriously up in the air, all four legs folded under it in a great push, and bounded off into the bush. The dogs scrambled after it and in a moment the barking grew faint.

Terrified, he turned back to his mother. She had dropped to one knee, and was waiting. When she saw she had his attention, she threw her arms wide open, fixed him with one rolling, sparkling eye and suddenly belted it out, " 'Mammy, how I love yuh, how I love yuh, my dear old Mammy . . .' "

In the dense African twilight he looked down at his minstrel mum, this golliwog in a housedress, and began laughing and crying. There were many times after this that she would appear in blackface, a fact his father would choose to ignore, but this first time and the last were lodged forever in his memory. He looked around frantically to make sure no servants were watching. He thought to flee. But then, there was a wantonness in her conviction, and a seduction in her rhythm that played havoc with his shame and dared him to transcend it. Sobbing and giggling, he found himself dropping to one knee beside her and coming in right on the beat—" 'I'd give the world to see . . .' "

Zeus started and awoke himself. Liu was opening the door to admit Florie with the tea tray and Doron, who was slumping more than usual and looking grave. Florie set up the tray, unfolded the legs and slid it over his knees.

"Come now, Zeus, you must eat," she urged. "If you must take these medicines, well, I cannot be the one to stop you, but I must be the one to make you eat."

Zeus smiled and gazed down at the tray. There was the letter covered with animals stamps, in his father's strange scrawl.

"A letter from Dad." Zeus picked it up. "Greetings from Zimbabwe. I wonder what's new? Perhaps they've changed the country's name?" He tore it open and began to read. He burst out laughing. "Eh, Doron, he's moved into the worker's kraal!"

Doron grimaced. "Is it?" he asked in disbelief.

Florie was amazed. "Do they want him?" she asked.

"No, of course not. But he still pays them, so they have to let him live there. Poor bastards! That's all they need, eh? God, he's got his own pondokkie there and he's paid *lobolla* for a wife. A hut and dowry animals, Liu," he added by way of explanation. Liu looked nervous.

"What, Zeus, he's gone kaffir, then?" Doron was peering over his shoulder and reading.

"Well, I, well he says he's lonely and the wife, well he misses Mum." Zeus looked over his shoulder at Doron and after a beat added, "A blackfaced wife, eh? Well, Mum was onto something after all."

Zeus started to giggle, then he burst out laughing, as did Doron when he realized what Zeus meant, even though surrounding the laugh was insanity and dreadful death. Zeus was joking about it in spite of everything and Doron wanted to laugh too because after this he would have to tell Zeus that, no, no, there are few more ironies yet to be faced: your woman's leaving you, your career's in shambles, and there may be no sanity left.

Eventually they stopped laughing and a silence fell. Florie switched on a table lamp and the warm glow of the light changed their mood and kept the rain from lodging in their hearts.

"Well, he's all right then," Zeus said after a time. "He sounds happy. Strange end for a racist, eh?"

"Yes," began Florie, pouring out the tea and offering the cups around, "but the other night, I was watching TV and there is a story about the New Guinea people and the first time the white man came to them. They show pictures from a long time ago, maybe sixty years, when the people were very simple hunters, pictures that the white men took then and kept. They show pictures of some young girls wearing leaves and feathers and then they show these same girls today and of course they are old wimmen in Western clothes. And one of these wimmen she says that their fathers and husbands sold them to the white men for some shells that were very dear to the people. And they ask her, 'Were you afraid of the white men?' And she says, 'Oh, yes. At first we thought they were gods, but then we had sex with them and we knew they were only men.'" Florie laughed heartily, as did Liu and Zeus. Doron looked uncomfortable.

"Eh, Florie, don't say such things in front of Doron, he's a modest bloke." Zeus smiled mischievously at his friend. "But I recall an evening at a shebeen . . ."

Doron moved to the fireplace and began laying a fire.

"We got the theater, Zeus," he said in an odd voice, his back to the company.

"The Jed Harris?" Zeus asked, and sensed a sudden tension in the room, a flight of the warm feeling in the face of an atmosphere that augured pain. "Did you tell Clca?"

He said her name and an anxiety took hold of him that made him pull a tiny bottle from his pocket and empty it into his tea. "Pardon me, my friends," he said as he did this, "I am not well. I am just not well."

Liu dropped his eyes and thought of himself in his cubicle in Hong Kong, all alone, writhing in grief. Florie set down her teacup and took Zeus' hand. "I think you must take a trip home, Zeus."

"Where is that?" he asked softly, releasing his hand. "What is that?"

"Afreekah." The name came out of her in a throaty purr.

Doron stood up and turned to face his friend. His tall body contracted so with anger, he looked almost small. "Listen, my brother, she is very angry at you for not going tonight."

Zeus grinned sardonically. "Why? She's going with Billy Butler.

She used to love him. He still loves her. It should be a treat. Maybe she still loves him. Maybe it's very dangerous."

Doron barreled on. "Look, mon, she wants to call the show—"

"No." Liu stood up and tried to stop it. If one man tells another of his wife's doings, it is almost impossible to put right, the loss of face is too great, but Doron blundered on.

"*Clea and Zeus Divorce.* She wants a divorce, mon, and she's bloody crazy. She seems to think the big bomb is going to drop any time now."

Depleted, Doron hung his head and threw up his arms. Florie stood up and began to gather up the tea things. Liu glared at Doron and then looked back at Zeus, whose body was so slack, he looked like a crumpled tuxedo that had been discarded in the chair.

"Look here," said Florie, "I think perhaps someone has put a bad spell on her. And perhaps on you, Zeus. I am going to find out." She picked up the tea tray and headed for the door.

"Wait," Zeus called hoarsely, resurrecting himself in the chair, staring at them with red-rimmed pupilless eyes, smiling an odd smile. "Do you know how many fake passports we possess among us?" he asked. They looked at each other and shook their heads. "Six," he said bitterly. "One for each of you, and three for me. Get them, Doron, let's look at them."

Doron went into his office and they listened as he opened his safe, closed it again, and returned with the contraband. He handed the six passports to Zeus. "All right," he said, shuffling them one under the other, glancing at the company like a rat caught in a trap, "here's a British one: Florie Amaxhosa. Florie, how did you get this in South Africa?"

Florie was standing, holding the tea tray, growing nervous. "I don' wan' to."

"Come, Florie," he pressed, "we're all runaways here. We're sworn to secrecy."

Florie sighed. "From a mon in Jeppe Street in Jo'burg. He made it for me."

"And what did you pay him?" Florie blushed. Her deep black skin took on a bright reddish hue and she averted her eyes. Liu went to her defense.

"Zeus, there is no need—"

"There is a need," Zeus snapped, "to know how much we paid for our so-called freedom. Florie?"

"I slept with him," she said bluntly.

"Aha!" Zeus pounced on her with his eyes. "A victim!"

"Zeus," Florie said, seething, "a woman does not always have sex from the point of view of the victim, even when she is in need. He gave me something precious, you see?" She gestured at the passport with the tea tray. "I was glad to do it. I was even in love with him for it."

Zeus shuffled the next one up. "Royal Crown Colony of Hong Kong," he read, and then glanced up. "Liu?"

"I got it at a small shop in Kowloon which specialized in such things. In the front it was a tailor, in the back a passport office for escaped mainland Chinese."

"And what did you pay?"

Liu sighed. "The marriage rings of my dead wife."

"Your wife?" Zeus was taken aback. In ten years this was the first he had heard of her.

"Yes," Liu said icily. "We were married for a short time when she was killed in a shelling. She gave me the rings off her finger as she lay dying, so the Japanese wouldn't take them. But, Zeus, I too traded them for something more precious than memories."

Zeus shuffled once more. "Doron? Possessor of the only American passport?"

Doron covered his eyes with his long bony hands. "You know this, Zeus. Some missionaries were ambushed, mistakenly. We came upon them during patrols and stole their passports. A bloke in Salisbury changed the photos, which we paid him money for."

"We?"

"Me and the Lieutenants."

"Ambushed mistakenly?"

"It was during the troubles. As they were white men and traveling in convoy, the rebels thought they were us. They were a seminary tour from the Midwest. We picked their holy bones and left the country immediately. After independence, we would have been shot you know."

Zeus shuffled again. "And these are mine." Zeus fanned them like a hand of cards. "British, Malawian, Rhodesian. All quite legal in a sense. Given to me when Rhodesia was censured, by the tobacco monopoly. So that I might continue to travel and sell our sanctioned tobacco."

Florie and Liu looked blank.

"We did business through Malawi, but they knew. Ethiopia, Cairo, they knew. We called Rhodesia 'Wiltshire' as a code name. Do you understand?"

Liu shook his head.

"When Ian Smith seceded, they banned us from existence. No calls home, no telexes, no letters. When I was out, my home was gone like a fairy town on a mountain swallowed up in mist. Only not really, not where it counted, where money was concerned or trade. I was like James Bond, only it made me cry. It was on one of these trips that I met Clea."

Doron stooped down and gathered up the passports. Florie shoved the tea tray against the door to Doron's office, which opened it a bit so they could squeeze through and slip away. Liu moved over to a far corner of the room and took up his pi-pa. He spent a few moments tuning it and then began to play.

Zeus lolled his head back against the chair and stared out the window at the thunder clouds. The rain fell like tiny metal missiles into space. He closed his eyes and instantly he was small again and trapped in one of the curing cubicles on the farm. He and Doron had been playing hide-and-seek. He had run along the line of curing rooms and finally pulled up one of the outside doors, darted in, and rammed it down. It was pitch black inside and stifling hot. The air was funneled in through midget doors at both sides of the room.

The air rose upwards, curing the wads of tobacco leaves, which hung, like washing, from a clothesline. He lasted only a moment before he realized he could not stand it. When finally he pulled up the door again, after much panic and almost fatal sweatiness of hands and fantasy of death, overcome by the thick smell of yellowing tobacco, he flung himself out into the oxygen and found his father standing there. "You've lost the game, you fool," his father had taunted. And he had run, into the house, into the arms of the first woman who would have him and hold him, in this case a friend of his mother's who smelled of gin and who, as she comforted him, secretly rubbed his little prick till it got hard.

Thirteen

TWO MINUTES," Charlie was calling. Liu turned and rushed onto the stage. He hurried across the proscenium to the pulley mechanism that ran the flying wires. Taking a flashlight from his pocket, he carefully examined the apparatus to make sure it was in working order.

Around him, the stagehands were murmuring, setting up the skeet shoot, testing it to release the clay pigeons, oiling it and cocking it for the next scene. Roger, the lighting designer, was on a ladder changing gels. Jim, the set designer, was adding a bit of paint to the backdrop. The cameramen had set down their cameras and were smoking cigarettes and chatting to the director through their headphones.

"It's fine," Liu said to Ruth Ravenscroft as she rushed past him toward the stage-right wing.

"What?" she asked.

"Tell Clea the flying mechanism is secure," he explained.

"Oh," Ruth replied uneasily, "I hadn't planned to—oh. Oh all right." She proceeded offstage and up the stage-right corridor to Clea's dressing room.

Florie opened to her knock.

"Ruth, you are here." Florie seemed relieved. "Clea, it is Ruth. Come in, Ruth. How are the apes?" Florie gave her a big smile and stood intently waiting for her answer. Ruth blushed.

"She's not dating them, Florie," said Clea, appearing from behind the door half made up. "Or are you, Ruth? It can get hairy out there in the jungle, I know. Oh for a cuddly man who can't speak and forages for his own food. I'd say you're lucky, sister."

"Hi, Clee," said Ruth, and hugged her. She took in her friend as she repeated her message. "Liu says the flying mechanism is secure."

"Christ, that's luck," replied Clea, sitting down at her dressing table. "We wouldn't want to die before we die, would we? That would be a joke, eh girls?"

Ruth forced herself to smile. She wanted to say something. She wanted to ask questions, like, What has happened to you, Clea? Why have you lost you mind? What has possessed you to bomb out this love? Are you so sure you'll get another? Are you so sure it's worth the agony? Think, woman, think hard. There are millions like me who will never have it, who can't have it. But instead she laughed. Clea scared her like Joan Crawford, the mother ape who beat her baby over and over, to the shame of the others. But the troop did nothing, knowing somehow that it was a mobius strip, this kind of love-hate, and their protestations would have no effect.

"The apes are fine," Ruth said to Florie. "They know their names. The book is coming well. I've built this lovely tree house, you must come see . . ."

"Ach, Afreeka," Florie murmured. "I miss the food, the big sky, the warmth."

"Oh sometimes, Florie, there comes a cloud of butterflies so big it blots out the horizon, nothing but yellow wings. It's like a god visiting, you know?"

Florie nodded. "No African gods in this place, Ruth, not for a long time." She shot a glance at Clea, who was painting eyeliner on her left eye.

"No," Clea agreed, looking at her in the mirror, holding the eyeliner brush delicately aloft, "she's right. Only Greek gods here now. Patriarchal ones of Western civilization. Thunder and fire, rain and cracking of cheeks. Did you notice, Ruthie, that we've got old?"

"Hey?" Ruth took a chance and met Clea's eyes. Clea gestured at a crow's-foot beneath her eyelash.

"Look here, baby. One morning I got up and I was older. This crack was here to stay. No stroke of makeup, no good night's sleep can change it. I walk down the street surrounded by baby sex goddesses. I understand them, but I am not one of them anymore."

"Look at me, Clea, for God's sake. The African sun has beaten me to death."

"You took another route. You live with gorillas and don't own mirrors. But we ruled the planet once, do you remember?"

Clea smiled and her huge eyes filled with light. Caught in their radiant beam, Ruth smiled too, widely, happily remembering such a time. "Oh yes," Ruth whispered, "of course I remember."

Athens. When she first escaped. She got a fellowship to study zoology at Cambridge and she came up out of Rhodesia like a jackal on the run. Scared that she wouldn't know how to behave, a farm girl with one dress, a pair of lace-ups, and a sweater and a beautiful fountain pen, given to her by Zeus when she did her O levels. Doron was there already, and the Seven, escaped but truly escaped, never to return. And Zeus, who she'd thought would always be damaged, would never be whole, a wanderer for sure. Oh no, the drumbeat had it, not anymore, now there's Clea.

In a taverna overlooking the Parthenon, the floodlit Acropolis apostrophed by a white full moon, she had looked across at them in wonder. Clea and Zeus had taken the town by storm. Their act at the Athens Hilton had become a cause célèbre. The English speaking community and the Athenian aristocrats alike had made them their new best friends. Their poster was everywhere, superseding even that of the Marlboro man. She saw it twice on the drive from the airport. Pasted on wide billboards alongside the Aegean, two brightly painted third world lovers, giant heads together, a single arrow piercing through both of their hearts. *Clea kai Zeus! Eseis agapoume!* Clea and Zeus! We Love You!

Of course Ruth knew Zeus was a dancer, he was born that way. Just as she was born an observer, always taking notes and cataloguing, her dolls, her books, then butterflies, then, for a short time, men. And Doron was a born protector, the littlest security man, always on recon patrol as early as she could remember, running ahead of them as they walked, beating the bushes for a hidden invader.

In all the grit and slime of civil war, she never thought of dancing as the key, their ticket out. But it was always there, in every memory. Zeus and she and Doron all age eight running around the lawn in underpants, spraying each other with hoses, sopping wet and screaming with delight. Zeus, bounding into the air with strength and grace, holding the hose like a long green peeing penis, a bawdy lawn elf come to life. Zeus, on the perimeter of her farm, aiming his machine gun, dancing out the bullets as she shot, keeping the staccato rhythm, making creativity of his killing. And here it was again. This Clea saw it and she knew. She snapped him up like a bottle of great wine mislaid in a bargain bin. She opened him and let him breathe.

And as Ruth sat across from them in that taverna, watching the famous come and go, kisses, compliments, and drinks heaped on the table like spoils and supplications, she realized that when she thought of who his wife would be, so long ago when sex was just beginning, she did not have the mind to think of Clea. She simply wasn't bright enough. She thought of women as opposites to men. If Zeus was tall, then she'd be short. If Zeus had black hair, then she'd have blond. If he was rough, then she'd be smooth. It never occurred to her that his wife would be exactly like him only female. Equally charismatic and sparkling, equally talented, equally larger than life, equally—what was it?—lost, no, hidden, no, bereft.

She remembered staring at Zeus and the way Zeus caught her eye and smiled the most peaceful and surfeited of smiles.

"Look here, Ruth," he said, glancing at Clea by his side, "look what fate sent me."

He turned, put his arms around Clea, and pulled her to him like a security bear. Clea, riveted by his passion, stared up at him and smiled in return. And out of this engagement rose a vapor of sweetness and utter faith that was palpable. This steam hovered around their dual outline and permeated the atmosphere. Ruth got goose bumps. Doron blushed. Liu, whose attention was elsewhere, for no reason felt compelled to turn their way and look. Florie grinned and bobbed her head in assent. The Seven Golden Lieutenants, their machine guns concealed in guitar cases in deference to the Greeks, dropped their eyes and thought of sex.

It was as dramatic as any performance. As pure as two toddlers embracing. It was, Ruth thought, their focus that created such a membrane around them, their ability to concentrate so fully on each other that they blocked out all else. They made each other godlike with their worship.

And then, down in the street below, a truck backfired with a boom. Zeus and Doron instinctively turned over the table and pulled the women down behind it. There were screams, a shattering of glass, and then dead quiet. Ruth remembered peering up from her crouch on the floor and seeing the Seven Golden Lieutenants, their machine guns miraculously out of their cases, forming a laager around the table.

She remembered the rest of the taverna, the patrons, the owner, the waiters, staring at their party, silent and unmoving. And Clea, struggling out from under Zeus, who had thrown himself on top of her in that second of terror, looking slowly around the taverna, letting a beat go by and then asking, "Zeus, honey. Is there something I should know?"

"What are you thinking?" Clea was watching her in the mirror, questioning her thought. Ruth looked up. Clea's eyes were painted now, her face powdered and rouged like an old bisque-headed doll.

"The taverna, 1974, when Zeus and Doron turned over the table," Ruth replied. Clea and Florie laughed.

"You were all so jumpy," Clea said. "Later, when we came back to America, I found my friends who had been to Vietnam were like that too."

"We had been through so much. We were drained. Your success, the festive freedom was like a dream. We never thought that Zeus would be a star or even in show business. It was such a wild card, the farthest thing from our minds."

"Yes," agreed Florie, "I didn't know what I sought when I came up from Jo'burg. I thought that I would teach small children."

"That's what you're doing, Florie." Clea stood up. "We are children. We don't have it in us to be anything more. Our bodies will grow old but we'll still be children, cursed with the minds of prepubescents." She turned to Ruth. "And as for Zeus, well, he was all there just waiting to happen. He was so exciting. I was just a trigger."

Clea and Florie hurried toward the dressing room door. Ruth, forgetting herself in the spontaneity of the moment, grabbed Clea's arm. "How can you divorce him? How can you do this? You loved him so much. I saw it. How can you do this to us, you're our family, for God's sake, we count on you."

Florie put her hand to her brow and sighed heavily.

Ruth, flustered, muttered, "I'm sorry. Now's not the time, I know."

Clea looked at this woman and the bond between them pulled some hidden sanity into her mind. "There was a vacuum I couldn't fill, Ruth, a grief in him I couldn't even hope to assuage. Over time, with the aid of his Lieutenants, he formed a laager round this meteoric crater. Outside, I was like a tribesman with a bow and arrow fighting against a weapon I couldn't even imagine."

"Under that analogy," Ruth snapped, "your love for Zeus is a colonial conflict. I rather thought it was more democratic, that you annexed him like a city-state."

Clea's glance turned inward and she softened perceptibly. "Oh no, Ruth," she murmured. "If you love a man, really love him, love is always a colonial tragedy."

"And if you want to dominate?" asked Ruth.

"It isn't love," said Clea.

"And if you want equality?"

"In love as in law, it is a concept only."

"You mean you never felt equal to Zeus?"

"Not when I was loving him. I thought him better than me, that's why I loved him."

"But when you performed together?"

"I wasn't loving him. I was loving it."

"But you had fun, surely?"

"Of course."

"But how will you live without him?"

Clea looked her squarely in the eye. "There's a possibility I won't live, Ruth. I'll be wearing my radiation suit, but there's always the possibility that at ten o'clock we will all be dead."

"No!" Ruth shook her head angrily.

"We have an extra suit for you, Ruth, if you'd like to put it on when the time comes."

"I don't know," Ruth muttered.

"I'll miss you," said Clea, and left the dressing room, followed by Florie.

. . . .

Fourteen

. . . .

OKAY." The director sighed. The long commercial break was coming to a close. "What time is it?" He turned to the A.D. "Eight forty-three. One hour and seventeen minutes till doomsday." The A.D. chuckled and asked hypothetically, "What if something does happen? What if the atom bomb does drop?"

"Then we're out of a job, ol' buddy, union or no union. Okay, let's see 'em. Camera One."

Onto the monitors popped a wide shot of the stage transformed into an open-air nightclub by the Nile.

"Nice set, Jim's a genius. Camera Two, please."

And up shot a closeup of the skeet shooting mechanism that released clay pigeons.

"Charlie," the director spoke into his headphones, "this pulley thing work? Anybody test this thing? Okay, good. Camera Three."

And up shot a closeup of the flying mechanism suspended above the stage in the center of the proscenium.

"Where are they? Are they getting strapped to it? Where's Clea?"

"She's here, boss." Charlie was standing stage right watching as Bobette and two stagehands buckled Clea into the flying wires and then helped her into the Chinese junk. "So's Eddie." Eddie Witz, with whom she would make her entrance, was standing by. He looked into the lens of Camera Three and waved.

"Hi there!" he boomed. The director laughed.

"The guy's unflappable," he said.

"Yeah." The A.D. palmed his stopwatch. "Good thing we don't have to fly him, then we'd really be worried."

"Zeus is strapped in," Charlie's voice spat over the headphones. "Extras are set. Ready when you are."

"God, I love this set," murmured the director. "This is my favorite scene, reminds me of the old days. Raise curtain."

"Ten seconds," said the A.D. and counted. "Ten, nine, eight—"

"Hit the lights."

". . . four, three, two, one."

"Go! Hit it!"

Arabic music snaked through the theater. The mingled din of hawkers and laughing patrons crowded the stage. The set was open-air nightclub by the Nile. Upstage along the back wall ran a mock Nile River, bounded by an iron railing. Downstage tables filled with jovial men and women littered the stage. Waiters navigated through them, selling jasmine flowers and delivering trays of drinks. Down right was the skeet shoot which, every now and then, with a re-sounding bang released clay pigeons above the patrons into the starry painted night.

Over the tables, tiny strings of colored lights were strung that twinkled festively. The male patrons were dressed in uniforms of the Egyptian army or in galabias, some with turbans, some without. The women wore evening gowns of teal blue, mustard, and deep red ocher. The tables were iron and white and heaped with foods like offerings to the gods. From the audience, the set seemed like an Egyptian tomb painting set in modern times.

Up right, in the center of the mock Nile, Clea, dressed as the Chinese junk, bobbed angrily and began the scene, addressing Sid, who was leaning over the railing and making placating gestures, to her.

"Nobody does promotion in Egypt, Sid. There's no room to get noticed."

"Trust me, baby." Sid was shushing her. "After this you'll have a sold out show. Ladies and gentlemen—" he began to introduce her but the report of the skeet shoot blasted him out.

"Jesus!"—the junk sank in the water—"What was that?"

Sid looked over his shoulder. "The skeet shoot. This is an Egyptian nightclub, alternate nights of dancing and skeet shooting. They told me at the hotel it was dance night."

"Great." The junk sank lower. "Now what?"

Downstage left, Zeus entered, dressed in his brown third world suit, wearing a hat and carrying a briefcase. Accompanying him were Mr. Zaki-Sayd, the head of the Egyptian tobacco monopoly, played as a cameo by the Arab rock star Abou Ben Adem, and Rita and Peg as high-class Egyptian bimbos.

"Have you shot skeet, Zeus?" Abou Ben Adem's voice was high and shrill. He had a Peter Lorre air to his orientalness. He was a small and graceful man, though not effeminate, who was part Arab, part busker and had an aura of intelligence about him that was attributed to his interest in electronic music.

"No. But I've shot men," said Zeus. Zaki-Sayd chuckled as he settled the bimbos at a table. Zeus abandoned his briefcase and hat, and the three men headed across the stage to shoot skeet. The Arab at the skeet mechanism handed Zeus a rifle.

"Look at him," Rita said to Peg as Zeus took aim. "Can you imagine sleeping with him?" A table of Greek sailors nearby responded unanimously.

"Yes!" they cried, "yes!" The audience laughed.

The clay pigeons were released and Zeus swung on his heel and fired at them one, two, three, and splintered them into shards above center stage.

"Fucking amazing," Eddie Witz mumbled under his breath to Clea. "Your husband's a crack shot!" Through his gun sight, Zeus could see Clea's head behind her costume. He took aim and fantasized popping it like a breadfruit. The nightclub was cheering. Eddie swung into character.

"Out of the Nile, baby, they can't see you."

"Here, give me a leg up."

Sid helped the Chinese junk crawl over the railing.

Zeus was again taking aim. New pigeons were released with a bang. Clea, encased in the junk, was struggling now to get over the rail. The audience was laughing at the physical dance she and the rotund Sid were doing.

"Look, kid, we'll go through the nightclub instead."

"What a great idea." The Chinese junk was annoyed. "Too bad you didn't have it an hour ago."

Zeus swung around and fired at three clay pigeons and got two of them. The third, it happened, thanks to the propmen, hovered right over the Chinese junk now navigating through the tables. He shot it and it shattered and the pieces fell and thwacked onto the junk's prow and sails.

"Shit!" bellowed the junk and fell onto the nightclub floor.

"What was that?" Zeus asked Zaki-Sayd.

"A small boat in distress," replied the Egyptian and turned toward the commotion.

Sid was quickly righting Clea, who, due to the weight of the junk, was on her back like a turtle. The extras gathered around so the audience could not see as Sid stood her up, readjusted the straps, and Velcroed pieces of clay pigeon to her sails. Finally the extras parted and the Chinese junk, littered with pigeon parts and a few feathers, sailed forth down the crowded stage. The audience laughed.

"Look at that, Zeus." The bimbos massed around him and pressed their curves against his skin. "What is that, baby?"

Zeus gasped. "Oh my God, it's—"

Sid began hawking as they paraded through the tables. "Ladies and gentlemen, straight from the Isis Lounge at the Cairo Hilton, it's a boat, it's a plane, it's—"

"Sid for Christ's sake," said the junk, "that is the most demeaning—"

"Shush."

Zeus planted himself at the end of their route and waited for the Chinese junk to reach him.

"Uh-oh!" Sid shrank back.

"What, Sid." Clea stopped in her sail.

"It's that guy with the weird name."

"Where?"

Sid did not reply but continued hawking. "It's Clea! The great acrobat and storyteller in the Chinese tradition. Appearing nightly, at the Isis Lounge."

Clea peeped around the sail and saw Zeus in front of her. She tried to float backwards, but he grabbed her prow.

"Hey!" she said, trying to wrench her prow out of his grasp.

"Hey!" he said, holding it fast.

"Hey!" Sid said, shoving Zeus' hand away and deftly unstrapping Clea from the boat. In a flashy movement he lifted the junk off her body and revealed Clea in a turquoise tulle evening gown.

"Ladies and gentlemen"—Sid held up her hand—"it's the beauteous Clea!"

Clea bowed low. The nightclub cheered. A spot came up on Zeus and one on Clea. Zeus stared at the big black heart earring dangling from Clea's ear. "You're human," he said softly, innocently.

"Sort of," Clea replied, and with a grand flourish of harp strings, they both flew up above the stage and hovered in midair.

The audience gasped and clapped. The music softened to a plaintive Arab love lament. Every eye in the audience was gazing up at Clea and Zeus. There had been other performers in the theater who used the flying wires but not like them, never like them. They always began, as they did now, by hanging slackly like stored puppets.

"You were the boat," said Zeus turning only his head toward Clea. His body, clad in the third world brown suit and wing tips, swayed a little. His arms hung motionless at his sides.

"Yes," replied Clea, nodding. Her body in the turquoise tulle evening gown sagged lifelessly. Her arms hung motionless at her sides. "I trained in China where festival boats are important."

The audience was waiting. The energy ruffled through them like wind through wheat.

"China," Zeus asked, swaying still.

"A kind of China-Taiwan. And you're from—" Clea asked, swaying too.

"Africa. Rhodesia. Land of Ian Smith," Zeus said and hung his head. "I was born of racists."

The Seven Golden Lieutenants shifted their guns nervously out in the audience. They didn't like this part of the show.

"I was born," Clea said after a beat, "of militarists. In the history of the earth"—she hung her head too—"our pasts are damning."

He nodded. "When they look in our brains, they'll know. Militarism and racism secrete sclerotic fluids. Alzheimer's of the soul."

Clea looked up to heaven, clasped her hands in prayer, and stretched her legs out behind her. She looked like an attendant angel in a religious painting. The audience rustled. This was the beginning. "Perhaps," she said hopefully, "the sins of the fathers are not visited on the children?"

Zeus stretched his legs out behind him and became an angel himself. "Self-deception is inherited," he said cynically. "I know it. I'm sorry."

Clea dropped limply again but snapped her head toward him in anger. "*You're* sorry," she said feistily. "*You're* sorry? The whole world is sorry!"

Zeus dropped limply too and snapped his head toward Clea. "I want you," he muttered with such intensity that the women in the audience got wet and adjusted themselves in their seats. The men felt it too and whistled and stomped at the thought.

And suddenly, they were in it. Suddenly, Clea and Zeus began to hold the air as firmly as ever they held the stage. The audience cheered. This was their magic. They called it a 3-D mime. With the aid of tiny weights sewn into their clothes and the muscle control of the blessed, they were able to simulate gravity while hanging in space. Five feet above the stage they walked, they ran, they danced and did their stage crosses with a conviction and solidity that defied the fact that they stood on illusion. Roger lit them with the E.T. special, the blue overlight of the alien being, which increased the magic and lit up the dust particles in the air so they seemed to be playing in floating diamonds. "Cathy and Heathcliffe suffering in the strato-sphere," a critic once described it. "It's the concept of love in the mind's eye brought out for all to see. I don't know how they do it."

Though they made it look easy, it wasn't. The flying mechanism corsetted their torsos and they were always afraid it might break. The infinitesimal muscle movements they were making to simulate weightiness made them sweat buckets. The odor of the makeup was suffocating and grew worse in the hot glare of the spotlights.

"I want you," Zeus muttered again. He strolled in a diagonal across the void and took her arms and held them out so he could see her. Clea twirled, a perfect pirouette in space, landed firmly on noth-ingness and curtseyed low.

"I want you too," she replied, staring into his eyes. He pulled her to him and she ran trippingly over the heads of the audience and into his arms.

And it was all in that kiss. The audience stared up at them, their attention so focused that they all got sensitive, all at once. A bodily shiver rose up off the crowd and stroked Clea and Zeus. And when they felt it, they started to spin themselves, slowly and sensuously at first like a human pinwheel . . . Then faster and faster; like cats in heat which have just been screwed. They became sexual frenzy. They became intense desire. They dug their nails into each other's souls until they were just a blur. It was something they were great at but only on stage: antigravity love.

Within themselves, as their lips touched, Clea and Zeus realized that they hadn't kissed for months. They hadn't wanted or known how to anymore. They had reached that stage of distance where one touch would be a trigger and they pleaded conscientious objections and shunned engagement. But in this second of play-acting, they retrieved emotions that had once been theirs and lay on them as if they were a net.

Finally, they ceased revolving and hung for a moment entwined in each other's arms like a living wasp nest under an eave or Christ and his girlfriend on a cross. Their projection of human love was three dimensional. The audience sighed deeply.

Beneath them, the stage lights had dimmed. Only the tiny bulbs strung over the tables still glowed. Eddie, Abou, and the company were silent and posed. A sole Arabic flute charmed the atmosphere.

Clea and Zeus stepped down solidly onto nothingness and pulled apart.

"Look here," Zeus said in his almost-British voice "we'll be all right if you just manipulate me." He walked forward on ectoplasm toward the audience. The effect was 3-D. They trilled with excitement.

"You know what I want on my tombstone?" Clea asked in reply. She too walked forward and joined him. He looked at her quizzically while she deftly turned her back, snuggled into his chest and put ·her cheek to his. She looked up at him and said, "She could understand being into bondage."

There was terrific *twang* and from out of Clea's midriff and out of Zeus' back popped the two ends of a mean-looking arrow. The audience gasped. Blood drops fell down their clothes. The Arabic flute was a lonely moan. And Clea and Zeus posed there, five feet above the stage, their feet planted solidly on the unsubstantial, their hearts pierced together by a huge black, viciously pointed projectile of love until deftly, artfully, Roger pulled the lever down and softened their vision to a silhouette.

THE LIGHTS snapped off and the audience broke into applause. In his house seat, Clark Lincoln, four-star general in the American air force and Clea's father, turned to his date, the newly crowned Miss Hollywood, and whispered, "What did she say about militarism? That it was a crime?"

"I don't think so, Clark," Miss Hollywood said, squeezing his arm.

General Lincoln sighed. "Well, the Chinese got her. There wasn't a whole hell of a lot I could do about it with her mother not being there."

As Clea and Zeus landed on the stage floor in the darkness, Zeus leaned over and whispered something into Clea's ear that he knew would endanger the evening's proceedings. He did it out of pure malice and conscious perversity and because he was so furious at what she was doing to him that it was the only way he could think of to fight back.

"I'm not wearing the radiation suit," he snapped and then fled away to the stage-left wing, where Liu was waiting to unhook him from the flying mechanism.

"Make it fast, Liu," he said, "there's going to be trouble." And he fidgeted nervously as Liu went about freeing him.

Clea was crushed. In performing the flying walk, she had conjured up memories, memories that she had hidden away like intimate snapshots of a former boyfriend. She had drawn them out for the performance: Moments Of Bliss With Zeus, and they had made her sentimental. It was therefore a perfect hit when Zeus whispered in the darkness, out of breath, ardent, that he would not wear the suit. His decision cleaved into her, like a coring device in a vast archeological dig, plummeting down through her levels of being, making history of her sacred beliefs.

She stood there staring after him, boring her eyes through the back of his skull until finally he looked back at her. They stared at each other across the stage, with mutual fury, until she said, "Fine. It's your funeral." And she pranced offstage.

Fifteen

THE DOOR to the War Room slid shut and Clea leaned back and spread her arms across it like a human barricade. Her head fell on her chest. Her eyes were open, staring down into blackness. Divorce, her mind murmured, divorce. How will you do it? How can you do it? Can you do it and make a joke of it too? How far can you go, really, how far? Frankly, my dear, you've overextended yourself, dontcha think? Her feet materialized out of the darkness and she began to see the floor and it became comforting. "I don't care. I don't care." She spoke out loud, lifting her head, her voice rising as she relaxed. "I do not fucking care." She looked around the War Room and she smiled. I'm safe here, she thought, this is mine, and like a taped loop, this phrase began repeating over and over in her brain: *This is mine. This is mine.*

The War Room had originally been Clea's office. When they moved into the apartment, she had purchased a word processor and that's how it began. Now, from that one computer seed she had grown it into a vast system, a long ell of gun metal machinery with red lights that blinked the time and the date and the temperature. She could take her blood pressure and her pulse rate, summon up articles from *The New York Times*, and talk porno with Tokyo. Lately, Jerry, her Vegas astrologer, had gotten his computer and together they had cracked NORAD.

For a while she stood in the darkness, focusing on the red blinking digital readout, and then she snapped on a dim lamp, switched on the system, and sat down at the console.

Above the computer was a long, low black and white photograph of Hiroshima after the blast. It extended the full eight feet of the wall, and its grim and ceaseless devastation made it transcend horror and achieve art. She looked at it for a moment and then thrust her arms into two metal wrist guards that hooked into the console. Her blood pressure and pulse rate appeared in red digital numbers and blinked on the board. She looked up at the photograph and imagined being in Hiroshima at the moment of the blast. She felt it. The great flash of light blinding her eyes, the enormous earth crack of an explosion in her ears, the terror numbing and shaking her body, the smell of her own burning flesh, the sound of her own soundless scream. She was just about to leave the edge of sanity when she looked down at the console. Her blood pressure and pulse rate had risen amazingly.

"Incredible," she muttered and said in the style of Alan King, "you know, I kid nuclear war, but I love it." She typed the data into the computer, but then remembered that she was in a rage when she began the experiment so at best her results were suspect.

"Fuck!" she spat as she leaned back in the chair. "Fuck! Fuck!"

She turned her head and looked at herself in the full-length mirror that was hanging to her left opposite her chair. There were a lot of mirrors in her life and she consulted them frequently, partly out of vanity, but mostly out of professional interest in her outer shell, in the fleshy casing that was her living.

Today she was young and very beautiful, an outer image that was completely at odds with the beaten-up crone that today was inside.

The beaten-up crone who wanted out of the marriage, out of the career, out of the web of responsibilities that had entrapped her. The word *divorce* had popped out of her mouth like a piece of undigested food. It was as though Zeus, in his refusal to go with her to the awards taping, had executed a psychological Heimlich maneuver and out it came, the chewed-over-but-undigested-concept divorce, separation for all time.

Clea wept and watched herself weeping, the mascara running, the Medea-like mask of her young, beautiful crushed-up face while the crone inside grinned a toothless grin and cackled: Who really is the loner here? The one who survives alone, who never links up, who revolves in inner space like a lost satellite transmitting only when tracked and then every one million light years? It isn't true! Clea rejoined, blubbering. I love a lot of people. The cat, my child substitute, and Zeus, I did love Zeus until he went away from me. She sobbed now, her little shoulders shaking, her head in her hands, staring backwards at her memories, wildly searching them for something or someone to blame.

"I loved him very much." She spoke out loud now and the sound of her voice was that of a grieving war widow from a forties movie. "But I couldn't get to him. He was surrounded by men. Constant testosteronics. Made me damn nervous."

She laughed, and then she really began to cry. Where before there were tears of frustration, now a deep, yawning pit opened inside her. A black mist descended behind her eyes, shutting out the light. And she began, as she did so often in confused moments of panic, to hallucinate stabbing herself to death. It was her hand that she saw, plunging the knife in her stomach over and over again! I hate you, her mind muttered, I hate you so much. Why can't you be normal, you insane cunt, you sick bitch. I hate you I hate you!

Just before the murder was completed, she threw herself onto the computer and lay there, quiet. Her headbones pushed down the cool keys and her intellect started to plan. You can go, Clea, a clear solution, matter-of-fact, you've done your time. A hut on a tropical island. Bright white sun and sand leading to a quiet, shimmering

sea. You'll be there just a person, just living, like you've done sometimes. Exchanging greetings, smiling and squinting, living on the
earth, simple, predictable. You drink milk from a coconut as the sun
sets and you sleep lulled by the lapping waves. Did I mention your
tan?

She was calming now with the plans. She listened. Or a dim
moody apartment in Berlin. Arty and bleak. Alone, in black tights
and a long dress, you write of your anguish and pain, you live in
your imagination and no one can touch you. You don't do business,
you wouldn't know how. You die of TB but you've done great work.
Not a bad trade-off.

And then the mother's voice all sweetness and comfort, the good
witch at last muffling the demons, cuddling the nerve-charged brain:
Clea, my baby, my little one, Clea, Clea, relax, little love, I'm here.
I'm with you. Mama! The brain gives one rueful cry before it sur-
renders to comfort, and Clea, now a spectator on the sidelines,
straightens her body and sits up and waits for the pain to fade.

"I must," she said brokenly, out loud, "fix myself. The time . . ."
And she turned and, like a carpenter following blueprints, began
to do so.

The simple mechanical act of painting her face calmed her as
it always did. The murderous shaking rage was diluted in a bath
of brain opiate that secreted in spurts as she disguised her visage. As
she fashioned herself the face of an idol, the personality retreated
behind this front as behind a nanny's skirts, peeking out only in
response to the instinctual entreaties of hand/eye coordination. She
drew back, back in time, to the Five Enjoyments Teahouse.

SHE STRUCK the woodblock on the high podium, and the sound
that emanated through the teahouse was homey and hollow. The men
and old women who sat beneath her drinking tea and smoking looked
up and waited. Some of the men leered at her, uneasy with this
break from tradition, but she didn't take it personally. She smiled
sweetly at them, dropping her voice modestly, and cleared her throat.

Clea had graduated from the Taipei Acrobatic School several weeks before. As she had for the previous three summers, she was telling stories in teahouses for spending money. She had painted her face in the Chinese manner for the occasion, pure white with bright red cheeks and lips and heavy black eye makeup. The Chinese believed in makeup for a performance, or it might be more accurate to say they could not take a performance seriously without it. Even tiny children in their school dramas wore it, looking like so many baby courtesans and dandies as they trod the village roads to school on festival days. Clea pursed her lips and began speaking in perfect Mandarin. "The Return of Tiny Tears" was the story she had chosen for today, a favorite in the teahouses, a true story as it happened, though the listeners were unaware of it.

"The small female foreign devil had no sisters and brothers."

A murmur swept through the teahouse. The story was to be a tragedy. They prepared themselves for sadness. Clea went on.

"When her mother fell ill and was taken away, she left home and traveled the longest journey a child can travel, to live with her father the General in his house on Pei Lin Street. Her father was in the American air force."

The denizens of the teahouse grunted here and Clea paused. It was unorthodox to speak of foreigners in the teahouse and it made them aware of their wholesale indenture.

"And on her journey," Clea forged ahead, "she had been entrusted to a series of military men who had lodged her for the night. She was, as I have said, a small girl only six years old, born in the Year of the Mouse, which was a good thing as she needed the mouse's luck. On her journey from Hawaii to Guam to Wake Island to Okinawa, from airbase to airbase, through foreign lands up to the borders of China, she carried with her her dear friend and confidante, the doll Tiny Tears. Together they had come to trust the thick odor of fuel on a runway, the glint of sun on a military medal, and the steady nightbeat of rain on a banana leaf that so characterized the airbases where she stopped along the way.

"Finally, after several weeks of traveling, the child arrived in

Taipei and the General took her home to Pei Lin Street, where together they would henceforth reside. In the confusion and joy of reuniting with her father, the small girl failed to notice that a tragedy had occurred. It was only the following Tuesday that she awoke with a start in her new room which, when it rained, smelled of teak and camphor and seven kinds of tea and knew that the doll, her friend and confidante Tiny Tears, was gone. Disappeared, lost on the great journey, vanished from her clutch.

"The child mourned, but truly, losing things and people was something the small female foreign devil was used to at this point in life and so when she told her father of her loss, it was with great sadness but greater resignation. 'She is gone,' the child sighed, 'that is all there is to it. Tiny Tears is gone for good.' Her father looked pained. 'I wonder where she is?' he said thoughtfully. 'I'm very sorry.'

"In the month that followed, the small female foreign devil grew accustomed to her new home. And it is true to say that in the absence of her mother, the child hopped right into the lap of the lady China and suckled from her fragrant breast."

The listeners murmured here in appreciation of the embrace of their country, in appreciation of the discernment of the child.

"But," Clea went on ominously, "always there was a bare spot, as with a tree when one of its roots is cut. It grows, but spindly, deprived of a nourishment that would make it fully flourish."

The listeners moaned. Stifled growth was one of the worst things they could imagine.

"One day, some time after these events, when the child's father had, as was his duty, flown away to Japan and the child and her amah were alone in the house, there was a knock at the front gate. The small female foreign devil had been playing in the bomb shelter at the back of the yard when she heard the gate close. She ran round the house and into the front courtyard. There, standing in the jasmine grove talking to her amah, were two American generals in crinkly silver flying suits covered with zippers. Each man carried a silver helmet under his arm and both were blue-eyed and square-jawed and in that place of delicate shadows and pagodaed roofs quite startling to behold.

" 'Hello,' the child said in her most lady-of-the-house manner. 'My father isn't here. He's in Japan getting his flying time.'

"The cook appeared from the kitchen now, as did the gardener. The amah went and scurried over to them and the three stared wide-eyed at the heavy-booted men wrapped in silver. The first one smiled and said in a kindly American drawl,

" 'We're here to see you, Miss.'

"The child stared at the helmet under the man's arm with its decoration of air force wings and wondered if there was going to be a loss. She looked around for a hand to hang on to, but there was only the amah whom she didn't know very well, or the cook and the gardener whom she didn't know at all. In the end she hung on to her own hand behind her back and waited for the inevitable. The second man stepped forward and said seriously, 'We're on a mission from General Matson from Hokusai Bay. We have something for you.'

"And from beneath his great silver helmet he produced a brown paper parcel. The child took it and unwrapped the string, and the paper fell open to reveal her dear friend and confidante, the doll Tiny Tears. The child gasped. The three servants broke into laughter. The two men beamed.

" 'Oh, thank you.' The small female foreign devil rushed forward and shook the outstretched hand of the silver-suited officer. 'Thank you,' she said again, inspecting the baby doll. 'I see she has her blanket. That's good, I was afraid she was cold.'

"The two men, smiling broadly, turned toward the gate and said, 'Well, mission accomplished, we've got to go now.'

"The amah hurried over and stood by to let them out. The sun, which had been watching from a corner of the sky, came out overhead and shone down, firing up the silver suits and helmets, igniting an explosive aura around the men that made them seem like gods. They lowered their heads and went through the gate. The small female foreign devil ran after them and watched. Clutching Tiny Tears to her flat warm little chest, she tried to say thank you again but her tongue had gone soft and she couldn't. They got into the shiny black staff car, turned back to look at her, and she waved. As they drove away, the tofu man on the corner let out a high-pitched cry and beckoned the neighborhood to buy his wares."

Clea pounded the woodblock on the high podium, and the old women and men began chatting.

"Propaganda," chortled one man, "but beautiful propaganda."

She climbed down and went from table to table to collect her tips.

"You've got the knack, dearie," said an old lady, grabbing her wrist and stroking it, "foreign devil though you may be."

"Small feet too," cried one man. "Will you marry me?" Clea laughed.

THE SMELL of bland boiling water and tobacco smoke, the oilcloth smell of China. Sometimes, when she was in a department store and there was an oilcloth umbrella or a hat, she would catch a whiff and she was back: skinny and silent, padding down an open-sewered back street, at one with the cacophony of poverty, the industrious buying and selling and creating of magic that was China. She would be standing in Bloomingdale's, an umbrella pressed to her nose, inhaling her early life like an illicit drug, and the images would drown her: the return of Tiny Tears, the man with the wax lobster cart who made thousands of wax sea creatures that she bought day after day—she was his collector—the knee-length hair of the girl next door drying over a chair in the sun, pitch black and straight, she combed it, helping, once a week. The antique store where she couldn't breathe. Trying on brocade death robes, her face would swell and she'd cry and choke, but the image of herself as a dead empress would prevail.

They knew her in the neighborhood, always alone, a tiny girl, she wandered in and out of shops and houses like a friendly, curious animal and they nodded to her and went about their business. Sometimes, though, she'd wander into other neighborhoods and then a crowd would gather round her and, expressionless, they'd stare. Ragged and muscled and inscrutable, they'd stare around her in a circle and in her horror she'd shout and scream and finally, having elicited no response, she'd caper, dancing first, then juggling stones, a thousand-year-old egg, whatever was at hand. And then she'd run down the open-sewered, foul-smelling streets, through the front gate of her house, which she'd slam behind her, her lungs heaving in her chest. Perhaps it was there, born out of embarrassment, horror, and guilt, surrounded by filthy babies and Buddhist shrines, that the seed was hatched: the desire to perform. Or before, way before, on a sun-drenched Texas morning, struggling out of the crib onto the floor, chatting the garbled chat of prespeech, waving her arms and crowing with freedom. All this as she snorted an umbrella on the second floor of Bloomingdale's and got high on the memories of her youth.

"And now," she said to herself, sitting in front of the mirror in the War Room painting her face, "I am a star and married to a man who no longer loves me. What a sadness. What a violation of innocence. I was so strong when I was alone. Sexual love has made me weak."

The computer began to beep and she turned from the mirror and looked at the monitor. A message was typing onto the screen.

"Darling," it read, "what's this about a divorce? Call me. Jerry."

"Amazing," she muttered, and put down her makeup brush, switched off the harsh light, and wheeled her chair to the console. She picked up the receiver, and as she punched in the number, she rose, stood on a small rubber box, and waited. As Jerry picked up the phone, her weight appeared in glowing red digital numbers on the console. "One-oh-eight," he said in his gentle, all-knowing voice.

"Exactly," she replied, and relaxed in the security of his vision.

"Clea, I saw divorce. What's going on there?"

She sat down heavily in the chair and stared at the console. "I don't know. I'm locked in. He's locked out. Ten years. No marriage should be longer than the average cat's life. What do you see?"

"It's murky, dear. It's too soon to tell."

"I haven't told Zeus."

"No?"

"No, just Doron." Her tone was bitter. "Zeus is closeted in his wing with his goddamn boats, stoned out of his mind on laudanum. We were supposed to be going to an awards ceremony. We're up for an award for last year's show. But he's not coming for the ninetieth time. I've got a blow up Zeus I'm taking with me. I had it made a couple of weeks ago 'cause he never goes anywhere anymore. As a joke, you know. I'm taking it with me tonight, that'll show him."

"Umhmm," Jerry responded. "Try and relax, dear."

"I am. I am. Any news from NORAD?"

"Yes, there is." Jerry's voice slid from soothing to serious. "They had a map up today of missile silo locations across America. They're everywhere, Clea. But we might have a chance either near the Oregon-Washington border or in upstate New York, or—"

"That's where I'll build a bomb shelter," Clea interrupted. "I can do it during my vacation. It'll be ready by September."

"Good. It's the Oregon-Washington border for me. Ohh, ahhh," Jerry was crying out in what sounded like pain.

"What is it, Jerry?"

"My head. I've been getting these pains all day since I tapped into NORAD. At first I thought it was just tension, but no, something's trying to break through, Clea, and it's big. It's very big."

"Are you all right, Jerry?" Clea was very concerned. Since the day she had met Jerry in Las Vegas, she hadn't made a move without consulting him. There was something about him that made her trust him with her life.

"Yes, but I must lie down, dear. Oh God."

"'Bye, Jerry. I wish I could be there to help you."

"Thank you, love," he said softly and then, very weak but sure, "you will win the award, dear, so plan your speech."

"Thank you, Jerry. 'Bye."

She had met Jerry at the casino in the Imperial Palace Hotel in Las Vegas. He was a tall, thin gay man with perfect skin and a boyish, thoroughly midwestern, rather nondescript face. He was standing amid the rows of slot machines in a button-down collar shirt and chino pants with his eyes shut and his fists clenched. He seemed in pain. She had gone up to him and said, "Excuse me. Can I help? Are you ill?"

For a moment he didn't respond. Then he sighed deeply, opened his startlingly piercing blue eyes, and said, "Follow me. I'm going to win a jackpot. Clea, isn't it?"

She assumed he knew her from the show poster in the lobby. She and Zeus were performing in the hotel's theater club. It was 1978. They needed the money.

She followed the young man over to a corner slot machine. He put in a quarter and then stood back. As the bells rang and the three cherries came up, a torrent of quarters cascaded out of the machine onto the carpet. The tourists around them applauded and laughed, and she and the young man bent down to gather the booty.

"Did you really know?" she asked, incredulous.

"Oh yes," he replied, mischief sparkling out of his eyes, "I'm a psychic."

"Are you really?" she asked.

His reply was interrupted by the appearance of a big, burly thuggish individual clothed in polyester who grabbed his arm and muttered, "Okay, Jerry, you're outta here."

"Hi, Bud," said Jerry sweetly as he was lifted to his feet, "I love your outfit."

"Very funny." The goon was moving him toward the door.

"Do me a favor, cutie," Jerry went on. "Tell this darling girl why you are ousting me."

The thug turned to Clea. His face had the tomato-end look of an aging boxer. "The guy always wins. He's got a scam. We don't know what it is, but we know he's got one."

"I'm a psychic, Bud. I get a vision." Jerry rolled his eyes heavenward.

"Yeah, that's what I said. You got a scam."

Clea laughed and followed the two men out into the glaring desert daylight. "Don' come back for a while, will ya, Jerry. I get trouble from you." Bud was eyeing him with some respect. It was a request. Eighty-sixing the young man without cause was illegal. "Only the next time, I have to pay my phone bill, Bud." Jerry smiled and waved as the goon reentered the casino.

"Hi." Jerry focused on her and grinned. "My name is Jerry. I don't go by a last name. You don't either."

"No, my husband Zeus and I have an act. We're in the theater club at the hotel. It's—"

"Your first time in Vegas."

"Yes. You know us?"

"No. I saw you in a vision."

"Did you?"

"Yes, it was destined for us to meet. I'm not sure why."

The sun was right overhead. Clea's eyes were slits. It felt like they were in a kiln. Clea looked up the strip and saw a water mirage at the entrance to Caesars Palace.

"Are you barred from every casino?" she asked.

He nodded. "Once they know me," he replied. "But they have no grounds to evict me. So I can win once a month at each and pay all my bills. I never take money for seeing."

"Why?" asked Clea.

"Because I'm not offering a service to people, I enlighten them."

He looked at her kindly. Despite the heat, he was not sweating. The sun was bouncing off his blond hair and white shirt, creating around his ageless face a kind of halo.

"Have you always had this power?" she asked.

"Since I was thirteen. I found out I was gay and had the power in the same moment. A man on a train offered me a baseball mitt in return for sex. At that instant I saw that he would forget the mitt at his stop. I saw it lying on the seat. But I gave him the sex anyway. And of course I realized I had to face it right then: It was the sex I wanted, not the mitt." He looked at his watch. "I must go. I have a client."

Clea felt a strange fear at his leaving.

"Will you come see us? I'll leave comps."

"Leave one for tonight. I travel alone."

He turned and strolled away down the strip. His stroll, she noted, was the stroll of a holy man, of a yogi or Gandhi, purposeful yet calm, accessible yet contained. The passion in him was pure white and there was something else she couldn't put her finger on, something homespun about the way he looked. Much later she discovered it: he made his own button-down collar shirts and chino pants, wove the material and sewed them by hand, according to the purist tradition.

THE DOORBELL to the War Room pealed and Clea wheeled back on her chair and pushed the button on the intercom.

"Bill Butler's here." It was the voice of Liu.

"In a moment," she said icily into the box, and turned back to the mirror. Ah, Billy, you wag, you menace. What do you want here, she thought to herself. She hadn't seen him for some time now. He had moved to Hollywood several years previously and was writing and producing comedy films with such extraordinary success that it defied the laws of commercial probability. Once he had called late in the night and she had picked up the phone and he had said, "I hate it here, Clea. I have the house and the car and the drugs and the dames and I hate it here. I hate it." And then he had hung up.

She picked up a longtail comb that sat in a jug filled with eyelash curlers, tiny brushes, and mascara wands and quickly teased her hair. When it was done, she looked into the glass as at Butler himself and smiled her most seductive power beauty smile and purred inwardly, Good timing, Bill. Doron was looking to shill for Zeus and you stepped right up. And with that, she whipped out of the chair, gathered up the deflated Zeus blow-up doll from a corner, buzzed open the door, and fled down the hall to her date.

Sixteen

BILLY BUTLER was pacing the front vestibule in a small circle, smoking a Camel. He turned at Clea's footstep, took her all in, and said, "It's not just the sex I miss, Clea."

She laughed and kissed him quickly on both cheeks and then flitted past him to the hall closet, from which she retrieved a bicycle pump.

"I have a limo," he said, staring at the pump.

"No." She rushed over to the hall chair, picked up her evening bag, and slung it over her shoulder. "It's for Zeus. I've got to blow him up on our way." She unfolded the blow-up doll and displayed it proudly.

"Christ." Butler examined the balloon. "You've sucked him dry."

"Very funny." She was irked.

"Trouble in paradise?" Butler asked, grinning. Butler took the doll's head in his hands and examined it as if he were Hamlet and it were the skull of poor Yorick.

"Where'd you get this? It's beautiful. What's the head made of?"

"Bisque." Clea was stuffing the bicycle pump in a plastic shopping bag. For reasons that escaped her, she did not want to be seen carrying it in an evening gown. "An artist fan made it, one who's in love with Zeus. I went to her studio, it was all Zeus, everywhere, floor to ceiling. Zeus masks, Zeus busts, Zeus puppets, oven mitts, unbelievable. Paintings, T-shirts, decals for the fridge. She sculpted the head out of bisque." Clea walked over and traced the line of the doll's cheekbone. "It looks just like him. Don't you think? It's just a tiny bit smaller than life-size, like his heart. Then you blow up the body, which is plastic."

Together they peered at the bisque head and then Butler tilted toward her and said wistfully, "Do you think she could switch her obsession to me? I need someone dedicated."

She smiled at him and then a wave of grief engulfed her and with a trembling lip she said, "It's so ironic. She doesn't even know him, but she loves him so much more than I ever could. Why is that?"

She opened the front door, carrying the shopping bag, and gestured for Butler to come along and lay the Zeus doll over the crook in her arm. He did, and she clattered into the hallway, the bisque head of Zeus bumping at her side. She pushed the elevator button several times, and then bounced on the plush carpeting, tapping her deer-hoof boots and jiggling the shopping bag.

"Obsession"—Butler was leaning against the wallpaper, staring amusedly at her—" is not love, they say."

Clea stared back. "Yeah, well they're goddamn stupid whoever they are because no one does anything over the long haul unless they're obsessed. Where would you get the energy? Why would you? Listen, baby—" The elevator door opened and she swept into the movable room, nodding graciously to Fred, the elevator man, whose heart melted with adoration when he saw her.

"Hi, Fred." She turned back to Butler. "There is more pseudo-psychological crap in the world than can possibly be stood. People make fortunes off telling you what's normal. People love to be herded. They love to be chastised."

"Like Minnesota Vikings fans," said the elevator man. Clea looked closely at him. "That's right," she replied. The elevator landed.

The big, fancy lobby could house fifty people. She never got over that. But at least it was old, built before she could possibly be responsible for its wastefulness. The building would never hold in a blast, never. Some could escape to the basement, maybe. The doormen, hopefully.

"Hi, Joe." She smiled at the doorman standing in the center of the great baronial entrance.

"Hi, Clea." He smiled and then said concernedly, waving toward the outer door, "They're out there." She stopped.

"Damn. How do they know, Joe?" she asked, frustrated. "How do they always know?"

"Who?" Butler was behind her, observing her trot along, muttering to herself, the big doll hanging over her arm, her mane bristling in the humidity.

"The gawkers. The fans." She hung her head and breathed deeply. Butler crossed to the center of the lobby and looked out.

"Yeah. They're there. Photographers, strange-o's, dog walkers, the lot."

She did not lift her head, but began to speak in a low voice to herself. "Well, you know, if Zeus is going to behave like Elvis Presley, I'm going to treat him like Elvis Presley."

Butler looked over at Joe, who was getting his umbrella. "Come on, let's flank her," he said, and the two men went over and grasped her by the elbows and walked her to the outer door. Fred left his post and held the umbrella over her head.

"No, but the thing is . . ." She was pretending they were talking. She was laughing, showing her teeth, throwing back her head, looking relaxed as she emerged onto the street, buffered by masculinity, crushing the bisque head of Zeus to her breast. A scream went up from the crowd when they saw her, and they rushed forward. Her being was stiff as a board. The two men holding her, feeling her fear, rounded themselves like football players staving off a tackle.

"Clea!" the crowd screamed.

"Hello." She waved her shaking hand, smiling adorably, picturing in her mind the face of her cat, its puffy cheeks and wavy whiskers, its tiny pink tongue. She could not see anything else. The two men moved her toward the limo.

"Where's Zeus?" the crowd screamed. Still seeing the pussycat face, one ear down, a nervous reaction, like a dipping airplane wing. Funny and sweet, so sweet.

"Here," she cried, holding up the bisque head, dangling the plastic body. The crowd laughed. They had reached the car. Butler pulled open the door. She clambered into the luxury cave. Butler jumped in after.

"Bye," she cried, waving. The doorman slammed the door. The chauffeur clicked the locks. She started to cry.

"I'm crying *again*?" She was mumbling through unruly lips, frantically pulling tissues from her bag, a mirror, dabbing scientifically at the makeup round her eyes, more panicked about the tears than the grievance that brought them on. "Shit! This is the third time in two hours. I'm going to look like a badly restored oil painting. I really don't have the time or energy . . ." The limo slid away from the building.

"What's wrong?" They were both floppy in the velvet atmosphere. Butler sprawled on his side and looked at her.

"No." She closed her eyes and waved her fingers defensively. "Let me just sit quietly for a moment and relax. My eyes are like baked potatoes already. I must send the tears away." She leaned back against the baby blue velvet seat and sighed.

"Man trouble?" Butler asked, and began to stroke her arm and massage the palm of her tiny hand.

"No, no," Clea pulled away and sat up, businesslike and detached again. Scanning the floor for her shopping bag, she rummaged in it and removed the bicycle pump. She busied herself attaching the pump to the nozzle on the blow-up doll, and then got down on her knees on the limo floor and began to pump.

She tried not to notice Butler. When he had touched her, a stab of sexual desire had suffused her system so fast and so thoroughly that he might have stuck her with a syringe. She had thought she was frozen stiff. She had walked around for months in a state of pious purity, refusing to warm to Zeus, punishing him for his withdrawal or perhaps simply reacting to it. She had thought she was impenetrable, perhaps forever, until Butler touched her and she nearly fainted from the physicality. She pumped furiously at the blow-up doll, which was beginning to puff up.

"This is truly," said Butler, "the most erotic scene I have witnessed in real life. Pump a bit faster, will you, baby?"

"Shut up," said Clea, but she did pump faster, putting all her muscles into it, pushing down, pulling up rhythmically, perfectly. Long before Zeus, Butler and she had been an item. He had been that man in her life about whom women, gathered together, smoking cigarettes and reminiscing, are wont to say, "Well, you know, it fit." The great sexual union that only in later life is differentiated from love. She had, by means of Zeus and her career, excised his hold, slamming hormonal doors and locking them with commitment.

And it had worked. Until this moment, on her knees, her spirit steeped in loneliness, her skin starved for affection, when she felt the longing of this randy man and lost resolve.

On the limo floor, she pumped up and down, making the puppet of her husband swell, spreading her knees in the black sequined gown so the heat within her might escape before it was too late. He watched her, like a hawk with a mouse, licking his lips, surmising her lusciousness. Glancing at the back of the chauffeur's head beyond the partition, confirming his obliviousness, he reached over and unzipped the long back zipper of her dress. Lined as it was and heavy with sequins, it fell off her like a bomb shell and snagged around her elbows. She continued to pump, pausing only to release her arms from the heavy dress, which dropped with a rustle to the limo floor. He got on his knees behind her. She heard some zippers and rustles and then his hands were on her hips maneuvering, positioning, setting up the exact trajectory for the docking. She dropped her head and scooted back against him, forgetting the bicycle pump, her face pressed against limo carpet. She raised one thigh, disentangled it from the dress, and set it down again, opening herself still wider. I am, the thought whipped through her molten brain, like a bottle of wine that will go bad if not corked, immediately, pronto. She was boiling, swirling, muttering between clenched teeth, when he grabbed her shoulder with his hand, braced his knee against her thigh, and pushed inside her. A growl escaped her throat, and then she fucked him, stroke for stroke, fantasy for fantasy, her consciousness lost to the outside world except for the dim awareness of a persistent hiss next to her ear. On an outstroke, she opened an eye and discovered the source. It was, of course, the plastic body of the Zeus puppet slowly deflating near the toppled pump.

Seventeen

Zᴇᴜs had been standing at the window for so long, he had forgotten he was standing at the window. It was only a rumble of thunder and a whip crack of lightning that jerked him from his half sleep and reminded him he was in his wing. From his aerie, he had watched a tiny Clea being herded into a tiny limousine. He had seen the tiny limo drive off down a doll-size Central Park West. He had spied a miniature Doron and Seven troop into the park for their nightly drill. After that he had concentrated on the light grains, observing them darken to deeper and deeper purple, until they merged into blackness. The park lights had come on during his lapse, like diamond stick pins, between the trees. Once again, the city wore the evening clothes of night. It was the beginning of a new party. He lurched toward his armchair, his intention to call for a cocktail.

The carpet around the armchair was littered with cigarette butts, beer cans, and empty laudanum bottles. It seemed odd until he recalled that he had sent Liu and Florie away. Sometime earlier, he had had a fit. He hadn't wanted anyone near him, though in this moment he could not remember why. It was too bad. He was getting as moody as a woman.

He dropped to his knees and began to gather up the garbage around his chair, crawling over to retrieve a wastebasket from a corner and crawling back. He was meticulous in his cleanup detail, an old army habit, he thought, and then shook his head wildly to keep any army recollections from entering his brain. "No, no no, no no, in that direction lieth horror. Hearts of darkness, hearts of palm, broken hearts."

Clea. That was it. He knew it now. That's why he'd had the fit. Clea was divorcing him. He dropped what he was doing and laid his head on the nearest cushion, the seat of his armchair. He felt suddenly glum, terribly glum. He needed to talk to someone. Ruth.

Ruth would help him. She wouldn't let him die in anguish. All right, Ruth. He tried to focus on his watch and started laughing when he couldn't. What time is it in Zaire? He thought about it. A big problem for you right now. You've got to add—what? Eighteen hours to the time you can't see, or subtract them. He grabbed his address book off the table by the armchair and turned to R. There were twenty-five numbers he had to dial. He'd never called her. Doron always called and put him on. She had written the number in his book during her last visit, neat European little crossed 7's. He dragged the phone from the table and set it down on the carpet next to him. Then he tried to dial. It took him twenty times until finally the old cricket chirp of an African phone sounded in his ear and a heavily accented white African male voice answered,

"Yes, hallo."

Now he had to speak. "Ruth Ravenscroft!" he shouted, for she was what he wanted.

"Yes?"—the whiny voice answered, pompous and posturing—"well, you must leave your number and she'll ring back."

"Where is she?" He said this angrily. Who was this guy?

"She's in the bush, of course. You've got the district office here. You can't call direct. She's only got a radio up there. You leave your name. She'll call you when she's down. She was just here, shame. It'll be another three weeks."

"Fuck off!" Zeus screamed this into the phone.

"Well," the whiny voice shouted back, "fuck off yourself, you rude bastard—who—"

Zeus slammed down the phone. He threw himself against the armchair. In his mind he pictured the district office, a shack at the base of a mountain range, overhung with banana leaves, the blond white man inside smug and effete, his brown shirt and shorts stained with sweat, a pistol strapped to his waist. He fantasized the man being surrounded by kaffirs, his phone lines being cut, the fear on his face, the helplessness . . .

Zeus shook his head. No, no, but he couldn't stop himself. He lay against the chair and closed his eyes and the memory he fled from grabbed him by the scruff of the neck and strangled him in its grip.

The servants were nowhere to be seen. It was the afternoon, the sun was high, the house was dark inside and shady. He had gone to call Doron about mending a game fence but the phone was dead. On the side of the house, he saw the phone lines had been cut. Quickly, his heart pounding in his chest, he walked to the front yard and rang the great bell, the prearranged area signal, two then one, two then one: we are surrounded. We are surrounded. He grabbed his machine gun from its stand and pulled the clip, then reentered the house to look for his mother. She too had vanished.

He went out the back to the servants' quarters. They were deserted. His father was running over the rise, rifle in his hand. He waited by the door.

They had known it was coming for some time. Their farm was near the border of Mozambique and Zambia, right near the guerrilla bases. As Ian Smith became more and more intransigent about majority rule, they knew they would be hit. Sooner or later, the guerrillas would have to cross their farm to move into the country. They had lasted this long only because of their decent relations with their workers.

Every farmer in the area had a signal. For the last year they had had drills. That Zeus' farm had been hit first was a bit of a surprise. They thought it would be Doron's. His father was so antikaffir, you wondered how he could live in Africa with the black blood in the earth and black tears in the sky. This was no white man's land. It was way too loose, jiggling with fecundity, and white men here often lost it completely. The lack of restraint loosed their screws, and without their rigidity to hold them together, their perversity ran out and stained them with its pus.

His father reached the back door, and said,

"Take the front."

Zeus had run through the cool, dark house and stationed himself at the front door. When he heard the jeeps coming up the front road, he took aim, the sound of his terror thundering in his ears. But it was Doron and Ruth and some of the boys from the outlying farms. Doron braked the jeep and the men and Ruth, armed with machine guns, ran and stationed themselves around the house. Doron, like the others, filthy and covered with blood, squatted down near him.

"My father's dead," Doron spat frantically. "Beatrice killed him," his voice broke. Beatrice Gwelo, Doron's nanny since birth, an old Matabele woman. Tears were running down his face. "Zeus, my God, what's going on?"

Zeus was cold as ice. Over the rise, black men were running toward them, dressed in strange army fatigues.

"Secondhand Chinese," said Doron, seeing his look. Zeus was stunned. His cook, his houseboy, the foreman of his workers were running toward him, armed and screaming at the top of their lungs.

"Shoot! Do it, mon," screamed Doron over the sound of gunfire coming from behind the house.

And Zeus fired, aiming at the hearts because he could not bear to see the faces of the men he had trusted with his love twisted in their death.

After a time of clashing and screaming there was a lull. Zeus and Doron looked up from their gunsights. A few men were dead in the front yard, fallen on top of each other like pickup sticks, the cook and the houseboy among them. The others, strangers, lay moaning, their wounds steaming in the sun. Suddenly from the side of the house, into a shaft of light, darted a black-faced woman laughing uproariously. She pounded across the lawn, fleeing the gunfire from the back, and stopped short in front of Zeus. Wreathed in smiles, she tore from the pocket of her housedress a large handgun and shot at him. Zeus slapped his gunsight to his eye and fired right into her shiny black forehead. As the face spasmed into atoms, he knew what he had done. He was so scared that he was sitting in his own piss and weeping rain.

"Oh God," Doron began wailing next to him, leaping up, running forward. Ruth came round the side of the house and vomited in a sudden spit take. Zeus dropped his gun and crawled forward on his knees, screaming in agony, sobbing and chewing the African dirt in his dragging wet mouth. And somewhere above that moment of terrible recognition, the cool English voice of his father defined the horror, buttoning the scene for all time. "Oh dear Zeus," he said calmly, "you've killed your mother."

. . . .

Eighteen

. . . .

CLEA rushed to the stage-right wing and stood, immobile, arms outstretched, while Bobette and Miss Florie quickly unhooked her from the flying mechanism. Bobette took the apparatus and moved back onstage with it, maneuvering the lines and gesturing to stagehands as slowly they pulled the harness above their heads to the top of the house.

The stage was revolving now. The eight conical heaps were nosing up through the stage floor. The stagehands, catching the yellow rope off the whirring cones, were sliding it along the stage floor as if it had always been there, as if nothing more had transpired in an hour than when it was last seen. The lawn chair and martini glass were put back, the American Indian sled heaped with objects, the backdrop of the strange planetary sky, aqua and violet, with its two great setting suns, was lowered in place. The propman ran on with the live creatures, the goldfish in a bowl, the cockatoo, the Siamese cat, and tethered them to the sled.

Clea was standing in a shaft of backstage light as the evening gown was pulled off her and the cocktail dress slid on over her head, yanked down her body, zipped up the back. She didn't move, only, head turned toward the dark active audible stage, hissed through clenched teeth, "Zeus will not wear the suit. That fucker. That limey swine. That third world suicidal brat."

Bobette and Miss Florie glanced at each other, horrified.

"No," Clea reiterated, catching their look, "no, he told me he won't. Can you beat it? An entire escape set up for the poor bastard and uh . . ." She suddenly stopped and Bobette and Miss Florie followed her look across the proscenium to the stage-left wing, where Zeus, arms overhead in a similar activity, being unhooked, fussed over, and fitted by Liu and Doron, was smiling defiantly and holding up the middle finger of his right hand in a fuck-you gesture.

Out in the control truck, the director started as Charlie, the stage manager, witnessing the act, gasped and said to himself and inadvertently into his headphones, "Oh my God."

"What? What?" The director was panicked.

"What?" asked Charlie, not understanding.

"What! Oh my God! For Christ's sake?"

"Zeus just gave Clea the finger."

"Oh," the director was calmed then not calmed. "Oh, great. What's she doing? Can we see her?"

First minicam swung to the stage-right wing, and a three-shot of Clea, Bobette, and Florie popped up on the monitor. They were all staring in one direction like nervous prey at a stalking predator. As the director and the A.D. watched, Bobette and Florie moved from terror to anger. Their expressions and bodies relaxed and retensed. Clea, whose body was in the hands of the women, changed only in her face. She went, they thought, through every emotion possible in a human and registered each one clearly. Fear, anger, despair, humiliation, humor, excitement, challenge, love, serenity, indulgence, defiance all were felt and finally covered with a businesslike control. They heard her as she turned to Florie and Bobette and said,

"Fuck him too, let's end the act."

First minicam followed her as she trotted onstage to take her place and disappeared in the darkness.

Clea was exchanging her emotions. She was syphoning off her bitterness, trying to infuse herself with the whimsical cynicism she would need for the scene ahead. That one of these emotions was real and the other an imaginary construct made no difference to her. It just made the exchange more painful as the real emotions clung on more fiercely, waging what she felt was their rightful territorial battle. Pain was a bath, so liquid and swampy, anger so hot and smoky, fear so icy cold. But love, pure love, so prismatic, was the hardest to conjure up. Few, if any, actors had ever done it fully. It was nearly impossible, and left, usually, to a matter of visual chemistry, a fantasy of how lovers look and talk and not to what went on within them.

The secret of Clea and Zeus was that they loved each other madly and could make others feel it too. Their love made them invincible, and the audience believers. This was their last show because, of course, it was the end of time. But because they had lost hold of their love, even without the bomb, they would have stopped performing. They would just have been another act, just another man and woman mugging and hoofing to an engaging beat.

But it was very painful this time because there was so much anguish and she had to perform right now and she really didn't want to. She knew as she watched the dim outline of Zeus lie down on the lawn chair and take up the martini glass that she might blow the scene. The bitterness might seep out and soil the whimsy mix. The audience might feel how real the hatred was and be upset. She might feel how real the hatred was and lose control. Control, that was it—or was it lack of control? You never really knew until the exchange was over.

The lights were coming up. They helped. The hot golden rays of the mock setting suns tricked her brain and an excitement rose in her, a desire to dazzle and trick, to amuse and seduce, to appear so perfect, to achieve such perfection that all else was eclipsed: real hatred, real pain, real anger, and of course the first one to go, real love.

"I don't know." Her voice flapped out of her mouth like a fish out of water. It was surprisingly strong. She was, as prearranged, addressing the audience, feeling the light catch her eyes, feeling their sparkle, the pull of irony lifting the corners of her lips. She waved the ends of her fingers in gestures of adorable martyrdom.

"You fall in love." She took the bowie knife from her waist sheath. "You accumulate objects"—she pointed with the weapon at the conical heaps amidst which she was pausing—"which, over time, meld together and lose their sense of ownership."

She picked up an old footstool upholstered with a flowery, feminine needlepoint cover. "And then one day it's over and you have to"—she took the knife and drove it under the upholstery seam—"cut these things apart"—she ripped the cover off the stool—"which at the beginning you would have sworn you'd never have to do."

She tossed the cover in her shopping cart, which she retrieved from behind one of the cones. The footstool, she carried to the sled and balanced it on top of the science fiction books. "That," she said, sadly pointing to it with her knife, "belonged to Zeus' grandmother. I made the cover in petit point, thank you very much, as a present." She trotted back to the cone, picked up the cover, and displayed it proudly to the audience.

"Do you like it?" The audience cooed. "Gorgeous! Lovely!" people called out. "I spent months on it. Months and months of delirious joy, working my fingers to the bone for my man." She examined it carefully. "My blood's on it in several places. I would have made six more if he'd asked me. When I gave it to him, he said, 'That's nice, love. Thanks,' and then switched the subject to a new destroyer they had gotten in at the model boat store. At the time, I thought his reticence was darling. Now, I'm taking it back." She dropped the cover in the shopping cart. "He won't miss it, if he ever noticed it."

On his lawn chair, sipping his martini glass of beer, Zeus was laughing.

"Well," he spoke to the audience, "I look like a major shit here, don't I?" The audience gave an iffy moan.

"Of course I did notice it. The woman is an artist, we all know that." The audience applauded and yelled, "Yah, we know." "She's always doing something talented. Perhaps I took it for granted. Yes, I would admit that: taking things for granted could be one of my crimes." Clea marched over and dropped the footstool on the sled. It made a dull thud.

"But women,"—he gestured toward her with the martini glass—"are so definite. They love to plan. Everything must be known and have an end. This could be only another stage in our association."

"Divorce? A stage?" Clea spoke sardonically, looking first in exasperation at the audience, then slowly timing her glance to fall on Zeus as she said, "He never could admit culpability. When he's guilty, he cowers behind the voluminous skirts of the existential. But believe me"—she cut loose a stack of Conan comics from a nearby cone and balanced them on the sled—"that's the only time. When it comes to believing in God or love, he's an atheist." The audience laughed.

Zeus set down his glass and popped up out of the lawn chair. He walked crisply over to one of the stage-left cones and began inspecting it. He pulled at the yellow rope and out came two pairs of worn, scuffed dancing shoes—one pair of little white go-go boots, hers, one pair of winkle pickers, black suede, his—both from their first show at Carnegie Hall in 1975.

"Remember these?" He held them up for her to see. Roger spotlit them with a cold blue tint. "We wore them in the 'Coming of Age in the Sixties' number. You had waist-length hair then." He smiled fondly.

"So did you." She smiled too. The audience laughed. "I realized recently,"—she cut a facial sauna from the yellow rope and dropped it in her shopping cart, interrupting herself with—"I'm taking this. I'm sorry, you'll have to get your own."

"Tell it to Marvin Mitchelson," he replied and added, "I'm taking these," and took from his pants pocket a large pair of poultry shears and cut the dancing shoes off the rope and dropped them on the sled.

"Fine," she went on. "I realized recently that never again will I have the experience of making love to a man who has waist-length hair. It was, I see now, a once in a lifetime experience, peculiar to that period. Long hair for men will come back but not for my kind of men. I remember the feel of it cascading over me. It made the sex seem so innocent. Men *are* so innocent in some ways, you know? In spite of the rotten things they do. *You* do."

"That's what I've said all along." He smiled.

"Do you know"—she was trotting around the cones, snipping off petticoats and four-way bras, boxer shorts and single sweat socks, and stowing them in their respective places—"that some people still have not gotten over the idea of men with long hair? I think the most ridiculous issue in our lifetime, or perhaps any lifetime on this planet, was men's hair length. Without question the stupidest, symbolic though it may have been. Grown men and women, world leaders, screaming about male hair length. And you know, once people behave that stupidly, they never can recoup. The planet has gone right downhill since.

"Zeus," she asked suddenly, changing the subject, "what is marriage?"

Zeus paused. The lights began to lower into a series of rays of reds, golds, and yellows playing around him. A warm pink spot uplit the beauty of his face and he said sadly,

"Marriage is a long yellow rope on which are tied the accumulated possessions of each party and which is wound into tall skinny heaps which over time collect upon the landscape. Marriage is bloody difficult." Clea did a long, slow take, looking around the stage, nodding as if she just understood something. The audience laughed. Then she said to the audience, "It's interesting, you know, how the depth of a man's sensitivity is so often measured by the depth of his inability to be sensitive."

"Okay," he said. "You're right. Marriage is a master/slave dialectic in which women are unjustly imprisoned by the society in a thankless—"

"Sexless," she added.

"—juiceless role pursuant to the perpetuation of the species."

"Well put." Clea cut three pans of Jiffy Pop off the rope and dropped them on the sled.

"As his wife, I often felt like a giant-size mother figure, much larger than life, as big as Michelangelo's *David*, towering over everything, clumsy and unfeminine, neutered by the advancement of age."

Zeus cut a large makeup mirror off the rope.

"Ladies and gentlemen," he began, approaching Clea, holding the mirror at different angles to her body, like a hairdresser who has just done her hair, "Mrs. Clea is a bit wacko. Does this beautiful middle-aged bird look like a monstrous mother figure to you?" He laid the makeup mirror on his sled.

"Middle-aged?" She stood in the center of the stage, her head hanging. With her eyes closed, without the peepholes to her soul which in its thirty-five years had seen some trouble and some joy, and which, it was clear, had been chosen as a storehouse on earth of infinite memories of the two, she appeared to be a child of about eight. The big head on the delicate little body was part of it. But, really, it was something less tangible. Perhaps it was the long years without a mother, no one to grow into. Or perhaps she was like the baby tooth she had in her mouth, which never fell out because beneath it there was no adult tooth to push it or because she had no children. Or maybe it had something to do with her talent, which was so isolated from questions of age, feeding instead on harvests of truth.

"I often felt like her father," Zeus went on, flashing the mirror around her, showing the audience different views of her, "when I wasn't feeling like her son." She stood silently, head hanging, eyes still closed. "After a while it was as if she never saw me, as if I wasn't there."

"You weren't." The phrase spat out of her mouth much harder than planned and surprised her and Zeus and the audience and those backstage and out in the truck and in the wings. It was loud and rage filled and accusatory, not at all the nightcap cynicism that was wanted, that had been rehearsed. Zeus laid the mirror on his sled and quickly cut off some Connie Francis forty-fives from the rope and put them in her cart as a diversion.

Clea was rigid, eyes wide open, staring at the exit signs along the back wall of the theater, at the silhouettes of the mercenaries with their machine guns flanking the aisles. She was trying not to vomit vitriol. Zeus began to improvise.

"Remember this?" he asked, holding up a palm-size sea urchin skeleton. After they had closed the show in Athens, they had taken a honeymoon in the Cyclades, spearfishing, collecting sea urchins off the sea floor, cutting them open with scissors, eating them raw. "I still have some spines in my finger. Look." He held it out for her to see. He was trying to snap her back, hoping she wasn't broken. "Now they call these Uni. People pay three bucks a piece for them in Japanese restaurants." He addressed the audience, going on with his lines now, praying she'd come in where she was supposed to, desperately, horribly sorry that he'd refused to wear the suit. "This is the sort of thing"—he held up the sea urchin—"that you cannot divide. That represents the whole damn loss. One of us will never see it again. Here, you take it."

He offered it to her, palm outstretched, and Roger, up in the lighting booth, going with the flow, muttered, "Bring up number two," and bathed the object in a magic ray, and, "bring down three," realizing that Clea, still silent, unmoving, a human grenade with a pulled pin, was better off dimly lit.

"Yah, he's right," muttered the director. "Let's do it. Closeup on the urchin, uh, two, get off her quick."

And there it was on the line of monitors, Zeus' hand palming the sea urchin skeleton, a delicate and deep purple dome like a little soufflé. And then suddenly, coming into the shot, a small booted foot punting it out of Zeus' palm, out of the frame, all the way to the back of the theater over the heads of the audience. It shattered against the proverbial fourth wall and dropped to the carpet in shards. The audience, thinking it was part of the show, applauded the perfect punt. The director, left with a closeup of an empty palm and no landing shot, scrambled.

"Shit, uh, two, go to Zeus. Be happening, Zeus baby—please."

Zeus was happening. The look on his face was priceless. He was looking off after the punted urchin, amused but deciding whether this was the moment to run for his life. Out of the corner of his eye he saw the glowing red light on top of the camera, blanched, and then blushed, for he had no lines and no movements that could rationally follow the event.

"Well," he began, shrugging, nodding his head, vamping while he flipped through the files of his brain, searching for old material that might fit the time, and maybe even the situation.

But Clea saved him, crazed pro that she was, suddenly walking into his shot, putting her arms around his neck, and saying, "There now. Neither one of us has to have the dead thing. We might get salmonella. Want to fight?"

"Pull back," the director snapped as she leaped away and struck the cat stance, a kung fu pose.

"What's going on?" Ruth was whispering to Doron, who was entranced by the action on the stage and looked, she thought, as if he had seen Death, the destroyer of worlds, and would have to have drinks with him after the show.

Florie and Liu glanced at each other in the stage-right wing and bowed their heads. Jim, the set designer, and Max, the producer, both out in the house leaning on the orchestra wall, grabbed each other's shoulders and waited. Up in the lighting booth, Roger told his assistant to move and took the controls himself. The conductor of the orchestra tapped his music stand and brought the musicians to attention. The extras and the dancers massed into the backstage green room and gathered nervously around the monitor. Peg, slouching against the doorjamb biting her nails, turned to Rita and muttered, "She's lost it, now. Oh boy."

On the stage, Zeus leaped back and collided with one of the cones. A feather boa, five or six old rusted razors (his), and a picture of the first woman he ever slept with fell on and around him and crashed to the floor. Clea was serious, he could see that. She had been schooled from adolescence in martial arts and was an expert. In a battle he would prevail through brute strength, but to do so would be an ugly, tortuous exchange and one not wholly consistent with the standards of prime-time television.

Clea was above or perhaps beyond such considerations. She had assumed the cat stance and was poised to deliver a monkey blow. Her eyes were narrowed, right heel was raised and her elbow bent back, just as the Master had instructed her. She was growling a compact motorized growl. In this, her most fetching dragon lady mode, the camera went to her, and Zeus, his face left to himself for a moment, began to giggle. It was nerves really and fear that set him to it, but there was some genuine amusement too at this, his final public predicament. And there was a neatening up of loose ends here which had begun to unravel during his first appearance at the Cairo Hilton so long ago. That was a fight turned theater as well.

IT HAD BEEN their first fight. He could not remember the particulars, just that it had been about power and who was in charge. Clea was appearing at the Isis Lounge, a star of sorts, and he, having traveled with her up from Addis Ababa, had decided to chuck the tobacco business and follow after her wherever she would lead him.

"I have to leave Africa," he had said as soon as they arrived in Cairo. He was sitting on their hotel balcony looking down at the narrow snaky Nile. On the opposite bank, an aged muezzin was slowly climbing an intricately carved, disturbingly phallic minaret. It would take the man until late afternoon to reach the top and make the call to prayer. It would take him till nightfall to hobble down again.

"May I come along with you?" Zeus had asked.

"Of course," she had replied, sitting down beside him, taking his hand, staring too at the snaky Nile, at a woman washing clothes on the bank at the base of the minaret. "I'll just tell Liu."

"I'll make myself useful," he added.

"What can you do?"

Zeus thought for a while until it happily came to him. "I can dance."

She nodded.

And they sat in silence, as the long, columnar barrels of the vast Egyptian sun sprayed them with sunfire, waiting for the muezzin to ululate his song.

And then, some days later, they had the fight. Just before showtime, she, nervous and bossy, treating him as entourage baggage. He, rebellious and brutal, enraged at her lack of care. She stormed out finally, late for her curtain, running down the hotel hall to the elevator bank, making up in a nearby mirror. Three minutes later she was onstage in the Isis Lounge, a bit out of breath but reciting her patter and juggling her plates on sticks.

He had followed her, betrayal firing his jets, missing her elevator by inches, stalking into the Isis Lounge, fuming, putting up with her audience's smiles for but a few moments before he dashed to the edge of the stage and wagged his finger at her and said loudly, accusingly, "You need me, you sniveling little minx. Don't ever forget that."

The audience gasped. The bouncer moved forward but hesitated. There was something right about this. He waited to see. Shocked, Clea swiveled her head toward Zeus and as quickly as possible removed the juggling sticks from between her lips and caught the plates. Then she erupted.

"How dare you interrupt my show? Can you believe this?" She addressed the audience. "Men are the most domineering creatures on the planet—"

"Except for women," Zeus snarled, and the audience laughed.

"You white African wretch. You covert racist scum," Clea was shouting.

"You pompous little bitch," he shouted back. "You loveless shrew."

"What?" she asked, softly then, dissolving, tears dripping down her cheeks, "how could you? Oh my God, is that what you really think?" The helplessness in her voice melted him, and drew him up onstage to shield her in his warm embrace.

"No, but baby,"—he was hugging her now, bending her over backwards, trying to penetrate her with his words—"you've got to let someone love you."

The audience was spellbound. Zeus lowered his head and kissed Clea hotly on the lips and then they began to dance.

Liu, leaning against the proscenium, at this point propman, roadie, director, bodyguard, and costumer, nodded to himself amusedly and composed a telegram that he sent afterwards to the Master. "Clea has found a partner," it read, "he demands equal billing." "Box him," was the Master's reply.

Some weeks later, Zeus was installed in the act and all Cairo was lining up outside the Hilton to see this lovely pair fight and make up. "She is the flute to his snake," the *Egyptian Gazette* stated in headline and then went on, "unless she's the mongoose."

THE CAMERA remained on Clea. She was in the tiger form now. She had assumed the horse stance, then stepped back with her right foot to deliver a rock smash blow with her right hand. Zeus dodged. She turned counterclockwise, pivoted north, and delivered a scorpion blow with her right hand. Zeus ducked. Moving clockwise, she stepped around with her left foot to face east, advanced, and struck a tiger-claw blow with her left hand. Zeus bobbed. The audience was mesmerized. She took a short step east with her left foot as she landed a ram's-head blow with her right hand smack in the middle of Zeus' nose. The sound was that of a thwack. Zeus gasped and fell backwards.

The Seven Golden Lieutenants aimed their machine guns at Clea and rushed the stage.

"Blackout!" Roger spat into the headphones, and shut the lights. The drummer hit the cymbals.

"Go to the card," the director barked, and up came the logo and the signature music.

"How is he? How is he?" the director called frantically into the headphones.

"Bleeding," was Charlie's reply.

The director flopped back in his chair. The sweat from his brow flew around him in a Saturnian ring. He looked over his shoulder at Max, the producer, who had just rushed into the control truck.

"Okay, Max," the director boomed, a strange grin illuminating his face, "it's intermission."

Nineteen

THE STAGEHANDS rang the curtain down with a whir and a bounce. The audience broke out instantly into frenzied chatter about what they'd just seen. Doron halted the frothing Lieutenants at the proscenium's edge. People rose from their seats to head for the lobby, and there was a mass squeaking of elderly seat mechanisms and a mass rustling of party dresses crushing up the aisles.

Roger immediately bumped up the stage lights and left the lighting booth for the stage. After the double ram's-head blow, Zeus had fallen down, bringing one of the cones with him. He was struggling to get off the floor now, untangling his feet from some balls of wool and knitting needles and trying desperately to capture two tropical fish that had fallen out of their bowl and were flapping wildly on the stage floor. The propman ran out with a small net and assisted him.

Florie, Ruth, and Charlie had run onstage during the blackout and grabbed Clea. She had been struggling against them, but when the lights suddenly flipped on and she saw Zeus squirming on the floor clutching at his nose and the fish, blood streaming between his fingers, she stopped and laughed. Liu had rushed out to stop the Lieutenants. Doron appeared and helped Zeus to his feet.

"Let me see it," Doron said, gently removing Zeus' hands from his nose and dabbing a handkerchief around his nostrils. "She hasn't broken it," he pronounced. "That's something. Come on, let's get some ice." And he took Zeus' elbow and guided him toward the stage-left wing.

Zeus and Clea looked at each other in shock, like two auto drivers who had suddenly crashed. Clea dropped her eyes and allowed herself to be escorted offstage by a furious Florie, who was shaking her head in disgust and muttering in the click language. Ruth, left to herself, followed the two women into the stage-right corridor and then peeled off, going through the door into the house and up the right orchestra aisle into the theater lobby.

THOMAS DE QUINCY, as he called himself, was lounging by a vase in the outer vestibule of the theater smoking a cigarette through a long, carved silver holder. He was dressed, as he lived, in the manner of the mid-nineteenth century. He had his tailcoats made by an aged English tailor in the West End of London, from nineteenth-century patterns handed down to the man by his tailor father and grandfather. His shoes, with their ornate silver buckles, were hand sewn in Paris from original patterns. His tall hats and his suede gloves were antiques as was his walking stick, with its secret hollow core, purchased in the Chelsea Antique Market in 1968 for a mere ten pounds. In it he carried his wares: the tincture of opium called laudanum, for by profession he was a nineteenth-century drug dealer dealing only in nineteenth-century drugs.

De Quincy lived in a nineteenth-century flat in London illuminated by gas light, without central heating, and he refused to have a telephone, communicating instead with meticulous notes in delicate script penned by quill and ink. He was usually alone. Occasionally he found girlfriends who would throw themselves into his period for a time, but the lack of central heating got to them in the end and they threw him over for modern men with convertible Rabbits and boilers.

Ruth knew De Quincy from Cambridge. He had been nineteenth century even in those days, having developed the fetish at his public school, where he was deemed "a bit old-fashioned." His refusal to accept his own century and live in it had gone virtually unnoticed by his masters.

She had found him fascinating at first, though she had not slept with him because of his ban on all modern forms of birth control. He had offered as a carrot some odd herbal abortifacients for after the act, but she had refused. Later, after she had introduced him to Clea and Zeus when they were appearing at the Hammersmith Odeon and Clea had informed her of his drug dealing, she dropped him, livid that he had not told her of his profession. She felt that she had been duped, and worse, that she had been an instrument in Zeus' decline.

So, given that she had an old score to settle and plenty of pressure and jet lag to blow off, when she saw De Quincy in the outer lobby, she strode over to him and spat out,

"Damn you, you wretched creep, for your part in what's happened to Clea and Zeus. I hope you rot!"

"My dear," De Quincy said shrinking from her and nervously tapping his cigarette in an ashtray behind him, "haven't you heard: the world is going to end tonight." He removed a gold watch from the pocket in his silk vest and snapped it open. "At precisely ten o'clock. As this will probably be our last conversation, let us not end it on an unpleasant note."

"You beast!" She bared her fangs.

"Do the apes do that, dear?" he asked, referring to her facial expression. "It's really rather effective. Scary, is it, or do they mean it as an enticement?"

She snarled.

"Anyway, it's not our Zeus who's singing the global dirge but our Clea, who as far as I know remains uncorrupted by yours truly. Any man faced with similar bedlam would seek lethe. I rather think of myself as his savior during this unfortunate episode. I received a desperate missive several months ago and I booked passage on the first Concorde I could get out of Heathrow."

"You took an airplane?" She was incredulous at this lapse.

"Only for Zeus," he said adoringly.

"You pig," she began, but he spied someone over her shoulder and interrupted her tirade.

"Now, dear, if you will excuse me . . ." and he turned on an elegant heel and disappeared back into the theater.

Ruth swung around and came face to face with General Clark Lincoln, Clea's father.

"Ruthie," he boomed, smiling a broad smile of welcome and giving her a hug. Then, grimmer, more appropriate to the moment, he said, "Welcome back! What the hell's going on backstage? Do you know?"

Ruth smiled wanly avoiding, after the initial glance, the kind but piercing eyes of this craggy-faced military man.

"Oh, General Lincoln," she began, "I . . ." and then stammered, panicked, wondering how to describe to a father a daughter's madness. Among the gorillas, there was no guilt. There was no self-blame, no personal recriminations. There was madness. There was grief, but there was also simple acceptance, a mournful shaking of a great fur head, and then on to a new place to build a sleep nest.

"She still believes this stuff about World War Three?" Ruth nodded. "Uh-huh."

The General was looking around inside his brain, casting about for some linear credibility. "Well, goddamn if she's not far off, you know. The Middle East is a powder keg, or there could be some damn accident. Look at Bhopal. Give those third world guys a fancy machine and they'll fuck it up pronto."

"Yessir." Ruth was trying not to cry, trying to appear supportive, unable to offer a verbal life raft to this man, who had fathered them all. Stationed in foreign climes, he had always traveled to see their shows, even during Vietnam, when, still in battle fatigues, he flew in from Khe Sanh, attended an opening, and afterwards went right back to war. "My daughter's just as important as the Viet Cong," he had told the Joint Chiefs, "and don't you sons of bitches ever forget it."

"Well, Ruth," he said thoughtfully, "you know her mother passed on a few months back?"

Ruth stared at his eyes now, sobered.

"No," she said, "I didn't know."

"Hmm," he seemed surprised. "I wonder if Zeus knows."

"Maybe; Doron doesn't know. Or at least he didn't write me about it. If he does, he might have forgotten. He could avoid something that tragic. There was another death too: Billy Butler."

"Oh yah, I read about that in the *Herald Tribune*. An old boyfriend. I met him a long time ago. Never liked him. A weak sister. A father's bad dream."

"I'm sorry about Mrs. Lincoln," Ruth said softly, touching his uniformed arm.

Miss Hollywood, thinking Ruth was making a pass, trotted smartly around the vestibule and encircled the General's waist and kissed him on the cheek.

"I'm back, Clark," she chirped.

"Welcome." The General smiled warmly at the bosomy little blonde and hugged her to him reassuringly. Then he acknowledged Ruth. "That was a terrible business with Clea's mother," he began, his eyes softening with liquid sorrow, his stiff back posture drooping imperceptibly, "a real, honest-to-God freak-of-fate tragedy. Leprosy. You tell me, Ruth. You had to accept it and move on. It had no why or wherefore. It was nobody's fault. You had to be so strong, you had to be inhuman. You had to be like—"

"An ape," Ruth offered, understanding.

. . . .

Twenty

. . . .

WHEN CLEA RETURNED from the awards taping, it was eight P.M., prime—as the TV people were wont to call it—time, like prime rib, juicy lean time not fatty, gristly time, not, as they called the period one A.M., the graveyard shift. The taping had gone well. They had won the award as Jerry predicted and she had run onstage, smiling and laughing, accepting the prize with humility and humor, making the Zeus puppet quip and joke and the audience hoot and cheer. Her face was sore from smiling and lying, smiling at cameras, smiling at assholes, and lying about the whereabouts of her husband and the status of her personal life. All through the evening, the scent of Butler hung on her skin, like the scent of fire hangs on a burned-out apartment.

In the limo coming home, Butler had fallen asleep, mercifully drunk. She sat, clutching a piece of hollow tin sculpture in the shape of a TV and a bouquet of half-dead roses, appreciating the irony of her position. The Zeus puppet lay crumpled at her feet. How happy she and Zeus had been going to the first parties ever given for them. The one after Carnegie Hall where they walked in the door of this fancy townhouse and the place lit up like they were batteries. Young men slipped her their phone numbers. Young women slipped theirs to Zeus. They compared them afterwards to see if among them there were any couples.

They adored being pursued. They adored it for several years, until they got used to it. Once, Clea had asked two young hookers on Eighth Avenue, several blocks away from each other, how long it took to get used to hooking on the street. They both gave the same answer: ten days. Same as a bad haircut. In time you could get used to anything, abuse or adoration, the important thing was not to confuse the two.

It was also true, however, that people no longer approached them with genuine delight. The world was used to them as well, and often they felt like scalps that various film producers and TV execs were collecting for their belts.

"Poor stars," she murmured to herself as she rode the elevator up to her apartment, "poor stars," as the Zeus puppet banged against the woodwork. She let herself into the very quiet apartment. She replaced the bicycle pump in the hall closet, sat the Zeus puppet in a chair by the door and, taking the roses and the award, hurried down the long hall and vanished into her War Room.

It was dark in the War Room and cozy warm. A single rose-colored forty-watt bulb burned in a ballerina lamp at one end of the console. She was discussing her adultery with herself and fantasizing how, if found out, she would explain it to Zeus. "I felt so lonely, so unloved, so shut out and frankly, buster, so horny that I fucked him and I'm glad. It was fun. I enjoyed it. It made me feel alive. But it was nothing. Not that I'm sorry, don't ever think that. But, Zeus, I could kill you for driving me to it."

She was furious, she found, that she had been forced, as she saw it, to break a ten-year spell. They were the boy and girl on top of the cake, the spun-sugar couple inside an Easter egg, dependably pure, and because of his coldness she had—

Uh uh, you fucked another man, sweetheart, plain and simple. The cynic inside her spoke up, patience clearly tried.

Well yes, it's true . . . It was the endless dialogue of her disconnected mind, never a clear thought, so many levels of truth and lies, she knew them all, discussing them, examining them, feeling them too, as now she was feeling guilt, dense, sandy waves of it, clogging her stomach and heart.

It's true but you know I'm a very loyal person. It's not a threat to us really, if anything, it will make us stronger, so many people have been brought together by betrayal.

The cynic parried quickly, America and the Soviet Union, who else?

Japan and America. Iran and America.

Okay, touché.

Anyway, he'll never find out.

Unless you tell him.

Tell him what? she asked herself. She shivered and squirmed around on her chair and relived for a moment some intense sexual sensations from the car ride until they were shut off suddenly by a violent surge of grief. She had slapped the bouquet, still wired together, into the press and now was bolting the cover down, down, mashing and pulverizing the roses, pursued, it seemed, by the ruthless harpies of sin, when the phone on the console rang and, to divert herself, she answered it.

She thought at first it was England. The distant sound, the delay of the caller. She said "Hello" three times before it registered and a male voice replied, "Hello, Clea, it's Dr. Buckner," and then echoing itself "Hello Cle, it's Dr. Buckn."

It wasn't England. It was Hawaii. The leprosarium.

"Hello," she said again and waited, frozen with dread.

"I'm sorry, Clea," the doctor said, "I'm sor, Cle. Your mother passed away this evening—pass awa is even. It was merciful I think—mercifu think, Cle—Cle?"

"Yes." It was a squeak from a swollen throat. Tears splashed from her eyes onto the flower press, soaking the wood.

"There are two options—two optios. We can bury her here in our cemetery or bur ere awcemtry aw we can cremate her and crete eran send her to you, ender you. We can't eean ship the body ipod you know that, Clea ouohah Clee."

"Yes"—another squeak and then a big breath and a sentence managed—"Can I call you in the morning, Doctor?"

"Of course, awcse. I'm sorry, Clea. IsurCle."

"Yes." She dropped the receiver on its cradle and lay down on the floor with her head pressed against the wheels of her office chair. She moaned softly, "Mama, no, Mama," and she was back at the ranch in Texas, aged six, and her mother was at the big oak table in the taxidermy room. Her small, delicate feisty mother, Mrs. Clark Lincoln, with her whiskey cheroot voice and her buzzing bee energy, was working at her business. She skinned and stuffed armadillos and then sent them on to Oklahoma to a man who painted them gold and made them into gewgaws. She also stuffed them for museums and kiddie parks in the Texas area, sewing them in odd positions of dancing and juggling, and supplying the miniature props: the toe shoes, the bowling pins.

Her pride and joy, her mother maintained, was the one who juggled little plates on sticks, in his claws, in his mouth, looking up at them, his beady eyes concentrated and thoughtful. She refused to sell him in the end. He had been commissioned by a wild animal refuge in Waco but instead became her trademark. He stood, immersed in his act, at one corner of the vast oak table, a prideful symbol of the best of her art.

The previous day, Mrs. Clark Lincoln had gone out with some local Indians and shot two big ones. Clea had watched her leave, flanked by two run-down, pony-tailed Sioux, a twelve-gauge gun in her hand, her cowboy hat pulled down over her braided hair, the fringe of her Buffalo Bill jacket flapping as she hurried over the hill toward the back forty. It seemed scary, this parting. One of the Indians had mentioned wildcats. Clea clung to her mother's leg and wailed,

"Mama, don't go. Don't go."

"Shit, honey," her mother crowed, laughing her throaty laugh as she gently peeled her off, "this is business. The work of Mrs. Clark Lincoln is in demand. You gotta be proud about that. You gotta help me. We gonna bring two critters back tonight, right, boys?"

The Sioux grinned and nodded soundlessly. "And tomorrow when I cut 'em up, I'm gonna show you how it's done. I'm gonna teach you, honey, so we can carry on the tradition. Okay, baby?"

Clea stepped back and let her go. True to her word, her mother was back at nightfall. She and the Sioux had shot two large, old armadillos. And each of the men carried one in a tarpaulin bag swung over a shoulder. Mrs. Clark Lincoln was in the middle, the tiny white hunter, roaring with laughter at some Indian joke, striding gloriously over the crest of the hill toward the ranch, a great red sun setting behind her.

The next morning her mother was standing at the big oak table in the taxidermy room. She was bent over a stiff three-foot armadillo, a harsh white overhead light illuminating its prehistoric grimace of rigor mortis. Clea was loitering on the other side, her face level with the dead thing, peering closely as her mother poised the scalpel and explained.

"Okay, baby, we gotta cut the innards out of him else he'll rot. So you just make an incision here"—her mother sliced the creature's underbelly—"and git 'em out." She dug her bare hand into the wound and dragged out a jellyfish of guts. "Okay." She slung the grisly mass into a pail at her feet. "Now we got to debone him and dry him, and that's a bit more difficult, so you just watch. Shit!" She dug her hand into the cavity and winced in pain. "Shit, honey, he broke a bone on my bullet and that bone cut me. Honey, run git me that rag over there. Damn."

Clea brought her the rag and watched as her mother withdrew her hand and wiped it. There was a long gash down from her third knuckle to her thumb.

"Never mind, honey," her mother said, shoving her hand back in the cavity, "it's just gonna be that kind of day. It happens in any business. A small setback."

She continued to work, pulling out the odd skeleton piece by piece, dunking the carcass from time to time in formaldehyde to wash and preserve it. She was almost finished when Doctor Pete, a huge man who was the district physician, appeared at the door with his hat in his hands and an odd look on his face.

"Howdy, Miz Clark Lincoln," he said. "Hi, Clea, may I come in?"

"Hi, Doctor Pete," her mother cried, cigarette dangling from her lips, her white apron smeared with blood and bits of armadillo flesh. "Come on in here if you can stand the smell." She laughed raucously. "Not very pretty today, Doc. Don't tell anybody about it else I'll lose my allure. Okay?"

"Okay." He smiled weakly.

She stuck her hand in the limp armadillo carcass and made it dance like a puppet on the table. "Well, what's the story, Doctor Pete?" The creature was moving from side to side, its little arms flapping up and down. "What makes you come all the way out here?"

The doctor was staring with horror at the dead dancing pangolin and he blurted, "Put that down, Ms. Clark Lincoln, put it down right away!"

Her mother did as he said and removed her hand from inside the critter. "I know I should use gloves, Pete, but you just don't git the feel that way. Look here at this jugglin' fool." She was gesturing at her trademark, the plate juggler on the end of the table. "He would never have come out that good if I used the gloves. You soften the skin with your hands, like sewing silk."

The doctor was white. He was staring at his hat, fingering the brim and sighing deep in his great cavernous chest.

Finally he said, "I don't know how to tell you this, Neva." He looked her straight in the eye. "You got leprosy."

"What?" The word shot out of her mother's throat like the human cannonball out of the big silver cannon at the circus.

"What's that, Mama?" Clea asked, aware of the fear that had emanated from the two grown-ups and was hanging on the air like dew. Her mother didn't answer.

The doctor continued speaking. It was the armadillos, he said. About 15 percent of them had been found to carry leprosy in their bone marrow. Several armadillo wrestlers and hunters in the state had come down with the disease, and the National Hansen's Disease Center in Louisiana had made the diagnosis from blood and tissue samples.

"The way your hands been growin', Neva, that's not arthritis. It's called claw hand. It's leprosy. After I heard about the other folks that's in your same business here, I sent away your samples, hon'. I just got word back, so I came on out right away. Neva, it's the worst thing I ever had to do."

Her mother went to pat the big man's arm and then flinched her gnarled hand away before she touched him. Clea ran around the table and yanked at her mother's bloody apron.

"What is it, Mama?" she asked again, insistent, driving. "What's leprosy?"

Her mother was holding her hands out from her body and looking at them as if she had just discovered they were there. "It's the end, honey," she said matter-of-factly. "It's the end of the world as we know it."

Twenty-one

FLORIE ushered Clea into the dressing room and directed her to
lie down on the chaise longue. "You stay," she snapped, and
went to shut the door on a corridor teeming with jangled nerve
ends. "Florie," Clea was protesting, starting to get up. Florie pushed
her back and sat on her stomach and folded her arms. "Florie! Ow!
Hey! Florie, listen." Clea was grabbing at her arm and pushing her.
"I'm going to vomit. You'll make me vomit."

"Good. The badness will come out then. It will be good."

"Florie," Clea was pleading, "I've got to check on the radiation
suits. I've got to make sure there are enough for those who want
them. I've got to try and convince some stupid people like yourself and Zeus. No, maybe not Zeus, maybe I'll let him burn to
death."

At this, Florie began to bounce up and down on Clea's stomach.

"God," Clea was yelling, "God, please stop! Florie, it's not a joke
what I'm doing here. It's not madness. It's not." Florie bounced
again and Clea gagged. Florie leaped up, got a fire bucket, and set
it on the floor by the chaise. Florie grabbed Clea's head and pushed
it toward the bucket.

"Go, puke, my baby, try to get that spirit out. It is like a big fat
lizard with a long, long tail. If we cut off the tail, it just grows back.
We must drag it out. Some way." Clea vomited. "Good. Good. I
know these ones. Spirits of old, old sorrow. They sleep sometimes most
of a life and only to wake suddenly to the loud wail of a new grief.
Puke, my baby, puke. Maybe this lizard spirit he will fall out and
into the bucket and splash us with vomit. Think of it, Clea. Hope
for it." Clea continued to vomit and Florie peered at her.

When Clea was through, Florie looked in the bucket. "Noo, noo."
She was disappointed and picked it up and took it to the toilet
cubicle at the end of the room. "I don't see him. He didn't come out,

that one. He is still inside." She flushed the contents of the bucket down the toilet and rinsed it out.

When Florie returned, Clea was on her knees praying.

"Please, Florie," she pleaded, raising her eyes to the Xhosa woman, "please wear the suit when the time comes. Please just wear it for me. How will it hurt?"

Florie took hold of Clea's hand. "Maybe I must stand free to protect you. I don't know yet. I will ask the *benge*. I will do what it says. This thing is very dangerous, only the *benge* can speak without fear."

"All right." Clea was on her feet now, combing the box Florie had packed, looking for the statistical analyses of the evening's atomic bomb blast. She found them and laid them out on her dressing table. She pressed the intercom and said, "Charlie? Charlie?"

Charlie's voice came over the tiny speaker above the mirror. "Yes, Clea?"

"Charlie, send someone out for two live chickens, young males, and have them brought to my dressing room. Pronto."

"Where could we find them at this hour? Clea?" His voice was fearful and sweaty.

"This is New York City, Charlie. Pay and you shall find."

She clicked off and turned to Florie. "Do you have the oracular poison?" Florie nodded sagely.

"Oh yes, when the Zim are about, you must always have the *benge*."

ZEUS was sitting in the dressing room chair having his nose doctored by Mr. Liu. On a hot plate near the miniature boat pond, Liu was cooking up the Black Dragon tonic. From the wings Liu had seen Clea connect with the double ram's-head blow, and he had rushed to the dressing room and begun the decoction. First the four ginsengs, then the deer antler, then the astragalus, the schisandra, a bit of magnolia flower, ginger, and finally a dash of Ho Shou Wu to preserve the proper balance of the elements.

"It will be ready soon," Liu said to Zeus, who wagged a finger to show he had heard. "It smells like gas," Zeus said and dropped his head back over the chair. His eyes were closed and he pressed a piece of ice to his nose.

Doron, his giraffelike frame too tall for the room, was cantering about the tiny space in a fomenting fury.

"She's gone completely mad," he sputtered. "Do we have a hope in hell of finishing this show? She's your wife, Zeus, what do you think?"

Zeus grunted and shrugged. Liu grinned. "Ah," Liu said with pride, "she is truly a Mistress of kung fu. How beautifully she executed the monkey blow. Such precision cannot be learned. I shall send Liu Ah To the video of that one. He will be proud."

"You're bloody mad too, Liu. This is prime-time television, you stupid twits. Fifty thousand dollars a minute. We're now a minute and a half short, you do understand that? It's bloody big money we're talking about."

Liu went silent and continued to stir the decoction.

Zeus, laughing, removed the piece of ice from his nose and sat up.

"What time is it?" he asked.

Doron checked his watch.

"Nine-oh-one."

"Yah, well it's not going to bloody matter if the bomb drops in fifty-nine minutes, is it, boffin?"

Doron clenched his fists and flailed about in pure frustration. In Zeus' slightly feverish, pain-filled state, he thought Doron looked like Big Bird being butt-fucked against his will.

"Aw for Christ's sake!" Doron was bellowing. "She should have gone to a sanatorium for a month like a normal nut, not been coddled and allowed to put everyone's career in jeopardy. She's spoiled, that's what it is. She gets away with bloody murder."

Zeus' nose started to bleed again, so he dropped his head over the chair and reapplied the piece of ice. Somewhat muffled, he said, "Perhaps, but one of the best moments of my life was when Clea told the head of programming—what's his name?"

"Ralph Dodson."

"Dodson, that's right. When she told Ralph Dodson that halfway through the show she was going to announce the arrival of World War Three and direct all America to the outlets in their states where they could acquire radiation suits, this warning and accompanying location crawl to take approximately thirty minutes. And Dodson hastily pointed out that all America would either be leaving their sets to head for the hills or worse, switching channels. 'Right,' she says, 'and us too Ralph, but at least we won't be guilty of mass murder.' Wonderful, the look on his face, wonderful. Fortunately he thought she was having him on. Or unfortunately, as will transpire."

Liu was pouring the decoction from the saucepan into a bowl. He placed the steaming liquid on the dressing table before Zeus and next to it a silver spoon. Zeus sat up and handed him the piece of ice. The nosebleed had stopped, but a large bruise was beginning to show on the bridge of his nose where Clea had popped him.

"Aren't you angry?" Doron asked in a wheedly voice. "Doesn't it bother you that your wife socked you, fuckin' beat you up on national TV in front of the whole of fucking America?"

Zeus slurped his tonic soup. Liu peeled the shirt off Zeus' back and took it to the basin to remove the bloodstains. There was a knock on the dressing room door and Charlie opened it and poked his head in.

"Doron, it's Ralph Dodson on the phone."

Doron cringed. "Tell him you can't find me." Charlie nodded and shut the door. "You see. What do I tell him?" Zeus went on eating his soup. There was a pause. Then Doron said, "The boys would have killed her, you know that?"

Zeus looked up at this. "Yah, they're on too short a fuse. Doron, do something about that. Get them laid, will you?"

"Christ!" Doron exploded. "Well, what about it? Why aren't you angry?"

Zeus sighed. "I didn't get in this business to be Richard Burton and neither did you, *boetie*, so don't go on about it. It's all been pudding for us. It was a way to try to have a life, to try to cleanse my hands, and yours. In hell I'll be poked in the nose every day for eternity. This is just a little taste."

"Oh, mon,"—Doron said sadly—"let that go. It was an accident. Everything that goes wrong isn't payment, you know."

Zeus nodded and went on eating his soup.

Doron opened the dressing room door. "Liu?"

Liu looked up at Doron from the basin where he was cleaning Zeus' shirt.

"Will you see that she's all right to go on?" Liu nodded, and Doron, bending his stalklike neck, cantered out into the busy corridor.

Just as the door shut, there was a tap on it and the director's voice was heard to say, "Hello in there. Can I come in?"

"Come on," Zeus called and the director entered, saying to someone behind him, "Yeah, we want suits. Go set it up with the A.D."

He bent over and examined Zeus' face.

"Nasty bruise, there. Gives an interesting tinge to the second act, eh Liu?"

"It won't show," Liu said with certainty. "Zeus is drinking Black Dragon tonic. It promotes blood circulation. At end of break, the bruise will be small and easily covered with makeup."

The director nodded. "Great." He put his hand on Zeus' shoulder. "It's uh, it's going great. That last thing, surprise though it was, was just beautiful, Zeus. When she started in with those kung fu moves" —he shook his head in admiration—"it was just gorgeous. Whew! And good punt!" He laughed heartily and slapped Zeus on the back. "Okay. We're a minute and a half short now, so stretch a little. You're starting Act Two as rehearsed?"

"Yah, I guess," replied Zeus through spoonfuls of soup tonic.

"Okay. Okay." The director moved toward the door and placed his hand on the knob. "Well . . ." he began and then paused, searching for an innocuous platitude that would fit the bizarre situation at hand.

"Knock 'em dead," Zeus offered, scanning him with a mischievous twinkly eye. "Break a leg? Make it funny? Have fun with it?"

The director smiled slowly. "God bless us every one," was the phrase he chose, and he turned the knob and went out the door.

. . . .

Twenty-two

. . . .

IT WAS DARK outside and the rain was still falling. The only light in Zeus' room was the ice blue glare of a blaring TV set, that strangely unearthly glow that washes the warmth from everything it touches, the perfect lighting for the undead. The channel was tuned to the awards show. It was a quarter over.

Zeus was collapsed in his chair. With one part of his mind, Zeus was waiting to see if they had won, to catch the appearance of Clea. With another, he absently monitored the progress of the wild-haired young woman who was kneeling between his legs, her lips fastened around his dick, giving him the first groupie blow job of his career. About an hour before, the poppet had rung the doorbell, nattering nonstop about puppets and Clea. Liu had answered the door and was about to call the Lieutenants to remove her when Zeus strolled by on his way to the kitchen and the young woman swooned. Right there on the doorsill, she landed with a mighty crack and was quite unconscious. He and Liu carried her to his room, and as Liu was off to a poetry reading at the YMHA, he had undertaken to revive her.

Zeus didn't really do much anymore, so much was done for him by so many that it gave him some pleasure, stoned as he was, to be needed for a moment, and he bathed the young woman's brow and loosened her collar and cuffs with all the intensity of a child ministering to an ill baby doll.

She was an interesting looking person, with very long, wild witchy hair dyed black and fifties slanted glasses. She had peered at Liu, myopic and mindless, until she had seen Zeus. Only then did her eyes widen with joy and shock. She was very thin and dressed all in black with pretensions to punk, through in fact she had the look of a woman who knew how to sleaze through a backstage door and claim access to all areas without a pass.

Zeus had never seen a fan of his up close before. The diehard ones, like this one, the ones for whom it was Zeus or bust, who managed to get backstage in their fuck-me outfits with their fuck-me states of mind, he had seen from afar, across wide expanses of green room. They were sustenance, he said, only half joking, for the Seven Golden Lieutenants. He dispensed them to his troops as a field commander would the local girls of a conquered village. Though they were the spoils of his show biz war, he gave them easily away.

When she awoke and saw him examining her, she began to shake violently. He was embarrassed at first, deathly embarrassed, almost sickened, for he realized that the woman was shaking out of awe, utter awe and desire for the physical shell she perceived to be him. She was deeply, crazily obsessed with his persona to the point where the mere sight of him triggered a meltdown in her body chemistry. It was very like lovesickness, but more like perversion.

But in the hazy fluidity of his present state, amidst the jabs of pain that the abandonments of this day had brought him, his embarrassment quickly dissipated and was replaced by a mixture of arousal and rebellion, of power and self-determination. He became aware suddenly of who he was and what he was due and the snap of the fingers, thumbs up or down mentality made perfect sense to him. He took the shaking woman in his arms and stroked her.

"Relax," he said, not soothingly, but slickly, seductively. "Don't be afraid. I'm just a man."

"Not to me," she managed through blubbering lips. "To me you're a god."

Zeus thought of Florie. And it occurred to him that he might have been saved had there been another person present, a leavening factor who, when the accusation of deism was leveled at him, might have sniggered and thus pointed out the hubris of the charge. But, he asked himself, what lovelorn man, all alone in a room with a dewey-eyed fan of his every pore, when called a god would laugh and break the spell? None, was the answer, none but the wimps and wankers, the pussy whipped, or the born again. And Zeus was none of these. And for the moment, he was free on a technicality. His wife, it seemed, was divorcing him. Though she had not yet told him herself, she had informed his employees and entourage and perhaps even—he glanced toward the chattering TV—announced it on prime time. He would see.

So when the young woman, between hyperventilations of breath, informed him of her worship for him and then of the Zeus puppet she had made on commission and then, of course, of the undying respect and awe in which she held Clea, and then reached into his fly, brought out his dick, and covered it with burning kisses, he succumbed.

It had been going on for quite some time. He had come once and after that had directed the young woman to remove her clothes and his, which she did rather like a geisha on Spanish Fly, alternately giddy with lust or tittering and squinting, her hands covering her mouth.

He was quite amazed when she took off her clothes. Though in his work he was often surrounded by half-naked dancers, crotches stretched wide apart in positions too bizarre even for fantasy, it had been ten long years since any woman other than Clea had stood naked before him emanating sexual desire. He inspected this one closely, running his hands over the odd pointy-nosed shape of her breasts, the tubular torso, ribs protruding, the emaciated hips with their jagged hipbones. She was terribly thin, this woman, not at all rounded, though he liked the way her thighs met at the top of her legs: in a T square protecting her furry little crotch.

She excited him as someone new and dangerous will do, and yet she shamed him as well. Deep in the depths of him, beneath the thumbs-up brutal ego, he blushed, for the truth was that Zeus, Zeus the sexy, Zeus the heartthrob, Zeus the fantasy back-door man in a million women's minds from New York to Timbuktu, was a modest soul not into the perverse and strange, not even in his mind. He was an African farm boy, used to having tea, and had the perversities of the world not interfered, had he not had to answer for the long, ugly years of colonial S & M, he would have been on a tractor right this minute, plowing out the bush for tobacco plants, his own children playing on the seat beside him.

Or perhaps it was true to say that Zeus had had his fill of perversity. By the age of twenty, after twenty years as a white colonial in Africa, after twenty years of his mother's minstrel battle with it, Zeus had seen perversity in the best of its permutations and was done with it. So show business at its most malignant, or this woman with her screw-me-with-a-carrot-if-you-dig-it approach, was tantamount to child's play and somewhere made him blush.

Zeus knew, however, or he had come to know over the years, that once perversity has been your intimate, it marks you for all time. He was forever doomed by something in his face to be a magnet for the weird, the lawless, and the wild. The prim stayed far away from him, unnerved. The modest, the unassuming were scared to death of him. He was used, now, to this cross-the-board misreading of his character and accepted it. He no longer tried to make friends outside his entourage. To the outside world he was polite and kind but distant. And now, Clea was leaving, his only link, the only female understanding he had known except for Ruth, who was his sister and lived with apes. And had this odd young woman not stumbled onto his island he might have sat forever in his armchair until he faded away, nothing left of him but a rumpled monkey suit.

The young woman removed his clothes garment by garment. As she bent over him, she rubbed her nipples against his lips. He caught them in his mouth and she cried out, a wanton birdlike shriek. Her lust was shrill and trembly like her soul. He moved himself only when she forced him to. She maneuvered him to pull off his coat and then his shirt. She lifted up and flopped down his legs and stepped back to draw off his trousers and his shorts.

When he was completely nude, still in the armchair, still collapsed, as in a womb, he stared out and watched her take him in. Her eyes feasted on his erection as if it were a pickable lock to a room filled with gold and jewels. At last he beckoned her to him and pushed her head into his lap. At this moment, a voice simulating joy screamed his name and he turned his head and looked at the TV.

"Clea and Zeus!" Bobby Biceps, as he called the man, an actor who had made his career by taking steroids and building himself a body no flabby film producer could possibly resist, was holding his arms up in victory and waving an envelope. They had won. Zeus smiled. He did like to win. The young woman removed his dick from her mouth.

"Congratulations," she said and squeezed his wrist.

"Thanks," he replied and gently pushed her head down.

There was a long shot of Clea running up the aisle to the stage. She was carrying what looked like a large doll with a human-size head. When she reached the podium onstage, she pretended to kiss Bobby Biceps, and arranged the doll at the microphone next to her.

Zeus tapped the young woman on the head. She looked up, still sucking.

"Is that your puppet?" he asked. She turned to the TV and exclaimed, letting his dick fall ignominiously on his stomach. "Oh! yes!" she cried. "Can I watch this?"

"You can," he said, "but you must fuck me while you do."

Twenty-three

CLEA was in the green room. She had called a meeting of the cast and crew and was standing on a chair in a corner of the room addressing them as if they were her troops, "I just wanted to let you know what will be happening at ten this evening. Here are the facts as I know them." She turned to the wall behind her, where she yanked down a Nicaraguan tapestry to reveal an elaborate chart entitled "Blast Effects of Air-Burst Weapons at Optimum Altitude for Range Indicated." The company murmured. The expressions on the assembled faces ranged from blatant fear to sarcastic derision.

"At the top here where it says distance from explosion: we are approximately ten point six miles from Kennedy Airport where, our information tells us, a one-hundred-fifty-kiloton bomb will be detonated in exactly"—she checked her watch—"forty-eight minutes."

There was the odd sound of one hundred eyes glancing around nervously.

"So, if we follow the chart across the top to one hundred fifty kiloton and then down to where it indicates a ten-mile distance from explosion, we find there will be point six pounds per square inch of 'overpressure.' Now that's not too bad, so we're lucky there. Overpressure is the number of pounds per square inch of pressure exerted by the blast wave over the normal atmospheric pressure. It is this overpressure combined with the drag pressure caused by the wind that explodes buildings. As you can see, winds are predicted here—" she dragged her finger along the next line on the chart—"at below thirty-five miles per hour, so what will happen in the theater district of Manhattan is that doors and windows will be blown out but the buildings will still be standing. However, in the case of the theaters which have no windows, in order to avoid compression and explosion, it will be necessary to leave the doors open at the moment of the blast. So I will now ask you three stagehands"—she pointed to three burly men with sullen looks on their faces—"to open all the theater doors front and back at exactly nine fifty-nine, so that when the blast hits at ten, we'll be ready. Thanks."

She smiled and yanked down the chart so it flipped up to reveal another beneath it. This one was a map of the five boroughs of New York over which had been drawn six circles, each one wider than the next, exactly like a bull's-eye. In the center, at the location of Kennedy Airport, was a drawing of a tiny black bomber. The areas inside the circles were marked A, B, C, D, and E. The Manhattan Island location of the theater in which the assembled company was performing was marked with an X. This bull's-eye chart was so frightening that several people moaned, involuntarily, and others, Rita and Peg leading the way, began giggling uncontrollably. Clea was understanding.

"Yes, this is upsetting. I'm sorry. I did suggest that we not do the show on the night of the nuclear blast, but it was the only night the network and the theater would give us the time and that evidently was more important than our continuing life on the planet earth, so . . ."

The assembly laughed nervously.

"Yes," Clea went on, "I even pointed out that the ratings during such a blast would be shitty and make us look bad, but the network countered with the inescapable fact and one terribly seductive to any performer: For over two million people, ours could be the last TV show watched in recorded human history. I had to give in."

The company laughed again.

"They didn't believe me. You don't believe me. Everyone thinks I'm mad. But here's the thing: I believe me. And I intend to do the best I can to keep you and the audience and whoever wants to follow my instructions alive."

The company fell silent. Everyone was listening now. She resumed.

"Okay. Kennedy Airport is in Sector A. We are in Sector D, once again, lucky, for in Sector D what we can expect mostly from a one-hundred-fifty-kiloton blast is severe damage to doors, windows, roof tiles, danger from flying glass and, of course, the charring of exposed skin."

"God!" Bobette's voice rang out. Others nodded in agreement.

"Right, Bobette, which is why I have accumulated all the damn radiation suits and keep harping on them like a madwoman. They will protect you from flying glass, skin burns, and will allow you to get away from the area relatively unscarred or, I should say, uncharred.

"Outside on Forty-eighth Street, next to the control truck, is a moving van containing a radiation suit for each of you who wants it. Those in the last scene must of course wear the suits. To the remaining cast members and crew I strongly suggest you save your lives for in the next eon"—she paused here and her eyes seemed to wander a bit—"there's just got to be a return to innocence. Any questions?"

"What if it's not a one-hundred-fifty-kiloton blast? What if it's a ten-megaton blast?" It was Eddie baiting her. Fear had turned him to her adversary.

Abou Ben Adem called out too. "What if they miss the target and get the Statue of Liberty, which is a lot closer to us, instead?"

"Yeah. What then?" The director was watching in the control truck. First minicam was at the door to the green room recording the event. The director mumbled the question as he went to the door of the truck, opened it, and looked out. There was a giant moving van parked adjacent. The side of the vehicle slid open, revealing hundreds of radiation suits and masks stacked within. He looked back at the monitor.

"Ten megatons five miles away?" Clea was computing. She looked highly intelligent, strongly delicate, and rather beautiful. "Well," she began somberly, pulling on the tassel to roll up the bull's-eye chart, "then overpressure would be at fourteen pounds per square inch. Winds would blow at three hundred and thirty miles per hour. Reinforced concrete buildings would be severely damaged. And impairment to humans would include ruptured eardrums and hemorrhaging lungs."

"Jesus!" The Lord's name swept through the crowd like a brush fire at a game park.

"I'm sorry I asked," boomed Eddie. Some people laughed.

"Me too, Eddie," said Clea angrily, "because it's not going to happen and it just scares people. The blast, I repeat, will be one hundred fifty kilotons and if you wear the suits, you will avoid skin charring. Any other questions?"

Clea paused. The company stood silent before her. It was too much for them, too weird for them. The whole thing just smelled like madness and badness and made them cringe.

"Listen," Clea resumed crisply and efficiently now, "there's little time. I say, indulge me. Hate me. Scorn me if you like, but wear your suits at ten o'clock and if nothing happens, I'll gladly be the joke, the butt of any mockery. We'll meet back here and you can douse me with cheap champagne or paddle me with Ping-Pong paddles—whatever. But, please, wear the suits."

Clea stepped down from the chair, threaded her way through the crowd, and sped off down the hall to the exit door to check on the moving van.

"Do you think Clea will make it through the show?" Rita asked Peg.

"Do you think *we* will?" Peg replied anxiously.

Abou Ben Adem pushed by them, muttering savagely to Eddie, "She crazy, this woman. I thought the theater would be calm compared to rock and roll. Hah!" He pointed aggressively to himself. "Abou Ben Adem does nothing a madwoman tells him. I spit on your women's lib! Phew!"

"Great," Eddie said, disgusted. "Now that you've said that, I'd be a goddamn fool not to wear one. I just bet they don't have one to fit me."

Max, the producer, and Doron moved out into the corridor to allow the company to exit the green room.

"Max?" Doron smiled in sarcasm.

Max replied seriously, "I always do what my stars ask as long as it's within reason. Wearing a radiation suit for five minutes, Doron, this is nothing, believe me. Once a star of mine was into macrobiotics. We had sprouts growing in the corridors which had to be fitted with grow lights which cost a bloody fortune to power. The whole company had to eat the stuff. I had a heart attack. I sneaked out to Frankie and Johnny's for a steak and something happened: I internally combusted or something . . . I don't know—you can't eat both, it's lethal. A radiation suit to save my life. No star has ever cared this much. Where's the van?" Doron laughed.

"Not me," Doron said. "I'm not going to indulge her. She's caused a conflagration in my life, mon. This bomb stuff is only a symbol of her guilt about it. She has hurt Zeus and I tell you, if I can, I am going to hurt her." And with that he stalked away, neck bent in anger.

The Seven Golden Lieutenants were standing around in the corridor muttering sotto voce. Rita and Peg loitered near them to try to pick up snatches of what they were saying.

"Doron says not to," one began.

"I've got a wife in Harrare," said another, nodding to himself.

"Ach, she's mad, anyone can see that," said a third.

"So's Zeus, so what?" a fourth replied. Then one of them noticed Rita and Peg and said, "Shush." The Seven smiled enigmatic sexy smiles and protectively cradled their machine guns.

"Okay. Okay, we're going." Rita nudged Peg and they scurried down the corridor toward the exit door.

"Did you hear what he said about Zeus?" Peg asked.

Rita nodded sadly. "We should have gone back into *Cats*. We made a big mistake. This is too weird. Boredom would have been better than—"

"That what?" asked Peg as they got on line to get their suits.

"Megadeath," replied Rita.

Twenty-four

CLEA buzzed herself out of the War Room and trudged slowly up the long hall toward Zeus' wing. Her heavy sequined skirt dragged on the parquet floor as she slowly and sadly proceeded on her way. She was terribly confused. Her head was drooping with pressure.

In her hand, she carried the award, the tin sculpture in the shape of a TV. It was almost nine o'clock. She would be on in a couple of minutes. If Zeus wasn't comatose, they could catch the show together. Winning would take the onus off the things she had to tell him: that she was divorcing him, that her mother was dead, that they wouldn't be performing together any longer.

Perhaps he wouldn't mind the puppet so much. What she had done with it had been sweet. After the limo ride with Butler, the point of the puppet game had changed from an attack to a tribute, for such is the sad power of adultery, the reforming strength of its sin. She felt, now, transparent and foolish, for her mother's death had changed things too. She no longer possessed the cold military resolve to divorce as she had when it was just another boring day in a successful life that moved by itself, solid on the track, no problems. There were problems, she reminded herself, it was just, of course, that when death is hanging out, no problem really seems like a problem anymore.

In truth, she had wanted to run to Zeus. When she heard of her mother's death she had wanted to drop the phone and tear up the hall to his room and throw herself into his arms screaming as loud and as long as it would take to drive out the vandal loneliness that had squatted in her insides. But she knew Zeus might be out of it. He might be sprawled in his armchair, eyes at half mast, unable or unwilling to love her, too floppy to hold her tight. And yet this was Zeus, who in some sense was always there, even in his coldness he was there, for they had saved each other long ago. They were even blood siblings.

In Brown's Hotel in London over tea one afternoon, two years into their association as they called it then, they sat on ancient slipcovered armchairs in that matronly room and traded blood. The waiters watched in horror, removing the three-tiered bonbon dish as she sliced Zeus' finger, then her own, with Brown's porcelain-handled fruit knife and squeezed them together.

"We'll pay for the knife," they told the waiter, but he shook his head. He had heard Zeus' Rhodesian accent and gave it to them out of pity for the commonwealth and the loss of the British empire.

So, blood of her blood, perhaps she could go to Zeus for comfort, even though they were estranged, even though his coldness had driven her as far away as another man's lap. But death was hanging around like a lion at the edge of her herd. And she was dropping back, tired, weak, and if Zeus was weak too when she ran to him, death might peg her for a straggler and try to pick her off.

A phone began to ring. There seemed to be no one in the house and Zeus wasn't answering, a bad sign for comfort. She hurried up the hall, turned and went into the vestibule and picked up the receiver. It was Jerry.

"Oh Jerry!" She relaxed when she heard his voice and let herself go a little. "Oh God."

"What? You know?"

"About my mother, yes."

"No. What? I can't see. There's too much—"

"My mother died today, Jerry, didn't you know?"

"No. I'm so sorry, baby. Jesus, what a day for you, and now this."

"Can you tell a man you're getting a divorce and at the same get comfort from him because your mother's died, Jerry?"

"I doubt it, baby," Jerry said. "But Zeus is special that way."

"Detached, you mean?"

"Yes . . . Clea, something's happened." Jerry sounded scared. "I had a vision. The headache broke and out of it I saw . . . do you trust me, Clea? Do you think I'm for real, or am I a neurotic faggot with an uncanny eye for perception?"

"Both. What's wrong?"

"I saw the end, a conflagration, a blast of incredible magnitude and a date—September tenth of this year. I saw the end of the world, Clea, as clear as day."

Jerry began to sob. Clea held the receiver close to her ear and listened to the man's anguish. In her mind some odd things were happening: an armadillo face in rigor mortis was crossing over with her dead mother's face, both gimlet-eyed, both grinning, then Zeus' face, undead, drugged-up, grinning too. The phrase "We've got the theater on the tenth and for a bloody good price" popped up to confuse the issue.

"Clea?" Jerry was calling for her.

"Yes," she called back. She was a long way away now, off in a firestorm of fear, for she knew what Jerry said to be true. In her bones his words had caused a low-level hum, her blood seemed to be coursing. Her particular grief was drowned out by the screams of a world of humans.

"The bomb will fall on Kennedy Airport on September 10th at ten P.M. Eastern Standard Time. One hundred fifty kilotons. Write this down, now. Do you hear me?"

Clea took up a pen and scrawled the information on the wall in block letters.

"Uhhuh," she grunted. "Uhhuh."

"I saw something else, Clea." Jerry's voice was calming now, guru-esque and clear. "We can survive. If we prepare, you know, as we've discussed: bunkers, radiation suits, the lot. There's a good possibility we and whoever else we care to save can survive."

There was a long pause in which Clea and Jerry took turns sighing.

"Well," she said after a time of staring at the date with death she had scrawled on the wall, "we knew this would happen, didn't we? The first time we tapped into NORAD by accident, we knew our numbers were up, that something had sent us to it for some damn reason."

"Yes, it's funny how things happened," Jerry said. "Like the first time I saw you in a vision before I met you that day in the casino: I knew you would be crucial to my destiny, but I didn't know why. Now I see it all. You are the one person I can share this knowledge with, the one person I can save, the only person who would really believe me."

"What are we going to do about the other two hundred million people in America, Jerry?"

"I don't know. It's a real Cassandra special, Clea, but I'm not Christ. Up till now I've been a two-bit psychic, couldn't even do kidnappings. This is my first big gig."

"The tenth. We have a show on that night. Our last show, as I so presciently described it several hours ago."

"Doron will never believe us."

"No, it'll be a mess. I'll have to fight the whole way . . . well . . . there's some things I have to do now—"

"I'm sorry about your mother, Clea, but I expect she was spared."

"Not really. For her, an atomic blast would have been the perfect way to go."

"Clea, do you think it's possible that a series of nuclear explosions could destroy the AIDS virus?"

"Very possible, Jerry." Clea's tone had changed. It had become quite practical and matter-of-fact. "As you and I have known for a while now, there are some things about nuclear war we can all look forward to. Good night."

Clea set down the receiver and, still holding the tin TV, exploded into movement. She pirouetted out of the vestibule into the vast unused living room and then jumped into the air, splitting the seams of her dress as she sailed over the long art deco couch. Landing soundlessly, she swept her arms across the floor and twisted into a deep body contortion, feet covering ears, chest folded in half, like she'd been done at the Chinese laundry. She unrolled along the floor and then pushed off from a sitting position into a front somersault.

In the building across the way, two architects who were working late threw down their drafting pens and ran to the window to watch her.

After the front somersault, they applauded and cheered. When she saw them, she stopped abruptly. Then she ran out of the living room, back through the vestibule, and up the long narrow hall. Just before she opened the door to Zeus' wing, she took off her deer-hoof boots. She left them, one standing, one falling drunkenly over on the parquet floor.

Twenty-five

OUT ON FORTY-FIFTH STREET, Clea was talking with the drivers of the moving van about the coming nuclear holocaust.

"If I can change just one man's mind . . ." she was saying. The two burly white guys, around their mid-thirties, were hardhats turned dopers by their experiences in the sixties. They were listening seriously to Clea, who came to the end of her speech and simply pointed at the piles of radiation suits for emphasis. They were a bit taken aback by this adorable but frantic woman, not really inclined to do as she asked until suddenly she looked at them and said,

"What battalion were you in 'Nam?"

The two men glanced at each other. "How d'you know we were in 'Nam?"

"I always know." She smiled and thought back to the R&R club in Tai Chung Street where, among the American marines on R&R from Vietnam, she had discovered sex. "I used to live in Taipei," she said.

"One eighteenth," one guy said.

"Taipei, shit," the other exclaimed and then, pleasure flooding his face, "the R&R club!"

The three of them nodded, smiling, remembering.

"Did you," the first guy began and then nervously cleared his throat, "ever know a girl called Tzu-ki?"

"Wang Tzu-ki," Clea laughed. "Sure. Stunning woman. She's married now to a banker in Hong Kong."

"Shit!" The guy's face fell. He glowered for a moment and then broke into uproarious laughter at himself. "I think about her every time my wife and I have a fight."

"One eighteenth . . . did you ever know a guy called Billy Butler?" Clea asked.

"Butler, sure, a dandy dude. Funny guy. Scared shitless in every firefight and made us laugh so hard—"

The other guy interrupted, "He won some awards for comedy and then soon after he died, didn't he?"

"Yes," Clea said. "He OD'd on nitrous."

The first guy laughed. "Yeah, a great way to go if you got to go." He looked at Clea and then asked, a bit gentler, "Did you know him from the R&R?"

"Ya," she said smiling. "I thought about him every time my husband and I had a fight." The guys laughed.

"Do me a favor," she said earnestly. "Wear the suits at ten o'clock will you? For the sake of the R&R?"

"Okay," the guys agreed. "Sure."

The company was streaming out of the theater now and forming a line to claim their suits. The two guys went about helping them, and Clea squeezed through the exit door past the throngs and disappeared into the theater.

Those who were standing on line made way for Clea to push past them. Some, she could see, did so from fear of her madness. They didn't want to be too close in case she went berserk, took up one of the machine guns, and opened up on the crowd. Others still felt a lingering respect for her fame and talent and were willing to go through fire for her. She smiled at them all. They were getting their suits, that's all she cared about.

She hurried up the corridor, turned left, and tapped on Zeus' door.

"Zeus," she called, "it's me, Clea. May I come in?"

Inside the room, Zeus looked in the mirror at the door behind him and prepared himself.

"Leave your weapons outside," he said coldly. "And enter without expectation."

"That's a virtual impossibility," Clea said as she entered and quickly closed the door behind her. "Your suit is on the costume rack," she said this lightly, ignoring his previous refusal to wear one. "I think you know where that is."

He stared at her in the mirror and grunted. Her eyes avoided his and searched around the far reaches of the dressing room.

"I'm sorry and I'm not sorry about your nose," she said, still looking away. "I'm sure you understand that."

As he made no sound, she glanced at him. He was rolling his eyes heavenward in derision.

"What are you doing," she shouted at him, suddenly enraged, all pretension to calm gone now, rolling mouse thunder.

"What am *I* doing?" he said calmly, sarcastically. "I'm doing my show, Clea. I might suggest you do it too. There's a great deal of money at stake here, Clea. If your blast doesn't hit, we're going to need it. I sense we'll be out of a job for quite a while."

Clea quieted down and began chewing a nail. This was the first time she had been in Zeus' dressing room during this show. There had been no cheery visits back and forth as there used to be. They were in separate bunkers here, sandbagged in.

"It's like a boys' toy shop in here," she commented. "This is every boat you ever made, isn't it? I remember that one." She did a little jig of excitement, and pointed at a destroyer from the American navy. "You made that one in Egypt. Tiny piece by tiny piece, I hadn't seen such dedication since the Master. I still love you." Though she said this suddenly, they turned to each other in perfect timing and he replied, "I love you too. It isn't that."

"Then please wear the suit." She put her hand on his shoulder and posed with him in the mirror.

"No," he said gently, "I want to do the love dance unencumbered."

"But we must set an example. We must save lives. Don't you care if you live or die?" She eyed him curiously. Something was going on that she didn't understand. She stepped back emotionally and physically and lifted her hands off him.

"No," he said. There was that tension gathering around him again, shutting her out.

She tried not to let this statement hurt her. She tried, in this moment of revelation, to treat him as a friend, to understand as a friend would that his desire to die was not an attack, not something she should flip out and kill him for. But she had discovered in the last few years that she and Zeus were not friends. Though they were deeply in love, theirs was a union based on electrochemicals and spiritual coincidence. They had both had the same baby dishes and the same favorite first book, *The Tawny Scrawny Lion*, his purchased in a shop in Rhodesia from a woman owner who was thought quirky for her love of things American. And apart from a dizzying attraction, that deepest link of predawn taste had seemed enough to hold them for a lifetime. Or so they thought. That, and the fact that they had seen their mothers felled by crazy fate. But they weren't friends. They were both too isolated to be friends. When they tried to open up to each other as they saw other couples do, couples who were friendly-family-like, they got embarrassed. They couldn't bear to see each other's weakness, so they ran their lives in a parallel fashion. They were never intertwined and didn't miss it.

But it seems that lovers cannot win, and whereas most are felled by cloying familiarity, a sibling rivalry in the marriage bed, in the case of Clea and Zeus some hazy horror substance grew between them. It pushed them farther and farther apart until they were squinting at each other over a vast chasm of space. And so, this moment of revelation was one that she had wondered about for a very long time. And as he had verged so near, out of the blue, taking her by surprise, she took the opportunity and threw her arms around his neck and whispered in his ear,

"Why? *Why* do you want to die?"

Twenty-six

CLEA was running for her life up the long hall to Zeus' wing. Her bare feet slapped against the wood floor, her skunky punk mane flew behind her, and from the torn places on her skirt, she was shedding sequins. The round shiny emblems of performer's success sparkled on the parquet floor like a flashy trail of Gretel crumbs. Clea wrenched open the door to Doron's office, raced through the darkened room, and pounded on Zeus' door with the tin TV.

"Zeus!" she cried between heaving breaths, "Zeus!" And then she turned the knob and, finding the door unlocked, pushed hard against it and threw herself into the room.

The first thing she saw in the shadows was her face on the blaring TV set. Smiling, composed, slick as satin, her face was saying,

"I'm sorry. Zeus couldn't come tonight. He's got flu. You ever try to deal with a man who's sick? It's like trying to make Napoleon see the bright side after Waterloo." The TV audience laughed.

She winced. The corpse-colored TV light was the only illumination in the room. It spewed over the chairs and carpet in front of it and gradually she became aware of a huge shadowy figure on the floor near the armchair.

"So I brought what I like to call a Zeus substitute," her face said.

She looked back at the TV, which was now in closeup on the Zeus puppet. It looked funny. She smiled. The TV audience was cheering.

There was a female squeak of delight from the shadowy shape on the rug, followed by some rustling. Clea's heart thumped crazily in her chest. Her temperature dropped and she got goose bumps.

"Zeus," she tried to call out, but her voice on the TV echoed and drowned her. ". . . Zeus were here tonight instead of so cranky at home that the cat's picketing for better snuggling conditions"—the TV audience laughed—"he'd thank you too."

"Zeus." She whispered this. She could just make out her husband naked on top of the naked puppet woman, one hand supporting himself, the other covering his eyes. The puppet woman looked scared but triumphant. After all, she was ecstatically hoist on her own petard.

"Here," Clea gasped and ran forward and set the tiny TV down on the carpet by the shadowy beast. As she fled out of the room, Zeus uncovered his eyes in time to see an extreme closeup of Clea's face on the TV saying to him, "Congratulations, darling," meaning it, meaning it, "I love you."

Wearily, Zeus looked over at the place where Clea had been standing. All that remained was a little pile of sequins, the spoor of his fantasy wife, sparkling in the undead TV light.

Twenty-seven

IT WAS NOT intermission for the television audience. After the commercials, they were seeing a ten-minute film of Clea and Zeus getting married in a weightless environment. It was on in the theater too, and that audience wandered in and out, watching Clea and Zeus projected on the big video screen above the stage like fish in a tank, all dressed up, swimming in space. A preacher and wedding guests floated around them. Clea wore a wedding dress with a huge satin train that in its weightlessness stretched out behind her as if by magic: Four fake doves were sewn to it to look as if they held it up in their beaks. The flaps of Zeus' tailcoat flew up behind him like a funny Dickens costume. His top hat was wired to his head, as was Clea's veil to hers. When he lifted her veil up to kiss her, he removed the little weights that held it down and it stayed up, billowing around her like a halo.

They had made the film at NASA in the antigravity training facility. It was odd dancing in a weightless environment, but thrilling. The extension of their limbs was effortless. They jumped and sailed and twisted and pirouetted higher and with more grace than was indeed humanly possible. Through windows in the air lock, the latest set of astronaut trainees and NASA engineers watched their performance and wept. Delicacy in a weightless environment was something new, something that never occurred to them in their heavy suits, with their militaristic intent, and it stunned them.

On the monitor in the corner of Zeus' dressing room, Clea and Zeus were waltzing on air. In another corner, Clea and Zeus were locked in a weighty embrace. Zeus glanced at the monitor and recalled that they had been in bed for two weeks after the shoot. Their muscles had been strained beyond imagining. Clea, who had been a contortionist since adolescence, could not move for the first three days. The doctors at NASA had come to see them and Clea had said, "Dancing will be entirely different in the twenty-first century. It will not be the same galumphing thing we know. My muscles do not know how to return from the frontiers to which weightlessness has pushed them. I feel like I have been run over by a truck. It was worth it, but in future, we must plan it better. Perhaps Zeus and I will be the first antigravity choreographers."

But their waltz on air was magnificent and the sight of it so moved Zeus that he thought back to their wedding day on a tiny island in Greece and hugged his wife the tighter in his clutch.

He remembered preparing for it in the whitewashed house by the sea. The big room was bare save for a Byzantine Christ on the wall and an old armoire and an iron bed on which sat Doron and Ruth. Four of the Lieutenants lounged around, the others were on guard outside. Doron and Ruth were helping him dress and he was happy and laughing until he remembered. He walked to them and took their hands and said, passionately, fearfully, "You mustn't tell her. You mustn't ever tell her the truth."

"It was an accident, Zeus," Ruth had said softly. "You didn't do it on purpose."

"I lied to Clea," he snapped. "I told her my father did it. I told her that so she would understand the enormity of it, but"—Ruth looked at Doron—"she couldn't marry me if she knew I killed my mother. No woman could."

He paced around the room, holding his head, frantic. Ruth grabbed him.

"No, no. You're wrong. Tell her. It was an accident. I'll tell her if you like. I was there, Zeus, I saw it. There's no blame."

"No!" He seized Ruth and shook her by the shoulders. "Promise me," he hissed. "Promise."

Doron rose from the bed and sprinted across the room and pulled his hands off Ruth.

"It was a bloody accident, mon, for God's sake. If you hadn't shot her I would have. I thought she was a field kaffir. The blackface, mon—who?"

"I should have known. She was always in blackface in the afternoon when my father would go down to the curing rooms. She'd come out and do her minstrel act around the house and make the servants laugh. And about that time as things got tense, she did it more and more often and then for longer periods, not just as a show but doing ordinary things like peeling potatoes. And in the back of my mind that day, I knew and I didn't—"

"Stop this!" Doron pulled him to his great bony chest. "It is gone now, my *boetie*. We have left that life and are on the run, and nothing can ever save us from it. Not lying, not rebirth, nothing. We were born onto a mobius strip and there we will stay until the end of time. And this woman you love knows something of this state of mind."

"Promise me."

Zeus recalled staring into Doron's eyes and clutching him as tightly as he could. He remembered Ruth drifting to the window and staring sadly out to sea. The Four Lieutenants sighed heavily, for they were just newly escaped from the war and the wounds had not yet hardened into scars. The bell in the little church began to toll. The afternoon light was shot with gold. Liu was tapping at the door.

"Zeus, it is time."

"I promise," said Doron, and Zeus released him. Ruth came away from the window. "I promise too," she said, "but it is a mistake and I don't like to."

She wiped her mouth with a handkerchief from her pocket and went to the door. The Four Lieutenants murmured their promises and followed Ruth out into the sunshine. Doron took Zeus by the arm and shoved playfully.

"C'mon, my *boetie*, you're getting married." He was smiling now. "Please God that will give you some peace."

Clea was kissing his neck and whispering into his ear.

"Zeus, listen—listen. Here's what it's going to be like. Here's what I've planned."

She held him at arm's length while she talked. "The blast hits and we're onstage wearing the suits. We must make for the theater doorways because if the theater collapses, the doorways will be the last to fall. I don't think the theater will collapse, but of course I don't know. Anyway, the doorway of your stage-left corridor would be a good place to rendezvous in all the confusion—and there will be horrible confusion, darling. I've tried to warn you, but I know you don't believe me." She squeezed his arms lovingly and rattled on. "Once we're together, we make for the Volks, which is parked on Forty-fifth Street. It's still there. I checked. I don't think they'll have time to tow it before the blast hits.

"Now, if nothing has fallen on it, we get in and drive upstate to the bunker. The bunker is stocked and ready for two or three months' survival.

"The cat's up there. She loves it, Zeus. Life can go right on, is what I'm trying to tell you. It'll just be different, you know, maybe what it was like when the earth first began. We'll have to fight to eat, not fight to get dressing rooms stocked with fruit and cheese plates or fight with networks about whether our dances are too sensuous for the kids of a country with the highest rate of teenage pregnancy in the white middle-class world. We'll have to fight to eat, and make our own clothes and just be, baby."

Clea's eyes were glowing with visions of the future. She was like the narrator of a Leni Reifenstahl film. She was bursting with hope and strength. Zeus took her face in his hands and began gently, "But, Clea—"

She interrupted. "I know what you're going to say: nuclear winter. Okay. Let's say the earth goes dark, the temperature drops. Plant life dies. The bunker's heated for three months. I sent away to *Survive* magazine for a special generator. We'll spend some time together—a vacation without pressure. No phones, Zeus, no worrying about the next gig, no worrying about our immortality, NO WORRYING. BABY, THERE'LL BE NOTHING TO WORRY ABOUT!"

She leaped joyfully into the air, and gave a whoop. Then she sobered and said, "And when the food runs out, I have poison pills in the bunker, enough for you and me and the cat and whoever else comes along . . . I'm prepared for every eventuality, Zeus, okay?"

"Yeah." Zeus was smiling in spite of himself. He went over to the dressing table and sat in front of the mirror.

"Sounds like a roaring good time, Clea. I can hardly wait for World War Three now. Are there protagonists in this war?"

She came and stood behind him and they posed with each other in the mirror. "I don't know, Zeus." she said thoughtfully, "I mean after we tapped into NORAD, we checked it every day and there are missile silos all over the planet, so you know, if one goes—does it matter?"

"No, just asking."

There was a pause during which Clea hugged Zeus' head and kissed his eyes. "Will you come with me, darling?" she whispered. "Everything that's gone before will be wiped away. We can forget about the past, Zeus, please?"

"It's impossible, Clea," Zeus said softly, gently. "It can't be done. You can't wipe out the past. It's like a Siamese twin. You cut it off and you both die. We've got to get ready now."

"Zeus," she bent closer over his head, close to his reflection in the mirror asking it, a second opinion, "will you wear the suit? Will you come with me?"

He looked at her in the mirror and replied, "No. I'm sorry."

"Why?" she asked again angrily. "Why do you want to die? Why?"

He smiled and shrugged. In his mind he was seeing her in front of the little church on a hill overlooking the Aegean. She was dancing before the little whitewashed Byzantine holy place. The hot sun was shining off her white dress and creating a glare. Her white veil covered her face in a peekaboo purdah. She was laughing with such happiness he thought he would faint. She believed in him so deeply, he wanted to run. But she came up to him and hugged him so lovingly and so tightly that for a long time the fear had been squeezed right out of him.

"Zeus," she said. She had her hand on the door and was about to leave. "This is an absurdist world. It's goddamn unpleasant and smug. It's so greed-filled I figure when they die, half the planet will be going to hell. I don't know what could redeem it except a firestorm."

"No," Zeus repeated, nicely, sanely, as if they were talking about starch in his shirts, "I'm sorry, no."

OUTSIDE Zeus' dressing room, the corridor was oddly congested. Those who had waited on line for their suits had gotten them and were now trudging along, on the way to their various stations, lugging the bulky outfits, dragging the pants legs along the floor. The effect was eerie, as if the entire cast and crew were carrying the desiccated remains of an army of dead workers. Gas masks, like the faces of giant cartoon mice, were slung around their necks and arms. There was little conversation, just the occasional grunt or sigh or sometimes the strained laughter of a mass of people forced to do a horrid job on pain of their own mortality.

Clea weaved through her converts up the stage-left corridor, nodding and smiling encouragingly. When she reached the stage-left wing, she gave whoever was looking a "V" sign for victory and ducked into the opening.

Onstage, the propmen were dressing the eight conical heaps, diminishing them, placing more and more objects on the dog sled and in the shopping cart: Clea's wedding dress here, Zeus' top hat there. By the end of the show, should there be an end of the show, the heaps would be gone, divided into two mountains of possessions to be moved out. Only coils of yellow rope would remain on the stage floor. Clea crossed the stage and called out to the propmen,

"Do you have your suits?"

The propmen nodded. She gave her victory sign and vanished through the stage-right wing into the corridor.

The three cameramen were lounging against a wall smoking cigarettes. Clea rushed over to them and smiled.

"I'm sorry about the unrehearsed bit at the end. It won't happen again."

The cameramen laughed. "It was amazing," said first minicam. "You're a master, Clea. I didn't mind. It was exciting. I shoot the NFL. I'm used to surprises."

Second minicam nodded in agreement. "Will you teach us kung fu sometime, Clea? I'd like to bring my son in. He's a nut for that stuff."

"Sure," she said sweetly, "if there is a sometime. Do you guys have your suits?"

Camera three coughed nervously. "Clea, we can't shoot with the damn masks on. The suits are heavy, but we can deal with that for a few minutes. But the nosepiece on the masks—"

She thought for a moment. "Listen, just put them on for the one minute from nine fifty-nine to ten P.M. and I'll take responsibility. Okay?"

The cameramen smiled indulgently. "Sure," they said, and took long drags on their cigarettes.

"Thanks," she said and she kissed each one on the cheek. "And I promise: if we're still here after ten, I'll teach the kung fu class this winter. Okay?" The cameramen nodded, and she hurried off down the corridor.

At the door of her dressing room, she ran into Liu. He was strumming his pi-pa and seemed to be waiting for her. The lyrical pings of the instrument played against the military buildup of the atmosphere.

"That's nice," she said. "Do you want to come in?"

She opened the door, and he followed her into the dressing room and shut it behind him. Florie was out. The room was empty save for the photograph of Hiroshima after the blast, her costumes on the rack, the hanging pair of black satin toe shoes, and the bottle of stage blood sitting on the dressing table, near her makeup box. She sat down in front of the mirror and began to prepare her face.

"I had up here"—she pointed as she sponged makeup base under her eyes—"a photo from the Yan Min Shan Theater, but Florie packed it away. Do you recall it?"

Liu strummed her intro music from that performance on the pi-pa.

"Oh, yes," he said, "the first of your appearances in town. When first you foot-juggled live fireworks. You were always fearless."

"Liu." She was thirteen again and in need of comfort. Her talent was robbing her of her life.

"Yes," he replied.

"Zeus won't wear the suit. He wants to die."

She turned around and looked at him, one painted eye, one unpainted eye, questioning.

"You sensed that long ago," he said calmly. "Did you think this"—he gestured uncertainly in the air—"this—bomb business would alter that?"

"No," she said, "I thought love would."

"At best love calms," Liu said. "It alters nothing."

"Fuck, Liu." She bounced up and down in mock hysteria. "You mean love can't make the insane sane or heal the halt and the lame? Or make man want to live and strive for a better tomorrow?"

"Only the first bloom of love does that," Liu replied seriously, "after that, I don't think so. But it's just my opinion."

Clea smiled. "You're a cynical man, Liu."

"Oh, yes," he said matter-of-factly, "that's true."

"And will you wear the suit, Liu?"

The painted eye filled with tears and scared him, the unpainted eye filled with tears and tore his heart. "If it is very important to you," he answered.

"And why that?" She was staring at him, anguished, a tiny paintbrush poised in her fingers. "Because you love me?"

"Yes. I suppose so."

She whooped in triumph. "There, you see, you're not so cynical, haha!"

Liu strummed the pi-pa. "No, Clea. I am still in the first bloom, that's all."

Clea beamed gratefully and a tear ran down her cheek, streaking her makeup.

"Damn," she muttered, and set about fixing it.

"I have a wire from the Master. It is for you."

Liu handed her the telegram, and she ripped it open and nervously read it.

"It says, 'One billion warm hands on your opening. We will be wearing our suits.' Bless him." She bowed her head for a moment and was silent, then she said, "How I long for those days in the Moon Court. Squeezing myself into tiny and tinier packets while Mee Lan, the greatest of acrobats, bounded about like a beautiful beach ball with arms. And the others in the class, do you hear of them? Chiang-Tzu?"

"She is a main performer with the Nationalist Chinese Opera. They are coming in the spring."

"In the spring?" Clea was at first excited by this and then, remembering, repeated, "In the nuclear spring, ah."

"It is time to prepare, Clea." Liu put the pi-pa under his arm and started for the door.

"Ten Thousand Talents," he turned back, calling her by the Master's name for her, "you will do the show as rehearsed?"

"Yes. Of course." She grabbed his arm and entreated him, "Stand beneath a doorway when the blast hits, won't you, Liu?" He nodded.

"Then meet us by the Volkswagen on Forty-fifth Street." He nodded again and padded by her to the door. "Liu," she said as she rose from her dressing table and took his hand, "if something should go wrong, I want to say—I want to thank you—for spending your life with me—how can I? It's not possible, is it?" She hugged him then and he stiffened as he did when people touched him. Even though he felt the love, it was too big inside him to let out and so he patted her on her tiny-boned back until she released him. Then he smiled enigmatically and went out the door.

Florie was bustling down the corridor, carrying on her head a small bundle that seemed to be filled with leaves and grasses. She was followed by Charlie, the stage manager, carrying a crate containing two live chickens. The fowl were squawking in fear and protest and flapping their vestigial wings in a panic to escape. Charlie was swearing at them in disgust as he checked the watch hanging around his neck and discovered the time.

"Sonofabitch chickens! Florie! I've got to get working. It's four minutes to—"

"Put them down," she said in her deep African drawl, and he set down the crate in the middle of the corridor and rushed off toward the stage-right wing. Liu, who was coming up the corridor at this moment, stopped and nodded to Florie.

"Are you wearing the damn suit?" she asked him. He shrugged.

"I will see when the time comes. And you?"

"I will ask the *benge*. I know you know this, Liu, there is something here, around us."

"Yes. The elements are out of balance. Yes."

"The Zim are in the neighborhood, Liu. The suit may be some trickery of the Zim. I will ask. Then we will know." The chickens flapped and bleated at her feet. "But you have told her—"

"I will wear the suit."

Florie nodded. "And Zeus?"

"Will not wear the suit."

"Achhh, mon," Florie hissed in frustration. "It is *too* bad. They were the gum and the bark, those two. Somewhere in this business there is the foot of a baboon, I *tell* you."

She bent down and picked up the crate and held it to her chest. The chickens stuck their beaks out through the slats and clucked shrilly. Liu gestured that he would carry it for her, but she declined the offer. They bowed imperceptibly to each other and each went off his separate way to prepare for the second act.

Twenty-eight

DORON and the Seven Golden Lieutenants had just returned from Central Park and were crowding into the vestibule. In the early evenings until just after nightfall, they practiced their old Rhodesian army maneuvers, guerrilla bush fighting, just to keep their hands in, just in case.

This evening they had been doing antiambush drills. The old Sheep Meadow in the park had been the killing ground.

They were exhilarated by the evening's action, wet from the rain, and rowdy, and they jostled each other playfully, stick fighting with their machine guns as they wound down from their outdoor op.

"Eh, look ere," one of the Lieutenants shouted to Doron over the melee. He was pointing to the wall over the telephone where Clea had printed the date of the end of the world. A big childlike scrawl in red pen, it had seeped into the white damask wallpaper and bled a little at the edges. Its presence was clearly an outrage. The handwriting itself looked shaky and menacing.

Doron eyed the message suspiciously. Then from Zeus' wing he heard a door slam, followed by the pounding of bare feet on a wooden floor. Immediately he turned to the Seven and snapped his fingers.

They dropped, silent. He clenched his fist and pointed his thumb toward the ground. Bush signaling. It meant: Civilian Type in the distance. He put his hand up to his eye in the shape of a monocle: Reconnaissance. He moved across the vestibule to the corridor and popped around the entranceway. Clea, her dress ripped, her eyes the source of rivers, was running wildly down the hall, keening.

"Oh God," she was moaning, "no, no."

Doron whipped toward his men, put his hand over his face, and pointed toward Clea: Immediate Ambush. The men stiffened. Four set down their guns and approached the doorway silently. As Clea reached the vestibule, she was oblivious to everything except the sense of loss that threatened to desiccate her, the vision of her husband inside a heartless woman that promised to drive her mad. Doron, whose main concern at that moment was the welfare of Zeus, snapped, "Hold her!" and the four Lieutenants stepped through the doorway, ambushed her, and dragged her into the vestibule. Doron streaked up the hall to Zeus' wing.

At first, Clea was terrified and struggled for her life. Then she realized who was holding her and when they wouldn't let her go, she struggled for her dignity. She was soaked in fury from the day's losses and she shook this off now. She flailed and bit for her freedom and gave the Lieutenants such a run for their money that one detached himself from the rest and started off toward Zeus' wing to scout Doron. The Lieutenants were stymied. Had she been a real CT in Rhodesia, they would have shot her for such behavior. As it was, they didn't know how to proceed.

At this moment Doron reappeared in the hall, followed by a very unsteady Zeus, dressed only in his tuxedo pants, with no shoes and no shirt. Ever beautiful, in spite of the fact that he was literally lurching, Zeus looked as if he were part of a TV ad for some fabulous French perfume. The woman would be dressed perfectly—he'd look like this. To the Seven Golden Lieutenants, possessed of more animal perception than most, he looked like a man who had just had sex and enjoyed it. They glanced at Clea, *not* with Clea. They nodded sagely to themselves.

"Release her!" Doron snapped at the scout.

"Release her!" the scout relayed to the four in the vestibule who were struggling with the demon. They did so, and she immediately spun out into the hall, sputtering and spitting, a cloud of sequins flying around her like the malorbiting moons of her own universe.

Seething and fuming, Clea caught her breath, for a moment, and looked up the hall at her husband. Zeus lurched toward her. A look of terrible dismay, of woozy red-eyed vulnerability distorted his features. He held out his hands to her in supplication and staggered forward. But he fell over her deer-hoof boots and sprawled on the parquet floor like a mashed frog on a country road. Clea's heart melted for him. At that instant she remembered that he didn't know she was guilty too. But the stinging reality of this thought passed quickly from her mind in favor of the theatrical rhythms that had so long dogged her perception. She wheeled and sped off down the hallway, past the dining room, past the War Room, and turned left down the passageway to their bedroom.

Florie, who was standing by the bedroom door, surveyed Clea with concern. She stepped back as Clea picked up speed and slammed into the bedroom like a whirlwind. Clea swept her arm across her dressing table and brought down all the perfume bottles but her favorite, Florie noted, miraculously spared. Clea then fled to the closet and tore out clothes and hurled them to the floor. Paintings, books, award statues, her tiny Buddhist shrine, Zeus' offering to his ancestors, their wedding picture, all were torn down in a heap, broken and splintered.

"Clea, Clea," Florie was shouting over the noise of anger and destruction, "what has happened, my baby, you have grown wings!"

Clea wailed and threw herself on the carpet. Her mind was a quarter porn show on a loop: Zeus inside the puppet woman, slamming and slamming, like a nail in the brain, deeper and deeper. Betrayal. Betrayal. She rolled under the bed and clawed at the carpet. The dust packed her nose and eyes and the quarter dropped and it was she on her knees, Butler inside her, slamming and smiling, slamming and smiling, smiling and moaning. And the quarter dropped and it was her mother, dead, noseless and footless, stuffed and juggling plates in her gnarled claw hands.

Florie had knelt down and was peering under the bed. "What is it, my baby?" she said, soothing and clicking. "Someone has put down the pipe. Who is it?"

Florie was lying down now, one arm stretched under the bed trying to reach her. Clea hunkered to the middle, where she could not be reached, and flattened out.

"Mama," Clea replied, sobbing.

"Achhh. Shame." Florie felt a stab of anguish. She rolled on her back and hugged herself for a moment. "Neva has put down the pipe." Then she said comfortingly, "Achhh, shame, but with the spirits, my baby, she will be fat."

Clea sobbed again and fell away and in her mind the quarter dropped, and it was a million faces melting and burning, screaming and shouting, their hands stretched upwards, pleading and clawing. Another drop: Zeus slamming and smiling. The puppet girl laughing and mocking and strangling her mother's armadillo face, grimacing Zeus, fucking and sweating inside inside inside—

Now, Clea gave a low long animal moan. Florie went cold at the sound and turned slowly to look at the woman in the evening gown prostrate under the bed. Clea's eyes were fluttering in her head and she was twitching. Florie crawled around to the side of the bed and rolled under it until she was up against Clea. She threw her arms around the suffering woman and dragged her, rolling her and scooting her until she was out from under the bed. Clea lay on the carpet like a drowning victim. She was gasping and heaving and her hair was plastered to her head.

The Siamese cat, who had run when the tornado blew into the bedroom, sensed the calm after the storm and sniffed in a friendly manner at Clea's face while she recovered herself. The long, stiff whiskers brushed and tickled her cheekbone and Clea opened her eyes to see a serious little fox face very close to hers, peering at her with gentle expectation.

"Soong," she murmured, smiling through the Post-Blast wastes of her emotion. She drew the little animal to her and petted it until it lay down with its head on her shoulder, its body medicinally warming hers.

"Soong," she cooed, stroking it and imitating its purr. It was the only creature in the world who forgave her for being herself, who regarded her furies as avoidable eccentricities, who loved her, difficult as she was to love, without reservation.

"Soong," she whispered in the cat's ear, and the animal gazed at her adoringly. "Don't you worry, my little lambskin, don't you worry."

Florie, in an exhausted heap in a nearby corner of the carpet, watched the scene with mounting empathy and alarm. There was something eerie about Clea. She had not fully returned. She had not popped back. She had strayed into the thorn forests of madness and now, though she was visible among the trees, she was unable or unwilling to follow the trail and stumble on out.

"Clea, my baby," Florie called to her, but she didn't seem to hear.

"I promise you," Clea was whispering to Soong, stroking the cat's face and kissing its cheek, "that when the atomic bomb hits, you will survive."

Twenty-nine

OUT IN THE LOBBY, the lights were flashing on and off, signaling that it was nine-twelve, the end of the theater audience's intermission. Most people had already filed into the theater and the few stragglers who were left did so now, hurriedly crushing out their cigarettes, and running through the lobby door into the velvet maw of the playhouse. An older woman in a hat said over her shoulder to the young man who was her date, "The Jed Harris Theater was built in 1928, the year Jed Harris, age twenty-eight, had four hits running simultaneously on Broadway. These included a dramatic offering called *Broadway*, which defined forever the concept of the Broadway play. Forty years later he would die in obscurity, a man so mean that people refused to work with him and his career died. Now that's saying something in show business!"

The film of the wedding in a weightless environment wound to a close. The audience clapped and chirped appreciatively. The orchestra had wandered into the orchestra pit and was tuning up. The sound man had arrived at the sound board at the back of the house and was fiddling with the EQ. Roger was in the lighting booth. The Seven Golden Lieutenants had taken up their security positions and were chatting at random with young women in the audience. Suddenly, the houselights dimmed and a spotlight came up on the curtain. Charlie, the stage manager, appeared and greeted the audience.

"Good evening, ladies and gentlemen. This evening's second act contains several special effects that Clea and Zeus feel present a safety problem for you the audience. The ushers will now give out asbestos suits and masks to each of you. Please put on the suits now. The ushers will alert you when to put on the masks as the act progresses. Clea and Zeus are sorry for the inconvenience and beg your indulgence for what you know to be their quirky creativity."

The audience laughed and, as he disappeared through the break in the golden curtains, instantly began discussing his request. The ushers set down piles of suits at the end of each row. They gave piles of suits to the conductor, who distributed them among the orchestra.

Geneal Clark Lincoln leaned down and whispered to Miss Hollywood, "Honey, these are radiation suits."

"What does it mean, Clark?" She pressed his arm nervously.

"It means Clea's trying to protect us."

He rose up, received two suits from the usher, and began helping Miss Hollywood get one over her clothes. Others, reassured by the orchestra and General Lincoln suiting up, began to do the same. There was much hilarity as patrons made fun of each other's looks in the bulky outfits.

"What's it going to be?" one man joked, "trial by fire?"

"Funny," his date said sarcastically. "I don't like this."

In several rows there were people who declined to wear the suits. The ushers tried hard to convince them and in some cases they were successful. But as Doron had forbidden the Lieutenants to wear the suits, those in the audience who most identified with this oddly militaristic aspect of Clea and Zeus stood firm and refused to reconsider.

Clea was onstage, watching the proceeding through a rent in the curtain.

"Damn," she muttered as she realized there were people who were not putting on the suits. She came away from the curtain chewing a nail and deeply distressed. At this moment, Doron bounded onto the stage and crossed frantically to the stage-right wing. Clea followed him into the stage-right corridor.

"Hey!" she snarled after him.

He turned and hissed, "Dodson's just shown up. I'm making myself scarce. You deal with him. It's your goddamn fault he's here."

"Hey, you!" She snarled again. Doron didn't answer and kept moving. "Why aren't the Lieutenants wearing suits, you damn fool? There's people in the house thinking it's safe not to wear one 'cause they're not!" Clea ran after him. "They're going to die, don't you see that? They're all going to burn to death and it'll be on your head!"

Doron halted and seized her shoulders with his giant bony hands. His face was contorted with fury. "You're mad, woman," he said through clenched teeth, "and you would bring us all down to your ludicrous level of anguish. So your husband cheated on you, so fucking what? You made his life so loveless he didn't have a choice."

She stared stonily at him. "The Lieutenants are going to die. I'm telling you. Save them. Save yourself."

Liu, who had appeared onstage to check the flying mechanism and heard the shouting in the stage-right corridor, materialized by Clea's side and removed Doron's hands from her shoulders.

"Enough," he said simply.

Doron stood back, livid. His great bony body was twitching like a giant skeleton marionette. Finally he spat on the floor and slunk off down the corridor.

Some moments later, Ralph Dodson stuck his head out from the stage-right wing.

"Ralph!" Clea exclaimed effusively, "What are you doing down here?" Ralph blushed. He was a network man not given to effusive behavior but capable of being seduced by it under the proper circumstances.

"Well . . ." He was thrown off guard. He never liked to confront those who were giving him a hard time. He was most comfortable with their representatives. He lived the life of the once-removed and thrived on it. "I'm sorry about the end of the first act," Clea gushed with mock shame. "My art imitated my personal anguish. But no one noticed at home, did they?"

Ralph, flustered, shook his head. "No, not really."

"And, it won't happen again. I promise." She said this sincerely enough to relax the network man, and he smiled at her. "Now," she asked sweetly, "do you both have your suits?"

Liu nodded obediently for Ralph's benefit.

"Ralph?" Clea was like an adorable kindergarten teacher. Ralph looked dubious. "Liu, would you show Ralph where the truck is so he can get fitted?"

"Come," Liu said, bowing imperceptibly. Ralph held up his hands.

"No thanks, Liu," he said politely, "I'm going back to the network. Just dropped by to see Doron and how things were going."

"Oh." Clea seemed genuinely disappointed. "Will you take a suit with you?" she asked, as if it were a homemade cake.

"No. No." Ralph was falsely jolly as he said this, clearly humoring her. "I'm going to wing it, Clea. We decided over at the network we'd take our chances."

"I'm sorry about that," Clea said, meaning it. Ralph was getting nervous.

"Now, Clea, you do intend to do the whole show?"

Clea rolled her eyes. "Not if the bomb drops, Ralph." Ralph was sweating now.

"Fair enough," he said, placating. "But if it doesn't?" He peered at her.

"Of course I will. Of course. I have no interest in fucking you or anyone else up, Ralph. I'm only trying to save lives."

"Fine." Ralph smiled, but he was ashen. She was nuts, that was obvious. "I think I'll stay and watch the end."

"Oh good!" Clea clapped her hands. "But wear the suit at ten, please, Ralph, it's the house rule." Ralph realized that his job was at stake. If Clea flipped out at ten, he'd have twenty minutes of dead air on his employment record. "Okay, Clea," he said. Doron had glossed over her condition, that was clear, but then, talent was very strange and often unpredictably solid.

"Where's Zeus?" he asked Liu.

Clea answered, "In his dressing room, which is on your way to the truck."

"Okay." Ralph's expression was bilious. "Let me see this truck," and Liu escorted the network man into the stage-right wing and out of the corridor.

Clea looked around and realized she was alone. It was the first time she had been alone outside the dressing room in the entire show. Obviously it was a fluke. Bobette must be in the bathroom, the propmen dressing the stage. She stretched out her arms and luxuriated in the wide expanse of unoccupied air. She trotted over to the prop table, picked up a pen and paper, and quickly wrote five short notes. Then she ran up the corridor to the stage-right wing, darted through, and corralled Charlie.

"Charlie," she said sweetly, "take these out to the people who won't wear suits. It's my personal plea. After this"—she placed the missives in his hand—"there's nothing more I can do."

She wafted back through the stage-right wing, leaving him charmed by her language and saddened by her strangeness. He checked to make sure everything was under control and then went off into the house to deliver the letters.

Now, she thought to herself, I have done everything I had to do. Now I am free. She bounced herself off the corridor walls and did cartwheels up and down the center of the floor. A thought popped into her mind: What if I'm mad? as she bent her body around in space, balancing it against gravity. There was a possibility, actually a big possibility, if you considered the circumstances. She checked her watch: nine-fifteen. What if nothing happened at ten? She spoke out loud: "Then I'll yell, 'April fool, everybody!' And laugh very hard."

She laughed at the idea of nothing happening, of all that fear and no payoff, of the way everyone would look. She imitated the look on her own face and her body movements, the utter sheepishness, the neurotic anger, the fear of reprisal from the cast and crew. "Okay," she was saying, "I was wrong." She was guffawing raucously and wondrously at the possibility of her own sanity when Bobette walked into the stage-right corridor and froze at the sight of her. Clea tried to stifle her laughter but couldn't. Bobette's terror of her seemed comic somehow too. No one believes in me, she thought and might have tumbled into self-loathing were it not for the loud squawking of male chickens that suddenly emanated from her dressing room at the end of the corridor.

She tried to explain to Bobette, "Florie's consulting the poison oracle to see if she should wear the suit." Bobette's eyes grew wide with horror at the thought.

"No," Clea said through giggles, "it's quite a respected way of discerning the truth among some African tribes." Bobette nodded weakly.

"Never mind," said Clea, and sobered by Bobette's reaction, she turned and padded up the corridor to her dressing room.

FLORIE was preparing to consult the oracle. The crate containing the two live cockerels sat in a corner by the chaise. The two fowl poked their beaks through the slats, scanned the dressing room with their beady eyes, and rustled nervously as if in foreknowledge of the event. Perched on Florie's head was the round, little bundle which held the sacred constituent of the trial to come. She took this down now, untied and opened it on the chaise, and removed the *benge*, the *bingbas* grass, and several other types of African plant leaves she would need for the consultation.

The *benge*, the red paste oracular poison, she had been given by an old Azande woman whom she found lying sickly in an alley in Mombasa. She had recognized the old one for a stranded priestess, and had carried her home to the shanty she was squatting on the outskirts of the sea town. After a long fever, the priestess rallied and explained that her name was Badiabe and she was the mother of a Zande prince who had been murdered in a coup, after which she had been forced to flee. She had managed to get to the coast and she had bought her way onto a freighter bound for the Cape. She disembarked at Mombasa because she liked the feel of the place, steamy and humid, the air as thick as mealie pap. Then she had fallen ill.

It was her high social position and her advanced age that accounted for the *benge* in her possession, for, as she instructed Florie, the poison oracle is forbidden to women except, very occasionally, those of exalted age and state. When she said this, Florie recalled, Badiabe grinned mischievously. The tiny old woman was birdbone thin, with leathery skin that hung on her like a cloak. One egret feather struck out askew from a cap of beads that encircled her hairless head. She wore a faded trading store housedress that wrapped round her twice and was belted with a leather thong. She grinned and cackled and showed five missing teeth.

"But you," Badiabe said, "are a woman among women with your long trek to freedom. If I was a young one I would come too. Instead, I send the *benge*. Use it well, Amaxhosa, for you use it for me."

One day before dawn, Badiabe arose and decided to go home.

She took her little bundle and her walking stick, checked her face in her trading mirror and, satisfied with the results, she walked out the door and vanished. It did not surprise Florie that the morning she herself was set to leave, when she went down to the ocean to bid it goodbye, the single egret feather was waiting there, plunged and quivering in the sand like an arrow fired straight down from the heaven.

Clea opened the dressing room door, entered quickly, and closed it behind her.

"Hello, Florie," she said dejectedly, and flopped into the chair before her mirror. She examined herself for a moment and then recited:

"My Lord raised a flag of surrender
Over the Emperor's city.
Buried deep in the women's quarters,
How can I understand
Why a hundred and forty thousand soldiers laid down their arms.
All I can say is—there was not a man amongst them.

"Lady Hua Ji wrote that, Florie, in the tenth century. She was the wife of the King of Szechuan, who surrendered to the army of the Emperor T'ai, soon after which he died. She was, of course, taken by the Emperor for his harem."

She and Florie nodded in understanding and then Florie set about preparing the oracle.

In a space she had cleared before the chaise, Florie now put a shallow bowl which had belonged to her grandmother in the Transkei and which, here, would be standing for the earth. Into this bowl she placed a large leaf as a basin for the poison oracle. From the *bingbas* grass she fashioned a small brush to administer the poison, and from the other leaves she made a filter to pour the liquid poison into the beaks of the fowls. She went to the sink and filled a gourd with water and then from more leaves made a cup to transfer water from the gourd to the cup when it needed to be moistened. Finally, she took up some branches and extracted their bast to be used as a cord for attaching to the legs of the fowls. It helped with those who survived the test. It made them easily retrievable when the trial was over.

Such were the strange properties of the *benge*, such was its oracular nature, that sometimes it poisoned the fowl and killed them and sometimes it didn't. It was in that sense factually supernatural. It was not a trick. It was not a game. It was just that it was a poison that didn't always kill, and scientists seemed at a loss to figure out why.

As Badiabe had said, "Eh, well, they question it, but this is life. There are many people who walk the earth who have been poisoned but do not die. Hope does not kill."

Clea hurried through her makeup and hair and then got up, and locked the dressing room door.

"Bring me the fowl," Florie said, and Clea sprinted over to the crate and removed from it one of the cockerels. She carried the live squawking fowl in her two hands over to the chaise and sat down with her back up against it opposite the *benge*. Florie nodded to her formally and began.

First Florie smeared the red paste poison onto the leaf basin. Then she poured water from the gourd to the leaf cup and from the leaf cup onto the poison, which began to effervesce. She mixed the water and the poison into a paste with her fingertips, and when she was satisfied with its consistency, she took the fowl from Clea and drew its wings down over its legs and pinned them between its toes. The fowl stood facing her, stymied, and watched as she then took up the grass brush, twirled it in the poison, and folded the paste into the leaf blade filter. She set down the brush, grasped the fowl, and held open its beak while she squeezed the filter and a stream of liquid ran out of the paste and down the fowl's throat. She then bobbed the head up and down to compel the cockerel to swallow, picked up a wooden switch, and began to consult the oracle.

"*Benge!*" Florie beat the switch on the ground and chanted in sing-song voice.

"*Benge!* This woman who is my friend and charge"—she pointed with the switch at Clea—"Clea is mad and would shame my name. *Benge*, listen, kill the fowl. It isn't so. It isn't so. Clea speaks the truth and would save my skin. *Benge*, listen, spare the fowl. *Benge!* Listen, don't be deceived. There's a suit of thorns the madwoman gives. If I put it on I will come to harm. *Benge*, listen, kill the fowl! *Benge*, listen, it's all a lie. The woman is sane and the suit protects. *Benge*, listen, spare the fowl."

While chanting, Florie here administered a second dose of poison to the fowl and jerked his foot to ensure the substance was stirred up inside the bird. "*Benge!*"—she slammed the floor with the switch—"Listen! *Benge!* She is soiling our souls with her ruined mind. The suit she would give will kill. *Benge*, listen, kill the fowl. *Benge*, it's nonsense, Clea loves us dear. She would give her life in place of mine. Her suit is my shelter from deathly rain, *Benge*, hear me, spare the fowl."

Florie here administered a third dose of poison down the bird's throat. She took it up with its feet between her fingers so that it faced her. From time to time she jerked it as she intoned.

"*Benge!* Listen, now! This thing is important. Our lives are at stake. A madwoman rules us. She'd shorten our spans. She'd give us a suit so we never could run. She'd make us her captives in ruin and death, *Benge!* Listen! Kill the fowl!"

Florie, rising to crescendo, screamed this last, and Clea, fixated and praying for deliverance, dissolved in tears and chanted her denial.

"No, *Benge!* No, *Benge!*"

"No, *Benge*," Florie went on. "It's vicious slander. This innocent child is possessed with a vision. She sees our destruction, and would bring us to grass. Her courage is such she would never desert us. *Benge!* Listen! It's truth she is telling, truth as she knows it, truth we should follow. Listen! *Benge!* Spare the fowl!"

Florie jerked the fowl a few times more, then tied its feet with bast and threw it down on the ground. Immediately, the fowl defecated and unconcernedly began to peck. Florie looked at Clea. Tears were streaming down her cheeks.

"The *bambata simi*, the first test, is finished. The fowl has been spared. The second test, the *gingo*, we will do in the long commercial break. Then we will know for sure."

There was a tap at the dressing room door. "Two minutes"—the voice of Charlie, the stage manager.

"Yes." Clea's voice cracked as she replied, and taking a spare leaf blade and placing it on the spot where she'd been sitting, she rose from the floor and hurried to the costume rack to change for the first number of the second act.

Thirty

WHEN LIU ARRIVED home from the poetry reading, he was a bit drunk. The poetry he had heard was not of the highest quality, heavy-handed Russians on a lark in America, more reportage about the Russian steppes in winter interspersed with whining about the war. It amused Liu that the Americans so lapped up Russian horrors of World War Two. They couldn't hear enough of it. Chinese poets spoke of such things only occasionally, preferring not to trumpet their howling disasters. The Russian poets at the YMHA held out their totalitarian predicament as bait for literary groupies. There was nothing that warmed a capitalist intellectual girl's heart like fellating a man at risk of the Gulag. They all opened their legs to cheer sad rowdies from the Eastern bloc. Oriental poets, however, were a vastly different case, he thought with some resentment, scarce and, for some reason, sexually inscrutable. There was one woman who was attracted to him whom he might have picked up after the reading: with waist-length black hair and a flat round face. But she thought he was Japanese and her feet were so big that the combination chilled him.

Liu let himself into the apartment just as the ruckus was dying down. The Golden Lieutenants were milling in the hallway off the vestibule, gazing concernedly toward Zeus' wing. He padded past the telephone table and noticed a date scrawled in Clea's writing in red pen on the white damask wall. When he reached the hallway, he looked where the Lieutenants were looking and saw a collapsed Zeus being aided by a frantic Doron. He hurried up the hall.

"He fell," Doron said protectively, the least possible information.

"I see," Liu replied icily, and then something stole his attention, a sound in the doorway to Zeus' wing. The woman from whom Clea purchased the Zeus puppet was standing there buttoning her blouse. Her wild, witchy hair was wildly askew and she had the just-bedded look he had first seen in the pleasure houses of his youth. When she saw the collapsed Zeus, she cried out and would have run to him had not Doron intercepted and restrained her.

"Where is Clea?" Liu asked coldly.

"In the bedroom." Doron took the puppet woman by the arm and was leading her to the vestibule. "Get her things," he snapped at one of the Lieutenants, who ran up the hall and into Zeus' wing. Liu turned on his heel and hurried down the hall to find Clea.

When everyone was gone from the hallway, Zeus opened his eyes and tried to push himself to his feet. He was too physically liquid to do it, though his mind was sober enough to know that he must get to Clea and attempt to explain.

"How could you fuck this woman in our home?" he imagined her screaming.

"I didn't—"

"You didn't expect me home so soon from the awards?"

"No, I didn't know I was going to fuck anyone."

"You didn't know you were going to fuck anyone? You usually know? How many times have you done this?"

"No. I've never—don't leave me, don't leave me."

He realized that, limp as he was, the only way he could reach Clea was to crawl to where she was, which might—under the circumstances —make a good impression. He was in a lot of trouble, caught right in the act, very hard to forgive. He crawled by the doorway to the vestibule and waved to the puppet woman as Doron escorted her out the door, then he proceeded on.

When Liu reached the bedroom, Florie had just begun to tidy up. She was on her knees, picking tiny pieces of glass out of the carpet and dropping them in the wastebasket. The odors of the spilled perfumes had mingled crassly and the room had the reek of cheap seraglio in Aswan. The place was in chaos, clothes and mementos thrown about or smashed or ripped, and in the midst of it all, Clea, still lying on the carpet, the Siamese cat Soong clapped to her breast, reciting from the poetess Jung Tzu,

"My dressing mirror is a cat of Fate,
A squatting cat.
A cat. A confused dream.
No light. No shadow,
Never once the reflection
Of my true image."

"The poetess Jung Tzu," Liu said, "an interesting woman. I met her in Taiwan with her husband, the poet Lo Men. I tried to talk with them, but I so envied them their life, I couldn't hear what they said to me."

He was standing over Clea as he spoke, still wearing his overcoat, conversing calmly and nonchalantly, never betraying the anxiety he felt to see her in such a state so lately so clearly ravaged. In her anguish, her eye makeup had streaked all over her face, etching itself into her lines of pain so she resembled an ink sketch of a mask of tragedy. Her eyes were blood red. Her mane in tangles. And she was played out, prostrate and boneless on the carpet like the body of the deflated Zeus puppet he had seen on a chair in the vestibule.

"Clea." Liu spoke to her, but she did not reply. Liu turned to Florie. "There was a woman with Zeus?"

Florie looked surprised, then thoughtful. "Eh? And Mrs. Clark Lincoln has put down the pipe."

"Ah." This surprised Liu, then pained him. Mrs. Clark Lincoln was dead, the great-spirited old dowager whom he had met once long ago on Clea's first visit to the leprosarium.

"So," Mrs. Clark Lincoln had boomed when she saw him, "what kind of job is this for a sensate poet? Are you in love with my daughter?"

"Perhaps," he had replied. "I needed a life. I lost mine."

The gnarled one mulled this over, lighting a cigarette with the three fingers that remained on her hands, so at home with her handicap that she made it at once charming and normal. "And what of this Zeus? What do you think of him?"

"Honorable," Liu replied immediately, "but weak. There is something . . . absent."

The lepress inhaled deeply and released the smoke through collapsed nostrils. "Well, I hear he's real pretty. That can make up for a lot. Don't kid yourself, Liu." She winked. "You know, Liu, you took over for me, protecting my little chick and all, and I thank you for it. Consider yourself hugged and your hand shook and all the other forms of endearment. I mean it. I mean it sincerely." She slashed the air with her stumps as she said this, miming hugging and shaking hands, the smoke from her cigarette underlining the display. "Your brother writes me with the news. He's a sweet old poet, that one. Bless him too. Bless him. But since you're standing in for me, I got to ask you, Liu." She stared him right in the eye and asked with full intensity, "Do you think my daughter should marry this furriner?"

"Thought not relevant, Ms. Clark Lincoln. Too late for thought."

He replied quickly and concisely. It was what he believed. He recited some lines from a poem he wrote once.

"There has been a coup in the Kingdom of Thought.
Love now reigns in the Idea Palace.
Fiery humeurs are burning books
And mindless joy beheads philosophy.

"First bloom of love, Mrs. Clark Lincoln, takes no quarter."

"Ain't it the truth!" said the old dowager, slapping her thigh.

"Clea"—Liu squatted down by his friend—"we must put back your shrine and burn some prayer strips to your mother and her ancestors."

"Yes," she said weakly. And he repaired to the far side of the bed and set about resurrecting the shrine.

"Clea," Liu said as he worked, "you will burn the first strip. It is your duty."

Zeus appeared on the doorsill on all fours, shirtless, shoeless, gasping from the effort, and leaned there like a sleeping elephant. He surveyed the scene, the destruction of his bedchamber, and was hanging back, waiting for Liu and Florie to finish their ministrations, to calm her so he might have a chance. Florie was tidying up the chaos around the dressing table and humming rhythmically, soothing the air. He listened, for he needed it too. He did not know what had happened to him. Things had gotten out of his hands, it seemed, and he was confused. Florie began to sing.

"Cry, my babies, cry, for death is in the kraal. He has taken the cow, but if we cry louder, we might hurt his ears and drive him away before he takes the calf. Cry, my babies, cry."

Florie wailed, a drumlike African wail that seared through the apartment and into the souls of Doron and the Seven Golden Lieutenants. They had gathered in the dining room for brandy, and through this grievous sound they suddenly glimpsed their long lost homes. And they wailed too, suddenly, spontaneously, their sorrow spilling out of them like the blood their clan members had shed on the veld. It was the earth funeral they never had, the one no tight-lipped Christian church could ever give to mourn their loss.

Florie wailed again, and Zeus, hearing his comrades answer her, would have wailed too, but the sound would not come. He was open-mouthed and open-tailed, on his hands and knees, straining to expiate a grief that would not show itself.

Soong, interested in the wail of the Lieutenants, squirreled out from under Clea's arm and trotted out of the bedroom, pausing only to sniff curiously at Zeus' armpit on the way. Clea, her security lost, sat up and leaned against the wall. For the first time she noticed Zeus. He seemed to be in pain. He was rubbing his hip as he sometimes did and on his face was the odd bewildered look he got when he realized an unwanted feeling was interfering with his state of lethe.

"Hip hurt from fucking on the floor?" she asked sweetly.

"No," he managed, slurring. "From crawling here on my hands and knees to beg your forgiveness."

"For what?" she asked and then, strangely, "not for having another woman?"

He raised his head and looked into her crowded eyes and took the chance she offered him. He shook his head no. She looked away nervously and watched Liu and Florie. Florie was still wailing, but softly now, almost finished with her tasks. Liu was gluing together tiny pieces of the shrine intently, ferociously, as if in truth religion and not poetry was the cornerstone of his life.

"Many things have happened today, Zeus," Clea murmured. "Each event engulfing the next in size, like a nest of boxes. I don't know where to start."

Zeus moved himself into a sitting position and gazed at her hopelessly. "Start with the largest. Isn't that how it works?"

"All right," she said. "In the largest box lies Jerry's vision. On September tenth of this year at ten P.M., Kennedy Airport will be nuked by atomic bomb blast. Undoubtedly, although Jerry is hazy on this point, this will set off a chain of events around the world which will signal its end as we know it. Those of us who are prepared for this blast, in my family, in my company, will be able to survive it. The rest will die."

Zeus nodded sadly. "Go on."

"The second box contains the half-eaten body of my mother. She has died, Zeus. This morning. Bless her strong, little soul. And may she be reborn into a fateless, mundane life on another, duller planet."

"Oh, Clea," Zeus muttered.

"Come, children." Liu said and got Clea to her feet and then roused Zeus, holding him under his arms, dragging him to the shrine. Zeus had tears in his eyes. His heart had spasmed at her loss. He was trying to tell her, but no sound was forthcoming. He was babbling preverbal anguish. Liu handed them both lit matches, and as they set fire to the bright red prayerstrips, Liu intoned an ancient Buddhist prayer. As the red strips flamed, Florie cried out to her own African ancestors for protection. The air was pungent with burning incense.

Clea resumed plaintively, "And in the smallest box, my Zeus, is our divorce. A smaller, less prophetic death but, in our scheme of things, no less important. When the day began this was the largest box, a ton of sadness, but as the day went by, this box was dwarfed till finally it is just a tiny speck albeit a black hole of a density few humans can withstand."

Liu set Zeus down on the bed, and he fell backwards and lay like a wrung-out rag. Clea lay down next to him.

"Ten Thousand Talents," Liu whispered in Clea's ear, "the Master is with you." He took hold of Florie, still wailing softly, and together, the two exiles left the room.

Soong reappeared at this moment and bounced onto the bed, entranced by the smoking prayer strips. The animal peered curiously at the ravaged couple and then, after batting at some hanging sequins on Clea's dress, settled down at their feet and dozed.

"I am going to build a bomb shelter in upstate New York and for the blast we can all go there."

Clea was whispering this, her frantic survival plans, staring at Zeus. Zeus was looking at the ceiling, lost in thought, trapped in thought.

"At first when I heard of the nuclear war, it seemed unnecessary to consider divorce, for the war would change everything anyway. But then, habits die so hard, Zeus, you can't even blast them to bits. So I think, well, when it's safe to come out of the bunker, we'll go our separate ways. It couldn't be more lonely than it is now, could it?" She asked this softly and painfully.

Zeus was trying to speak. He was trying to tell her about his mother. In his mind he was saying clearly, calmly: I shot her, baby. She winged me in the hip and I shot her right between the eyes. And, so, I lied to you, Clea, I wasn't, you know, an observer of fate. We didn't have that in common at all. But I did truly think it wouldn't matter . . . He snorted a little laugh out loud.

"Could it?" Clea asked again. He swallowed and said nothing. "Could it?" she asked again, and fell silent.

There was a smell in the room of burning incense and hot perfume and paper smoke. They lay motionless on the bed as on a bier in a Shakespeare play in rep. She, trying not to dwell on the picture of him with the puppet woman, decided to spasm it and confess about Butler. He, pursued by the blasted-to-bits face of his mother, tried to outrun it and grabbed Clea, melting into her, inhaling her with all the relief of a scuba diver who has run out of oxygen and only just surfaced.

"Zeus . . ." she tried to tell him, hugging him, whispering into his ear, "Zeus," but all she could manage was, "don't feel guilty."

He was weeping. His body shook all over her.

She drummed the muscles of his back with her fingers and tried again. But what came out was, "I don't care, Zeus. The woman was just a symptom."

He laughed then, a blast of laughter which sent Soong leaping off the bed in annoyance. It scared Clea and she pushed him back and looked in his face. Anguished poetic beauty stared back at her, slightly corrupted innocence and deep macho shame.

"Could something change?" she asked him. "Could you include me like you used to? Could you help me now, for example? I am grieving for my mother, for the strange fate that separated us for life, and I think if you could tell me something of how you felt when your mother died— It isn't the same, but it is similar. Picked off suddenly and oddly, no one truly to blame. In my case an armadillo's bone marrow, in yours a father's stray bullet. Of course, she was dead, your mother, in a second, whereas mine . . ."

She trailed off, for she could see that he was never going to help her. He was staring at her with some fear and awe, remembering once when she had intuited something precisely and Liu had remarked,

"Well, the Master will tell you that one of the Ten Thousand Talents is knowing without knowing."

"What?" she asked, probing now, determined. "What is it?"

Zeus struggled up off the bed and lurched around the room, sobbing and bringing down all the glass that had been spared on the dressing table, including her favorite perfume bottle. Down came the wedding picture again, the offering to his ancestors; only the little Buddhist shrine remained untouched. Soong, ears back, raced from the room. Zeus staggered through the bedroom door, unable to look back, unable to face her. To keep his balance, he clawed the walls with his nails and struggled up the corridor in the direction of his wailing Lieutenants.

Thirty-one

WHAT TIME IS IT," the director asked.

"Nine-seventeen. Forty-three minutes to Armageddon."

"Want to make the bet now?"

"Sure, fifty bucks"

"Done."

Out in the control truck on Forty-fifth Street, the director was switching cameras in preparation for the second act. The door to the truck was open. Ruth Ravenscroft was struggling up the steps, lugging two radiation suits. These she laid on the floor inside the door, nodding to Max, the producer, who was standing at the back of the truck. She returned and waited, arms outstretched as the hardhat from the moving van handed her another two. She closed the door with a metallic thud and turned toward the monitors.

On the TV screens were the eight diminished conical heaps. Roger's afternoon suns on the wane were waning deliciously now, orange fires burning up the aqua and violet planetary sky, playing off the yellow rope and the African red rust floor, reflecting off the sparkly objects: the goldfish bowl, the Siamese cat's eyes, the cockatoo's diamond collar. Closeup to long shot, closeup to long shot, the abstract Africascape was no longer littered. The shopping cart and the sled were piled high with objects, ready to be pulled off a stage that was fast becoming the promised Post–Blast void.

"Okay." The director lit a cigarette as he muttered into the head-phones, "Let's have a shot of the flying mechanism."

Onto the line of monitors popped a dim picture of the pulley ap-paratus descending center stage.

"Liu checked this?" the director asked. "Well, get him out there, pronto . . . thanks, Ruth," the director said over his shoulder. "You got one for yourself?"

"Oh, sure"—Ruth forced a smile—"I only wish I had a lead brief-case for my notes about the apes."

"Think they'll survive the thing?" The director was being humorous.

Ruth was not. "Listen, Al, if they can survive the poachers, they can survive anything."

"That's the way I feel about my kids," the director said.

"Two minutes," the A.D. barked. "Well, where the fuck is he?" The director snapped into the headphones as the door to the control truck opened and Ralph Dodson, aided by Liu, stumbled up the steps, drag-ging a suit behind him. "Never mind. He's here." The director turned. "Liu, have you checked the flying mechanism?"

"Now," Liu replied, and bowing slightly to Ralph, he rushed away.

"Ralph, howaya." The director glanced out of the corner of his eye at the A.D., who rolled his eyes.

"Hope you don't mind." Ralph waved.

"Hey, it's your money." The director sighed and leaned back in his chair. Tension upon tension. "This is an odd one, Ralph, but it's going good. It's running on nuclear energy." The director laughed heartily. "Right, Max?"

Ralph jumped. "Max, I didn't see you there."

"No. I was praying in the shadows," said the producer.

"You think she'll get through it?" Ralph, it was clear, was terrified.

"Awww—" Max made a gesture of derision at the thought of failure. "Ralph, I once had a star who experienced the Crucifixion every Friday. She worked it into the performance. You could hardly tell except for the stigmata. I'm not worrying about it. If she's right, we've got our suits. If not, she'll do the show as planned. We can't lose." Ralph did not reply. He dropped his suit on the pile by the door and wandered woodenly to the back of the truck. He had stopped by Zeus' dressing room, but Zeus could not be found. It did not augur well.

When Zeus had heard that Ralph Dodson was looking for him, he had fled from his dressing room into the darkened wings and huddled there, trying to calm himself down. The gassy smell of the Dragon tonic had got to him too and had driven him out. His heart was skipping beats and his legs were shaking uncontrollably. He tried to go over his lines but couldn't remember them. He attempted to dance out the choreography but he tripped on his feet. The rest of the second act after ten o'clock, after the so-called blast, was a complete blank, as if they had never written it. No scene would come to him, no familiar prop, no rehearsal memory. Clea's obsession had wiped it out, obliterated the imprint, pushed the erase button. Her obsession and his terror of the future. I could . . . his thought began and vanished . . . I've always wanted . . . it vanished again. Do I bloody exist, he asked himself, without the act, without the wife? What was it Doron held out to him—a dancing Julio Iglesias?

"Iglesias gets a hundred dollars a ticket," Doron said gleefully one afternoon. "A pretty boy's got it made in this country, boffin, don't worry."

"Zeus." Floric's velvet tone blanketed the darkness. "Zeus, my baby, you are in the blackness?"

Zeus bolted out of the wing and searched, petrified, for the tribal woman. She was behind him and clucked displeasedly at the tension in his body.

"Oh my Zeus, come here." She beckoned him into her arms and hugged him tight. "I am struck by sorrow for you. You are too tight, my baby, like an overstretched drum. You will not give a good sound."

He nodded and clung to her for dear life. Florie, Florie Amaxhosa come up out of Jo'burg and trekked her way to freedom. They had found her at the temple of Abu Simbel, wandering around staring at the statues of Ramses the Second.

"Who are the little ones?" she had asked Clea, referring to the small statues between Ramses' legs.

"His wife," Clea had replied, and Florie nodded in understanding.

"She was not so much smaller than he?"

"Oh no," said Clea.

"He saw her that way," said Florie.

"Right," Clea said.

They had passed the afternoon together and then, as the plane did not come, the night. Abu Simbel was a nonplace. When the Aswan Dam was built, the Egyptians had built a false hill, onto which they had raised the temple. Behind the great statues of Ramses the Second, underneath the dirt was a bizarre James Bond-like geodesic dome which kept the temple standing. Outside was the huge temple and a few shacks and an airstrip. Florie had made it there by felucca. She was, as she pointed out, happily clicking, almost to Cairo, almost at the end of her journey.

"I come from the Transkei, but I left from Johannesburg, which we call the Pool of Cihoshe. It means place of never return. Nothing and no one goes to Jo'burg ever returns to the bantustan. I, Florie Amaxhosa, I never am going back. I am out of there a year now, on my feet. Ach! To travel is to see!"

Zeus told her he was from Rhodesia, whispering it lest anyone hear. The sun was setting behind the great temple and they sat stranded above the Nile, trading stories of the dark continent.

"It is too bad!" she said of his homeland. "I was there. It is bleeding too."

"And did you walk all the way?" Clea had asked in awe and amazement. "Three thousand miles?"

"Well, there were some boat trips and some rides in combies and I rested along the way. But Africans can walk, eh, Zeus?"

"Ach, Florie—" his eyes flashed in agreement, "—once, I went with a farmer to Kenya to buy some cows from the Masai. We met with the chief who was selling them, but we couldn't agree on a price. 'Think about it,' says he, 'and meet me down the road at the dingo store.'

"So, we got in the combie and we drove seventy miles to the dingo store. He was there to meet us with the cows and he says, 'Have you reconsidered?' The price was too high for my friend, so the chief says 'Well, you think about it and meet me down the road at the impi station.'"

"So we drive seventy more miles and again he is already there to meet us with the cows. And we laughed for we were tired of driving and we paid the price. And when we got back to where we started, he was once again there to greet us with the cows we had bought. That day he had walked almost three hundred miles. He was grazing them, he said, for the long journey to a new home."

Florie laughed heartily. "It is too true," she said. "Zeus, in your country, I stayed one night with a wonderful woman, a medium called Mbuya Nehanda, do you know of her?"

Zeus was startled. Nehanda was one of the great spirit mediums of the guerrilla fighters. The war zone around his farm was called the Nehanda sector, after her. The old lady in her mid-eighties had inherited the spirit of the first Nehanda, who was hanged in 1898. The first Nehanda had predicted that her children would one day liberate the country. Through Mbuya Nehanda, the guerrillas spoke with the spirit of Nehanda and asked about strategy, place to cache arms, hideouts, and routes to take. For all Zeus knew, she might have ordered the attack on his farm.

"What was she like?" Clea had asked, unaware of the irony.

"Oh, she was busy, the old one. All day, she was blessing the fighters and their guns and she would tell them if they wished to win they must not touch women and must not eat certain types of relish and must not fight with each other. And if a snake was to cross their path, they must take another way."

"My dad would have bred snakes if he'd known that," said Zeus morosely.

Florie didn't get it and looked to Clea for clarification. "The guerrillas were responsible for the death of Zeus' mother," Clea said.

Florie was horrified. "No! Forgive me! I am sitting on live coals now. It is too bad!"

Zeus leaped to his feet and turned on the two women. "Clea," he hissed, "this is not yours to tell. Keep out of my business, mate!"

"I'm sorry." Clea was frightened, cowering. Florie got up and began to sway.

"Eh, Zeus! Eh, Zeus!" Florie was beckoning to him and making him smile.

"A *ntsomi*," he said to Clea. "She's going to do a *ntsomi* for us," and he pulled Clea off the promontory and down next to him to watch Florie perform an age-old Xhosa narrative poem.

"FLORIE," Zeus was begging like a child who's got to have a present "do a *ntsomi* for me. Do the one you did when I first met you. At Abu Simbel."

Florie grinned. "Ay, Zeus, it has been a day. Everyone is growing wings and I am asking the *benge* about the bombing. I could sleep the sleep of the dance if I had the chance."

"Ay, please, Florie," he said, flashing her his most seductive smile and sitting at her feet. He clutched at her dress and rubbed his cheek into it. "Please," he said again so sadly that Florie's heart was melted.

"Oohhhhhhh," Florie moaned softly, her eyelids fluttering like hummingbird wings over the whites of her eyes.

There in the wing, in a shaft of backstage light, she began to recite, moving, backwards and forwards in a pulsating rhythm, her little round body swaying and thumping, her little round head nodding and nodding.

"There was a young girl called Nongquase—uh *huh*
She went to the spirit medium and she said—uh *huh*
Vision men have come to me. They say—uh *huh*
Eat the crops. Do not sow. Kill the herds—uh *huh*
Uh *huh* uh *huh* uh *huh* uh *huh*."

Florie was rocking. Her eyeballs were rolling. Her voice was a deep and a guttural cry.

"The spirit medium was shocked—uh *huh*
She said—Tell me again—uh *huh*
And Nongquase said—They say—uh *huh*
Eat the crops. Do not sow. Kill the herds—uh *huh*
Uh *huh* uh *huh* uh *huh* uh *huh*."

Florie was pitching and heaving and sighing. Her head was turning and shaking denial.

"The spirit medium grew wings—uh *huh*
She cried—Why? Why? Why must we?—uh *huh*
And Nongquase said—They say—uh *huh*
So our dead ones will rise
And bring us a wind
To drive the whites
Back into the sea—uh *huh*
Uh *huh* uh *huh* uh *huh* uh *huh*."

Florie was smiling and swaying and humming. Her eyes were open and beaming with glee.

"Then our dead ones will be young again—uh *huh*
And our grain bins will overflow—uh *huh*
The cattle will eat till they're fat—uh *huh*
And so will we—uh *huh*
Uh *huh* uh *huh* uh *huh* uh *huh*."

Florie was bobbing and miming the running, as fast as the wind, as fast as the waves.

"The medium ran to the chiefs. She repeated the story—uh *huh*
One chief thought the prophecy madness—uh *huh*
Another—a crafty plan—uh *huh*
Foot of the baboon was muttered
And muttered, and muttered—uh *huh*
Uh *huh* uh *huh* uh *huh*
Till Sarili, the chief of the Xhosa, declared—uh *huh*
Uh *huh* uh *huh* uh *huh*."

Florie was reeling and reeling and nodding. Her voice rang out with the sound of a man.

"Set the date. Make the plans. Do it.—uh *huh*
Eat the crops. Do not sow. Kill the herds—uh *huh*
Uh *huh* uh *huh* uh *huh* uh *huh*."

Florie was keening and sobbing and moaning. Her tongue trilled the warning to one and to all.

"Oh, even the mighty have dreams of the pipe—
Watch out! Watch out!
Oh, yes, the mighty have dreams of the pipe—
Don't kid yourself.
Uh uh
Uh uh
Ohhhhhhhhhhhhhhhhhhh."

Florie screamed this anguished scream. Zeus was shivering and shaking with grief. She took the man's face in the palm of her hand and forced him to listen against his will.

> "Sarili did it—uh *huh*
> He really did it—uh *huh*
> Set the date. Made the plans. Gave the word.—Uh *huh*
> Uh *huh* uh *huh* uh *huh*
> Ate the crops. Did not sow. Killed the herds—uh *huh*
> Ate the crops. Did not sow. Killed the herds—uh *huh*
> Nothing left—uh *huh*
> Not a grain—uh *huh*
> Or a calf—uh *huh*
> But our dead ones never rose up—uh *huh*
> No, our ancestors never appeared—uh *huh*
> And the whites never saw the sea—*uh* uh
> The whites stayed dry—uh *huh*
> Uh *huh* uh *huh* uh *huh* uh *huh*
> OOhhhhhhhhhhhhhhhhhhhhhh."

Florie was tearing her clothing asunder. She fell on her knees with despair and with dread.

> "False prophecy, false hope!
> Sometimes—
> Hope kills, Badiabe—
> Listen! Sometimes—
> It does!
> Uh *huh* uh *huh* uh *huh* uh *huh*."

Florie bowed her head.

Zeus applauded wildly, as did several stagehands who had happened by during the recitation and were caught up in its passion.

"Ach it is the saddest story in Africa," cried Zeus, helping Florie to her feet.

"Africa has too many sad stories, Zeus," said Florie.

"Is it true?" asked one of the stagehands.

"Oh yes, it's true," replied Zeus. "In 1857 the Xhosa destroyed everything they had as a result of Nongquase's vision. Twenty thousand died of starvation. Thirty thousand left their land. Thirty thousand others disappeared. Died of shame, they say. The Xhosa committed mass suicide in hopes of driving away the whites. But they didn't realize the whites burrow under a country's skin. They lay their eggs of destruction, and even when a country gets them out, their eggs remain hidden to hatch and multiply and feed on the country's health. Eh, Florie?"

"I don't know. The whites are still in my country. Perhaps."

The stagehands looked uneasily at Zeus and rushed away to complete their work.

"What did the *benge* say, Florie?" asked Zeus when they were alone again in the dimly lit wing.

"The *bambata simi* is with her. The *gingo* is yet to come."

Zeus nodded. "And now"—Florie was bustling—"I must go back. You have made me late, white boy."

Zeus dropped to his knees and hugged her around the waist. He was remembering the moments after the *ntsomi* at Abu Simbel when Florie said,

"Well you know, I am a selfish woman. My mother is dead of disease. My father is dead in the mine. So I have waited until my grandmother is dead and then I have left the place behind. The madness of the Xhosa is in my blood. I too could kill myself from false hope. I have almost done so in a thousand ways. I could not do it anymore. I am saving my spirit from the Zim. I am walking to freedom."

"Where, where are you walking to?" asked Clea, captivated by the tribal lady, dying to know where she thought freedom lived.

"I don't know. When I feel it I will be there."

"Come with us, Florie," Zeus said then. "I too must leave Africa, Florie. The Zim have stolen my home."

"Ayy," chanted the tribal lady, "I know what you mean."

"Eh, Zeus." Florie gently removed his arms from around her waist and helped him to his feet. He caught her hand as she was moving to leave the wing, and she turned with some anger. The look on Zeus' face made her catch her breath.

Once, long ago in the bantustan, a young man was whipped by the police for a political offense. As the big black tongue licked off his flesh, the man's face contorted into an expression so raw that those who had been forced to watch, she, among them, felt that their souls had been dipped in mud. For weeks after, purification ceremonies were held, but it did no good. They had seen a spirit seared, the long shaft of life peeled and stinging and no spell or ritual could wash them clean or make their souls like new. There was something of this rawness in Zeus' face now, and she dropped her head and snapped her eyelids shut.

"Florie." His voice was choked and threatened. "That freedom that you sought, did you ever find it?"

"Once," she replied, eyes firmly closed, thinking back, "in a Zambian rain forest, I had a glimmer . . ." The face of an angry spider monkey came to mind and she smiled to herself. "And once when I got a credit card and I knew I could visit the bantustan any time, there was a joy . . ."

"I could go back, Florie." He was chattering now at top speed. "I could farm. You could come too. Zimbabwe is free now."

Florie sighed. "You could go again, Zeus. I could go again. We could never go back." And with that, she hurried out of the wing and across the stage to Clea's dressing room.

"ONE MINUTE." Charlie was running around backstage, crying out, Clea thought, like Paul Revere. "Clea." He pounded up to her. "Ready, doll?" he said cheerily.

"Sure, what time is it, Charlie?"

"Nine-thirty." She set her watch and smiled warmly.

"You got your suit now?" He blushed and pointed to Bobette's corner.

"Over there."

"Good." Clea threw her arms around him suddenly and hugged him close. "Thanks for everything, Charlie. So lovely to have known you. I thank you from the bottom of my heart."

Charlie patted her on the back and crushed her to him. "Clea, don't worry," he soothed. "It will be all right, I promise you. Nothing will hurt you. I won't let it."

She looked up at him and kissed his cheek and then broke the embrace. Reluctantly, he hurried away, glancing at her over his shoulder as she drifted toward the wing.

"ONE MINUTE!" Charlie continued his call as he traversed the back of the stage and appeared in the stage-left corridor. Zeus was leaning against the wall smoking a cigarette. On one side of him stood Doron. On the other was a skinny young woman with wild witchy black hair and wearing slanty fifties glasses. She was standing in a provocative manner, pelvis thrust out toward Zeus, and in her right hand, on a lead, she had two Shih tzu dogs, snappy, unpleasant creatures that snarled at him as he approached. Charlie took an instant dislike to her. There was something sleazy and untrustworthy about her, as if perhaps she'd sneaked into the theater without a pass. She was obviously after Zeus, and so it was with some familial loyalty and protectiveness that Charlie rushed over and said officiously to Doron,

"If Soong sees these dogs, there'll be hell to pay."

"Soong's in the bunker in upstate New York," Doron replied sardonically. "Soong's the only one of us who's truly safe." Zeus inhaled deeper on the cigarette. The young woman giggled. Charlie was angry.

"One minute, Zeus," he spat and hurried to check the props.

LIU RUSHED offstage and hustled Zeus away from the puppet woman and Doron and into the stage-left wing. Zeus stepped on his cigarette and then looked up and across to the stage-right wing, where Clea stood motionless, like a doll in a box ready to be given to some lucky little girl.

"Good fortune, Zeus," said Liu, and handed him his flask.

Zeus put the silver bottle to his lips. While he drank, he scrutinized his wife, as he had done so many times before so many acts, acts of performance, acts of love, acts of mercy, acts of revenge. She looked the same as she always did, even though she claimed she was about to die.

"Well," she once said, "performing is a kind of death, when it goes right."

"Thanks, Liu," he said, turning back to the Chinese man, returning the flask. "I suppose we're going to need good fortune. I'm bloody terrified." The two men walked onstage to where the flying mechanism was being lowered from the ceiling.

Clea opened her eyes and trotted nonchalantly onto the stage. In the background, Charlie was giving the call, "Thirty seconds. Places, please."

"Hi, kids," she said to Liu and Zeus and smiled. She was wearing black stirrup pants, her deer-hoof boots, and a white angora sweater that was covered with rhinestone sequins across the shoulders and around the neck. At her ears she wore giant rhinestone flowers, and her mane stuck out straight from her head and rode down her back to her waist like she was some kind of new feminine animal. Zeus was wearing black pants and a white shirt trimmed in black leather. Around his wrist he wore a black leather bracelet. Together they were very classy and very beautiful.

They stood side by side, center stage, while Liu hooked them to the flying mechanism. Charlie ran onstage now, and as soon as Liu was done, he said into the headphones,

"Okay, we're taking 'em up now."

And he waved to a stagehand in the wings. Clea and Zeus rose slowly off the stage. When they were about seven feet off the ground the mechanism stopped and they hung there in midair.

"Ten seconds," the A.D. said.

"Okay," the director said, "get 'em entwined, Charlie."

Charlie pointed at Clea and Zeus and they turned to each other, raised their legs, and threaded their bodies around each other, so intricately, it was hard to tell where one ended and the other began.

"They're beautiful," Ruth murmured.

"Yeah," said the director, "they're like rubber. Roger? Lights out, my man, let's raise the curtain, Joe." The six monitors went dark. The seventh was carrying the end of the commercials. "Five," the A.D. was saying, "four, three—"

"Christ," Clea whispered to Zeus, "it looks like the audience is full of Michelin men." Zeus opened an eye. Indeed, almost everyone in the house except for De Quincy, in his nineteenth-century kit, was clothed in a bulky white suit. "Theater of the Absurd," he replied.

"—two, one. Lights! Hit it! Okay, everybody, Act Two, we're off!" the director said, and lit up a cigarette.

On the monitors, Clea and Zeus appeared to be a giant ball which occasionally unraveled and revealed a limb. As they were constantly moving, the ball would change size and shape or move to the right or left. Roger's golden light of twin suns flashed off Clea's rhinestones and made prisms in the air. Clea and Zeus were, in fact, like a third sun, a black and white sun hanging against the purpling backdrop, or like one of those mirrored disco balls. After a few moments of creating the illusion, Clea spoke. "After you're first married . . ."

Her voice seemed to come from the center of the ball. Out in the house, the sound man was mixing wildly to keep her from sounding muffled.

". . . you're inseparable."

The audience laughed.

"You can't get enough of each other. You go everywhere together." Two legs shot out from the ball, entwined, then two arms, then returned. "You do everything together."

Their two heads suddenly appeared out of the ball side by side and looked to the right and then to the left as if they were watching a tennis game. The audience laughed. Her head disappeared into the ball. His head remained, he spoke, and her voice was heard. "You think and speak as one." The audience laughed.

His head merged back into the ball and the ball began to move again. It waxed and waned, shooting out loose ends and dragging them in, like a ragged comet orbiting across the sky.

From the depths of the ball now gushed an amalgamation of their voices, half his, half hers, an androgynous mingling of sentiment, a technical achievement in sound that some weeks ago had been effected in a studio in the West Forties.

"You were"—the voice trilled through the theater—"the sweetest thing I ever knew. I imprinted on you like a baby duck. The energy I got from loving you was superhuman."

At this, the ball began to expand. They bent their bodies and elongated them at the same time and the ball got bigger and bigger and looked as if it was going to explode. The audience ooed in amazement.

"There were times I felt so strong, I thought my heart would burst."

The percussionist smacked the cymbals and the ball shrank suddenly and hung motionless, a neat and glistening chiaroscuro orb.

"The first time we had a fight . . ."

The ball started to shrink and the audience gasped and went on gasping and finally broke into applause, for the effect was startling. The black and white human ball was getting tinier and tinier. In fact this was achieved by Zeus rolling himself into a fetal contortion and Clea wrapping her rubber-band body around him more and more tightly. She had on the back of her costume a special design of black and white that made it look as if it was Zeus' body when in actuality it was hers. It was one of their tricks which the audience adored. Now they were cheering and screaming,

"No! No! Come back! Come back!"

Within the ball, Zeus was muttering, "Hey, hey, I'm suffocating. It hurts."

Clea's body enveloped him like contact paper on a shelf. Her legs and back were so strong and so flexible that she was able to squeeze him almost senseless. This she was doing both for the optimum stage effect and to torture him. Her face was pressed into his stomach, but she managed to slide her right eye over to the end of its socket to steal a look at him. The eye was full of mischief and revenge. His left eye, forced as it was to stare at his navel, flapped open for a second and glared. He heard her laugh. The tape played on,

"I thought the world would end. I remember you said, 'Oh God, this is the first time you haven't been glad to see me and I . . .' "

The ball got smaller and smaller. The audience was screaming. Zeus sputtered, "I'm dying. Help me," and began to lose consciousness.

Clea relaxed her legs and expanded her body. She allowed the ball to grow and Zeus to emerge from the fetal position; she blew on his face and revived him.

"Okay?" she whispered as she pushed away from him. He was silent.

"I wept inside for the first loss of control. My cover was broken but I did try to warn you, that first date. I said, 'I'm odd, you know. For many reasons. I'm not all there.' But I had hid it well enough until then."

The ball shot off appendages again now, two entwined arms that unwound slowly from each other like vines following separate suns, one turned stage left, one stage right. Two heads popped up again, side by side, heads back to audience and then turned away, his to the right, hers to the left.

Zeus was himself again, woozy inside, but crisp in his attack, muttering, "Bitch," under his breath. Their top halves were apart now, their legs and groins were still entwined, like two hydras joined at the hip. The light flashed off Clea's earrings and shoulders and off the sweat on Zeus' face, making them angelic, a two-headed religious thing . . . There was a sting from the orchestra and down from the ceiling dangled objects that engaged each head and focused its attention.

On her side: a bunch of lit-up earth globes, a live Siamese cat, a handful of sparklers. On his side, a model of Hitler's great battleship *Tirpitz* and six midget X-craft submarines of the royal navy. Each head and pair of arms pursued its group of objects tentatively, hesitantly, turning back to the other head for encouragement and grounding, and an occasional kiss. But after a short period of uncertainty, the two torsos began to ignore each other and to play intently with the objects they'd been given.

The Siamese cat was wearing tie-on slippers with rubberized soles. These were the same color as the animal's seal points and could not be detected from the audience or on camera. These made it easier for Clea to juggle the creature. They gave it a bit more traction in her hands and took away the danger of being clawed. This was not her beloved Soong, but an animal actress with a résumé that spelled trouble: one cat food commercial after another, a career of downers and starvation. Never encouraged to leap and jump, to be a cat, the creature had an expression of tranquilized peevishness on its cross-eyed face and its fur and whiskers were too perfect and fluffy. They looked, as they in fact had been, shampooed and blown dry.

There was another Siamese cat Clea preferred to work with that did film and possessed a more jovial nature, but the creature was on location with a good-size role in the new Bertolucci picture and was unavailable.

"Marlena is in China playing the favorite pet of the last emperor," Doron announced at a casting meeting.

"How lucky for her," Clea said ominously. "She may well be out of range there. But unlucky for us. We'll have to get that bitch Pilar. Ah well. At least we know her trainer will make her a suit. You can bet on that."

And indeed her trainer did. An obese cat breeder from Long Island, the woman had only lately discovered, through the success of Pilar, that her cats could quite literally make her fortune. She had therefore set about a bizarre agenda of dressing and grooming her pets, as she put it, "like the stars they are," which made the animals both nervous and hard to handle. As the woman was hysterical about Pilar, Clea did not tell her about the blast, but gave her the same story she had given the audience, about volatile special effects. And indeed, the woman had made Pilar a tiny four-footed radiation suit which had arrived at the theater in the cat's steamer trunks earlier in the evening. Pilar herself arrived wearing a seal point-colored Chanel suit made by Chanel in Paris from sizes sent to the workshop by her trainer.

"The designers will do anything for money now: tub toys, cat litter pans," the trainer said. Pilar's ears were pierced like Bastet, the Egyptian cat goddess. The feline wore tiny gold hoop earrings which did look divine. "The earrings," the trainer explained proudly, "are from Zolotas in Athens, specially made."

Getting the trainer to allow Pilar to perform "nude," as she saw it, was not easy, but Clea finally won out. She argued that while being juggled Pilar might hang herself on her own jewelry and suggested the boots, which satisfied the trainer's urge to clothe her. This was why Pilar was now dangling over the stage unadorned except for the slippers, yowling like a banshee.

Roger brought the setting suns down now and pushed up several spots, which illuminated the upper torsos of the two players and the objects each was playing with.

Clea placed her palm under the dangling feet of the cat and batted her up into the air. Pilar's ears flattened against her head, but she stopped yowling and concentrated instead on falling on her feet, righting herself as she sailed upside down through the air, thus giving the illusion that she was doing somersaults. The audience cheered. Clea then added to the trick an earth globe and a sparkler, throwing the three from hand to hand in a figure eight.

In the light, the sad, dark beauty of Zeus' face, the glory of his bone structure, was accented as he turned his arms and head in profile to the audience. He cradled the model battleship in his hands and cried, "The *Tirpitz!* Sister ship of the *Bismarck.* Proudest battleship of the Third Reich. From Great Britain, round the North Cape into the White Sea, the Allied convoys chugged toward the Russian port of Archangel till Hitler gave his order. 'Crush their lifeline,' " Zeus screamed, " 'crush it with the *Tirpitz.*' "

The orchestra struck up the Korngold music now, a cruising, sneaking-through-dark-water tune, while Zeus shoved the *Tirpitz* across the pulley wires and the sound man brought up the slap of choppy sea waves.

"Silent and slimy like a great snake, the *Tirpitz* slithered through the North Atlantic to its hidden naval anchorage at Altenfiord along the ragged coastline of occupied Norway. There she lurked, an eerie predatrix, striking at the vital artery between the Allies and the Russians on the Eastern Front. Soon, few convoys were reaching Archangel."

Clea was juggling four earth globes, two sparklers, and the Siamese cat. She and Zeus were hanging in the air, facing the audience, their inner legs still entwined but untwining now as she batted her globes and he followed his battle. The audience went back and forth, ooing and ahhing at each performance, sometimes at both.

On Clea's side, it was all visual grace and beauty, save for an occasional yelp from Pilar as she defied gravity and sailed through the air. On Zeus' side, it was militaristic flash, metallic sound and fury, the bombarding echoes of male history.

"Without the vital convoys, the Russian war effort would be smashed. Something had to be done."

There was a sting of strings and suddenly there appeared at the far end of Zeus' stage, near the wing, three tiny submarines dangling from the flying mechanism. Roger shot them with a spot.

"Look!" Zeus cried out, and pointed. "The secret weapon of the British Admiralty, the X-craft midget submarines, designed to hold four men, to avoid minefields, to slink stealthily into a battleship's lair, to do the job that bombers couldn't do, to annihilate the *Tirpitz*. A plan was made."

Liu's pi-pa was heard now, a spooky, creeping plaint that set the tone for secrecy. Clea and Zeus both glanced into the orchestra pit and saw him there stroking his only lover, making her wail.

"Six X-craft subs steamed toward the guarded anchorage at Altenfiord and lay their charges beneath the *Tirpitz*. But on passage through the North Atlantic, misfortune ruled: two subs were lost and one developed defects. Now there were only three."

Down from the ceiling dropped a circlet of rubber cliffs and rocks which formed a fiord round the *Tirpitz*, leaving one skinny channel open to the North Sea. Zeus detached himself completely from Clea and flew behind the *Tirpitz* to where the midget subs were hanging in a line. He was now over by the stage-right wing.

Clea, freed of her entanglement, turned her body so she faced up-stage. She curled into a fetal position and began to juggle with her feet.

On cue, the fishbowl dropped down from the ceiling and the audience groaned. Pilar's eyes lit up. She fixated on the fish whenever she passed them. Clea began to foot-roll the fishbowl without spilling the water. The audience ooed.

Zeus continued guiding the first of the little subs with his hands as he spoke.

"The X6 was the first to strike. It dove at the entrance to Altenfiord and followed a German supply boat through the torpedo net into the *Tirpitz'* lair. But then disaster!"

Orchestra joined pi-pa in horror.

"While maneuvering into position to lay its deathly charges, the X6 crashed into a rock. The tiny craft was catapulted to the surface. Onboard the *Tirpitz*, the sub was sighted."

An alarm, a piercing wa-wa like that of arriving Gestapo, rang out through the theater. Zeus grabbed the tiny sub and plunged it beneath the battleship.

"Undaunted," he cried, "the X6 dived again and, right beneath gorgon's mighty hull, planted its charges. But there was no escape. The X6 surfaced now and her courageous crew abandoned ship. The men were hauled aboard the *Tirpitz* and the X6 sank to a watery grave."

When the alarm went off, Pilar's tail puffed up like a pine tree and a fur ridge rose on her back. It happened in rhythm, and the audience laughed. The cat, terrified, scuttled in the air and made as if to run. With her foot, Clea gently brought the animal within reach and petted her, while never losing the motion of the juggle. It was extraordinary. Clea was twirling and spinning four earth globes, two sparklers, the Siamese cat, and a fishbowl containing two goldfish.

She was bouncing in space counting the count. Rather than seeing, her eyes were counting too. She heard nothing except the alarm and only when Pilar passed right by her nose, a spitting puffball, did she realize something spontaneous had occurred. She smiled, never losing the count. She was not aware of Zeus or his story or that she petted the cat, she was that deep into the physical flow. World War Three couldn't have gotten her attention. Zeus went on.

"The second midget sub, the X7, snapped in the torpedo net. At a depth of seventy-five feet, the commander struggled with his tiny craft and finally got it free. It dove beneath *Tirpitz* and laid its charges. Then, as it tried to escape, once more it floundered in the nets."

Zeus, as if underwater, was trying desperately to free the sub. His was a swimming battle with death. He plunged and twisted in the air, doing a crazy dance of disentanglement. His tortured movements kept the time of Clea's juggling, complementing it, in spite of the difference of purpose.

"The explosives were on a time fuse and time was running out."

Zeus lashed this way and that with the tiny sub, trying to free it from the invisible net. Inside himself, he filled with mounting terror. Some of it was fear of the night ahead, and some of it was age-old fear, stored in his cells, waiting to be tapped. That moment before the attack on his farm spewed out from a dormant brainstem. That past combined with present gripped his body and made it dance. He was the tiny sub, trapped in the torpedo net, awaiting the concussion of four tons of explosives, counting the minutes till the blast.

Clea was counting beats, and on the tenth, she slipped onto the soles of her feet a string of firecrackers that had been lit by a stagehand and dropped by pulley. There was so much going on around her that few if any noticed the tiny maneuver she made to detach the firecrackers and place them on her feet.

Pilar had gotten into the juggling game and was posing in midair now like a trooper. Whenever she came near the goldfish bowl, she stuck out her paw and tried to dip it in the water. It was very funny, and though some felt for the goldfish, most understood they were symbolic of the lowest rung on the cat-eat-fish ladder that Clea and Zeus had climbed.

Suddenly there was a huge explosion. The firecrackers exploded.

The stage lights flashed. The Korngold music raged. Pilar puffed up and spat. The fish leaped in the bowl. The sound of crashing waves rose and fell. Zeus cried out in anguish.

"Thirty minutes after the charges had been laid, explosions rocked the forty-two-thousand-ton *Tirpitz!* The great crash thundered down the fiord, echoing like a reverb in hell. The mighty battleship, sister to the *Bismarck*, listed to one side, her great hull torn to shreds below the waterline. Oil from her fuel tanks eddied like blood on the water's surface. On the bridge of the *Tirpitz*, hysteria reigned."

The tiny sub jerked from underwater, where Zeus held it up to the surface, level with the battleship.

"Underwater shock waves blasted the X7 to the surface. German gunners hurled grenades and peppered the tiny sub with bullets."

Firecrackers were going off all around the juggling earth globes. Pilar was like a cartoon cat, head snapping around at each crack, running in the air, still trying to grab the fish, which were leaping from the bowl.

"The X7 had to be scuttled. Only two of the four-man crew escaped with their lives. The third sub, the X5, entered the fiord after the explosion. She never had a chance. The Germans scored a direct hit and she was lost."

Clea now had the four earth globes, lit up and shining, balancing in a line. Pilar and the goldfish bowl were right in the middle, side by side. As the last firecracker exploded and sputtered, Pilar grabbed a goldfish in her paw and put it in her mouth.

The lights came down. The sparklers sparkled. A spot lit the listing *Tirpitz* and cast a sheen over Zeus' agonized face. The orchestra built to a crescendo of pure Korngold tragedy, and Pilar ate the fish, first biting it in half so that fish guts and blood were visible on her fur. The audience gasped and then all went quiet.

Clea righted herself and ceased juggling. The globes, sparklers, cat, and fishbowl did not fall, but hung limply on the flying wires, as did the battleship, the rubber rocks, and the three midget subs. She and Zeus were lowered to the stage and landed with a thud.

"God," Clea and Zeus spoke simultaneously to each other, very excited, very proud, "did you see that, honey? Did you see what I just did?"

They stared at each other for a beat, both looking blank, then shook their heads, a little bored. "No. What?" They asked each other politely, not really interested to know.

"Blackout!" spat Roger.

"Roll commercial," barked the director. "That was an Oscar winner for Pilar, don't you think? What time is it?" he asked the A.D.

"Nine-forty," the A.D. replied.

Everybody in the control truck looked down at their watches and nodded.

"Nine-forty," the director repeated.

Thirty-two

CLEA knew something was wrong when Zeus met her at the elevator door. He looked too calm. In him, the absence of intensity was chilling. As he carried her bags into the apartment and dropped them in the vestibule, she noticed that the date of the end of the world was gone from the wall. Someone had papered over it with a white damask that very nearly matched. She wondered what the paper hangers had been told. The Manson girls came by for a visit! Or, his wife's gone mad. Or, Clea, you know, of Clea and Zeus, is virtually starkers. Or, more likely, nothing. In their tax bracket, you never had to explain any oddity, anything at all.

"Clea," Zeus said, taking her hand, leading her into the rarely used living room, sitting her down on the velvet sofa but remaining standing himself, in case, she could see, he had to run, "Butler's dead. I'm sorry, baby."

"Oh, oh," she cried out loud, each exclamation accompanied by a little shake of anguish, as if trying to throw off a cloak of hopelessness that had suddenly settled over her. She raised her eyes to Zeus. He looked like a man who's underrehearsed and knows there are critics out front. "How?" she asked.

"Right, well . . ."

He began it like a college professor, like it was a historical subject. He might have had a pointer in his hand as he paced around the room trying to minimize the perversity.

"It seems Butler decided to have a party. He made a party list and, through a friend who works at a dental equipment rental, ordered two tanks of nitrous oxide, so everyone could do balloons."

Clea caught the professor's eye and they both began to smile. He went on.

"Due to the fact that the friend was going on vacation and would be away the week of the party, he sent the tanks over to Butler's early."

Clea closed her eyes and shook her head slowly, a hot flash of hilarity rising through her system.

"It seems that Bill decided to break one open and try it out. It seems he forgot about the party, or at least to invite anyone else. They found him, nitrous mask strapped to his face, smiling, quite dead, the party list and invitations on the couch next to him."

Clea patted the couch seat next to her and acted, for a moment, Billy's death. She leaned back, felt the streaming hollow of nitrous gas, and relaxed into nothingness. She brought her hands up and pushed a spectral mask into her face. She inhaled.

"Was I invited?" she asked, pulling out of it.

"Yes," Zeus replied.

"Were you?"

"Yes," he said. "The police rang us because we were both on the party list. You missed all the excitement, really. It's done wonders for our prestige."

"Ohhh," she murmured, remembering who they were, that there were some bastions they had to defend. "Have they dropped the show, then? Can I, please God, build my bunker and be in it when the bomb drops instead of on national television?"

"No," Zeus snarled. "We are so lovable, the network forgave us instantly."

"Zeus," she began and would have told him about the limo ride had not an old scene popped into her mind that tapped her grief and struck her mute.

She was seventeen and standing at the bar in the R&R club in Taipei. The year was '68, the club was filled with Chinese bar girls and American soldiers on leave from Vietnam.

At the end of her day, telling stories in teahouses, she would wander to the R&R club to smoke some hash and wallow in its dark, red-lit opium den cum honky tonk atmosphere. She was fascinated by American boys. She had lived in China so long that they seemed to her like luxury imports, in the same category as fresh cow's milk and Dylan albums.

She would stand at the bar with the doll-faced, doll-bodied flower-drum girls and together they would make a study of these soldiers on leave from Vietnam.

"They either laughing or crying," said May Ling one evening. At the R&R, the free drinks at happy hour were for military men to lure shy soldiers into the web.

"That could be the war," Clea ventured.

"They good in the bed but afterwards always cry," said Jade Flower.

"Really?" asked Clea. "*Post coitum, omnis anthropus est* assholes. Cicero's wife said that." The girls laughed.

"One said, 'I give you hot meat injection.' What is, Clea?" Winter's Hope looked at her seriously.

"I think it means he wants to penetrate you, Hope. The hot meat is because it's like a big sausage."

The girls were confused. "Why is he calling his privates meat?" asked May.

"I don't know. It's unusual. Usually women are meat or fish. It's rare men call themselves meat. Perhaps it has something to do with the war. Watch out, girls, General Clark Lincoln says the war has driven them nuts."

"No, no, no." Clea turned and a young man with blond hair and wire-rim glasses, dressed in army fatigues, was mumbling, shaking his head. He looked smart as a whip and drunk as a skunk.

"No," he said. "The war has not driven us nuts; it's made men of us. I know. I used to be an asshole before I went to Vietnam, now I'm a napalm reader."

Clea glanced sideways at the girls. "A napalm reader?"

Rather stiffly, the soldier lit up a Camel. He was like a highly inebriated, angelic toddler.

"Yup," he said, fixing her with a magnified eye, "I read the future in napalm burns. If you've been torched on the arm, you'll never carry your baby normally. On the leg, you'll never dance at your daughter's wedding. And so on."

"What's your name?" Clea asked.

"William Butler," he replied proudly. "I am nineteen. I went to Andover. And I'm here because I got my draft counselor's daughter pregnant and my draft board refused to believe I had homosexual tendencies. I have committed no specific atrocity. I hide when the going gets rough. In twenty years' time, I should have no problem running for senator."

"Be careful," Winter's Hope whispered in Clea's ear. Madam Wu had appeared and was shooing the girls off the bar into the lounge. "Be careful. This one not live long."

"Clea?" Zeus asked. He was sitting now in an armchair next to the couch, staring at her. "What?"

"A flower-drum girl once told me that Butler wouldn't live long. I thought she was talking about the Vietnam War. Thirty-five seems like a long time when you're eighteen. Just like our parents said. Is there any difference between us and our parents, Zeus?"

Zeus thought of his father, now living in a pondokkie in the worker's kraal, eating mealie pap, dancing and laughing in the early evenings after the cows had come in and the tobacco was hung and graded. He was trying desperately, the old man, to become one of those he tried to destroy. Or maybe it was simpler; he was hoping to feel any feeling as deeply as a black would feel it. Too many years of seeing the laughter shake their souls, of seeing them light up like lanterns in spite of their plight. He was envious, that's what it was, and maybe horny.

"Not much," Zeus replied.

Clea began to sob. She sank into the down cushion of the rarely used sofa and wept for her childhood friend. That Butler had deflowered her was one thing, an important thing to be sure. But far more important was his association with all the faraway places of her Chinese youth. Their bond of place and time was so precious that the pain of admitting that he was dead, and possibly out of choice, caused her to have an out-of-body experience. Her personality disintegrated in one massive sob and her spirit swept out of her mouth and hovered above the living room scene.

Her spirit gazed down at her body slumped and wetting itself with grief and said in the sweet voice of Glinda, the Good Witch of the South, "Oh my Clea, know that it is your mother you weep for, as well as for him." On the couch, her head nodded in agreement, for there was a link between Butler and her mother and that link was China.

The Chinese house with its pagoda roofs to which she and the General escaped after her mother got leprosy. The years of hot, longing afternoons when she lay in her cotton shorts and shirt, hair matted behind her head, sprawled in the grass of the back tea garden. The little pool with its lily pads and tiny bridge, the fat, droopy tropical trees, and in the corner, near the bamboo grove, the concrete bomb shelter, built by the Kuomintang, where she played with her vanished mother.

Inside the concrete tube were spiders and lizards, which she swept away with an odd Chinese brush. Then she and Tiny Tears would crawl inside and they would begin it: "Mom, there's armadillos here. I have seen them on the roads running in front of the cars. But we don't touch them. Not anymore. Don't worry. Is lunch ready? It is? Thank you, Mom!" And she and Tiny would pretend to eat dead leaves and berries until the sing-song call of the Chinese amah flushed them from their lair and brought them in.

And years later, after loving Butler in her room that smelled of teak and camphor and seven kinds of tea, strolling with him in the garden, stopping by the shelter, and his laughter when he says, "Funny they thought this dinky thing could protect a person from bombs. They were so fucking ignorant about what they'd wrought." Defensively, she answers, "It could protect from flying glass or falling trees."

"Just barely. Just fucking barely."

"I remember when we first met," she heard Zeus say. She turned her head and tried to focus on him. Tears were pouring from her eyes now. She felt as if she were leaking love, old deep love, as if inside her was an ancient jug that had cracked and was losing its precious childhood contents. Zeus was bending over two cups of steaming tea, sprinkling in each a few drops from a laudanum bottle.

"It was in our dressing room at the Hammersmith Odeon," he continued in his gentle, almost British voice. "He didn't like me much."

Zeus handed her the cup of tea. She sipped it, and then discarded the saucer, and held the hot cup near to her chest as if with its steam it might warm her ice cold heart.

"It wasn't that," she replied in a choked growl. "He was a bit jealous and he thought . . ."

"What?" Zeus asked finally, after a pause.

"That you were too much like my father."

Zeus chuckled. "Yah, well, he was nothing like your father, then."

"Oh, no."

General Clark Lincoln, the rock on which she built her church, was a young man when she and he arrived in China, younger than she was now. The slim, handsome U.S.A.F. officer, hero of the Second World War, with his crystal-blue eyes and his flashy smile and his purring Texan drawl, sat opposite her at the teakwood dining table, looking perplexed. It was a few weeks after they'd arrived and set up in their quarters. It was the beginning of the rainy season and the rain beat on the roof and on the screened porch like a frantic drum message from heaven. The lights had gone out, so they sat across from each other in candlelight, a little girl of six and a good-looking American soldier. She had just told him that Tiny Tears was missing, lost on the long flight from Texas.

"I think I had her in Japan or maybe Guam. I don't remember. She's gone, that's all."

"I'll look into it, honey," he said, frowning. "Damn. We've already had a casualty. We've got to be more careful, you and me. Can't lose any of our troops right now. We're in a vulnerable position."

The Chinese cook padded into the room and carefully removed the soup. They both smiled humbly, unused to being served.

"We've only got each other now, Clea," her father said seriously. "We each got to take care of ourselves, now, when we're not together. Be aware of where we are, who we're with, what we're doin'. Besides that, we can make sure of one thing, that we have dinner together every night and see how it's going."

And they had, over the years, even if, as often happened, he had diplomatic dinners or wars to attend. When she found the acrobatic school, she told him over dinner. She was eight and sitting opposite him and explaining it. She was wandering, she told him, down a skinny little alley at the end of which two pigs and a scraggly cat were eating sewage when she came upon a most beautiful door. It was carved in the shape of a flower vase. The door or base part of the vase was an oval of ancient dark wood. Around it was a carved stone rim which led up over the oval door, forming the neck of the vase. In the neck was a carved stone peony. It was centuries old, this graceful door, even a child could see that, she told him proudly. She stood in the alley, rain pouring down, staring at the door, sniffing the scent of the dark wood, panting to know where it led, when it opened with a creak. She stepped through it, and found herself in a courtyard before an ancient Chinese house, bright red in color, with yellow dragons guarding each pagoda of the roof. A Chinese man in yellow silk robes appeared suddenly. His hands were long and slender and the nails on his pinky fingers extended for several inches and then curled inward like claws. He smiled and bowed, did three back flips very suddenly, and then asked,

"Who are you?"

"Clea," she replied. "From Nan Lu," giving her address.

"This is the Flower Door Acrobatic School," he said, nodding, "and I am Liu Ah To, the Master. You have come to enroll?"

"Yes," she said, sure, suddenly, of something powerful crystallizing in her chest, of something that she must have, better than a new doll, better than her own dog, equal, almost, to a mother. "But, of course, I must ask my father."

The Master scratched his temple with his pinky nail. "Of course," he replied.

Her father looked a bit pained.

"Is something wrong?" Clea asked.

"No, honey. I'd just like to meet this fella, that's all." She stared at her father through the flicker of the candle.

"It's just I'd have more to do while you're flying."

"Yeah," her father said, forcing a smile. "Yeah. That does make sense."

It was the same look of momentary sadness that flickered across her father's face the night she first made love to Butler and he stayed to dinner. By this time, her father was a general and commuting back and forth to Vietnam. "How are you getting along?" the General asked Butler across the table. Butler, always a little drunk, always sarcastic, replied,

"Well, sir, if I could only get seriously wounded—I stand, literally, right out in the open during firefights. I don't take a gun. I yell,

'Shoot me, for God's sake, get it over with,' and nothing ever happens. Back home, I could get beat up in any bar, in Vietnam, I can't even get a head wound."

Clea stifled a giggle. The General stared at him somberly. Billy went on.

"In spite of this behavior, sir, I can't even get a psychiatric discharge. No, you know who gets a Medevac? A guy in our platoon who *fucked a dead girl!*"

The General got angry. Clea gasped in shock.

"Pardon my Vietnamese," Butler said, "but there this poor fucker was, after a battle, screwing this lifeless thing, its eyes rolled back in mock ecstasy. Anyone who had to witness that should have been Medevac'd too. And I know, sir,"—Butler picked up the General's anger and threw it back at him—"that while this is going on, my buddies back home are going to rock concerts, taking acid, and fucking live, warm girls indiscriminately on auditorium floors, and that knowledge, sir, is the only thing that has ever made me want to kill."

There was a silence around the table. Clea glanced at her father and saw a look of sadness flee across his eyes. It was pursued by a steely indomitable expression that sat itself down on his craggy face and stayed there for the rest of the meal. He stared at Butler, and then, after a time, he said in a fatherly tone, "Too bad, Butler." And then, after a little time more, in a tone of such chilling condescension and visceral disgust that Butler never quite wanted to meet him again, the General reiterated, "Too fucking bad."

THE AFTERNOON light was waning. Long spears of sunlight crisscrossed the rarely used living room and stuck in the walls at odd angles. For a while, Clea and Zeus were in a shadow and then a cloud moved and Clea was shot between the eyes by a ray of light so fierce, it obliterated her vision. She felt warm and gold and fuzzy-edged, and obliged somehow to perform now the great spot was actually on her.

"Oh God," she murmured, "the light is so beautiful. Light has sustained me through so much."

"Yes," said Zeus in the blackness beyond her. He was thinking of the light after the battle, the dark gold African sunlight which caressed, with its incongruous splendor, the cold blasted body of his mother. The light did not accept the carnage, did not endorse its tragic aspect, but instead lit the scene as if it were a festival.

"It's like the bloody Creation today," Zeus remembered saying, madly, as he dragged the bodies of his servants into the shade.

"She winged you, Zeus," he heard his father say, and he looked down to see the blood running from his hip, its color turned to black by some science change of the hot sunlight.

Clea spoke again. She looked like an alien in a Hollywood movie, wildly overlit, eyes almost closed, face upturned toward the home planet.

"Just now, in Texas, after I hired the light plane and we were flying over the armadillo brush of the old farm, I leaned out the open door, clinging with one hand to a piece of interior fusillage, the other hand clutching the strange soft dust that was my mother. I thrust my fist out into the warm air and let the ashes go and they eddied into a circular wind current. And the light, the light was so goddamn beautiful, so hot and yellow and steamy sweet on the armadillo brush, like so many days when she rooted through the undergrowth in search of her quarry, never, never losing her focus though the sun beat down on her like a bully."

"That's part of it, Clea, the beating you have to take," her mother said once, "the way the brush cuts your arms and the sun burns your skin."

It was night. They were sitting on the porch of the nineteenth-century house that was the leprosarium. The grounds, unvisited, unchanged since the house was built and willed to the lepers, were stunning and fragrant. The old Hawaii, the Hawaii of the settlers and the innocent conch eaters, persisted here in this shunned place. The long low porch was ringed with strings of fairy lights, tiny and deep ocher. The sound of the sea at the end of the lawn was rhythmic and soothing. Palm trees fanned lethargically in the breeze. The air smelled of orchids and frangipani all mixed up, like a matron over-doused in perfumes.

It was the last time she saw her mother, six months before she died. Mrs. Clark Lincoln had gone blind. Her eyes, perpetually open, were opaque white like an old dog's. Her face had collapsed inward. Her body, though tanned as a coffee bean, had lost its hands and feet and her limbs ended now in neat little balls. She sat most of the time, her legs twisted under her like a sadhu's, and gestured with her batonlike limbs as if conducting an orchestra. Her hair, now white, hung in a braid down her back. She wore her fringed jacket. Her life force was as strong as always, fairly erupting out of her velvet skin.

"By the time you've hunted down the critter and bagged him"— Mrs. Clark Lincoln let out a whoop through her collapsed mouth— "you've been through something so alive! Oh, baby!" her mother continued, whooping again, her two remaining teeth gleaming in the fairy light, "what a feeling!"

The night hummed with her energy for a moment, then calmed. "Do you know that feeling, baby?" she asked softly, exaltedly.

Clea stared at the little brown nut of a creature perched on the rattan sofa next to her. The pleasure in her mother's face moved her so deeply she thought she would die. "Yes," she managed to get out of her strangling throat in a somewhat normal tone, turning her thoughts to the first time in the Moon Court when she was twelve and suddenly was juggling sixteen plates on sticks, the ring of glory in her ears, her mind and body meshed and sated, not existing, not existing, just a living shriek of life. "Yes," she repeated, turning to her mother, flinging out her hands and doing something that she hadn't done for thirty years: running her fingers up and down her mother's bony arms, touching the leprous body, enfolding, lifting it off the rattan cushion onto her lap and crushing it to her breast as she once crushed Tiny Tears in its absence. Her mother stiffened her neck and flailed for a moment, then laid her head on Clea's shoulder and sighed. "Yes, Mama." Her lips touched her mother's ear as she whispered to her mother's soul, "I know it very well."

For a long time, Clea and Zeus sat in silence. The sun sank below the windows. The fringes of the rarely used living room glowed with gold wisps as the afternoon wore on. Occasionally, the phone would ring then stop as someone would answer it in another wing. It had a strange quality to it, this afternoon of motionless mourning. They felt as if they were ill and in a foreign land.

Clea looked over at Zeus. He was staring out the window, deep in himself, his eyes glistening with poetic conscience. But they always did. Even if he was contemplating buying paper napkins, he looked to be mourning the death of the human race. She knew this now, just as he knew that beneath her dolly exterior lurked a raging little animal that bit and clawed and threw itself around rooms, causing destruction.

She married Zeus because she had seen God in him onstage. It was because she had never seen God in her husband offstage that, ten years later, she was divorcing him.

"Zeus?" she asked. He was holding his head in his hands now in a posture of male misery. "What is it?"

He did not react.

"What is it?" Louder, more insistent. He shook his head, shook her away.

She sat up, looked around nervously, and reached for her purse. Back to business, her mind was repeating, back to business. Get back to business. Goodbye, Mom. Goodbye, Billy. Have a nice death. I see you in Elysian fields with gods and muses. I hope it's that way. I hope so. I might be there soon, or not. But I won't see you here anymore. Not on earth, no. NO. She rifled through her purse. Zeus looked up at her.

"They won't be here anymore, Zeus," she said to him. "Not anymore."

She removed some papers from her purse, and unfolded them. Pushing the laudanum bottle and the teacups to one side, she spread the papers on the coffee table. Then she leaned over and snapped on the table lamp.

Frantically she and Zeus shielded their eyes. A few moments passed before they could see. Zeus squinted at the papers on the table. They were blueprints.

"The bunker," Clea said, "the biosphere bunker. Here's my plan." She pointed to some little boxes in the drawing. "Here's the atomic garden: tomatoes, lettuce, beans, all fresh vegetables will grow here, including your favorite, brussels sprouts." She smiled at him. "You see, I didn't forget you in the planning." He nodded.

"Okay—here's the irrigation system. I'd like a few flowers to keep us cheerful but I can't promise, you know, without sun."

Zeus sat back and stared at his wife. He felt like an old man in a glass booth on trial for war crimes committed in his youth.

"And here's the surprise!" Clea switched one blueprint for another. "Your own wing! Here's the boat pond for your boats. And something you've wanted for a long time—your own sauna!" She beamed at him triumphantly.

"A sauna?" he said, smiling in spite of himself, picturing himself sweating in a wooden box while outside the world was being consumed in a firestorm.

"A sauna?" he asked again, not knowing what to say, then finally, saying the polite thing, the mindless thing: "Won't that be awfully expensive?"

"Don't worry about that." Clea smiled at him. "I'm spending everything I have on this. Money will be worthless after the blast."

Thirty-three

ONCE she had been unhooked from the flying mechanism, Clea rushed off, stage right, and stood while Bobette redressed her for the cones' scene. Off came the angora sweater and the black pants. On came the rhinestone-studded cocktail dress and, of course, the little boots.

"Oh, that was lovely, Clea!" Bobette was chattering nervously.

Clea powdered the sweat off her face, reapplied her rouge, and touched up her mane. Bobette's fear, well placed though it was, irritated her.

"Thanks, dear," she said with a condescension that she felt was expected of her.

Bobette cringed. "I have the suits here." She pointed. "Hanging here. See—I have them." It was an offering of solidarity.

Clea patted her shoulder. "Thank you, Bobette. I appreciate it." Clea pushed her face muscles into a smile. She knew she had achieved one when the corners of her eyes were squeezed and warm. She no longer trusted her mouth to lead. It would only have grimaced.

She trotted into the stage-right wing and waited. It was odd that the truckers had known Billy Butler, odd that it had come up at this time. Perhaps his spirit was hanging around, waiting for the big one, confident he had nothing now to lose.

The last time she saw Butler was in front of the Sky Bookshop on East Fiftieth Street. She had gone there to get *Survive* magazine and whatever other books on nuclear war and its aftermath they were currently stocking. It was a strange shop, militaristic and macho, devoted to war in its every permutation. Her father had introduced it to her once when he was in town and they went to the Plaza for tea. Afterwards he had walked her to Fiftieth Street and said suddenly, "I must check something," and led her up the stairs of the small building into this inn of male happiness.

It was the period of the Falklands War and on the wall was a map of naval encounters, victories, and losses that was changed every day as the war progressed. Her father checked the map and jotted down some notes.

"What are you doing?" she asked.

Her father replied mysteriously, as always, "Some stuff with NATO."

"I saw some footage of some British sailors after they'd been hit with an Exocet missile." She stood with her father and looked at the map. "They had the fear of God in their eyes. The same look I saw in the firemen who had just come off the twenty-fifth floor of a plastic-lined skyscraper after it had imploded. In both, their fear was tinged with surprise. The heat was more terrible than they thought possible. They could never have imagined it would be so bad."

"That's always the way it is with war," her father said philosophically. "War is like childbirth, Clea. If men could remember the pain of the labor involved, they'd never have another one."

She bought the books, said goodbye to her father, and hurried down to the street, where she ran into Butler, who was emerging from a cab with a beautiful blond girl of about eighteen. One of the odd things about the Sky Bookshop was its situation above the studio of a well-known photographer of debutantes and socialites. As you emerged from the macho world, you fell into soft lens of the land of flawless women. Rich, blond, and oblivious, they stared at you over their shoulders in posed color photos that trumpeted their ignorance of tanks and planes and guts and sweat and anything that smacked of men. The blond preppy girl rushed by her into the studio, leaving her with Butler. He was slightly drunk, slightly askew.

"Ah," he said smiling, "perfect. I have something funny to tell you."

"What? The limo driver's blackmailing you?"

"No. I went down to Washington last week to see about a project and I visited the Vietnam War Memorial."

"You're kidding?" She was surprised then angered. "You didn't cry, did you, you stinking hypocrite?"

He smiled enigmatically. "No," he said, "but guess what?" He could hardly conceal his glee.

"What?" she asked.

"My name's carved on it."

"What?" They burst out laughing. "Are you going to get it changed?"

"No, of course not. I love it. It's perfect. And it's beautiful, my name chiseled there, very moving."

"How weird," she said.

"How fitting," he answered as the blond girl came to the door of the studio and beckoned for him to follow. "I'll call you," she said as he rushed away. She wanted to tell him about her mother and the divorce and prepare him for the coming blast, but she never got hold of him. But by the time she had been to Hawaii and back, he was dead.

CLEA looked at her watch: nineteen minutes to ten. She walked on-stage and took the bowie knife from the top of the shopping cart where it lay. Zeus was already in his lawn chair, sipping from the martini glass. The bottle of beer had been replaced by a bottle of gin. The cones were small now. Many of the objects had been removed and divided up. Clea's shopping cart was overflowing, as was the American Indian dog sled. Charlie stood behind the cameras, and as their red lights came on, he waved the players to go.

Clea bent over the stage-right cone like a dowager about to cut roses. She turned her head toward the audience and said,

"It's funny, but when you really pull away from each other is when you feel the most secure."

She snipped a pair of black satin toe shoes off the yellow rope, and held them up by their satin ribbons.

"Look at these beautiful objects: these are female opiates." She dangled the toe shoes so they caught the light. "When I was no longer mesmerized by him, I got into ballet. I approached it in the manner of Zelda Fitzgerald, and it gave me what it gave her—"

"Delusions of grandeur," said Zeus.

"A sense of identity," finished Clea.

They slowly turned and stared at each other across the stage. Clea dropped the toe shoes in the shopping cart. Zeus took a sip of gin. Then he rose and, taking the poultry shears from his pocket, approached the stage-left cone.

"I know what she means," he said, and cut a giant key ring with hundreds of door keys off the rope. "You develop a false sense of freedom. You feel free because you have a home base and when you feel free, you want to roam. So you roam, and inevitably, you chuck the home base, and right then, you don't feel free anymore. Life"— he tossed the key ring onto the dog sled—"is bloody perverse."

"Yes." Clea trotted to the middle cone and cut off a framed autographed picture of Peter Sellers. "It's damn grisly," she agreed, and threw it on the dog sled.

"Then, there's the sexual boredom." She cut off a football and bulleted it to Zeus. He caught it, snipped off a vibrator, and bulleted it back. The audience laughed.

"Yes," Zeus said, and dropped the football on the dog sled.

Clea examined the plastic phallus. "I mean, hey, you have steak for dinner every night, you get gout. Am I right?" She addressed the audience. The men hooted. "Yeah, you've gotta have green vegetables. That, I suppose, is why men leave their wives for tomatoes with pea brains." The men groaned. The women hooted.

Zeus smiled. "And women?" he said, snipping a pair of baby-doll pajamas off the rope. "Women cheat on their husbands with sex machines."

Clea dropped the vibrator into the shopping cart. "Men are in it for the adoration, women for the release. What's wrong with this picture?"

Zeus cut the baby-doll pajamas into little pieces and flung them like confetti into the air.

"What are you doing?" Clea asked.

"I don't recognize these. I've never seen these. I don't want them to be here. Now, they're not."

Clea rolled her eyes. "I wore those on our wedding night."

"You wore nothing on our wedding night," he snapped.

Clea cut off the rope a huge threaded needle stuck in a pin cushion.

She pulled out the needle, dropped the pin cushion in the shopping cart, and ran around the stage retrieving the scraps of pajama. Then she fled to the edge of the proscenium and sat down and began to sew the pajamas back together.

In the lighting booth, Roger slowly brought the stage lights down behind her while bringing up her pink spot. Simultaneously, his assistant followed Zeus as he walked to the front of the stage, bringing the lights down behind him and a blue follow spot up on his face. One of the Golden Lieutenants was running the follow spot from his security perch in the balcony. He set his machine gun against the balcony railing and hugged the giant light like a weapon.

"I guess," Zeus began, "you want to know what's gone wrong." The audience murmured their assent.

Clea looked up from her mock sewing and scanned the theater. Besides the Golden Lieutenants, there seemed to be only one person not wearing a suit. Third row, aisle seat, she focused her eyes outward through the darkness while referring to Zeus with her head. She looked like she was listening to him, but she was only listening for his last word. De Quincey, well, she recognized him from his tailcoat and bow at the neck, well, he'd been warned. She brought her eyes back, sadly, modestly. Zeus was speaking.

"I don't really know. How can you know? It's been so many years. There were so many things." Clea looked up.

"Like the time you told the interviewer you didn't know if you'd ever been in love."

"I never said it, Clea."

"I'll never know." She went back to sewing.

"She never forgave me for that. She decided I didn't love her. But it isn't so." His throat caught with emotion. "I do love her. I'll always love her."

She sprang to her feet. "The kiss of death," she snapped, and the lights bumped up. She ran upstage and stood by the cones.

"Okay. Look. I think it's better if we don't see each other for a long time." The audience groaned, "No! No!"

She addressed them. "You'll be okay. You've got videos. Actually, you're lucky. We can break up in life but go on being married in video for at least ten seasons of television." The audience hissed.

"Come on!" she shouted at them. "One out of every two marriages fails in this country. Why should we be any different? Because we're your fantasy?" "Yes!" the audience shouted back. "Yes!"

"Well, fantasize this." She held up the reconstructed baby-doll pajamas. "He slept with another woman!"

The audience gasped and went silent. En masse, their heads turned toward Zeus. A glass booth of the sort Adolph Eichmann sat in while on trial lowered like a shot from the flyloft, encircling him and crashing onstage. Zeus placed a set of earphones on his head and stared nervously out at the audience. There was an echo on his voice when he spoke.

"I was only following orders."

The audience winced.

Clea cut from the middle cone a British barrister's wig and black robe and quickly donned them and turned back to the audience.

"Here we have the architect of an emotional holocaust and he says he was just following orders? Whose orders? Sir?"

"My groin's." The audience laughed. Clea redressed.

"Is a man's groin such a terrible dictator? . . . Well?"

The women in the audience turned to their mates. There was a long silence.

"Well?" Clea asked again.

A man called out, "Sometimes!" Then another, "Sometimes." Then all the men, "Sometimes!"

"What times?" Clea shouted. "What times?"

Inside the booth, the heat was so intense, Zeus was dripping with sweat. He was trying to get the line out of his mouth, but he felt so faint that he fell against the side of the booth and in so doing inadvertently glanced at his watch. Nine forty-seven. The digits flashed before his eyes and he suddenly felt as if he were going to have an epileptic fit. He went weak.

"Holy shit!" Out in the control truck, the director forgot that Ralph Dodson was right behind him and bellowed into the headphones. "What's going on? What's happening? Go to her and snap back instantly when I tell you."

Clea saw the red light flash on camera two and very theatrically turned her profile toward Zeus. When she saw him slumped against the glass, beginning to slide down, she glanced beyond the camera to the cameraman and led him with her eyes into a stage cross.

"Follow her, follow."

She trotted, the camera following her, over to the booth and she rapped on it with her fist.

"Hey! I asked you a question! What times?"

Zeus, terrified he would go out of control, spoke fast. "She became obsessed with nuclear war. She paid no attention to me."

The feeling passed and he collapsed.

The director sucked in his breath and closed his eyes. "Oh no! I can't look. Tell me."

Max, the producer, spoke up. "She didn't hear him. I don't think she heard him."

The director opened his eyes. It was true. Clea was going on as rehearsed. He checked her face. No concealment. Though Zeus had said *nuclear war* instead of *ballet*, she was so programmed, so intent, she had heard *ballet* and missed his blunder. Zeus never knew what he had said. On camera three, he was bleeding sweat and weeping terror, but smiling because he hadn't had a fit. He dragged himself up and the glass booth rose off him and disappeared into the flyloft. He responded with an odd grin to the men in the audience, who were now murmuring, "Aha!" "You see!" "That's it!" "She ignored him."

"We lucked out, fellas," the director boomed over his shoulder. "That makes me feel good! Camera two! Hit it!"

Clea took off the barrister's wig and robe and threw them into the shopping cart. "So," she said, her dolly face registering disbelief, "not paying attention is grounds for emotional holocaust?"

Zeus retrieved the assegai from the sled, and with newfound courage, brandished it menacingly over his shoulder. "You must be on your guard. You can't go slack."

She began to dodge him, sidestepping around the now tiny cones, skipping over the yellow ropes as he followed, threatening her with the spear. In the orchestra, the drummer started beating the kettle drum, a slow rhythmic rumble, low at first, then louder and louder. Roger muttered in his headphones to the sound man, "One, two, three, GO!" There was a flash and crash of lightning. The audience screamed.

Zeus plunged the assegai into the stage floor, where it stuck and swayed to an orchestral sting. "It was nothing!" Zeus shouted.

"But it hurt me!" she shouted back.

"I don't love her. I love you!" Zeus grabbed Clea by the lapels and barked this in her face. There was a pause, then he let her go.

The camera dollied in for a closeup on Clea. Tears were fleeing from her eyes. "I will never," she mumbled through shaking lips, "trust you again." Clea turned on her little deer-hoof heel, ran upstage, grabbed the shopping cart, and pushed it defiantly offstage.

Zeus picked up the bottle of gin and took a swig of it. Then he dropped it on the dog sled. He walked slowly around the remaining cones and cut from one a bunch of videotapes, and from another a bunch of his résumés, and from a third a stack of eight-by-ten glossies of himself and Clea. The videotapes and the résumés, he dropped on the dog sled. The eight-by-ten glossies, he held up to the audience and then took his poultry shears and cut the sides picturing Clea right off and let them flutter to the stage floor. The remaining half-pictures of himself, he wedged in a pocket. Then he bent down and put the sled harness over his shoulder. As the kettle drum beat like a dirge and the lights slowly dimmed, he bowed his head and, like an Egyptian slave with a pyramid stone, pulled the heavy sled out of sight.

As the commercial popped onto the monitor, Ralph Dodson asked nervously, "What time is it?" There was a pause and then everyone in the control truck chorused, "Time to put the suits on, Ralph!" And the place broke into laughter.

Thirty-four

CLEA pounded up the stage-right corridor and into her dressing room. She slammed the door and locked it behind her. Florie was waiting, sitting before the poison oracle, humming to herself.

"Bring me the fowl," Florie directed, and Clea moved quickly to the crate behind her and removed the second cockerel. The first cockerel, the one who had been spared, squawked at her as she did so. She handed the second fowl to Florie and picked up the blade of *bingbas* grass she had left to save her place, and sat down.

Clea's heart was hammering in her chest. She peered at the fowl as Florie drew its wings down over its legs and pinned them with bast between its toes. She watched the fowl teeter as Florie set it on the floor and took up the grass brush and twirled it in the poison. The fowl hopped around Florie as she bent over and folded the red paste into the leaf blade filter. The fowl began to wrestle against the bast, emitting a high-pitched squawky scream, then Florie grabbed it, held open its beak, and squeezed the red liquid down its throat. She bobbed its head up and down, compelling it to swallow, picked up her wooden switch, and began the *gingo*.

"*Benge!*" Florie beat the switch on the floor and chanted in a singsong voice, "This woman who is my friend and charge, you said she is sane, you spared the fowl. *Bambata simi*, wear the suits! If you are truthful, if you speak truth, then slay the fowl, slay it now!" She poured a second dose of poison down the fowl's throat.

"Listen, *Benge!*" She jerked its foot and took up her switch and beat the floor. "Our lives are at stake. In a matter of minutes our world may end. Slay the fowl if this is the case. If she speaks truth, then slay the fowl!

"Spare the fowl if the woman lies." Florie poured a third dose of poison down the fowl's throat. "It's up to you, we do not know." She held the bird upright with its feet between her fingers facing her and jerked it from time to time as she intoned.

"Spare the fowl if her soul is mud and her vision a nightmare that must get gone. Listen, *Benge*, spare the fowl."

Florie's voice rose as she intoned this last and she jerked the fowl's feet one more time. "*Benge!* Hear me, for I must know, should we wear the suits the madwoman gives? Should we run when it's time as she tells us to do? Will a great wind come and blow us away? Does she speak the truth, the truth of *benge*? Will you give her your blessing and slay, oh *Benge*, oh *Benge*.

"Slay the fowl!" Florie threw the fowl to the floor. There was silence. Clea and Florie peered at the bird. It didn't move.

"The fowl is dead," Florie said, poking it with her switch and pushing it over so Clea could see its lifeless, beady eye. "The *gingo* is done. Eh, my baby,"—she jabbed Clea with the stick to make her look up— "you speak the truth. Now, where is my suit?"

"FOUR MINUTES. Four minutes," Charlie's voice rang out of the speaker.

Two minutes for the long commercial break. Two minutes for the film of the atomic life blast. Four minutes in which to make sure everyone was wearing the suits.

The hotline buzzed as Clea was scrambling to leave the dressing room. She grabbed it in a hand that was shaking with adrenaline. "NORAD is quiet." Jerry's voice was joyful. "I see nothing yet, so I've been watching the show. You're wonderful."

"Jerry, listen," she said out of breath with anxiety, "Florie asked the *benge*. It said we were right."

"I'll check NORAD again. Oh, Lord . . ."

"God keep you safe, Jerry."

"I'll call you on the shortwave from the bunker."

"Roger. Over and out."

Clea set the phone on its cradle and rushed from the dressing room. Florie gathered up the *benge* in its leaf, folded it, and put it in her pocket. She went into the bathroom, got a plastic bag, and returned and stuffed the dead fowl into it and tied the top with bast. She padded toward the costume rack, swinging the bagged fowl in one hand. As she hurled the corpse into the wastebasket and wrestled the radiation suit off its hanger, she thought to herself, ah well, I thought it was a *Nongquase*, but it was not. The foot of the baboon, but it was not. This is one storm with giant drops. Ah well, I have eaten life and eaten full. But, oh Badiabe, we are under your arms now, are we not?

BOBETTE helped Clea into her suit and hood and handed her the mask.

"Leave the boots in the wing, Bobette. Get yours on now," Clea said, and hurried down the corridor.

All around her, people were struggling into the radiation suits: the cameramen, the stagehands, leaning up against the corridor walls and pulling the bulky white pants legs over their feet.

"Great!" Clea called as she passed. "Thank you so much for this. Thank you all."

She rapped on a door and opened it. Inside, Pilar's owner was fighting with the cat, trying to get her suit on.

"Let me help," Clea said, and set down her mask and held the four-footed suit while the owner slipped in the cat and fastened the hooks up the back.

"What is this," the fat woman asked, picking up her own suit and letting go of Pilar, who instantly rolled on her back and began biting at this latest costume, "some special effect?"

Clea nodded. "A big one, dear, a very big one. I just want everyone to be safe. Can I help wtih the hood?"

The owner picked up Pilar and Clea pulled the hood over the Siamese face. Pilar looked like a medieval monk.

"Don't forget to stuff the whiskers in the mask," she cautioned the owner and, with that, left the room.

Clea maneuvered through the stage-right wing and onto the stage. Roger was standing on a ladder, changing gels.

"Where's your suit?" she demanded.

"In the booth, Clea. I'll change when I get up there."

"Are you sure?" She asked this suspiciously, hands on hips, legs spread.

Roger thought she looked like the Pillsbury Dough Boy with a girl's head. "I promise, doll. I can't get up a ladder in the thing, look at them—"

He pointed to the stagehands who were lumbering about, trying to set the stage for the love dance. Every now and again, one of the white-clad figures would stumble and curse. They were moving an automobile onto the stage, as well as some streetlamps, and the suits interfered with their balance.

"I'm sorry," Clea called to them, "but you'll see—" They nodded resignedly and continued their work.

"Your assistant's got one too?" she asked Roger.

He nodded reassuringly. She sped across the stage and pushed through the stage-left wing into the stage-left corridor.

The dancers were in the corridor, getting on their suits. They lined the walls and leaned against each other, laughing and hooting and stepping gracefully into the bulky garb. Charlie, the stage manager, already suited up, was directing the endeavor, helping to drag on boots, snapping on hoods, tromping here and there as quickly as possible. He was wearing his headphones under his hood, and the mouthpiece in conjunction with the mask slung around his neck made him look like a grandfatherly robot.

"I can't believe we're doing this," Rita screeched as she fell against Peg. "It's so crazy. All to satisfy this madwoman! Boy! When I'm a star—"

She stopped midsentence. The sight of Clea froze her voice and she blushed and turned away. The corridor went silent and the dancers stopped moving and stared.

"Good," Clea spoke curtly. "Good, Charlie. Great, everyone. Go on, get your suits on. There isn't much time."

The dancers did not budge.

"Do it!" she snapped, and the dancers jumped en masse and hastily returned to their fumbling. Clea jostled her way through the madding crowd to the door of Zeus' dressing room.

Zeus was standing at the back of the cubicle, alongside his plastic boat pond. A minute earlier, when Charlie's voice had come over the speakers, "Four minutes, please. Get on your suits," Liu had come through the door carrying their radiation suits and he had waved him away. "No, Liu," he had said, having decided, "no." Liu had hung the two suits up on the costume rack and retreated into the bathroom, where now he was ironing the neck ruffle Zeus was meant to wear in the show's finale.

Zeus had listened to the muffled commotion out in the corridor, the laughter, the hoots of derision, the mocking threats, until he could stand it no longer. He had gone to the door, opened it, shouted "Quiet!" and then slammed it shut and returned to his boats. He knelt down by the plastic pool and pushed a tiny galleon with his finger. It glided across the water in a perfect sail with all the majesty of history in the sure balance of its hull. Once, he had sailed such a ship on the great Zambezi River, the summer that he turned fifteen.

They were given to him by his mother, a fleet of tiny galleons in a wooden box. In a lucid period, she had gone to Salisbury and found them in a British import store and saved them in a closet. On his birthday, she produced them and said, "Take them with you on your camping trip and sail them on the Zambezi and I swear, my son, you'll have a time!" Her voice cackled off into peels of painful laughter then, uncontrolled and uncontrollable. She was by this time ill at ease with joy. But he did as she said and took them to his room and stowed them with his gear.

The next day he left with Doron, the Lieutenants, and Ruth and journeyed to the Hwange game reserve to camp by the Zambezi River. They tromped through the high grass of the veld until nightfall. They could not see the river, but as they pitched their camp, they could hear the rumble of Victoria Falls, the mighty waterfalls the natives called *Mosi O Tunya*, "the smoke that thunders." They built a fire and lay around it gazing at the stars, listening for the high-pitched bark of the hunting hyena and the deep roar of the eating lion. While they slept, their tents were buffeted by buffalo and elephant passing through their camp on their way to drink at the river. Once, Ruth screamed with terror and had to be comforted and taken into Doron's tent. But after that, all was quiet.

At dawn, they broke camp and pushed on toward the sound of the rumbling waters. When they had gone quite a ways and the noise of the water thunder was all around them, they hit a patch of forest and stopped. It was very hot and the insects hung around their eyes and whined annoyingly in their ears.

"Where is it?" Doron asked, removing his machete.

"Yes," Zeus agreed, chopping into the forest, "where is the bloody thing?"

Chopping, chopping, slicing and whacking, they suddenly broke through and emerged onto the bank. There, there it was before them, thundering from the heights, exploding at their feet: three thousand gallons of water per minute, the most astonishing natural force they had ever seen. The waterfall was huge, four hundred and twenty feet high, and out of the top of it rose two rainbows. At the foot of the thundering gorge where they stood was the Zambezi River, deep blue and dotted with kelly green islands along its center.

They had known it would be here. Victoria Falls was on the map. But for a moment, each in his own heart, each a third-generation white African, each a descendant of an English pioneer who stepped out of a tea room and onto the African plains, they each experienced discovering it. And Zeus reached into his pack and took from it the box of galleons, opened it, and set them, one by one, on top of the boiling white water at the bottom of the gorge. And one by one, the proud little ships were carried away, down the Zambezi River. They bore as their cargo a white boy's love for a land he was destined to disown.

After Zeus had screamed, "Quiet," Clea had stopped to help Eddie fasten his hood.

"Orson Welles wore this at Three Mile Island," Eddie roared, and she laughed.

"Shhh," she whispered. "What about Abou?" Eddie rolled his eyes. "I see," she muttered and hurried on, making a mental note.

She rapped discreetly on Zeus' door and entered and closed it behind her.

"Zeus!" she cried, running over to him and kneeling on the floor beside him. "Florie has done the *gingo*. The *benge* says I am telling the truth: the blast will come. Zeus, put on the suit."

Liu came out of the bathroom. "Liu," she said breathlessly, "did you hear? The *benge* is with us." Liu nodded. He had not known what he would do. But such was the thread of his life that his lot had been sewn in with Africa's and it was fitting he should follow African law. He took his suit from the costume rack and retired into the bathroom.

"Zeus." Clea shook her husband by the shoulders and pleaded with him.

"No," he said. "No."

Charlie's voice squawked out of the speaker, "Two minutes. Two minutes."

"Zeus!" She burrowed her head into his chest and spoke urgently, feverishly, afraid to look at him. "I love you. I love you. The *benge* spoke. Zeus, the fowl is dead. African fate, your fate. I beg you."

Zeus' eyes filled with tears. "I love you too," he mumbled. "It isn't that."

"Zeus, you went away from me. It was revenge I was taking."

"No, Ten Thousand Talents, I was never really here," he whispered, hugging her close. "It was none of it your fault, my baby."

"Please, Zeus." She buried her head in his neck and spoke between furious kisses. "Give me this chance. Believe in me, and after the blast there will only be our love left. Nothing cheap and dazzling, just the pure raw love that drew us to each other in a coffee shop so long ago."

"Clea . . ." He stroked her hair and said gently, "I killed my mother."

He went on stroking her hair and she buried her eyes in his shoulder and listened.

"It wasn't my father. *I* shot her—right between the eyes. Piouuu!" He mimicked the sound of a bullet hitting steel.

"It's not that I don't believe in your blast, my baby. On the contrary, I hope for it. I long to die in it."

There was a pause and Clea drew her head up without looking at him and whispered in his ear, "Surely it was an accident, Zeus?"

Above her head, he whispered back, "No."

She whipped her head over her right shoulder and away from him and stood up. Liu was standing at the bathroom door, clad in the suit, holding the neck ruffle limply in his hand.

"Meet me by the Volkswagen after the blast," she said to Liu, and without ever meeting her husband's eyes, she fled the room.

OUT IN THE control truck, the men were snapping up the final snaps on their suits and making jokes.

"Ralph," the director chortled, "no one would ever know you're a network man. You look like something out of *On the Beach*." The men laughed.

"What's this thing made of—asbestos?" the A.D. asked.

"I guess so," replied Max, "do I know? I produce musicals."

"You think this thing can really protect you against radiation?" the A.D. asked.

"Sure," the director said, "and Hollywood's off drugs—what—do you trust anything anyone's ever told you since the Korean War? What, Charlie?" He spoke into his headphones. "Okay. Ralph—can the cameramen put on masks for the blast? A request from Clea. We could have picture wobble."

Ralph sighed. "Anything to keep her happy."

"Buck up, Ralph!" Max clapped him on the back. "There's only a few minutes to go."

The director and the A.D. sat down in their places. Ruth was climbing into her suit in the back of the truck.

"I think you people are awfully callous. This is one of the saddest experiences I've had since one of the mother apes beat her baby to death."

"Well, Ruthie, the show must go on," said Max. "And look, if the blast comes, well, in a way, it'll be a happy ending."

Everyone turned to look at him and then the director began the countdown.

"Looking toward the end of time, everybody: five, four, three, two, one—hit the film!"

The commercial faded and on to the monitor popped the film entitled *Clea and Zeus Atomic Life Blast*.

"This film is amazing," Max said to Ralph. "Made by a company on Long Island that simulates atomic blasts. Look at this!"

On the screen was the original set with the eight conical heaps, untouched, undivided, as they had looked at the opening of the show. The backdrop was the strange blue and violet planetary sky. In one corner the two great setting suns, dripping reds and yellows, cast two sets of rays across the termite hills of Clea and Zeus' possessions. The yellow rope coiled along the red rust floor between the heaps like a whimsical carton snake. The many objects piled on the heaps, the books, the clothing, the mementos, the shoes, the photos, glittered in the waning light, and the whole scene, both bizarre and beautiful, reflected a quirky and complex peace.

The live things, the goldfish, the cockatoo, and the Siamese cat, were matted into the film, there but not really there, a piece of technical wizardry that went unnoticed by the uninitiated.

Liu's pi-pa music underscored the shot, a lovely, soothing trill that rose and fell in emphasis as the camera combed each heap and inspected its contents. When the camera was done with its search, it pulled back to a wide shot and the voice of Clea was heard.

"Goodbye, Zeus," she said.

And then the voice of Zeus: "Goodbye, Clea." Three beats passed: one-two-three, and then, a flash of light and the earth crack of a massive nuclear explosion rent the eyes and ears of those in the control truck. On the monitor, the heaps flew apart and the objects, still attached to the yellow rope, whirled in a crazy tightrope dance of destruction.

At this moment the door to the control truck smashed open and Clea, clad in a radiation suit and hood, entered, screaming.

"Ralph! Ralph! I want to see Ralph!"

In a move of terror, Ralph looked behind himself, as if to find himself, and then, realizing what he was doing, lunged forward.

"Clea! Clea! I'm here. What's wrong? What is it?"

Max rushed over to Clea and put his arm around her flailing body. "What is it, dear, tell Max."

She was sputtering. "If Zeus does not wear the suit, I am not going on. I will walk out of here so fast, so fast. I should be in my bunker now. This whole thing is ludicrous, it's criminal. Millions of people are going to die, and I know this, and I am being forced to do this stupid show, this meaningless piece of pop trivia. Don't you people understand? I will not die for you! A one-hundred-fifty-kiloton bomb is dropping in exactly one minute and a half—"

"Let me understand this, dear," Max said calmly. "Zeus won't wear his suit?"

"No! And if you think—" Clea was screaming at the top of her lungs.

Doron appeared at this moment outside the truck. He ran up the metal stairs and addressed Max.

"She's out of her bloody mind, any fool can see that. Leave Zeus alone, leave the poor motherfucker! Let him do his dance—the one thing in the show he's enjoyed and she wants to spoil it. For God's sake, Max!"

Ralph and Max glanced at each other.

"Get out of my way," Max snapped, and pushed Doron roughly to one side and leaped down the metal steps. The two Vietnam vets, suited up, had emerged from their van to observe the commotion. Max spotted them and beckoned.

"C'mere," he cried. "You want to make some extra money? I got a job for you!"

And with the two vets running behind, Max rushed into the theater.

"Take your place now, Clea," Ralph said sternly. "Go on."

Clea was still screaming, "Yes, all right. But I'm warning you—if he's not wearing the goddamn suit—" She broke off abruptly as she caught sight of Ruth cowering in the back of the truck.

"Ruth." Clea's voice was hoarse. Ruth had experienced great apes running at her at top speed brandishing tree stumps, but she had never been this scared.

"Yes, Clea," she found herself shouting.

"Was it an accident?" Clea was wild with emotion.

Ruth panicked. She knew exactly what Clea was talking about.

"Yes and no," she answered before she could stop herself.

"What do you mean?" Clea croaked.

Ruth spit it out. "His mother shot first! I saw it. She stopped. She shot him. Then he fired. But he knew what he was doing."

Clea turned and ran down the steps and vanished into the theater.

OUT IN THE HOUSE, the lights had come up and the audience was checking their programs to see who had made the film of the blast. They had booed en masse when the lights came on midfilm, for they were thoroughly enjoying the spectacle and did not wish to be interrupted.

On the huge screen now was an extraordinary mushroom cloud swirling with the objects Clea and Zeus had divided: the science fiction books, the wing tips, the Connie Francis album, the giant Ortho-Novum, even the Siamese cat, the cockatoo, and the goldfish bowl were somehow caught up in this gloriously colorful nuclear explosion. The audience persisted in watching, but chuckled as Charlie made the announcement:

"Put on your masks, please, there could be radiation from this blast."

General Clark Lincoln shifted uneasily in his seat and put on his mask. "Put it on, honey," he said to Miss Hollywood, and checked the location of the theater exits as the ushers pointed them out.

In the back of the house, Jim, the set designer, all suited up, was standing next to the puppet woman and Thomas De Quincey.

"Zeus isn't wearing a suit, so I'm not either," the puppet woman was saying to an usher.

"There was no bomb in the nineteenth century," De Quincey said. "Though Verne thought of it later. No."

The usher shrugged his shoulders and hurried away. The Shih tzus were tethered in the lobby by order of the health department.

BOBETTE was shaking like a leaf. Clea had charged her, screaming like a banshee, and it was all Bobette could do to fasten the radiation boots on the hysterical woman's feet. But she did it. Then she grabbed Pilar, all suited up, placed the animal on the shopping cart, and tied her leash to the handle and pushed the cart into the wing. Then, with every ounce of courage she possessed, she seized Clea by the arms and propelled her into the wing after it. She watched the stagehands open the theater doors at the end of the corridor and she prayed.

"Okay, fellas," the director was saying, "wind machine. Wind sound. Picture—go!"

THE LIGHTS came up on a nuclear wasteland. The backdrop was a grim cityscape, blasted-out buildings, mounds of rubble, broken windows in grays, blacks, and greens. On the stage were some mangled streetlamps and an abandoned auto, its doors flung open, its interior gone, its windshield smashed. The wind machine blew pieces of the broken streetlamp and whindshield ominously back and forth. The noise of the wind was a giant whoosh and howl of a million muffled voices, of a race tricked to death.

In the wing, Clea was heaving with dry sobs. The mask was hot and rubbery against her face. Through the mask window all was gray and hazy, visible but distorted. She was out of control, gone. Her body was hyperventilating, sweating and pulsing. She couldn't keep still. Her mind was careening. Pilar, atop the shopping cart, still trying to bite her way out of the suit, looked up at Clea, rose on her hind legs, and entreated the woman with her paws. Clea untied the leash, took the creature up, and cradled it in her arms.

Zeus, who had been strongarmed into his suit and escorted to the wing by the two vets, looked across the stage at this moment and saw the murky vision through his mask. Jesus Christ, he thought, it's like a nuclear madonna and child.

"Don't be afraid," Clea was murmuring to the animal in the radiation suit. She was staring kindly into the almond eyes, visible through the tiny mask. The whiskers were all mashed up, at odd angles around the furry face. This made Clea so sad, she thought she would break.

"I don't know why he didn't tell me. Why didn't he tell me?" She wailed, and placed Pilar back on the shopping cart and buried her head on the handle. Charlie came up behind her and tapped her on the shoulder. She jerked up and whipped around. He was gesturing across the stage to Zeus to go. Charlie's eyes, piercing her through his mask, were filled with pity.

"You can do it, Clea," he said. "I believe in you. Now—go!!"

Slowly, Clea trudged onto the stage, pushing the shopping cart. Zeus trudged from the opposite wing, pulling the dog sled. They were the street people of the future, the lonely gatherers, searching the blasted planet for signs of life.

The wind howled in Clea's ears. She was moaning to herself. Her blood was backed up and pumped furiously in arteries constricted by grief and overtaxed with foreboding. She was going by rote now, moving her body into prearranged positions as if it were a mammoth burden she was being forced to carry. To the audience, it looked like acting, some of the best they had ever seen. As her body twisted in agony, the audience's tears clogged their masks and they snuffled behind the rubber. It was "The Love Dance," it said in the program, perhaps of reconciliation? The audience was waiting to see. The special effect was coming too. The audience sat mesmerized, as finely tuned to their idols on the stage as to a sudden accident in the street.

Turn away. Clea's brain was directing her. Turn back and we

see each other—something living for the first time in months. Turn away. She glanced at her watch: 9:59.30. Look back. Counting in her head-35-36-37-38-No! Zeus! No!

Zeus was ripping off his mask, then his hood; 41-42-43. He was tearing open the front of his suit, bumping and grinding, a macabre striptease.

She pounded across the stage, screaming the muffled scream, "No, don't!" She tackled him and with the strength of atomic conviction, flipped him onto his back and tried to dress him.

The audience cheered. They thought they were following it. Zeus fought like a beast. They grappled on the stage, rolling over and over, 55-56-. She wrenched the hood on his head, and then, realized the mask was gone. She dropped his head 57-58, and scurried about the stage, searching for the mask, sniffing for it like a hound on the scent of a rabbit. She found it near the album of birth control pills and fled with it back to Zeus. She cleaved it to his face and in doing so saw her watch numbers click 1-0-0-0.

There was a flash of light so white that she went blind. There was an earth crack so terrible that she went deaf. She was blown across the stage into the automobile with such force that for a moment she thought she had died. Then dimly, through the scratched mask window, she saw a whirlwind of debris funnel upwards, the mementos of her life with Zeus tornadoing through the air. She felt heat, a ghastly heat, and watched fire rain from the fly loft. Her body rumbled and shook and the organs crashed around inside her bruising her heart and collapsing her chest.

She looked for Zeus and he was still stage left but the stationary camera had fallen on him and was turned shooting into the audience. Instinctively, she checked the monitor stage right, hoping for a shot of her father, hoping for salvation, but what she saw there was Doron and the Seven Golden Lieutenants, still flanking the orchestra pit, their machine guns still clapped to their breasts, still in an orderly line but unrecognizable: charred, their blond hair singed off, their skin hanging in strips from their beautiful faces.

RALPH DODSON screamed when he heard the explosion and the control truck toppled over. His eyes were fixed on the broadcast monitor, on the charred row of Lieutenants. "Oh my God!" he screamed as he plummeted into the console.

ROLLING FIREBALLS swept the stage. Clea could still not hear and now her mask was smeared with grit and, once more, she could not see. She raised her hand with a great mental effort and wiped off the mask with her glove. "Get up!" she was yelling. "Get Zeus and go!"

She staggered across the stage to the American Indian sled. It was empty now. Its contents—the science fiction books, the Jiffy Pop, the wing-tip shoes—blew around her like dead leaves in a storm. She pulled it, dodging flying objects—the facial sauna, the needlepoint stool—until finally she reached Zeus.

She was going to drag him out, to push the camera off him and drag him on the sled like a squaw with a drunken brave. But when she knelt down, she discovered he was dead, his lovely features fused beyond imagining, his Florida Keys blue eyes half lidded with a deadly fatigue. "Oh, Zeus," she muttered helplessly, touching his still warm cheek, searching the floor around him for something to cover his face. What she found was the cockatoo's wing singed off the dead bird's body, and with that she covered his eyes.

With the maelstrom swirling around her, she rose and bid him goodbye. *"We could have survived!"* she screamed suddenly, a soundless scream, *"I loved you!"* And then coming to her senses, remembering her duty, she left him and staggered off stage.

In the stage-right corridor, she stopped to get bearings. The smoke was as thick as cotton batting. Tongues of fire lashed out and burned at the fallen beams of dressing rooms and melting television cables. Something tripped her, and she looked down to see Pilar running around her feet like a cat possessed. She picked her up and plunged forward into hell.

The first person she found was Bobette. Pinned by the costume rack, costumes aflame, she was jerking and twisting and trying to get free. Clea tied what was left of Pilar's leash to her waist and dragged the costume rack off Bobette. She seized Bobette's head with her hand and wiped off her mask and made a following gesture with her hands. Bobette staggered forward and took hold of Clea's belt loop and hung on while Clea forged ahead through the fire and smoke.

Pilar's owner was wandering, flinging her hands above her head, probably, Clea thought, screaming. Clea caught a flailing hand and jerked it hard. The fat woman looked at her. At this moment, a beam fell behind them and whips of flame surged down the corridor. The woman made to run, but Clea held firm and the woman fell to her knees. Clea caught her chin and yanked it up so she could see the woman's face. She pointed at her feet. The woman looked down. Pilar was running for her life in ever smaller circles around Clea's legs. Clea untied the leash and handed the woman the cat and then gestured for her to follow. The four proceeded on through the smoke.

Through the fires of the great blast, Clea gained strength. She pushed beams from their path, ran through heat so intense she saw her gloves melt and the ends of the mask adhere to her face. But she grew more lucid. It had happened, just as she and Jerry predicted, and people were still alive. She had saved them. For what, she did not know. But there was life still on the planet, human life that might build a better world, and the thought of this cleared her mind and gave her the energy to strive for the open door, now dimly visible at the end of the corridor. The line of beings behind her stopped suddenly and she stumbled backwards and fell. She looked where the others were staring—at the corridor wall. Abou Ben Adem was melted into it, unsuited, his clothes burned away like some grim oil painting of the wages of male chauvanism.

She gestured sharply at the others, "Come!" And the line turned, and all on their hands and knees now, they crawled over shattered lights and burning cables, around flaming evening gowns of teal blue and red ocher, past mangled café tables and splintered miniature galleons to the open door. The last thing Clea saw before she crawled out into what was left of the Times Square area was the long long photo of Hiroshima after the blast, which burst into flames just in front of her and shriveled into ash.

Her mask was covered with grime. She still was deaf. She kept her head bowed to the ground as she crawled so she could be sure she was going forward. She wiped her mask again and saw that there was a great pile of broken concrete in front of them which they must crawl over to get to the street. Gray smoke and debris curtained whatever was beyond, though she thought she saw a flash of lights through a break in the pile. A broken neon sign perhaps, or a crashed police car. She began the climb. She scratched her way with her melted gloves up, up, over the crashed lintels of the theater, over the grimacing gargoyles of the 1930s master builders, over the brass door that once adorned the backstage entrance, to the summit of destruction, where she stopped and wiped her mask again and looked out to survey what the ignorance of man had wrought.

There was a blaze of light. She looked toward it and saw that it was shining around a man, a man who wore a strange helmet on his head. She refocused her eyes for they were tearing from the smoke, and looked again. It *was* a man and he seemed to be preaching. A savior perhaps, a savior for the race, a savior from the wasteland that men had made? She blinked her eyes several times, then focused once more. No. No. It was Ed Koch, the mayor of the City of New York, and he was wearing a fireman's hat.

He was speaking into a microphone, she saw now as her eyes adjusted further, and a man holding a minicam on his shoulder was taping him. The mayor was standing behind a cordon surrounded by firemen and police and a crowd of ambulance attendants who seemed to be looking right at her without seeing her. Beyond, she saw firetrucks and Con Ed vans and police cars with their lights flashing. And, in the midst of all, Florie, Liu, Max, Al, the A.D., Ralph, the Vietnam vets, the General and Miss Hollywood, all clutching their masks and hoods to their chests, scanning, scanning the rubble where she lay with anguished concern.

Suddenly Florie jumped and ran to the white-coated attendants and pointed at her. She became aware then that Bobette and the others had reached the summit and were flanking her and madly waving.

The din in her ears subsided now and she could hear sirens and shouting. "Look! Look! Survivors!" And the mayor's voice saying, ". . . gas explosion, uh, that's what we know. When we, uh, know more, we'll tell ya'about it, okay? I can't, uh, tell you what I don't know, now can I?"

When the ambulance attendants reached Clea and tried to pick her up, she fought like a netted psycho. She reacted, they told the news team later, as if her world had come to an end.

About the Author

Emily Prager grew up in Texas, the Far East, and Greenwich Village. She was graduated from the Brearley School and Barnard College, where she majored in anthropology. She has been a contributing editor for *The National Lampoon* and *Viva,* and a political satirist for *Penthouse;* she currently writes humor and TV criticism for *The Village Voice.* She is the author of four books, three of which are fiction—*World War II Resistance Stories, A Visit from the Footbinder and Other Stories,* and *Clea & Zeus Divorce.*

VINTAGE
CONTEMPORARIES

"Today's novels for the readers of today." — VANITY FAIR

"Real literature—originals and important reprints—in attractive, inexpensive paperbacks." — THE LOS ANGELES TIMES

"Prestigious." — THE CHICAGO TRIBUNE

"A very fine collection." — THE CHRISTIAN SCIENCE MONITOR

"Adventurous and worthy." — SATURDAY REVIEW

"If you want to know what's on the cutting edge of American fiction, then these are the books you should be reading."
                              — UNITED PRESS INTERNATIONAL

On sale at bookstores everywhere, but if otherwise unavailable, may be ordered from us. You can use this coupon, or phone (800) 638-6460.

Please send me the Vintage Contemporaries books I have checked on the reverse. I am enclosing $ _____ (add $1.00 per copy to cover postage and handling). Send check or money order—no cash or CODs, please. Prices are subject to change without notice.

NAME _____

ADDRESS _____

CITY _____ STATE _____ ZIP _____

Send coupons to:
RANDOM HOUSE, INC., 400 Hahn Road, Westminster, MD 21157
ATTN: ORDER ENTRY DEPARTMENT
Allow at least 4 weeks for delivery.

VINTAGE
CONTEMPORARIES